The STRANGE PATH

D Jordan Redhawk

Bella
BOOKS
2012

Bella Books, Inc.
P.O. Box 10543
Tallahassee, FL 32302

Printed in the United States of America on acid-free paper
First published 2012

Editor: Katherine V. Forrest
Cover Designer: Linda Callaghan

ISBN 13: 978-1-59493-275-5

PUBLISHER'S NOTE

Anna Redhawk—you could never love you like me—standing next to you will always be me.

Acknowledgment

No book is written in a vacuum, and this particular series has seen years of writing, editing, proofing and rewriting. So many people have helped me throughout its creation, and I know I'm missing people somewhere along the line. If your name isn't here, my apologies. Know that you were vital to the finished product, and I couldn't have done it without your support.

Those not among the missing include Janet Redhawk (no relation), Agatha Turko, Carol Dickerson, Teresa Crittenden, Jean Rosestar and Jaq Hills. You stuck with my first efforts through the years, added your two cents where appropriate, and kept me interested enough in the project to continue writing it. Thank you for the emails and critiques! And Mr. Dommie? You da man!

Anita Pawlowski, Shawn Cady and Anna Redhawk (definite relation!)—my first readers. You guys suffered through reading four different versions of the same story. My apologies for taking so long to get it right, and I appreciated your time and effort on my behalf. You guys ROCK!

Most of all, my thanks go to Karin Kallmaker, Katherine V. Forrest, and everyone else at Bella Books. They took a single manuscript and agreed to a trilogy, sight unseen. Thank you so much for taking a chance on me!

About The Author

D Jordan Redhawk lives and works in the Pacific Northwest. She shares her life with her wife of twenty-four years and two black cats. She's a geek, Apple fan, metal-head, enjoys sharp pointy things and science fiction/fantasy books.

To know more, check out her website, In Shadows - http://www.djordanredhawk.net

CHAPTER ONE

Whiskey woke, unable to see, lurching to one side as all motion stopped. The sudden stillness puzzled her. *Why does my head hurt?* Car doors slammed, rocking her with the reverberations. Fear kicked her heart into overdrive. *The boys, the car, the attack.* Someone thumped the trunk lid. She flinched, barely kept from crying aloud as footsteps crunched past. They spoke just out of hearing, their voices nothing more than a murmur that she registered above the roar of her pulse in her ears. Blood still oozed from the cut in her mouth. She hadn't been unconscious long. That meant they hadn't traveled too far from where they'd attacked her.

Struggling, she turned onto her side, reaching out to the walls of her cramped prison. Rubber and dust filled her nostrils, the spare tire digging into her side. Other unseen items pressed against her, her backpack a hindrance as buckles and straps tangled her arms. If she got out of here in one piece, she'd at least have her personal belongings with her. She strained against the lid. It didn't budge. *Maybe I can reach the latch from in here.* She searched blindly for the nooks and crannies inherent in any vehicle trunk. Stiff carpet met her touch, slight dips and hollows indicating where metal chassis gave way to engineering cavities. If she could get the carpeting pried up, she might be able to access—

The lid popped open. They dragged her from the trunk. Swearing, she punched and scratched and kicked anything within reach.

"Ow! Shit! She fucking *bit* me!"

Pleased, Whiskey had no time to dwell on the distinctly different taste of the boy's blood compared to her own. One lost his grip on her arms, and she threw a wild roundhouse swing that connected with another's temple.

"Hold her! Fucking hold her, you idiots!"

That was their ringleader, Paul. She remembered that much at least from their initial meeting.

Despite the strength of desperation, she succumbed, outnumbered. She stood pinioned between two nervous boys, Paul gloating before her. In the dim glow of a distant streetlight, she made out a prone body a few feet away. Satisfaction shot through her. *Knocked that bastard out, at least.* Two others nursed their wounds nearby. One wrapped his bleeding hand in a T-shirt. Beyond fear, she sneered at him, making a production of licking her lips.

Paul backhanded her, knocking her head to one side. She slowly turned toward him, defiance simmering. Lights sparkled in her vision. She shook her head, but they remained in the darkness beyond Paul's shoulder. *They look like eyes.*

"Hope you clean up good, bitch, because we're going to fuck you until you scream. But first—" He punched her hard in the abdomen.

Whiskey tried to double over from the impact, but her captors held her upright. Paul hit her again in the same place. She sagged and dry-heaved, unable to breathe. The boys let her drop to her knees between them. Nothing but bile came up. She couldn't help a weak chuckle. *Good thing I haven't eaten all day.* Movement flickered from the corner of her vision. She looked into the night, and saw the sparkles nearing. *Dogs?* The lights weren't at ground level. *Awful big dogs.*

Paul yanked her head up by the hair. Grinning, he said, "You're going to regret fucking with me, bitch." He delivered another punch, his fist crashing into her cheek, knocking her back to the ground.

Whiskey struggled to retain enough consciousness, to stand and defy the bastard. Everything ached. Her ears rang, and her stomach threatened to make another vomiting attempt.

"Come on, get up, pussy. Thought you were going to kill me."

Anger flared in her chest. She forced herself to her hands and knees. Maybe she'd die tonight, but she'd be damned if she'd go down without a fight. Impatient, Paul ordered his friends to pick her up. The reality of her physical state hit her. Panting, she tried to unfold her body, unable to straighten from the pain in her belly. She sagged between her captors, the edges of panic tickling her resolve.

"Let's get her to the water."

"A bit cold for that, isn't it?"

Whiskey blinked as a woman coalesced from the darkness where the sparkles had been. Others materialized with her, sliding into the clearing from every direction. *Were those their eyes?*

"Hold her," Paul muttered. He turned to the newcomer. "It's none of your business. Beat it. There's nothing here for you."

The new arrivals ignored him. They threaded their way through the group, seven Goth street punks—four men and three women. Even in her half-beaten state, Whiskey felt a measure of envy for their leather and latex. They had a small fortune invested in their wardrobe. All four men had mohawks, though only two had dyed and spiked them. Of the women, one had the telltale dyed black hair of a Goth. The others had red and blonde hair respectively.

The redhead had come out of hiding first. She now slinked among the boys to stand before Paul. "I'm hurt." A fake pout perched upon her lips. "You're having a party, and you didn't bother to invite us."

A couple of the boys sniggered, obviously feeling they had the upper hand. The male punks were slim and silent. None swaggered with machismo despite tattoos, multiple piercings and clothing that bristled with metal spikes. The lead of a woman enhanced their inherent weakness, magnifying it by the placid way they'd infiltrated the scene. Rather than put up a united front, they'd sprinkled themselves among the rich teenagers, mingling with the enemy, weakening their advantage.

"What kind of party did you have in mind?" Paul leered at the redhead.

The woman with dirty blonde hair sidled up to Whiskey and her captors. Without asking permission, she reached over and fingered Whiskey's hair. One of the boys tightened his grip, but didn't interfere. The blonde brushed disheveled hair from Whiskey's face, caressed her cheek with a thumb, swiping through the blood trickling from her nose. The woman's dark eyes slowly scanned Whiskey's form before returning to her face. She smiled, tasted the blood on her thumb, and turned away.

Whiskey shivered as the woman's eyes flashed golden from the reflection of a distant streetlamp. *Just like a wolf.* She shook her head; she couldn't deny the points of light she'd seen in the darkness before their arrival. *They must wear designer contacts.*

The teasing conversation had continued between Paul and the redhead, all attention upon them. Beside Whiskey, the blonde murmured in a barely audible voice, *"Aga ninna."*

Whiskey wondered what it meant. She blinked at the abrupt attention from the punks. As one, they turned to stare at her. She saw several sets of eyes flash like the blonde's. What the fuck's going on? She'd barely heard her. How the hell did they? Who are they?

Suspicious with the sudden tension, the boys shuffled in the crowd, their movements childish and awkward compared to the dangerous grace of their visitors. First to turn away, the redhead reached up to caress Paul's cheek. "This party's just getting started." With a laugh, she raked her fingernails down his face, gouging the skin with razor-sharp swiftness.

He yelped in pain, reaching out to backhand her.

The blonde spun around, and delivered a punch to one of Whiskey's guards. The boy released Whiskey, and crumpled to the ground.

"One punch?" Whiskey stared at the boy writhing on the ground. She saw no blood, and the blonde didn't have a weapon. *Christ, she's strong!*

"Fuck this!" Whiskey's other guard turned, and ran into the darkness.

Without the support, Whiskey dropped to her knees, her body reminding her of the toll that had been taken. Staring stupidly around the clearing, she saw her tormenters lying on the ground, some unconscious and others moaning in pain. She smelled the sharp aroma of blood, though it didn't look like any of them were seriously wounded. Peering at the aftermath, she attempted to wrap her mind around the speed and power of the punks' attack.

"Let me assist you, *ninna*." The blonde helped Whiskey stand, and offered her body as a brace.

Whiskey grunted, her stomach roiling at the abuse. She couldn't stand straight, and wondered if she'd received internal injuries. She glanced around, amazed at the efficacy of her saviors. Her gaze narrowed on one of them crouching over his victim. He looked ready to bite the boy's neck.

"Manuel, not now," the redhead ordered.

"I'm hungry." Long canines flashed.

Whiskey closed her eyes, shaking her head. A sharp stab of pain made her stop.

"Later, dude," the man with the blue mohawk said. "Let's get out of here before the cops show up."

"We're too exposed, Manuel," the redhead said. "I don't want the *Saggina* coming down on us. Not now." Her gaze flickered to Whiskey. "You know why."

Disgusted, Manuel released his opponent, who dropped to the ground with a thump. "Fine. I'll go catch the one that got away."

"Do that." The redhead approached Whiskey. "Are you well?"

Whiskey tried to speak. Relief and shock clogged her throat. She nodded.

The woman smiled, held out her hand. "My name is Fiona. Shall we leave, my little *lamma?* We have place of safety nearby."

Clearing her throat, Whiskey finally found her voice. "Uh, okay." If anyone came by now, all of them would be locked up, and on their way to prison. She glanced at the unconscious Paul, unable to tell if he still breathed. A part of her hoped not. She gathered up the moisture in her mouth and spit on him, blood and saliva mingling to slide down his face.

Laughing, Fiona took Whiskey's hand and tugged, pulling her attention away from him. "Come then. We'll keep you safe."

Whiskey allowed herself to be guided, hardly noticing that her backpack ended up on the shoulders of one of the men. Fiona held one hand, and the blonde supported her as they walked. The rest, except for Manuel, ranged around them in a loose circle. They flanked and surrounded her, leaving no escape. Whiskey couldn't help but connect her situation to the book she'd recently read about children captured by some of the roughest Indians in the west who were either adopted into the tribe after a period of testing or killed before their arrival at camp. Whiskey limped into the unknown, resolving to make it through any tests these punks could come up with.

CHAPTER TWO

The pain in Whiskey's abdomen didn't abate, making a ten-minute walk drag on for hours. She couldn't stand straight which made the going rough. If she moved too fast, she stumbled beyond the blonde's ability to keep her upright. The group paused while Fiona helped get Whiskey back on her feet, and moving. Something tickled along her right cheek. With her free hand she rubbed at it, fingers coming away with blood.

"His ring," the blonde said. "When he hit you."

"Which he'll never have the opportunity to do again." Fiona squeezed Whiskey's hand. "We're almost there."

Whiskey nodded, biting back a looming nausea. In light of her apparent safety, the adrenaline had fled her system. It left behind a shakiness she couldn't afford. These people might have saved her ass, but they had no reason to do so, and weren't harmless.

She didn't know who they were, or why they'd interfered. Heroes didn't exist; everything came with a price.

They broke through the trees onto a typical suburban street. Far off, a dog barked, and Whiskey heard the faint hiss of traffic from the highway in the distance. She hadn't been here before, didn't recognize the location, but she saw downtown Seattle over the rooftops. It looked like they were probably at Portage Bay rather than Lake Union. It eased her mind to know she remained near her territory, though she'd never succeed in a try for freedom. At this point, she could barely walk.

Fiona directed them down a side street. Whiskey didn't know what to expect. Most street punks she knew—herself included—lived hand to mouth, traveling on foot. Her saviors had so much money invested in their clothing, she thought it possible they had a fleet of Harley-Davidsons with which to terrorize the city. Her stomach turned. She couldn't imagine riding a motorcycle in her current condition. They stopped beside a black Lexus, and she weaved, blinking at the vehicle. These people were much more affluent than the kids they'd just dispatched. Paul's attack on her had been motivated by anger and revenge. She'd kneed him in the nuts when they'd initially accosted her on the street; she expected nothing less of him. *But what the hell do these people want?*

Fiona tugged gently on her hand, reaching to open the rear passenger door. "Come, my little *lamma*. We've a safe place for you."

Whiskey glanced around at the others. Her nerves were oddly soothed by the apparent disregard of the others. Only Fiona and the blonde seemed interested in her. The Goth woman argued softly with one of the two spiked mohawks while the other watched in boredom. At the trunk of the car, the third man held her pack, waiting to put it inside.

"Who are you? Why did you help me?"

Fiona gave another mock pout, and tsked under her breath. She released the door, and stepped in front of Whiskey, reaching up to caress her cheek. They were the same height, and Whiskey caught that reflected flash of gold in the woman's eyes. *Have to be contacts.* She reminded herself that Fiona had just laid a boy's face open with those fingers, and steadied herself. *Damned if I'm going to flinch like he did.*

"They had an unfair advantage. We take care of our own. As for who we are, I told you my name. This is Cora showing such provocative attention to you. The man holding your belongings is Daniel; Alphonse is in deep discussion with Bronwyn; and my other colorful colleague is Zebediah." She smiled. "And you, my sweetness, are my little *lamma*. Unless you have another name?"

Whiskey stared at Fiona's wolfish grin. Should she worry about the fingernails gently tracing her jaw, or be more concerned with the sudden image of Fiona ripping out her throat with those teeth? *What does she mean, 'taking care of their own'? That's a crock of shit.* They and Whiskey were worlds apart.

Fiona awaited an answer, a mocking smile on her lips.

"I'm Whiskey."

Cora whispered, "Whiskey." She spoke again, a bit louder. "I like it. Are you well-aged, slow and smooth? Or are you young and rough, burning your way down?"

She attempted a little bravado. "I can be either. What do you have in mind?"

The two women laughed, not unkindly. Fiona stepped backward, drawing Whiskey with her. "What I have in mind is to get you home. You need rest and food."

Whiskey paused a moment longer. The women remained silent, not pushing, giving her time to think. They'd saved her from a life-threatening situation, whatever their reasons. Had they wanted to do her harm they'd already had the opportunity, yet rescued her instead. In her current state, Whiskey couldn't protect herself. The thought of strapping on her pack, and lugging it to the youth club, Tallulah's, caused her knees to quiver in preemptive weakness. The shelters were closed, she had no options for medical attention, and she seriously needed to eat something and sleep as Fiona suggested.

On a more calculating level, Whiskey knew that at least one of these people had outrageous amounts of money. She couldn't deny the allure of hanging out for a while despite the alarm bells clanging in her head. Maybe some of that cash would trickle down to her. It could simply be a case of a hard-core group of rich bitches wanting to piss off their parents by socializing with a street kid. Although that didn't explain how they had handled themselves.

With a single nod of her head, she allowed herself to be helped into the car.

"Come along, children," Fiona called. "Let's get my little *lamma* home for the nonce."

Whiskey wondered where they'd put everyone. She sank into the backseat, the plush leather cushioning her aches, driving the thought from her mind.

Cora slipped in beside her. "Lean on me, Whiskey. Stretch out."

Whiskey concentrated on finding some level of comfort for her bruised body. She didn't note who got into the car until Fiona settled in the driver's seat. Only Daniel had joined them. "Where are the others?" She peered out the window.

"As you know, Manuel was hungry." Fiona shrugged as she started the car. "Bronwyn and Zebediah decided to join him for a bite to eat before coming home. Alphonse is keeping an eye on them."

Whiskey saw Manuel in her mind, leaning over one of the boys they'd beaten. He'd gone after the one that got away. *Do these people believe they're vampires?* The idea both intrigued and worried her. She'd read about people who thought that they needed human blood to live. She gave Cora a surreptitious glance, but didn't see fangs. Whiskey had always been drawn to stories and movies about vampires, but she'd never been swayed to believe she had anything in common with them. *Other than a morbid curiosity and sense of humor. It'd be fun to pretend though. Maybe I'll have a chance to play the game.*

The city blurred past the passenger window. Cora produced a bottle of water from somewhere and, after Whiskey drank her fill, used the remainder to wet a piece of cloth. She gently cleaned Whiskey's most apparent facial injuries. At first skittish with Cora's proximity, exhaustion and pain took a toll on Whiskey's ability to guard against danger. Her body relaxed into Cora's, a distant part of her noting the softness of the woman's figure. Her eyelids drooped.

"You must stay awake, Whiskey." Cora shifted to rouse her. "You may have a concussion."

Whiskey blinked and sat up a little, the movement causing her stomach muscles to throb in protest.

"Very true." Fiona glanced at her in the rearview mirror. "We'll have Doctor Daniel here have a look at you when we get you home."

Whiskey looked at the blond punk in the passenger seat. "Doctor? He's no older than me."

Fiona laughed. "You'd be surprised, little *lamma*. Our Daniel has a medical doctorate. Certainly you know better than to judge someone by appearances alone."

A stab of jealousy soured Whiskey's curiosity. Paul and his crew were privileged assholes, but eventually they'd get into a fix from which their parents' money couldn't rescue them. Whiskey had a suspicion that Fiona's pack didn't have that problem. *God, what would it be like to have the money and the parental support to become a doctor at eighteen or nineteen?* The idea simply amazed her. She knew that not everyone had loving parents, they were an extreme rarity in her world. They did exist, though, and she studied Daniel's profile. Did he rebel against his parents by dressing and acting like this? Maybe he hadn't wanted to become a doctor, and that's why he hung with Fiona. She felt a faint wash of disgust. *Spoiled. What a fucking waste.*

Fiona guided the car off the road and into a driveway. A garage door widened, brightening the darkness. She pushed herself up to see where they were, falling back with a groan. "Shit, that hurts."

Fiona laughed as she shut down the engine. "We're home, children. Let's get our visitor inside and comfortable."

With creaky movements, Whiskey disengaged herself from Cora's lap, trying to keep from expressing how much pain she felt. Looking out the window, she anticipated some wildly decorated flophouse, a la *The Lost Boys* movie. Instead she beheld an immaculate three-car garage. A black Porsche skulked next to the Lexus, low-slung and gleaming danger in every curve. Past that a fleet of Ducatis and Triumphs crouched on their kickstands, ready for action.

The car door behind her opened, and Cora eased out of the backseat. She helped Whiskey swing around and exit the vehicle, once more supporting her. Whiskey still couldn't straighten, but at least her knees had stopped shaking.

Fiona tossed the keys to Daniel. "Get her things and bring them into the house." She took Whiskey's free hand, and escorted her toward a door. "Welcome to our humble home, my *lamma*. I hope it's to your liking."

"Why do you keep calling me that? What's it mean?"

She received an enigmatic smile in response. "It's just a pet name from the old country, sweetness. Something I picked up from my family."

The house substantiated Whiskey's assumptions about Fiona's wealth. Tasteful wood and marble marked every surface. The vast kitchen held the latest quality appliances. A polished dining table gleamed under decorative light. Fiona had to be bucking parental authority by bringing her here. Whiskey wondered when Mommy or Daddy was expected home. Her mouth watered at the sight of a bowl of fruit artfully placed in the center of the table. It'd been hours since she'd eaten. Her stomach growled in distress even as it spasmed with sickness.

Fiona released Whiskey's hand. She reached for a banana, and handed it to her. "You should be able to eat this without much pain. Daniel, why don't you bring her things to the guest room, and get your medical bag."

Daniel's unspiked mohawk hung over his eyes in a dark blond mop. He was dressed completely in latex and his tank shirt stretched low enough across his chest to reveal an intricate medallion and chain tattooed across his skin. He sauntered by the women, Whiskey's pack on his shoulder, and disappeared into the next room.

As much as she wanted to eat, she couldn't peel the banana. Cora supported her under one arm, and Fiona had reclaimed the other hand. Her queasy stomach bitched at her. *Just as well. I'd probably throw it up. Maybe later.*

"Shall we?" Fiona led the way through a living room just as richly adorned as the kitchen and dining area. Plush leather dominated the room, with a wet bar in one corner. A couple of game systems and stereo speakers were hooked up to a large screen television. They passed the front entry and stairway to continue down a long hall as Fiona kept speaking. "I believe I could tempt you with a shower if Daniel deems it safe, yes?"

Swallowing, Whiskey fought a blush. The boys who'd grabbed her had commented that she stank. It'd been days since she'd been able to do more than wash in a public restroom. Showering at the Youth Consortium meant leaving her belongings unguarded and subject to theft. It was much easier and safer to let nature take its course. Fiona didn't seem to mean anything snide by her question, however, and Whiskey nodded. "That'd be cool."

"I'm sure Cora would be delighted to assist you in that endeavor." Fiona gave Whiskey a knowing smile.

Fiona threw open a door and gestured for her to enter. The "guest room" was, in actuality, a suite decorated in white and crimson. Polished dark wood, contrasted with the color scheme, shone in the light of a crackling fireplace. Whiskey stared around her, unable to take it all in.

"As you can see, this is the sitting area. Through there is the bedroom." Fiona gestured through an archway toward a vast bed with an intricate iron frame. She led Whiskey to a door. "But I must say that the bathroom is a religious experience."

Encased in black marble, the white of porcelain clashed stark against the darkness. A huge shower held multiple faucets, and a built-in seating area. On its back wall, the face of a lion had been carved from the marble, a design re-created on the side of an equally vast bathtub nearby. Thick scarlet towels and washcloths hung on silver racks, awaiting her need. Subdued overhead lighting gave less illumination than the several large candles glowing about the room.

"Fuck." She gaped at the splendor.

Fiona chuckled at Whiskey's murmur. "Yes, well, that does depend on one's religion, doesn't it, dear Whiskey?" She glanced over her shoulder. "I do believe the doctor is in," she said, stepping back. "Let's see to your injuries."

CHAPTER THREE

Waking up in a strange place wasn't a new experience. Registering the strange softness of clean sheets, Whiskey remained still, eyes closed and breathing even, until she remembered the events that led her here. *Walking to the U District. Paul and his cronies. A beating. She opened her eyes, not stirring. Blood-red sheets, black comforter, a nightstand made of ebony. Fiona's crew, Doctor Daniel.* The warm comfort felt disquieting, alien. She shifted, testing her ability to move. Stiff and sore as expected, she forced herself to sit up.

Although alone in the large iron bed, it looked like someone had slept beside her. Murky and dark, thick crimson curtains blocked what appeared to be the tail end of daylight from entering the room. She glanced at the digital clock beside the bed. If it could be believed, she'd slept through the night, and most the following day. With ginger movements, she edged out of bed. She didn't remember getting undressed the night before, and frowned at her nakedness. Lifting her arm to her nose, she smelled soap. Someone had stripped and bathed her. A stab of fear lanced through her. *Shit! How could I let that happen?*

She recalled sitting on the bed, letting Daniel examine her. He'd asked the right questions, poked and prodded the right areas, and seemed knowledgeable enough with the stethoscope and blood pressure cuff he'd produced from his medical bag; he had to have had medical training. He spoke with a faint German accent as he applied butterfly bandages to the cut on her face. At one point he'd injected her with something, a deep red liquid that looked very much like blood. He'd said the injection fought possible infection, and accelerated healing. Not long after, she'd lost consciousness.

He drugged me! She went over herself again, finding nothing else wrong. No other apparent needle marks marred her skin. In fact, the bruises and scrapes on her knuckles looked days old. *What the hell did he give me?*

Damned if she'd be found any more vulnerable if Fiona walked in. She forced herself to stand. Her knees had lost their earlier infirmity. Both her stomach and her bladder demanded attention, one grumbling loud enough to wake the dead. No banana in sight. She wondered as she stumbled toward the bathroom whether she'd eaten it, or if it had been returned to the kitchen once she'd passed out.

After urinating, she peered into the toilet. No blood. Grateful for that, she turned toward the large mirror. She grunted at the view, fingers tracing a multicolored map of bruises across her abdomen. Yellow and green blotches stood stark against the skin of her upper arms and her left cheek. If she hadn't known better, she'd have thought days had passed since they'd been inflicted. She leaned closer to the mirror. Her lip wasn't swollen near as much as she thought. The butterfly bandages on her left temple itched when she frowned. An inch or so to her right, and she'd be half blind today. She reached up, tugging one aside. The scab beneath appeared to be healing too well to need them. Wondering if Daniel had been overreacting when he'd insisted on them, she pulled both the butterflies off. Seeing the damage, slight though it was, made her shaky again. She leaned heavily against the black marble counter, gathering her energy. Whoever had washed her the night before hadn't gotten all the blood and dirt from her hair. Streaks of rusty red marred the light blonde tresses at her scalp. She had an overpowering desire to be completely clean, and she looked at the shower through the mirror.

Experimenting with the various knobs and showerheads, she soon had three streams of hot water pouring across her body. She luxuriated in the immersion, her skin humming with joy. A niche carved into the marble near the shower controls held a handful of items—a bar of soap, a selection of shower gels and shampoos, and a razor. "Oh, my God," she groaned, reaching for the razor.

Thoroughly scrubbed for the first time in weeks, she rinsed off the last vestiges of shampoo from her long hair. She wasn't finished, not by a long shot. Blinking water away from her eyes, she studied one of the shower gels she hadn't yet used.

"Mmmm...Very nice."

Survival instincts functioning at top peak, Whiskey whirled about with the razor in hand. Her world spun a fraction of a minute at the sudden movement. It cleared, and she saw Cora standing at the shower entrance.

Cora's hands rested against the walls above her head, effectively blocking the entry. The stance caused her silky white shirt to ride up, revealing lacy bikini panties and nothing else. She smiled at Whiskey, ignoring the rudimentary weapon as she sauntered forward. Water hit her blouse, making it translucent, and Whiskey's mouth went dry.

CHAPTER FOUR

Cora didn't leave the bathroom until they were both breathless from their exertions. Languid from the sex, Whiskey loitered in the hot water, leaning against the dark marble to recuperate. She scrubbed herself a second time before turning off the water. On the counter by the sink she found a comb, toothbrush, toothpaste and deodorant. She gladly took the opportunity to clean her teeth.

Wrapped in a towel, her wet hair hanging loose, she left the bathroom. Cora lounged on the wrought iron bed. She'd had time to dress, and wore a black gypsy skirt and corset, the skirt slit up the side to reveal an enticing expanse of thigh.

"Breakfast's almost ready." She licked her lips. "I set out clean clothes from your pack."

While Whiskey had hoped to gain something of monetary

value out of this mess, her hard-won paranoia caused her to stand taller. "Why are you doing this? I've got nothing to offer in exchange for any of it. What do you want from me?"

Cora's face sobered as she studied Whiskey. She rose from the bed and approached, pressing against Whiskey as she snuggled her cheek on a damp shoulder. "Maybe you have nothing now, but someday you might. All we ask is that you remember who assisted you when you needed it most, *Ninsumgal.*"

That language again. Whiskey frowned. She wondered what it was. She'd never heard its like before. Maybe she could do an Internet search at the library to locate some of the words.

Everything had a cost. If she continued with these people, she'd be obligated in some unknown way. It had already happened. They'd ask a favor in the future. She'd learned on the streets to take more than you gave. If Fiona's little pack of loaded rabble-rousers wanted to spread the wealth on the off chance Whiskey would have something to give in return, so be it. She'd pay that bill when and if it came due. *Hell, it's not like I'll be around long enough to deal with it. Once I get back on the streets, chances are good they'll never find me again.*

Deciding to play their game, Whiskey tilted the woman's face. "I'll always remember you, Cora," she said, and kissed her.

It took some prurient time before Whiskey stood clothed. Cora assisted, more a flirtatious hindrance than help. Whiskey wore a pair of form-hugging latex pants, showing off every curve of her legs. She donned her studded belt and the black leather wristband that her best friend, Gin, had given her for her last birthday. Gin's birthday party was tonight.

Cora tucked Whiskey's crimson camisole into the latex waistband, pausing to slide her hands along the smooth, tight-fitting plastic.

"Stop that," Whiskey growled playfully, feeling another swell of arousal as the woman's hands glided down to her crotch. "We'll never get out of here at this rate."

"Would that be such a tragedy?" Innocence glowed in every line of Cora's face.

"Yes, it would," a voice said from the door. "We've plans tonight, sweet Cora."

Whiskey turned to see Fiona enter the room.

"You look stunning, though I'm surprised you're not abed. Cora can be quite the minx when she's of a mind."

"I noticed." Whiskey glanced at Cora, who grinned wickedly at the accusation. *Take more than you give.* "What kind of plans? I have to be somewhere later tonight." She turned to the vanity to finish brushing out her hair.

Fiona approached and took the brush from her, working her way through the black-streaked blonde tresses. "Oh, I was thinking drinks, dancing, perhaps a hunt or two." She stopped, and ran one hand up and down Whiskey's right arm. "What would you say to a tattoo? I think a black dragon would look marvelous there."

Whiskey stared at Fiona's reflection. Tattoos were expensive enough that she'd never thought to have the money for one. The best she could hope for was an ex-con who'd do the deed for fifty bucks, and a blowjob. Gin wouldn't begrudge her this opportunity regardless of what day it was. Besides it wasn't like they'd get to hang out much with her boyfriend underfoot.

Cora had returned to splay across the bed. "I think a red dragon would be better."

"How about both?"

Cora sat up and scooted to the foot of the bed. She licked her lips. "Let's pierce your nipples, too."

Whiskey quelled a sudden shiver. "Sounds like a plan."

The two women escorted her to the kitchen, where a fluffy omelet stuffed with mushrooms, ham, cheese and olives awaited her. Whiskey swooned from the aroma, weakened knees buckling when she sat at the dining table. Separate platters held toast and bacon, the latter still sizzling. Daniel dished up a plate for Cora before serving himself, and sitting at the breakfast bar.

Badass street punk, doctor, and now chef. Wonder if he cleans windows?

Alphonse had been in the living room when they'd passed through, kicking ass on some first person shooter video game. He came in long enough to grab food, piling a large amount of bacon onto his plate before returning to the other room, presumably to continue laying digital waste. None of the others appeared to be in residence. Cora joined Whiskey at the table. Fiona retrieved a cup of coffee, setting it before Whiskey before sitting across from her. She had no plate, instead cultivating a glass of deep burgundy wine.

As much as she tried to pace herself, Whiskey couldn't help but wolf down her meal. She hadn't had more than a bagel—and maybe a banana—in the last thirty-six hours. She consumed half her omelet before her ravenous appetite abated. Glancing at the others, she flushed at the spectacle she made of herself. Daniel ignored her; Cora gave her a sympathetic smile. Whiskey reddened more. She didn't know whether she felt miffed at Cora, or embarrassed. She didn't want anyone's pity. She'd lay odds on any of them having starved before. Her gaze slid to Fiona, the woman's expression raising her hackles.

Fiona smiled indulgently at her over the rim of her wineglass. Whiskey had seen the look before, usually on the faces of parents cooing at their ill-mannered, pampered brats. The facial expression hinted at parental possession, and a familiarity Fiona didn't possess. Whiskey didn't belong to a street family for exactly this reason—nobody owned her. On the streets, she'd take Fiona to task for her presumption. Here she didn't know the group dynamics. In any case, a confrontation might get her thrown back onto the streets. *Too soon.* She had too many questions, and wasn't willing to end this little adventure so quickly. She scowled and forced herself to slow, an easier task now with the worst of her hunger abated. Straightening in her chair, she grabbed a slice of toast, slathering apricot jam on a slice.

The more leisurely pace gave Fiona the signal she awaited. "So, dear Whiskey. Tell us about yourself."

Whiskey recognized that Fiona's pleasant tones concealed the interrogation about to begin. It would be to Whiskey's benefit to show strength from the onset. While the rest of Fiona's little pack might bow and scrape upon command, Whiskey would not. She wasn't interested in becoming a member, even with the offers of shelter, money and sex. She took her time responding, eating a bite of toast, and washing it down with coffee. "Not much to tell."

Fiona gave her a knowing look. "I find that difficult to believe.

A beautiful youngling such as yourself, out alone at night, all of her worldly possessions in a backpack?" She tsked. "Where is the family who is taking such little interest in a fascinating child like yourself?"

Bristling at the choice of words, Whiskey eyed her. "I'm no more a child than you are." She jutted her chin at Fiona. "You're what? Twenty? Twenty-one? Only two or three years older than me."

Their amusement met her words. Even Daniel, who'd remained stone-faced from the beginning, snorted. Whiskey's scowl deepened.

"Thereabouts. That still doesn't answer my question. You're under my roof, eating my food, and enjoying my...hospitality." Fiona's gaze slid to Cora to complete the innuendo. "Surely you can give us the opportunity to know you better."

The words sounded sensible, but Whiskey wasn't fooled. Still, Fiona was the leader of these people. Whiskey debated whether to show strength or rudeness in response. One would gain her respect. The other would get her tossed out like so much garbage, probably in worse shape than she'd been in had she stayed in the clutches of her attackers last night. Though Fiona had been pleasant to the extreme, Whiskey remembered the blood flowing from that boy's face. She maintained eye contact, not willing to show the least amount of weakness. "I don't have parents. They're dead."

She watched a flash of something cross Fiona's face. What was that? Beside her, Cora made a noise of sympathy, and stroked her bicep. Whiskey refused to be distracted. She didn't want Fiona to think she could gain the upper hand with this knowledge.

"Pity," Fiona murmured. "Though that would explain—" She trailed off, looking away.

Whiskey felt a moment of elation as her opponent broke the stare first. Emboldened by the unexpected win, she leaned forward. "Explain what?"

Fiona's sharp green eyes focused back on Whiskey. "It explains why you're out in the cold rather than snug in your family's confines." She smiled, returning to that faint superior amusement. "Did you even know them at all?"

The words, lightly spoken, brushed painfully against Whiskey's hidden regrets and nightmares. She brushed Cora's hand off, not wanting to feel any touch upon her abruptly sensitive skin. Pushing her plate away, she glared at Fiona. "I don't want to talk about it." Her voice sounded foreign, even to herself.

Fiona's eyes glittered knowingly. After a moment, she agreed. "As you wish, my little *lamma*." She raised her chin.

Many people used the gesture to indicate stubborn resistance. Whiskey blinked, slouching in her chair. Fiona conceded the point—chin lifted, countenance haughty, baring her throat in capitulation. Whiskey recalled the flash of vision she'd had on the street of Fiona ripping out her throat with sharp teeth. *They really do think they're vampires. Is that where that gesture comes from?* Fiona's lips curved into a smirk, and Whiskey schooled her features to indifference.

"Are you finished eating?" Cora spoke softly.

The food, once so delicious, left a nasty aftertaste in Whiskey's mouth. She pushed her plate away. "I'm done."

Fiona raised the dregs of her wine to Whiskey in salute before draining the contents. "Time to go, children."

Hours later, Whiskey stared at herself in a mirror. A scaled tail circled her right wrist, the dragon it belonged to coiling up her arm, ending at her collarbone and shoulder blade. Mere outlines of black ink at this point with hints of color here and there, its ethereal wings sheltered her, protecting her as it struggled to rise. Antibacterial ointment caused the artwork to shine, making the dragon scales glisten.

"Magnificent," Fiona murmured.

Whiskey nodded. "Yeah it is."

Cora smiled. "Red was a much better choice than black."

Whiskey moved her arm. The dragon writhed along her muscle. Her skin felt lightly bruised from her fingers to her neck. The burning sting had subsided, and the last two hours had been sheer agony. The worst had been those areas closest to the bone. It had been worth the pain. Once the job had been started, she'd insisted they finish as much as possible. She didn't know how long she'd be hanging with this crowd. It'd suck to have a partially completed tattoo for years on end. This thing cost an outrageous sum; she'd never have the cash to color it in, too. The artist, a petite Asian woman exhibiting dozens of tattoos on her exposed skin, had attempted to halt the process twice, and Fiona had backed Whiskey's request by offering a substantial tip to complete the outline. She turned to the tattooist. "This is fucking killer! Thank you."

"You're welcome. I'd say it's some of my best work. Mind if I get some pictures before you go?"

Whiskey turned back to the mirror in fascination. "Go ahead."

The tattooist went to the front counter for a camera.

"A definite success." Fiona smiled at her. "Are you certain about Cora's suggestion, my little *lamma?*"

Whiskey glanced sharply at Fiona's reflection. Her voice sounded mocking, but her face was serene. "Why not?" She sensed a subtle challenge. "If I'm going to do it, might as well do it all."

Cora clapped her hands in glee. "I'll tell her." She scampered toward the front of the shop to get the tattooist.

Fiona conceded with a sly grin, raising her chin. The action increased her naturally haughty appearance, something that didn't need work.

"Where's everybody else?" Whiskey asked. When they'd arrived, Daniel and Alphonse had both decided to add to their collection, getting into a deep discussion with one of the other tattooists.

"They finished early, and got bored. We'll run into them later."

Whiskey nodded, and looked out the front windows. A clock by the register showed nearly midnight. The place had quite a few customers at this hour. Friday nights were busy. She returned her attention to the dragon. *No wonder, if this is the usual quality of their work.*

Normally she'd be tired at this point, but sleeping through

the day, and an endorphin high from the tattoo had boosted her energy levels. She didn't know how long it would last. It didn't look like her benefactors were anywhere near crashing, either. Their money made things a lot easier for them, giving them the opportunity to run with impunity, knowing they'd have a safe place to crash in the wee hours. She'd gotten far more than she'd hoped for since meeting them—a shower, sex, new clothes, a full stomach, and now a tattoo worth eight hundred or more. Still, as easy as it would be to remain in their care, she knew things would end badly. They always did. Fiona would get tired of her new toy, and toss Whiskey out eventually, not before softening her up with easy food, sex and money. It might take days or weeks, but it would happen.

After tonight, Whiskey would cut and run. *Take more than you can give.* She'd catch a nap somewhere; maybe head over to Tallulah's to see if Gin's party still progressed. She also had to be at the Youth Consortium at eleven in the morning to meet with Father Castillo.

"Piercing your nipples, too?"

Whiskey turned to the artist. "Yeah. What the hell, you know?"

The smaller woman grinned. "All right then. Let's go into the back room for that." She led the way toward a curtain.

Swallowing her sudden trepidation, Whiskey followed, Cora and Fiona trailing after.

CHAPTER FIVE

"You've got to be shitting me." Whiskey studied the upscale club across the street from the car. The word Malice dripped bloody red across black-colored brick above the door. A spotlight brought out the glossiness of the paint. At nearly one in the morning, people still lined up, waiting for admittance from the two bouncers at the door. The air pulsed with the muffled bass of the music inside. Someone threw open the double doors to leave, and a flow of ambient trance music washed over the street.

Fiona laughed, locking the vehicle doors. "When it comes to raising hell, my friend, I rarely joke. Have you been here before?"

"Hell, no." She raised her voice to be heard over the crowd. "I'm not twenty-one." *Not to mention I'm not pretty enough to be let into the hottest club in town.*

Cora wrapped herself around Whiskey's left arm. "I think you'll like it. It's not as much fun as Crucible, but—"

"Cora."

Fiona's sharp voice redirected Whiskey's attention. She saw Fiona give Cora a glare. For her part, Cora didn't wilt, but her pale skin flushed as she looked away.

"What were you going to say?"

Cora's discomfort faded. She smiled at Whiskey. "I was going to say it's not as much fun, but I like the music better here."

Whiskey always knew when someone lied to her. She'd expected it sooner or later. Fiona ruled this roost. For whatever reason, be it fear or greed, she engendered loyalty from her people. She'd probably ordered Cora's intimacy with Whiskey whatever Cora's enjoyment of the activity. Whiskey ruthlessly quashed a faint sense of regret. *Take more than you give.*

"Shall we?" Fiona turned away from her guest, and crossed the street.

Whiskey allowed herself to be pulled along by Cora. She kept a neutral expression on her face as Fiona led them not to the end of the line, but to the door itself. *Shit. How much influence does she have?*

Glances smoldered with venom, especially from those who'd waited longest near the door. A handful verbally accosted them as Fiona spoke with one of the bouncers. The big man's black T-shirt strained across his pectoral muscles. He looked past Fiona to Cora and Whiskey. His eyes flashed golden in the streetlight, startling Whiskey from her feigned nonchalance. He nodded, and spoke with his partner. Another nod, a wave, and the door opened for them.

They mounted the steps, and entered the thundering music. The more vocal members of the crowd swore at them. Whiskey ignored the epithets, staring at the bouncer with the golden eyes. Up close his eyes were dark brown, a few shades lighter than hers. *He has to be wearing contacts, too. Is he part of Fiona's clique?* She had no more time to dwell on it as the doors closed behind them.

Light and sound. Multicolored flashes overhead illuminated the balcony onto which the entry opened. An industrial-style railing circled this level, an affectation permeating the club's decor. More brightness assaulted her eyes from somewhere beyond and below. She let Cora guide her as she gained her bearings. Gunmetal steel cabaret tables here held a handful of drinkers. A small bar huddled in the corner to accommodate them. Fiona smiled over her shoulder, and waved at Whiskey to follow. She descended a wide circular staircase.

As Whiskey approached the steps, she saw three cages hanging from the ceiling on a level with the balcony. A couple currently occupied one. A man and woman danced seductively inside, both partially undressed. From the looks of the clothing scattered in the corners of the cage, they'd be completely nude before long. The cage gently swayed with their motions, and Whiskey saw where a catwalk extended out to it. She wondered if they were paid workers for the club, or exhibitionist patrons allowed its use. Looking down, she saw the large dance floor packed with revelers moving to the hypnotic music. Squares of colored floor tiles pulsed in time with the music. Another cage hung against the opposite wall, this one a metal and Plexiglas contraption that housed the club's DJ.

Reaching the main floor, Fiona ushered them past a long bar, up some steps and toward the back corner. Whiskey squeezed past people to keep up. She seriously doubted they'd find anywhere to sit at this time of night. Malice was too popular for a table to go empty for any length of time, especially on a Friday night. She wondered if Fiona would resort to bullying her way into taking one over.

Cora was already enjoying herself. She clutched Whiskey's arm, but moved in time with the music as they walked. She smiled at Whiskey, leaning forward to give her a lingering kiss on the cheek. Whiskey raised an eyebrow, eyes darting around to see if anyone took notice or offense. No one responded, and she breathed a sigh of relief. Another fight after the one last night would wipe her out. She didn't want to ruin a good thing. Now that she'd been allowed inside Malice without showing identification, maybe she could sneak back in the future, preferably without her current companions.

Fiona pushed aside a curtain made of metal chain, and waved them past. "Sit down, children."

Whiskey stepped into a semiprivate area. She recognized Manuel and Bronwyn from the night before, lounging together on the booth seat of a single large metal table. Daniel also sat here, raising a beer in welcome. No other tables graced the room, giving the pack a secure, private base from which to party. Cora helped Whiskey into a chair across from the others, immediately taking residence on her lap.

The chain rattled back into place, and Fiona drifted behind Whiskey's chair, hardly pausing as she trailed her fingernails up Whiskey's recent tattoo. The tender skin stung. Before Whiskey registered the annoyance, Cora squirmed in her lap, drawing her attention to more pleasing things.

"Where's Alphonse and Zebediah?" Fiona sat at the head of the table. A waitress appeared out of nowhere with a tray full of drinks.

"Out on the floor," Manuel drawled. "They've found a couple of *kizarusi* for the night."

The waitress set two shot glasses and a bottle of Chivas Regal Royal in front of Whiskey. Cora wriggled in a pleasing manner, distracting Whiskey further. Her hands caressed and supported Cora's waist as the woman leaned forward to reach the bottle. Whiskey focused on her hands splayed out upon Cora's back. The conversation continued as she studied them. Clean healthy skin covered her knuckles where bruises and abrasions had been just this afternoon. *What did Daniel inject me with?*

"*Kizarusi* or cows?" Fiona accepted a glass of red wine.

Whiskey's left hand strayed to her new tattoo. The antibiotic cream had soaked into her flesh, leaving the skin smooth. She felt the slight raised scabbing along the ink. She'd never had a tattoo before, but she'd heard how much it hurt, had seen how long it took to heal with other street kids fortunate to have friends in the business. This looked days old, not an hour. She drew her hand from her forearm to her belly, pressing on the bruises, finding little discomfort.

Bronwyn and Manuel gave each other a knowing glance. "Cows." Bronwyn smirked.

"What are *kizarusi?*"

Fiona smiled at Whiskey. "A babe in the woods," she said to

the others, indicating Whiskey. Bronwyn chuckled, and Daniel's lips quirked in amusement. Manuel showed no emotion at all.

Whiskey's eyes narrowed at the vague insult. On a hunch, she lowered her chin. "That doesn't answer the question." Cora handed her a shot glass of alcohol. Whiskey took it without drinking.

"How to explain *kizarusi*?" Fiona looked inward for a definition. "They are a class of Humans who...serve us."

"Serve? Like maids or something?"

Bronwyn's laugh clashed with the music thumping in the main part of the club.

Fiona didn't hide her amusement as she sipped her wine. "No. Perhaps 'serve' was the incorrect word. *Kizarusi* offer us the ultimate gift so that we may continue life." She raised an eyebrow. "You must have been quite young when your parents passed the veil, little *lamma*. You don't even know the most basic of words of your native tongue."

Whiskey blinked. The mention of her parents' death hurt; it always did, some years more than others. This had been a bad year. She drained her glass without thought. The unfamiliar alcohol burned hot down her throat. She barely controlled the urge to wheeze, and slammed the shot glass onto the table to cover the unexpected physical response. "Native tongue? What are you talking about?" She glared about the table, pleased her voice didn't sound too rough.

"Surely you've known you were different from others, Whiskey." Setting her wineglass down, Fiona leaned forward. "Known that you were alone when surrounded by your alleged peers, felt a burning need as a child for something unimaginable?"

Cora poured another shot, and handed the glass to her. Whiskey sipped it this time. "Everybody feels that." It still burned, though the sensation rapidly became familiar. "Everybody thinks they're special, more important or different from the rest of the assholes around them."

"But you *are*, *Ninsumgal*," Cora whispered, leaning forward to kiss Whiskey's forehead.

"Bullshit." Manuel stood, and downed the rest of his beer.

"She's no more *Ninsumgal* than I am *usumgal*." He thrust a chin toward the curtain separating them from the dance floor. Bronwyn slid to her feet, and the pair walked out in a rattle of metal chain.

"How did—?" Whiskey turned to Cora. "How did he hear you over the music?"

"We all heard her, little *lamma*," Fiona answered. "We're Sanguire as, I believe, are you."

Whiskey shivered. Of all the strange words these people bandied about, this one meant something to her. "Sanguire." She'd heard it before, said it before, but couldn't remember where or when. "Sanguire."

"You recognize it?"

Sensing danger, Whiskey finished her drink. "Tell me more about *kizarusi*. They give the ultimate gift? What gift?"

Fiona smiled. "Their blood. None of us can live without it."

They do think they're vampires. "So, *kizsarusi* are...your victims?"

Cora laughed, wrapping an arm around Whiskey's neck to hug her. "No, silly! Most *kizarusi* are from well-established Human families who have served us for generations."

Whiskey did her best not to flinch away from the blonde. She searched through her memories of horror flicks she'd watched over the years. Almost all vampires had a human caretaker during the daylight hours, someone who'd been driven mad and protected their masters and mistresses with rabid devotion. "Like...Renfield?"

Fiona sneered. "Hardly, dear Whiskey." She took a sip of her wine.

Daniel decided to join the discussion. "You read too many trashy vampire novels, youngling."

Whiskey took his comment as an invitation. "What did you inject me with last night?" She shifted in her chair, automatically grasping Cora's waist to keep her from toppling from her perch. "It didn't just look like blood, it *was* blood, wasn't it?"

"Very astute," Fiona said.

A wave of light-headedness swept over Whiskey. "You gave

me your blood! You're trying to turn me into a vampire!" *What if one of them has AIDS or something?*

"I rest my case." Daniel snorted. "It doesn't work that way, Whiskey. You either are or aren't Sanguire. No blood transfusion can make a Human into a Sanguire." He took a swallow of beer.

"Drink, *Ninsumgal.*" Cora refilled Whiskey's shot glass.

The alcohol ripped through the curtain of weakness. Whiskey gasped, and held out her glass for a refill. "Well, it did something," she insisted. "My knuckles aren't wracked up anymore, and I think my bruises have gone away." She looked at the fine lines on her arm. "Tattoos sting for days, but this barely hurts now." *Come to think of it, my nipples don't hurt that much, either.*

"Which proves my theory," Fiona stated. "You are Sanguire, or you couldn't enjoy the benefits of Daniel's medical cocktail."

Whiskey stuttered, the alcohol in her system blurring her thoughts. *Jesus, this stuff's strong.* Fiona watched in amusement as she gathered her thoughts. "I can't be...Sanguire. I don't drink or need blood to live."

"Yet," Cora whispered.

Whiskey gave her a sharp look, seeing a beautiful smile on her face.

"It is the nature of our people to age slowly." Fiona stroked her cheek with one finger, lost in thought. "We have always hidden among Humans, and have evolved a bit of camouflage."

"In order for our offspring to survive childhood, they age like Humans until they reach physical maturity," Daniel said. "Once they attain adulthood they begin the *Ñíri Kurám*, to walk the Strange Path. It's a gradual phenomenon that takes many years to complete. Most of us utilize a *Baruñal* and the Book to accelerate the process."

Whiskey peered at Daniel as his light Germanic accent flowed over her. His words were nothing but noise to her. *Baruñal? Ñíri Kurám?* Gibberish.

Cora blocked her vision, gray eyes staring into hers. "Whiskey?"

"Three shots in under half an hour. She's had too much to

drink." Fiona suddenly appeared beside Whiskey. She took the shot glass and set it on the table. "Odd that you should carry the name, yet have difficulty holding the liquor."

Whiskey flushed, feeling overly warm. "It's jus' a nickname." She felt a moment of dismay at the sound of her slurred voice. Attempting to control herself, she enunciated her next words carefully. "I've never had whiskey before. Only beer or wine."

Fiona brushed her fingers through Whiskey's hair, an insincere parody of tenderness. "Not anymore, dear little *lamma*. From now on you'll eat and drink the finest the world has to offer. You're home now."

"It may also be a result of the healing and hunger," Daniel said. "She's using a lot of her energy to repair the damage." He appeared within Whiskey's groggy vision, leaning over her, lifting an eyelid to peek at her pupil, ignoring her sluggish attempt to slap him away. "It's been hours since she last ate, and her metabolism has accelerated as she's mended. She needs more food and sleep."

"Let's get her to the bench for a quick nap, and I'll order dinner."

The world swooped and rolled as the three got Whiskey to her feet. *It was only three drinks, damn it!* "I'm fine. Jus' lemme alone a minnit." They ignored her, manhandling her to the bench seat. She closed her eyes for a moment, opening them with a start at the deep sound of metal scraping metal.

The heavy metal table now two feet away, Fiona smiled at Whiskey. Dusting her hands, she headed for the curtain.

"Damn, she's strong."

Cora knelt on the floor beside her. "As will you be when you complete the *Ñíri Kurám, Ninsumgal*."

Whiskey wanted to ask what the words meant, but couldn't make her mouth form the question. Her eyes drifted closed.

She didn't feel it when it happened.

An overpowering copper aroma choked her nostrils. Hot liquid splashed down her inner thigh. These sensations told the tale of injury long before her flesh screamed, splitting beneath the thrust of a blade. With each pulse of her heart, she hemorrhaged, soaking her skirts with stickiness. The pain reverberated down through the arch of her foot, and up to her hip, spreading with each beat of her heart. She attempted to pull back, find something—anything—to put between herself and her attacker. Clumsy with the enervation already seeping through her body, she stumbled.

There was a shift of time. One moment she stood with her life's essence pooling in her boot, slicking the marble beneath her. The next she battled cold, icy talons wrapping her body in a freezing embrace. Bewildered, she didn't know how much time had passed. Unable to stop her teeth from chattering, she stared up at the vaulted ceiling of her private audience chamber. A shadow blocked the intricate gilded paintings. She took precious seconds to study it, making out the details of a strange woman looming over her.

The woman spoke. *Minn'ast.* Her musical words sounded both intimate and foreign. *So familiar. Is that my name? How can I remember a woman I've never seen?* Green eyes glittered with unshed tears above her, mahogany hair cascading down to brush her face. The woman spoke more words in a voice full of anguish. She understood no more than the tone of them. She heard herself respond, instantly recognized the slurred voice as hers, but the words were as strange as the woman's. Cold gripped her, deepening beyond ice. She no longer had the energy to shiver.

The world went dark.

CHAPTER SIX

Sharp, burning pain woke her. With a hiss, Whiskey sat up, clutching at her thigh. As she roused, the ache receded. She sat on the bench seat at Malice, music throbbing in time with the fading spasm in her leg. Alone. "Fucking nightmare," she muttered.

She released her leg to scrub at her face, and brush hair from her eyes. A glance around showed that Fiona's people hadn't left the bar, though they'd cleared out of the immediate area. A crimson filigree shawl Cora had worn adorned one chair, and a small shoulder bag last seen in Bronwyn's clutches sat in the corner of the bench seat. Drinks and half-eaten food were scattered across the table's surface. She'd been out at least long enough for everyone to have had dinner, and continue drinking.

Her stomach ached at the reminder of food. Whenever she

drank her metabolism went into high gear. She'd never suffered a hangover, but after a binge she'd be absolutely starving. Like now. Swinging her legs to the floor, she stood with little problem, the intoxication having faded to a minor buzz. *How long have I been out?* She didn't have a watch, and there weren't any visible clocks. *It can't have been too long. Don't the bars close by two or three?* Unless Fiona had greater pull than Whiskey suspected. Considering one of the bouncers appeared to be Sanguire, it wasn't too far a stretch to think closing time had come and gone hours ago.

She looked at the curtain of chain, not seeing much beyond except flashing light and shadow. Was someone standing outside the divider? Fully awake, she stared at the darkness, and listened intently for any movement outside. Was that the sound of cloth moving? *Dumb shit! You can't hear over this music any more than they can.* Someone yawned loudly on the other side, and she straightened in surprise. *Fuck! There's someone there.*

She couldn't imagine any of Fiona's people hovering over her. Most of them treated her with indifference. Only Cora and Fiona paid outright attention to her. Had they wanted to come in, they'd do so. Still unsettled by the drink and the bizarre discussion, Whiskey took some time to collect her wits. She returned to the chair she'd been seated in before she'd gotten so smashed she couldn't talk. Pouring herself another shot of alcohol from the bottle, she spun the chair around to face the curtain. "I know you're there. Might as well come on in."

The tinkle of chain links heralding his arrival, an outrageous figure took up her summons. Thin and lanky, the specter looked like he'd just sidled out of a comic book. His black hair stuck up in three spiked mohawks, one centered and one at either temple, sweeping to the back of his otherwise bald skull. High cheekbones made his long face appear gaunt and accented his deep-set eyes. He was dressed in black, and Whiskey felt a surge of jealousy mix with her apprehension. His outfit was a Goth's wet dream: leather pants, thick-soled boots, spiked knee guards, unadorned T-shirt and a leather trench coat. *These guys don't do things by halves.*

"Ah, the prodigal daughter awakes." The man's voice was a pleasing tenor. He pulled another chair away from the table, and sat across from her without invitation. "Sleep well?"

"Well enough," Whiskey allowed.

The caricature visibly tested the air, sniffing, his leather creaking as he leaned slightly closer. "I detect a certain...Cora about your person, do I not?"

Whiskey feigned nonchalance. "You know Cora?" Had Fiona requested his presence, or had he sneaked past her? "Who are you? Do you work for Fiona?"

He smiled coyly, dusting his clothes with an air of false modesty. "I am no one of import. Nor am I in service to a wild youngling such as that little temptress. I am but a mere servant of my *Ninsumgal*, here in this wondrous city to search her out."

Ninsumgal. The word annoyed her. She didn't know why, but she didn't think this man meant her harm. The use of that word cemented that for her. She gathered her indignation. "Look, I don't know who you are, or what a *Ninsumgal* is, okay? Why don't you just leave, and I'll be right behind you. You go your way, I'll go mine."

He acted shocked. "My apologies for my lack of manners. Allow me to introduce myself." Standing, he swept into a low bow. "Reynhard Dorst, at your service, *Gasan*."

His sudden movement surprised Whiskey. She flinched backward. When she saw he didn't intend to attack, she felt a heavy blush. "I don't care who you are. Get the fuck out of here."

Dorst peered up at her from his bow, a hairless eyebrow raised. "Hardly a proper response, my dear. It's customary to answer with your name at the very least." He slowly straightened. "A slight nod of the head wouldn't be amiss, either, since common curtsies have gone out of style."

She stared at him. Though he was quite a bit taller, she didn't feel a threat. Dorst, despite his garish appearance, wasn't here to hurt her. Sheepish at his lesson on etiquette, she said, "I'm Whiskey."

"Yes, you are." He rewarded her with a slight smile, and a nod. "You're also an enigma, my dear. Someone unexpected, possibly someone perilous. At the very least, someone who is in danger."

She thought of Fiona, and frowned. "How am I in danger?"

"By your very existence."

She watched him rummage in a voluminous pocket of his trench coat, and wondered if her instincts had been wrong. He remained between her and the doorway. There were no other exits. She mentally prepared to put up a fight.

He extracted a bag from a local fast-food chain. "Hungry?" He set it on the table and removed a greasy paper-wrapped bundle. "With or without cheese?"

The aroma of hamburgers overpowered her. "With."

"Excellent choice." Dorst tossed the sandwich to her, and retrieved another for himself. "There are those godawful potato strips in there if you'd like." He slid the bag closer to her. Stepping away from the table, he resumed his chair, effectively continuing to block her from the exit.

She accepted the bag of french fries. They dined quietly, the drumming trance music a loud accompaniment. She noticed his watchful eyes studying her, and returned the favor. He ate neatly, his paper napkin unfolded across one leather-clad leg. It perched with incongruence next to a knee guard sprouting long metal spikes. The soles of his boots were four inches thick with bright decorative silver plates riveted to them. He wore a leather harness of some sort over his T-shirt. She wondered why. He didn't look or act like a bondage type, not that she had much experience with those people.

Dorst finished eating first. He tidied himself with his napkin before leaning the chair back, neatly balancing it on two legs, one boot on the edge of the table. When Whiskey completed her meal, she balled up the waste, and stuffed it inside the empty bag.

"So, what do you want?"

"To meet you, get to know you. What are your thoughts on world politics?"

Whiskey grimaced. "I hate politics. It's just a network of powerful assholes swapping favors and money back and forth. It doesn't do anybody a damned bit of good."

"Really?" He intently watched her. "How would you do things differently?"

She shrugged. "I don't know." He didn't continue the

discussion, expectantly waiting for her to explain herself. "Throw them out and start over. Spread the wealth. Make sure everybody's taken care of, not just the top ten percent."

"Very idealistic, but not too practical."

"What difference does it make? No one gives a shit what a street kid in Seattle thinks anyway."

Dorst smiled. "One person can change the world."

"That's a load of crap."

He cocked his head. "Do tell."

Whiskey snorted. "One person is useless without power. It takes other people to give that person power. Besides, all one person can change is their perception of the world. The world remains the same shit heap it's always been; it's the person who's changed."

"Do you want that kind of power?"

She rolled her eyes. "This is a stupid conversation. Is that why Fiona brought you here?"

Dorst dropped his chair onto all four legs. Placing his elbows above the knee guards, he leaned closer to examine her. "Do you want that kind of power?" he whispered.

Whiskey glared at him, realizing he wouldn't take silence for an answer. "Fuck no. I'm not insane."

They stared at one another a full minute before Dorst relaxed his stance. "Not yet."

"What the hell is that supposed to mean?" His impish grin irritated and confused her. The longer she remained in his presence, the more familiar he became. With the familiarity came the certainty that he meant her no harm. If she wanted to walk out the door, he wouldn't stop her. "Have we met?" she blurted, automatically negating the question in her mind. She'd have remembered seeing someone like him.

His smile faded, and the keenness returned to his eyes. "Why?"

"I don't know." She shook her head. "You remind me of somebody, that's all."

"Who?" he asked. "An enemy? A friend?" He wiggled nonexistent eyebrows. "A lover?"

Despite herself, she chuckled. "No, not a lover. I'd remember *that*." She closed her eyes, trying to place him. "I don't know. Not a friend, exactly. But someone I can—" *trust.* Whiskey snapped her mouth shut before she revealed a potential weakness. How could she trust this garish man whom she'd never met? *Hell, I didn't even trust Gin this much in our first year together!* She opened her eyes, and they studied one another again.

"You are very like someone I once knew." She strained to hear his words. "I have been searching for her for some time now. I wonder…"

The emotion in his voice was so poignant, so filled with pain and loss, almost as much as Whiskey felt for her parents. She swallowed a lump in her throat, damning herself for the abrupt desire to be the person for whom this strange man searched.

Several minutes passed and Dorst inhaled deeply, breaking the tableau. He swept to his feet, and bowed again to her. "Thank you so much for dining with me, my dear."

She blinked as he moved the chair to one side, and headed for the exit. "Wait. That's it?"

Dorst grinned at her. "We'll meet again, dear Whiskey. I'm your *Baruñal.*"

She watched him stalk out of the room into the club beyond. "Wait a minute!" She scrambled after him through the metal curtain. "I don't understand."

He turned to face her. "You will, I think." With a flourish and a sweep of his trench coat, he bowed once more. "I am ever your humble servant, my sweet Whiskey." He spun about, and walked toward the stairs.

Whiskey stared after him, feeling an unacceptable sense of loss. She clapped her hand to her forehead. *What the hell is wrong with me?* Looking around the club, she saw that it had closed. Fiona and her pack lounged at a table near the dance floor, the only patrons in the vast room. The wait staff counted money, and figured the night's tips at the bar. Cora approached with a smile on her face. Whiskey looked up as Dorst arrived at the balcony above.

He turned with a flourish, tipped an imaginary hat to her, and disappeared beyond her vision. She smelled the faint gust of fresh air that announced his departure.

"Ninsumgal." Cora slid into her arms. "Do you feel better now?"

Whiskey resisted the urge to push her away. Cora was Fiona's whore, the carrot at the end of the stick to keep Whiskey under control. Had Whiskey been interested in one of the men, she had no doubt it'd be one of them sucking up to her instead. It wasn't Cora's fault that Whiskey preferred women, and she didn't deserve to be treated like trash because of circumstance. "Yeah, I do."

"Are you still hungry? The kitchen remains open. We can order anything you'd like."

Near the dance floor, Fiona watched them with golden flashing eyes. *Can she hear what I say over the music?* "What time is it?"

"Nearly five in the morning." Cora glanced back at her pack leader. "We were waiting for you to wake before going home."

Home. For years that word had meant nothing. She had no home, and didn't want one. Somewhere in her distant past she'd had one, and it had been destroyed. It could never be replaced. Afterward home meant a place of pain and neglect, a place where beatings and starvation occurred with dreary regularity. Whiskey lowered her chin, still staring at Fiona across the room. "I'm not going with you."

Fiona raised her eyebrow, her mocking smile unchanging. With a slight nod, she turned to one of the colored mohawks, giving him an order. Zebediah clambered to his feet and went to the bar.

"The *Sañur Gasum* said you might not want to," Cora said.

Like the word Sanguire, these words too had meaning for Whiskey, though she didn't know why. "You mean Dorst?" Somehow the words fit him.

"Yes." Fiona had crossed the distance between them in seconds. "That's his title."

Fast as well as strong. Whiskey swallowed in sudden dread, wondering if Fiona would put up a struggle. At least one member of the staff here had to be part of this, maybe all of them. She almost lifted her chin in defiance, but remembered Fiona using the same gesture to capitulate. "Thank you for everything, but it's time I was on my way."

"I think you're wrong, little *lamma*."

Zebediah walked up, and deposited Whiskey's backpack at her feet.

Whiskey blinked, glancing down and back up at Fiona. In her arms, Cora stiffened, her grip tightening around Whiskey's waist. Fiona smiled, elongated canines shining in the strobe lights.

"I had Daniel put it in the car just in case."

Cora's response to Fiona's toothy smile and Whiskey's instincts suggested a less than congenial send-off. The vision of Fiona using those teeth to tear out her throat flashed across her mind. *Never show weakness.* "Thanks. I guess I'll see you around." She disengaged from Cora, and reached for her pack, refusing to take the bait. As Whiskey shouldered her pack, Fiona stepped back to give her room, fangs still showing. What had she read once? If a wolf stalked you, walk away, don't run or it'll give chase. With her pack settled, and the hip strap secure, Whiskey paused. She also recalled what Cora had said earlier in the evening. *All we ask is that you remember who assisted you when you needed it most, my Ninsumgal.* Whiskey turned back. "Thank you. I owe you."

The gesture did what Whiskey expected. Fiona's eyes darted to Whiskey's outstretched hand, her feral smile fading to something a little less dangerous. "You're most welcome, Whiskey." She took the offered hand.

Whiskey shook Fiona's hand. Turning to Cora, she leaned forward and whispered, "And thank you." She received a deep kiss in reward.

"If you should have need of us, little *lamma*." Fiona held out a cell phone. "All our numbers are there. Don't hesitate to call."

"I won't," Whiskey lied, taking the phone.

When she reached the top of the steps, she glanced back. Manuel, Bronwyn and Alphonse danced to the music still blaring from the speakers. Zebediah nursed a beer at the bar, and Daniel's feet were atop the table where he slouched. Most of the employees appeared to have left, leaving the bartender, the bouncer and the DJ in the booth.

"You'll find Reynhard's number on the phone as well," Fiona said, raising her voice to be heard.

Whiskey gave her a sharp nod. Moments later, she stood on the street, inhaling lungfuls of cool, moist Seattle air. Not wanting to hang around and be discovered by Fiona's crew as they left, she settled her pack on her shoulders, and strode away.

CHAPTER SEVEN

Whiskey walked ten blocks before slowing, zigzagging through early morning downtown Seattle to throw off any pursuit should Fiona change her mind. The sky grew lighter, wisps of clouds drifting across an otherwise blue sky. It promised to be a day with plenty of sunshine. Whiskey scowled. She'd never been able to tolerate too much sun; it gave her migraines.

Easing down a steep hill, she looked out at the bay spread out before her. Ferries and fishing boats had already motored to their destinations. Someday she'd ride a ferry. She'd always wanted to, but just hadn't gotten around to it. It would be fun to go to Canada on a ferry, leave the States altogether. No birth certificate meant no state identification, however, let alone the passport required to get across the border these days. She didn't know where she'd been born. The fatal accident that had orphaned her at five years old had effectively erased her past. All she knew for certain was that her parents had hailed from North Carolina, and died on a road trip in Oregon. As a ward of the state, she knew that Oregon had to have located her birth certificate, but she'd have to tell someone here in authority her real name to get it. One of the first lessons she'd learned in the social welfare system was that the people in charge of her fate didn't give a rat's ass about her. She couldn't trust anyone in authority with her real name. Times were changing, though. Sooner or later she'd need real ID to get along in the world.

The ground before her leveled out onto a small park overlooking the piers. Across the bay sunlight hit the top of the hills. Along the sidewalk, between her and the Pike's Street Market, vendors had already set up tables and goods in preparation for the weekend tourists and local regulars. Whiskey stopped to get her sunglasses out of her pack, and debate what to do next.

She couldn't panhandle without being set upon by the old-timers who called downtown Seattle home. The youth club, Tallulah's, closed at six. She'd never get there in time to meet Gin, even if she had change for the bus. Which brought up another issue—she had thirteen cents to her name. Despite her early morning burger, courtesy of Dorst, her stomach informed her it needed breakfast.

Whiskey laughed aloud, rousting a nearby pigeon. "Got cool clothes and a tat worth hundreds, but didn't catch any cash. Just my luck," she told the bird. Deciding she wasn't a danger, it returned to pecking grit from the sidewalk.

It looked like she'd have to walk back to the U District. Maybe she could bum some money there this morning and grab a latte. She still had several hours before meeting with Castillo at the Youth Consortium. Slipping on her sunglasses, she vowed to ask him for bus tickets and food vouchers. Maybe after that, she'd check the University branch of the public library for that book she'd been reading two days ago. *And check the Internet for those words.*

Whiskey opened the main compartment of her pack. The smell of detergent and bleach tickled her nose. Her clothes had been laundered while she'd slept, to include the ones she'd worn when she'd been attacked. Brow furrowed, Whiskey closely examined the rest of her things, not liking that someone had gone through them. From the looks of it, her worn sleeping bag had been replaced with a similar brand, and the thin blanket she kept inside it cleaned. The exterior compartments held the usual amount of clutter—hairbrush, toiletry items picked up from various shelters and services, her journal, lighters, a pocketknife, and other detritus she'd collected over the years. There were other things, too—a slim leather-bound book with strange writing, a fresh carton of cigarettes in her brand, an aluminum travel bottle filled with water, a four-inch sheathed knife, a silver flask that sloshed when she shook it, and an ivory envelope. Whiskey opened the flask and took a sniff, the smell of alcohol burning her nostrils. *Of course, whiskey.* Sealing it, she put it back, and took out the envelope.

The elegant handwriting on the front merely stated her name. An old-fashioned wax seal with a stylized *F* graced the back flap. Whiskey cracked the seal. She held it open only an instant, glimpsing the contents before shutting the envelope with a crackle of paper. Looking around, she verified no one stood within thirty feet of her, and peeked inside again. A stack of twenty-dollar bills, and a folded paper met her gaze.

"Holy shit." She clumsily thumbed through the bills, not pulling them out of the envelope. She wasn't sure, but it looked like four hundred dollars or more inside, more money than she'd ever had in her hands in her life. "Jesus!" Her mind immediately went to the things she could purchase without worry—cigarettes, lighter fluid for her empty Zippo, socks. She could get a good pair of boots, some more pens, a portable CD player, and still have money left over for a couple of days of food. Her fingers met with parchment, undermining her elation. This money came from Fiona. Another in the long list of favors she'd use to call Whiskey back to her.

Whiskey pulled the paper out, stuffing the envelope back into her pack. Unfolding the note, she braced herself for what it might contain.

Dearest Whiskey,
If you're reading this, you've decided to go it alone rather than accept our hospitality. You'll never know how much this saddens my heart.

Whiskey snorted. "Saddened, my ass."

I hope this surprise finds you well. Considering your lack of a stable domicile, I took the liberty of doing what I could to assist you. You're a proud and noble woman, little lamma, much like your predecessor. Please accept the gifts in the spirit they were given.
Again, I reiterate—you have a cellular phone with our numbers. Call for any reason, no matter how slight. At the very least, I urge you to contact your Baruñal, Reynhard Dorst, at the soonest opportunity. He can assist you with the Ñíri Kurám you are about to undergo.
With Heavy Heart,
Fiona

Whiskey reread the note. *Who's my predecessor? Who do these people think I am?* She turned the paper over, as if expecting answers there. Folding it, she returned it to her pack. She glanced around her, seeing sunlight crawling down the trees across the bay. It was just a matter of time before it breached the cityscape behind her, filling the day with sunshine. More vendors had appeared on the sidewalk. A few hardy customers already dickered over vegetables just inside the covered market area. Her stomach reminded her that she'd been drinking, and a burger and fries didn't do much with her metabolism.

Keeping the envelope hidden inside her pack, she pulled out two twenties, and pocketed them. The rest remained inside. She secured the pack, and hefted it onto her shoulders. *La Panier*, a restaurant here at the market, remained open twenty-four hours. She'd have some breakfast, and try to make some sense of what had happened to her.

CHAPTER EIGHT

Whiskey stepped off the bus near the U District Youth Consortium. Her stomach comfortably full of baguettes and coffee, she'd changed back into her ragged cargo pants in the market restroom, carefully tucking the latex ones away. No need to advertise her sudden good fortune, and invite an attack by her peers. The tattoo publicized it enough. The sun beat down upon her, and she readjusted her sunglasses with a grimace. In another hour, the shoe place downtown would open. She'd already spent the better part of an hour staring into the window at the boots on display there. She'd promised Castillo she'd check in with him, else she'd have blown him off to make her purchase. Too many people broke promises these days; she didn't.

Whenever her mind wandered to the night before, she chastised herself for gullibility. Vampires only existed in books, movies and video games. Whiskey ridiculed the whole concept of a completely different race of beings living off human blood. These vampire wannabes said that to justify their lifestyle. She'd done some reading, heard some things; she must have come across the word Sanguire somewhere else before.

Hefting her pack, she walked the two blocks to the shelter. The sidewalks were crowded with people enjoying the early spring sunshine. Seattle skies were cloudy more often than not—a plus in Whiskey's book—so people always came out to catch rays on days like today. Her exposed skin stung with sunburn, though she hadn't been out in it for long. Her body always felt like that to her on sunny days, even as a child. When she arrived at the shelter, she gratefully pushed inside.

She nodded to the two street kids lounging in the day shelter, neither of whom she knew well. The rest of the regulars were probably at the nearest park or the campus, like everyone else. At the registration desk, she slouched out of her pack, and set it on the floor. "I have an appointment with Father Castillo."

The chunky little woman peered up at her through her bifocals. "Whiskey! How are you?" Her expression belied the welcome tone in her voice. She looked like she stared at a particularly ugly bug in a microscope.

Not put off, Whiskey spoke evenly. "Pretty good, Sister. You?" She mentally recited the nun's next words, doing her best not to roll her eyes.

"God blesses me in every way." The nun peered at a clipboard with the same loathing.

Whiskey wondered if she'd always had that look on her face. *Maybe there's truth to that saying, "Don't make faces or yours will freeze that way."*

The nun stared at Whiskey's right arm. "That's new, isn't it?"

Whiskey held her arm forward and turned it, showing off the artwork. "Yeah, it is. You like it?" She rubbed the light scabs with one hand, reminding herself to use the ointment again before heading out.

"I'll let Father know you're here."

She chuckled at the nonanswer. "Thanks, Sister." She moved

her pack to a nearby couch. The woman hoisted her bulk out of her chair and waddled down a hall.

"Big score?" one of the other kids asked.

"Kind of." Whiskey flopped next to her pack. "Got this out of the deal." She breathed a sigh as the teenager quickly lost interest, glad he'd accepted she had nothing else. She relaxed, her eyes drifted closed of their own volition. She'd use some of the money for a motel room today. With Gin's boyfriend, Ghost, back in town, she had a fifty-fifty shot whether she'd be allowed to bunk down with his street family. The longer she avoided him, the less jealous he'd act when she did show her face.

"Whiskey?"

She opened her eyes, and grinned. "Hey, Padre, how goes it?" She stood as he approached.

A handsome man with brown skin and black hair and eyes smiled at her. His shoulder length curls extended past his crisp white collar to brush his shoulder blades. A haphazardly trimmed beard adorned his narrow face. Whiskey bet if she ever saw him in civilian clothes, he'd pass easily among the street kids. She'd only ever seen him in the black cassock of his order, with a heavy silver cross at his neck.

He held out his arms for an embrace. "I'm doing well, Whiskey. How about you?"

She stiffened in his arms, unaccustomed to casual displays of affection. Her demeanor remained pleasant, however, as she extricated herself from his arms. "Not bad. Beautiful day out there. Why are you in here instead?"

"And miss seeing my favorite client? Never." His eyes scanned her, noting the ink on her arm. "Shall we head back to my office?"

"Sure."

Before she could pick up her belongings, Castillo had her pack in his hands, easily swinging it to one shoulder. A small man, no taller than she, he had a fine bone structure. It amazed her how easily he hoisted her laden pack. "You been working out?" she teased, trailing him through a door past the reception area.

He grinned, and winked at her. "Can't keep up with you young'uns otherwise."

She snorted. "You're not that old, Padre."

"You'd be surprised."

A frisson of suspicion whispered through her. *Oh, get over it! You'll be seeing vampires all over the place at this rate.* They entered his office, the best room in the building. Books lined the walls from floor to ceiling on two sides. A large secretary desk sat adjacent to the high windows along the third wall, and four beat-up file cabinets flanked the door.

Castillo gently set her pack in one of the two chairs across from his desk, and waved her to take a seat. "You want something to drink? I've got coffee and sarsaparilla."

"Still on that root beer kick?" She sank into the chair.

"Nothing finer on a hot spring day."

She grinned at him. "Sarsaparilla it is then."

"Fantastic." He sat down, and rummaged in the small refrigerator underneath the desk, pulling out two bottles of root beer. He cracked one open and handed it to her.

Whiskey took a long draught, scanning the room. Shade trees kept the sun at bay. A bank of high windows helped her cause. For now she was safe. No street kids preying on the loner that walked among them, no police officers busting her for napping on a park bench, or business owners throwing things at her for daring to sit on the sidewalk in front of their establishments. Father Castillo understood her need for this more than any other counselor she'd ever had. He remained silent, waiting for her to take the next step. He never acted too busy for her, never gave the impression that he had more important matters to attend to even when his next appointment waited in the lobby.

Maybe his youth kindled her trust. Whiskey immediately denied the argument. Her faith seldom manifested in anyone these days, and she hung around many people her own age. *Except Reynhard.* The memory of her emotions when meeting Dorst at the club troubled her. Now she thought of him by his first name? *What the fuck is going on with me?*

She had to give Castillo credit, though; he had a refreshing approach to dealing with street people. Most priests and ministers spent quite a deal of time bringing the word of God to the downtrodden masses, pounding His holy writ into their heads with zealous intent. Castillo rarely brought up the topic. His goal seemed to be putting street youth into stable shelters and programs, nothing more. He required a prayer only before dishing up meals at the soup kitchen, allowing the homeless to eat their suppers without proselytizing.

"Spent the night in a club?"

Whiskey blinked. "How the—" She barely stopped herself from swearing. "How did you know that?"

Castillo grinned, tapping the side of his nose with one finger. "I smell cigarette smoke, but not cloves. Obviously, not at Tallulah's last night."

"I detect a certain...Cora about your person."

Whiskey pushed away the incongruous recollection. "You're good, Padre. I partied at Malice last night."

He raised his eyebrows. "Malice? That's an adult club. How'd you get in?"

"Don't give me shit, Padre." A faint grin contradicted the harshness of her words. "My benefactors slipped me in the main entrance."

He conceded with a bow of his head. "They give you that, too?" His bottle gestured toward the dragons running up her arm.

"Yeah! Pretty cool, isn't it?" She rolled up the sleeve of her T-shirt to expose as much of the artwork as possible, turning in her seat.

Castillo stood, and leaned over his desk to get a better look at the tattoo. He gave a low whistle. "Top-notch work. When did you get it done?"

"Last night."

He stared intently at her. "It looks days old."

Whiskey swallowed. His expression mirrored one she hadn't seen since the first time they'd met—a sharp examination giving the impression he measured the breadth and width of her character in mere seconds. "Really? I didn't know you had a lot of experience with this sort of thing." Her joke sounded lame even to her. She didn't want to tell him about the last couple of days. The whole stupid vampire thing—Sanguire, her mind corrected. Besides, priests always fought vampires in the movies and books.

Castillo studied her a moment longer. He smiled without responding, and sat down. "What happened with Sister Rosa?" he asked, referring to a nun he'd introduced Whiskey to some weeks ago.

She busied herself with rolling down her sleeve again, her stomach fluttering with relief at the change of topic. Sister Rosa ran a three-bed girls shelter out of an apartment. Whiskey hadn't lasted long before leaving. Her biggest problem had been the imposed curfew. "Oh, she's nice enough and all." She looked away with a vague gesture. "Sleeping in a bed was pretty cool, but it's just not my gig."

Castillo nodded. "She came to the church to ask after you. She was worried you'd gotten hurt or something."

Whiskey scowled. "Tell her I'm fine, Padre."

"I will," he promised. "She has a good heart; don't let that color your opinion of her. She wishes to help."

Chagrined, Whiskey nodded.

Castillo took a drink from his bottle. "So, why did you want to see me today?"

Whiskey considered the question. Her initial reasons had been bus tickets and food vouchers, with a side order of visiting with the priest for a while. He wasn't exactly a friend, but she enjoyed the time they spent together regardless of the occasional rough spots. Flush for a few days, she felt greedy demanding things she didn't need.

Take more than you give.

For a change, she pushed aside the thought. "I was wondering if I could use the shelter as a permanent address so I can get a library card."

He leaned back in his chair, teeth gleaming at her. "A library card?"

Smirking, she nodded. "Yeah. It'd be nice to legally take a book out, and finish it sometime, you know?"

"You do realize you have to have state identification for a library card?"

Whiskey's face fell. "Really?" *Damn.*

"It'd be an easy thing to do," he continued, reaching for a pad and pen. "You've told me you don't know where your birth records are, but I could do a search on your real name." He slid the items across the desk to her.

She stared at the notepad. After four years in Seattle, she'd had nothing but minor scrapes with the law. No one here knew who she was, only her nickname. Years of foster homes and the fucked-up bureaucracy inherent in them had nurtured a desire to be completely clear of the system.

"We've talked about this before. I know you're allergic to the idea of revealing your identity to the social services," Castillo said. "But we both know you'll get nothing but scraps as long as you refuse to take the requisite steps."

Whiskey grimaced at him, but didn't argue.

"You've told me you're eighteen, legal age. That means the child welfare system is closed to you. I know you were in the system in Oregon. You don't have to worry about someone coming to cart you back there to a foster home or lockup—unless you have a warrant out for your arrest?"

"I don't. Not that I know of."

Castillo leaned closer, his hands in his lap. "Give me your name and birth date, Whiskey. I can do some research, find your birth records, and get you that ID. That'll open the doors for you—library card, Social Security card, GED courses, maybe college. You're a smart young woman who can do anything if you set your mind to it." He paused. "Give yourself the chance."

Whiskey rubbed her forehead, fingers drifting across the lightly scabbed wound left from Paul and his cronies. No one knew her name here, not even Gin who'd come here with her from Portland. But the padre knew the way of things. In a couple of more years, she'd be too old for the youth services. If she didn't play her cards right, she'd be one of those bag ladies downtown, wheeling a decrepit shopping cart through the city and sleeping under bridges. Not looking at him, she reached for the notepad and pen. Quickly scribbling the information, she shoved it back onto his desk as if the paper burned her skin.

Castillo just as rapidly snapped it up, not letting her change her mind. "Thank you, Whiskey. I won't say you won't regret it."

Despite her foreboding, Whiskey snorted. She gave him a lopsided grin. "You know me well, Padre."

He rummaged through his desk, and pulled out a stamped envelope. As he addressed it, he said, "Now take this out to the closest mailbox, and send it. It'll come back here, and be your proof of address." He slid the envelope to her. "Once we get your identification, we can get that library card."

Whiskey took the envelope. *Jenna Davis, c/o Father James Castillo.* "Thanks, Padre. I'll do that."

"Jenna Davis. J.D." Castillo gave her a gentle smile as he made the connection to her nickname. "Jack Daniels?"

She wondered why she had the urge to cry, forcing herself to swallow past the lump in her throat as she nodded.

He sensed her distress. "Need bus tickets? Vouchers?"

The desire to get away surged over her. She shook her head and stood. "No, I'm flush at the moment. Maybe next time."

Castillo rose, and came around her desk. "Shall we arrange for next Saturday? Same time?"

"Yeah, okay." Whiskey settled her pack on her shoulders, hoping he wouldn't insist on another hug. She didn't know if her brittle emotions could handle the closeness.

He sensed her need for distance. Opening the door for her, he stood beside it, smiling. "I'll do my best to keep your confidence."

She focused on him, gauging his words against his demeanor. He meant what he said. "Thanks, Padre. I appreciate that." *Doesn't mean he'll succeed.*

"Take care, Whiskey."

Whiskey nodded, and swept past him. In moments she stood outside, shards of sunlight stabbing her unprotected eyes. She fumbled for her sunglasses, trying to convince herself that the brightness caused her blurred vision.

CHAPTER NINE

Minn'ast.

Whiskey woke with a start, the sharp pain in her right thigh companion to her rousing. Once she waded through the resultant confusion and feelings of loss, she swore. She might eventually sleep through the nightmare, but she didn't hold out any great hope. The ache faded as she stumbled from the thin mattress toward the mildewed bathroom. She turned on the overhead light. A single bulb glowed in the ceiling, illuminating water stains and yellow drip marks marring the paint above. Discolored and pitted, the counter embraced a sink with rust stains oozing from the perpetual faucet leak. Rough linoleum floor scuffed her feet where innumerable dropped items had gouged the surface. *Definitely not Fiona's place.* She focused on her reflection in the spotted mirror.

The cut on her face had completely healed. When she lifted up her T-shirt, unblemished skin met her gaze. Not a single green or yellow discoloration marked where serious bruising had been two days before. She pulled the shirt off to examine the rest of her torso. Nothing. Poking at her abdomen caused no discomfort. The dragon tattoo snaking up her arm appeared completely healed, the scabs flaking away as she'd slept through the afternoon. She rotated the small silver bars piercing her nipples with little resistance. A tingle of arousal spilled through her, and she did it again for good measure. *Whoa. That's cool.*

Taking her shirt, she stepped back into the bedroom. The grubby decor matched the bathroom—nondescript brown carpet, white walls with odd splotches of dingy color here and there, and permanent shelves in place of nightstands and desk. The only true pieces of furniture in the room were the dresser and the bed; the dresser drawers were nailed shut to deter clientele from use of them. The sheets and blanket had been so dirty, Whiskey had used her new sleeping bag on the bed.

She turned on the lamp bolted to the shelf masquerading as a desk, and lit a cigarette. While she smoked, she rummaged through her pack for clothing and toiletries. After speaking with Castillo and mailing the envelope, she'd returned downtown and bought her boots. They'd cost almost two hundred dollars. She'd expected the purchase to raise her spirits, but it had physically hurt when she handed that much money to the clerk. In a wave of guilt at her extravagance, she had stopped at a drugstore to pick up the essentials she'd need for the next week. She also selected a belated birthday card for Gin, stuffing fifty dollars into it as a gift.

Whiskey brushed out her hair, examining the black-streaked tips. She could probably do with a trim and another dye job, and debated the wisdom of spending her dwindling cash supply. Swiping deodorant under her arms, she turned to her clothes and dressed. Not wanting to hide the dragons under cloth, she wore the deep red camisole she'd gotten from Fiona. She sat on the bed to put on her newest pride and joy, shiny black Dr. Marten boots that swept up her calf to her knees. She laced them over the top of her cargo pants.

Standing, she went to the window and opened the curtains. The motel she'd found wasn't far from where she'd done the majority of her shopping. Few hotels allowed guests to register without identification, so she'd had limited choices. She could have paid the offered hourly rates instead of a full night. Even now she heard the grunts and thumps of someone fucking in a nearby room. Across the street, a car wash gleamed in the twilight. Behind it, the Seattle sky turned a dark blue-gray.

With the night came the doubts. During daylight, thoughts of Fiona and her people faded into the distance. They told bizarre stories to freak and frighten people, nothing more. Just a game they played on unsuspecting marks. All the urgency and fear Whiskey had felt in the dark seemed laughable in sunlight. Vampires weren't real, therefore neither were Sanguire. Fiona and the rest perpetuated this delusion upon themselves and others around them. Whiskey's reality revolved around food vouchers, bus tickets and flops. Fiona was nothing but a rich bitch who'd targeted Whiskey for— *For what? A massive joke? A new toy for her friends to tease and torture?*

As the sky darkened, the idea of a race of vampires became more plausible, more concrete. Whiskey's sunlit rationalizations drowned in the spreading shadows. *What if it is true? Why else would I know the word Sanguire?* She knew she'd heard it before Fiona had said it, but she still couldn't pin down from where. Why did the sound of the word strike such feeling if she'd only read it in a book or on a website? *And where was the joke last night?* Fiona had given Whiskey well over a grand with the gifts, the tattoo and the entertainment. Whiskey had suffered nothing more than Fiona's malicious teasing, receiving a small fortune for the aggravation.

A door slammed somewhere below her. Moments later she saw a businessman climb into a sedan. He left alone. A couple of minutes later, another slam, and a woman appeared. She wore a skimpy skirt and high-heel shoes that showed off long legs. Strutting, she walked across the parking lot, and back to the street where she wiggled her ass for traffic. Streetlights had already come on, giving the woman a garish look under the yellow bulbs.

Whiskey studied the street, the traffic, searching. *Where's Fiona now? What are they doing? Have they targeted someone else tonight? Is this a nightly ritual for them, to find some unsuspecting idiot to fill with lies?* She rubbed the healed dragon tattoo.

What if they told it true?

Another door slammed, and she jumped. Scowling, she turned back to the crappy little room.

After a bento dinner, Whiskey hopped a bus back to the U District. Feeling foolish, she watched for Fiona or one of her people, even here. *They ain't gonna ride the fucking bus, idiot.* Regardless, she slumped in her seat at the back, warily watching every individual come aboard. She remained on guard after she reached her stop, eyeing traffic for the Lexus, Porsche or motorcycles.

Her mood lightened as she neared Tallulah's, the heavy bass beat thumping louder and louder. No way would anyone from Fiona's crew be found here. They partied at Malice or Crucible, upscale clubs more suited to their cash flow. Nothing more than a hole in the wall youth club, Tallulah's operated without a liquor license, and had little in the way of flashy decor. Arriving late, she paid a two dollar cover charge to a grizzled old man. She ignored his leer as he stamped her hand.

As she pushed inside the all ages club, the music hit her with physical force. She saw the usual crowd—street kids looking for a nighttime haven, local teenagers in search of risk and adventure, and adults either trying to relive their misspent youth or trolling for entertainment. She bypassed the pool tables and snack counter, passing the posturing youths smoking clove cigarettes. Whiskey breathed in through her mouth until she passed the noxious sweet smoke. Entering the bar proper, she looked around for her friend. Strobe lights flashed, illuminating the otherwise dark room. Tables sprouted here and there around a dance floor packed with people.

A handful of teenagers and young adults she recognized lounged in one corner. Most of them wore baggy pants and shirts in the typical skater street style, a striking difference to Whiskey's punk dress. She easily spotted Ghost among them, a twenty-something albino man sprawled in a chair with Gin in his lap. The fluorescent spotlights made his hair and skin glow like the specter for which he called himself. Gin spotted her. She waved, and then leaned over to say something into Ghost's ear. Whiskey saw him glance her way, a sour expression on his face. He didn't argue with Gin, though, just nodded and released her to stand. Gin gave him a kiss, and left his company.

"Hey, Gin. How goes it?"

Gin gave her a welcome hug. "*Hola, amiga*! I missed you last night."

Whiskey saw Ghost scowl at the intimacy, and quickly pulled away. "I know, but something came up. Forgive me?"

"Always, *chica*." Gin led her to the outskirts of her street family. She sat on a recently vacated chair. "Sit down."

Grinning, Whiskey dropped her pack, and did so. "So how was the party? Get anything good?"

"Ghost got me some really cool glass. And Lena gave me a teddy bear."

"Sounds cool. Is it a pipe or a bong?" Whiskey asked, bending over to rummage in her pack.

"Pipe, a little one. But it's shaped like a dolphin."

Whiskey winked at her. "You and your dolphins, *amiga*."

Gin gave her a light punch on the arm. "Better than vampires or werewolves, *chica*!"

Considering her recent meeting with Fiona, Whiskey's smile faltered. She forced away the desire to glance around the bar for Sanguire. *Don't be stupid.* She handed Gin the birthday card. "Here. For you. Happy belated birthday."

With a pleased expression, Gin pushed a stray strand of dark hair behind her ear, and took the envelope. "Thank you!" She made a production of opening it up, calling the attention of a couple of her street family to the proceedings.

Whiskey glanced beyond to see Ghost watching. *Bastard.*

"Where'd you get this kind of cash, *chica*?"

She turned her attention back to Gin who held the money in one hand. Behind her a kid craned his neck to see past the others. Whiskey recognized him as one of Ghost's newbies. He claimed to be sixteen, but didn't look a day over twelve. His face was partially covered by a large strawberry birthmark—the others called him Spot. "Hit the jackpot last night. Found some rich punks that had money, and wanted to go slumming. That's the last of it right there." She stuck out one foot to reveal the boots. "Got these today." The new leather sparkled in the strobe lights.

More of Gin's street family paid attention to the conversation, glancing from the boots to the money in Gin's hand.

"So, you got the boots. Anything else?"

Whiskey nodded, and shed her denim jacket. "Yeah. Check it out." She removed her sweatshirt, and showed off her dragon.

Several spectators whistled. "Wow. That's good work." She took Whiskey's hand to turn her arm. "How much did it cost?"

"Over seven hundred for the outline and shading. Maybe someday I'll scrape up enough to have it colored in."

The spotted kid pushed forward, jarring one of the others. "You just got this last night? It looks like it's a week old." The person he shoved aside punched him in the arm, and he glared at the perpetrator.

Whiskey stared at the wine-colored birthmark. *Dominick, that's his name.* Most of the members of Ghost's street family were jerks. This brat was fast becoming her least favorite. "I heal fast."

"You're a liar."

The throbbing music followed the same beat as Whiskey's heart. She didn't dare look away from Dominick or his challenge, but she didn't know what to do. The kid was raw—he'd been on the streets a month or so—and had a lot to prove to his street father. She could kick his ass in a fight, but would that cause Ghost to retaliate against her? The politics of the situation were too fragile.

"Shut the fuck up, *caja*." Gin stood to confront him, looking him in the eye. "She was with us in the flop two nights ago, and didn't have it then. What are you? Stupid?"

He obviously didn't know Spanish, or he would have immediately hit Gin for the insult. A few of the others did understand the slur, and laughed. He puffed out his chest, posturing, preparing to throw a swing at Gin. Whiskey edged between them.

"What's going on?"

Dominick turned to see Ghost behind him. He went from tough guy to adolescent in the space of a second. "She called me stupid and another name in Spanish, but I don't know what it was."

"That's because you are stupid, Spot." Ghost slapped Dominick, knocking him down.

Others in Ghost's family remained where they were, not offering their fallen comrade any assistance as he staggered back to his feet. Blood swelled at the corner of his mouth. He glared at Gin and Whiskey, but stormed away from the table.

Gin stepped into Ghost's arms with a smile. "*Gracias, mi corazón.*"

Whiskey watched as her best friend sucked up to him. She couldn't help the scowl on her face, which deepened as she saw Ghost grin at her. They both knew how things stood between them. He lived for moments like this, when he could flaunt his rising influence over Gin; he hadn't put out a hit on Whiskey yet for just this reason.

Eventually Gin felt she'd awarded his ego well enough. She must have asked him to leave them alone while they'd been kissing, because he drifted off to the bar with a couple of his crew when she let him go. She returned to her chair, staring at her hands.

They sat in silence for a long time, not looking at each other, the chasm opening wider between them. They'd arrived on the Portland streets within days of one another—Whiskey from a rural Oregon foster home, and Gin from San Diego—and had banded together for security. Fuck buddies since the beginning, she and Gin had both wandered elsewhere upon occasion. They'd dallied with others, both women and men, for variety and experimentation. Whiskey stuck with women; Gin sampled an even mix. They'd always ended up with each other when the dust cleared, and good sense prevailed. But this was the first time one of them had found someone for more than a temporary liaison.

Since Gin had hooked up with Ghost, she'd drifted farther and farther away from their friendship.

It surprised Whiskey how much this one hurt when all their past flirtations hadn't. Her heart literally ached with yearning sometimes, missing something she didn't have. Occasionally, she even felt that way in Gin's arms. For the most part the wistful longing subsided with Gin, becoming almost nonexistent. Whiskey had always known she felt stronger for her friend than the other way around. Knowing their permanent separation loomed in the future hadn't made the fracturing easier to bear. *Will we even be friends in a year?*

"Ghost found an abandoned building off the Ave to crash in," Gin finally offered.

Whiskey breathed a faint sigh. At least the breach between them wasn't insurmountable. *Not yet.* "I'll keep it in mind. I've paid for a full night at the Bella, so I think I'll nap there before I have to check out."

"Suit yourself." Gin held up the card, and smiled. "Thank you."

"You're welcome." Whiskey stood and leaned over Gin, giving her a long hug. "Happy birthday," she whispered into Gin's ear. Heartened to see tears in Gin's eyes to match her own, Whiskey released her. *Jesus, you've wanted to cry for days now. Get over it!* "You better get back to Ghost."

"Yeah, I better." Gin winked at her.

"You think you'll ever leave him?" *You think you'll ever come back to where you belong? To me?*

Gin frowned, looked away. "I love him, Whiskey. I love you, too, but not like this."

"Okay." Whiskey nodded. Uncomfortable with the silence, she took Gin's hand, tugging until her friend looked at her again. "You know I love you. I'm there for you, no matter what happens, no matter how many years go by."

"I know, *mi amiga.*" Gin gave her hand a squeeze. She sounded a little breathless. "You're the best friend anyone can ever ask for. I'm glad we hooked up when we did."

The urge to cry redoubled. Maybe the death dream meant the end of her time with Gin. Ghost had been a fixture in Gin's life for three months now. The dream had become increasingly intense during that time. "Me, too."

"Take care, Whiskey. See you around?"

She forced a smile. "You know it, *chica*. Can't keep me away." Whiskey's smile faded as Gin made her way back to her boyfriend.

CHAPTER TEN

Gin and her street family stayed on for a while. Whiskey kept her distance from her friend, remaining on the outskirts of the group. She stayed on sufferance because of Gin, and everyone knew it. Those low within the hierarchal group dynamics had no problem with approaching Whiskey for conversation. A handful sat with her, discussing tattoo shops, music and street fights. Dominick glared at her from a distance, his lip swollen. He didn't attempt to start another fight.

Somewhere around two in the morning, Ghost decided to leave. Gin gave her a wave, her fingers brushing Whiskey's shoulder when she walked past. Most of their family left with them. That began an exodus. The last of the teenagers still living at home trickled out, leaving their less fortunate counterparts to huddle around the empty spaces. Few adults remained in the crowd, having already picked up their jailbait for the evening. The music played on, though, and Whiskey grabbed her pack. With the floor sparsely occupied, she found a spot near the back wall to lay her gear, and began to dance.

She danced with her eyes closed. Oddly, she *felt* those nearest her. She sensed how far away they were, and which direction they moved. Making a game of it, she rode the music, senses reaching for people, opening her eyes to check her accuracy. Almost every attempt proved true. She made one error, positive someone lurked in the shadows at the far corner of the room. Closing her eyes she attempted again, sensing a presence, yet she saw no one there. Unnerved at the lurking phantom, she feigned boredom with the game, and resolved to pay no more attention, focusing on the pulse of music.

Quite a bit of time passed before she came out of her self-induced trance. Hot and thirsty, she retrieved her pack, and went to the bar. "Glass of ice," she yelled over the music.

The bartender grimaced. "Fifteen cents."

Whiskey snorted. "When the hell did you start charging for fucking *ice*?" Too intent on the bartender's response, she hardly felt the arrival of someone beside her.

"When half you kids barely buy drinks. We've got to make money or we close."

She'd be damned if she'd pay good money for ice, even with plenty of cash in her pocket. Whiskey glared as the bartender moved to the next customer.

"Two glasses of ice," the man beside her yelled.

The bartender rolled her eyes, and asked for payment.

Whiskey turned toward the intrusion, her irritation draining as quickly as the blood from her face.

Reynhard Dorst slid one of the glasses toward her. "Are you certain you wouldn't like something else, sweet Whiskey?"

She stared at him, her mind and mouth not working, her heart galloping hard in her chest.

"I'll take that as a no." He whirled in place, leaning back to place his elbows on the bar, and survey the room. "What an intriguing little place you've discovered. I must return here in the future."

Whiskey took the time to scan his relaxed form. He wore the same clothes as when she'd met him last night—leather trench coat over black leather and steel spikes. One booted foot tapped in time with the music, flashing lights gleaming off the polished surfaces of his accoutrements. As her mind caught up with the adrenaline coursing through her blood, she cleared her throat to test her voice before speaking. "What are you doing here?"

"I came to see you." He glanced at her, his gaunt face a parody of surprise. "Do you still have the cell phone our Fiona gave you? I've attempted to call several times this evening."

She glanced down at the pack she'd set on the floor. "I—I wasn't expecting—"

"No matter." Dorst waved an elegant hand. "I've found you, and that's what's important. Do enjoy your ice, Whiskey. You're no doubt thirsty after your exertions on the dance floor."

At a loss, she retrieved the glass from the bar. As the fight-or-flight response eased, her knees shook under her weight. She sat on a barstool. "How long have you been here?"

"A bit of time." He sucked on an ice cube for a moment. "It was difficult keeping out of sight. You almost caught me in the corner there."

"That was you?" Whiskey looked at the dark corner, her mouth dropping open. "I thought someone was there, but I couldn't tell."

"When you and I are finished, you'll be able to locate myself and any Sanguire in the immediate area with a mere thought." He grinned at her. "And know who they are."

The previous night's eeriness rushed through her anew, shoving aside the rational arguments she'd used throughout the day to placate herself. Her logical inner discussion couldn't stand up against the physical existence of Dorst lounging beside her. Whether or not she believed the shit Fiona spouted didn't matter. Dorst lived it.

Still, knowing where Fiona was at all times sounded comforting. *Yeah, like this is real.* "What do you mean, 'when you and I are finished'?"

Dorst looked at her, the surprised expression returning to

his face. "Did I not explain well enough last evening? I am your *Baruñal*, your guide as you go through the *Ñiri Kurám*."

Whiskey mouthed an ice cube, running through the conversation she'd had with Fiona at the club. It had gotten difficult to follow after three shots of alcohol, but she vaguely remembered the words. Cora had also referred to Dorst as *Baruñal* before he left, and Fiona's letter had used the strange terms. "You guys still think I'm a...whaddya call it? A Sanguire?"

"That is not in doubt."

She crunched her ice, staring at the dance floor, feeling a terrifying solace from his confidence.

"Tell me of your little Mexican friend. She seemed to be the only person you really wanted to spend time with, yet she kept you at a distance."

Whiskey scowled. "That's none of your business."

"I've found that Humans can be quite insightful upon occasion. Perhaps this aloofness is indicative of her perception that you are Sanguire. The nature of the Sanguire/Human relationship is that of predator and prey—she may be manifesting a simple inherent desire to flee, and survive your racial tendencies." He paused to study his manicured nails. "She was no doubt protecting the child that grows within her, albeit on a subconscious level."

Pregnant? "You don't know what you're talking about. You don't know anything about her!" *She would have told me! Wouldn't she?*

Dorst bowed his head. "As you wish, dear Whiskey."

They remained there for some time without speaking, the music pulsing around them. Four street kids, obviously hyped on some intoxicant, bounced around the otherwise empty dance floor. Twice that number drowsed at the tables, catching the only peaceful sleep they'd be able to get for the night. Whiskey turned on her stool, facing the bar. Beyond it, she watched three kids smoke cigarettes as they played pool. Thick metal bars blocked casual access to the closed snack bar. No one else moved in that section of the building.

Her mind whirled with his revelation. Gin's need to stick with Ghost come hell or high water made perfect sense if she carried his baby. *God, how could I have missed it?* Single mothers had it tough to begin with; living on the streets with a baby was a bitch. *Why didn't she tell me? And how does he know?*

Dorst remained silent, not interrupting her musings. She had trouble comprehending her ability to enjoy a comfortable silence with this stranger. The feeling she knew him from somewhere had gotten stronger over the course of the day. Now it towered rock solid in her heart. After her initial shock at his appearance here, she couldn't deny a sense of pleasure at seeing him. She had complete confidence that he had her best interests at heart. She might not like what he said, or how he said it, but he meant her no harm.

"Why are you here?"

He lifted his chin, and turned toward her. "To start you upon the path."

Whiskey swallowed. "What if you're wrong? What if I can't do this?"

His heart-warming smile warred with the image of a gaunt mutant clown. "I think you'll do fine, Whiskey. All you have to do is try."

She stared at him. Her common sense told her to get away from him, throw away the cell phone Fiona had given her, and head for California. The kindness in his eyes countered the desire, tendering acceptance and friendship, things she sorely lacked these days.

"Okay. I'll try."

CHAPTER ELEVEN

Still bent out of shape about her decision to bring him here, Whiskey scowled at Dorst as she set her pack down next to the bed. At least she knew the location. Her entire being might insist on trusting this stranger, but she still hedged her bets. No way would she step foot in whatever hotel or house he had set up for himself. For all she knew, he worked out of Fiona's home, the last place to which she wanted to return.

"How quaint."

Her hotel room looked no better than it had when she'd left. "Don't knock it until you see the alternative."

He grinned at her, giving her one of his magnanimous bows. "Of course, dear Whiskey. I meant no offense. One must use the resources at hand."

She sat on the bed. "So what now?"

"You have the Book?" He drew the desk chair toward her, and sat down.

"Book? That weird leather-bound one Fiona gave me?" She bent to rummage in her pack.

Dorst crossed his legs at the knee, primly placing his hands atop. "That would be the one."

She came up with the thin volume, and handed it to him. "I wondered why she gave it to me. I can't read any of it." He peered down his nose as he thumbed through the pages. Whiskey imagined a pair of spectacles perched at the end of his beak, and smothered a chuckle. He looked like a black-plumed bird with vision problems.

"Ah, here it is." He held the Book out to her. "Your first language lesson."

She took the Book, and looked at the incomprehensible scribbling. "You realize this means nothing to me?"

"And more's the pity, dear Whiskey." An expression of deep mourning sat upon his wan face. "Had you been raised among your own, you'd be completely conversant in our tongue."

It took a moment for her to pick up on his humor, a wicked combination of droll sarcasm. It fit him perfectly. *It must be difficult for people to catch him in a joke.* "So, what is this thing?" She waggled the Book in her hand. "How does this get me through the...whatever it is?"

"The *Ñíri Kurám*," he repeated patiently. "Far back in our history our young people walked down the Strange Path gradually. It takes many years to pass through from childhood to full Sanguire adulthood in this manner. Mystics and oracles eventually discovered a series of chants that opened the doors of the mind and body, accelerating the process. Now, what would take twenty years to accomplish can be done in a week or so. It can be a shock to the system, hence the need for a guide, such as myself, to assist the youngling through the traumatic experience." He pointed a long finger at the writing on the page before her. "This is the first chant, written thousands of years ago in ancient Sumerian."

Whiskey blinked. "We're Sumerian?"

Dorst peered over nonexistent glasses at her. "We're Sanguire.

My ancestors came from that region of the world. Just as with Humans, there are other...races of Sanguire."

She stared at him. This went beyond anything she'd ever conceived, blowing her perception of the standard vampire myth out of the water. "Other races of Sanguire?"

"Certainly. African, Asian, Indian." He leaned back, one hairless eyebrow raised. "I was told Daniel informed you we procreate through natural sexual channels rather than horror story blood-sharing, did he not?"

"He did." She frowned in thought, remembering something along those lines. "So what are we?"

Dorst smiled. "I and Fiona come from the European contingent. We are here on sufferance, as guests in this country." He tilted his head. "Until we know your ancestry, we do not know where you belong. It is assumed by your appearance that you are also European, but time will tell."

Her mind full of questions, she didn't know which to ask first. *Here on sufferance? Guests of whom?* She remembered their discussion on politics the night before, coming to the conclusion that if there were different groupings of these people, then there'd be government of some kind to rule them. "Jesus."

"A bit much to take in?" He smiled in sympathy. "Don't tax yourself overmuch with the details, dear Whiskey. First we get you through the *Ñíri Kurám*. Your education will follow in due time."

Whiskey swallowed, and nodded. She forced herself to focus on the Book in her hands.

Dorst carefully instructed her on the pronunciations of the required chant, pointing out with one long finger the syllables and words on the page. It took nearly an hour before she could recite it without error. When they finished, she recognized the strange letters that made up the words.

"How long have you paid for this room?"

"Just tonight. I check out by noon tomorrow."

He sniffed, eying his surroundings. "While it leaves much to be desired, you'll need a place to sleep after you've finished. I'll pay the landlord for another night."

Whiskey shook her head. "No, don't worry about it. I'll find somewhere."

Dorst swept into a low bow, his voice reverent. "I beg your forgiveness, sweet Whiskey, but I am your *Baruñal*. Until you've completed the chants, and come into your full power, I will keep you safe." He peered at her from his bow, his eyes sparkling with humor despite his stance. "When you've attained adulthood, you may take me to task for my presumption."

She stared at him a moment before giving him a slow nod. "Okay. You've got a deal."

"Thank you. I know how much of a sacrifice it is for you to give over control."

Whiskey's brow furrowed. "How do you know that?"

"Call it a hunch, one that I hope will pay off handsomely." He grinned, and swept toward the door. Pausing there, hand on the knob, he looked back at her. "Remember. Someplace you feel comfortable and safe. Not here. But return here as soon as you've finished. You'll need the seclusion and rest."

"I remember."

Dorst opened the door. "Do you still think we've met before?"

She examined her feelings. "Yeah, I do."

He lifted his chin in concession, and left the room, closing the door softly behind him.

Whiskey looked down at the leather-bound Book in her hand. It felt alive, the light tan covering warm against her fingers. After a few moments, she stood and packed it away, collecting her things. Even if she were staying here another night, she wasn't about to leave her gear to be pilfered by the management.

CHAPTER TWELVE

Whiskey stared over Puget Sound. She sat on a bench in Olympic Sculpture Park. Dawn prepared its approach in an hour or so. The park technically closed, the cops in passing cars wouldn't hassle her unless she lay down to sleep. Smoke from her cigarette coiled over her head. From here, the lights of Bainbridge Island sparkled in the darkness, reflecting in the water like sunken treasure. Traffic passing around her on Elliott Avenue and Broad Street picked up with early morning commuters, garbage trucks and delivery vans. There'd be more activity soon, though not as much as on a weekday. Overhead, stars sparkled faintly in a clear sky. *Looks like another sunny day.* The thought made her grimace.

She looked at the Book in her lap, idly brushing stray ashes from its cover. Taking a final drag off the cigarette, she sent it flying as well. The red glow disappeared into a patch of grass, a slow tendril of smoke rising above.

Wondering if she should get into one of those silly yoga positions, she frowned. She should have asked Dorst, but had been too baffled by the information overload he'd imparted. Too late. She supposed she could call him on the cell phone. With a sigh, she shrugged to herself and took stock. Seated, her legs crossed at the ankles before her, she assessed her body. Comfortable enough, she opened the Book.

She flipped gently to the page Dorst had shown her, mindful of the Book's age, and peered at the writing in the dim nearby streetlight. Relieved to see her memory held, she closed her eyes, and let her breathing slow and deepen. Around her she heard the intermittent traffic bypassing her by a few hundred feet. A hedge of flowers grew close to her, their delicate scent filling her nose as she inhaled.

Relaxed, Whiskey began the chant. The words rolled off her tongue with a strange sensation. Here, alone and in the waxing light, she felt a jolt of surprise. They came alive with her voice, something that hadn't happened when she'd spoken the phonetic pronunciations with Dorst. The louder she spoke, the more substantial the words became. Her eyes closed, she imagined them floating in the air before her in greens and golds, visible for anyone to see.

She finished her first recitation, and began the second. Dorst had told her to run through each chant four times. Her blood tingled. She detected each corpuscle burning a path through her body. The sensation solidified in her chest, growing stronger with each syllable and every beat of her heart.

On the third repetition, her senses heightened to extraordinary levels. The smell of flowers overpowered her, a seductive lure distracting her from the meditation. With an iron will, she ignored it, banished it. The scent all but disappeared at her command. Amazed, she continued to speak, the words so real that she tasted them as they spilled from her lips—sharp and sweet, hot and heavy.

A combination of giddiness and fear jabbed at her spine as she began the final run-through. *What's happening?* She felt a physical shift in her head. Fireworks exploded behind her eyelids, blinding her with their nonexistent glare. She heard her surprised grunt from far away, ears no longer hearing street sounds. As she uttered the final word, she heard distant music, a familiar tune. She couldn't quite place the slow, seductive beat that pulsed in time with her heart. It drew her, irresistibly tugging at her as the brilliant colors in her mind's eye solidified.

Flash.

She found herself in a darkened hallway, thick carpet cozying her bare toes. Clutched in her arms, a floppy teddy bear kept her company, and she squeezed him in wonder and recognition. *Upsy Downsy.* That was the bear's name. Her grandfather, a man with dark hair and benevolent eyes, had given the bear to her. She hadn't seen Upsy Downsy since the age of six when an older foster brother had torn him apart in front of her. Somewhere the music played, interlaced with snatches of conversation.

Lost in the dream, she followed the sounds, shuffling down a set of stairs, holding the banister that stood tall by her head. Strange and familiar faces turned to her, conferring indulgent smiles, touching her light blonde hair as she passed, speaking fondly of and to her. With a sleepy grin, she accepted their attentions as her due, hugging one or offering her bear to another for kisses. The air smelled of jasmine drifting in from the deck outside.

She wandered through the party, following the music, knowing instinctively what she'd find. They were in the living area, wrapped in each other's arms, dancing. Watching for a moment, she saw the love her parents shared, floating in a misty haze of gold and green around them. She laughed, and tumbled forward, caught by Daddy, and lifted high into the air.

"What have we here?" His sky-blue eyes sparkled. "A night owl come to watch over us?"

"It's *me*, Daddy!"

He peered closely at her. "Why, so it is! Look, darling! Our lovely daughter has joined us for a dance!"

She giggled as Mommy put her arms around both of them.

"Then we shall dance." The dark haired woman smiled, and kissed her forehead. "Afterward, it's back to bed for a story."

Delighted, she hugged an arm around Mommy's neck as Daddy cuddled her. "I love you very, very much! Can it be the story about the elves and the shoemaker?"

"Whatever you wish, beautiful lady."

The three of them danced together to the music as family and friends watched, and Whiskey wished that every night would be like this.

Flash.

Whiskey recoiled from the dream, if dream it was. With a cry she bolted to her feet, the Book sliding from her lap and along the concrete, coming to rest at the edge of the flower bed. Eyes wild, she took in her surroundings. The sound lay quietly before her, traffic still coursing upon the nearby streets, and the sky had begun to lighten.

At least an hour had passed, though it seemed ten minutes in her dream.

Feeling soaked to the bone, she wiped at her face. The thought brought a shiver as a gentle spring breeze caressed her sweating skin. Knees shaky, she sat on the ground beside the bench, wrapping her arms about herself, staring at the leather Book a couple of feet away.

What was that? A memory, yes; Whiskey now recalled it well. She couldn't have been more than four or five at the time. *It was so vivid!* She trembled again as she recalled the warmth of her parents' embrace, her mother's gentle perfume, the sound of her father's laugh. She could see them so clearly. She'd been devastated when she'd forgotten what her parents had looked like. Now she eagerly committed their faces to memory, hoping she could hold the images forever. She swallowed hard, eyes stinging. A hollow opened in her chest, a swooping, falling sensation that occurred whenever she pondered her parents on more than an intellectual level. She forced herself away from the feelings, lifting her chin and inhaling deeply of the dawn air.

When her emotions settled, she knuckled away unshed tears and rose. She stood over the Book, glaring at it with a curled lip. Tempted to leave it there, she remembered its venerable age. Dorst wouldn't be pleased if she dumped an expensive antique somewhere. Besides, there were more meditations to get through before she finished. With a dissatisfied growl, she picked up the volume. The cover pulsed thickly in time to her heartbeat. She almost dropped it again, Fascinated and repulsed, she shoved the thing into her pack, and quickly closed the flap.

The walk back toward the hotel became surreal. Colors leapt out at her, brighter than they should be, more vibrant. They rang with with a low-level tone, one Whiskey couldn't quite hear no matter how she concentrated. As the sky grew lighter, traffic increased. She walked along the Alaskan Highway Viaduct in wonder, eyes darting everywhere, trying to catch everything. A furniture delivery truck blatted past, and her mouth dropped open in surprise. She *smelled* the sound, a combination of turkey and onions!

What the hell did that chant do to me? She waffled between fear and delighted pleasure. Many a time in her life she'd taken hallucinogenic substances for just such a high. She'd never quite attained this level of clarity before. Somehow the chant must have physically changed something within her brain. *Just like Reynhard said it would.* She frowned at her familiar use of his first name in her thoughts again. Attention now focused on him, his face popped into her mind, picture perfect. But a full head of dark brown hair flowed past his shoulders. He looked maybe ten years younger than he did now. His black eyes held a deep devotion, and he bowed his way backwards and away from her.

"What the fuck?"

Turning off the main road, she puzzled over the vision. It replayed over and over in her mind, nothing more and nothing less than what she'd already seen. She couldn't see much else—not his clothes, or the place where they stood. Ten years ago, she'd been deep in the Oregon foster care system, already beginning to act out and get into trouble, a sullen eight-year-old girl with a huge chip on her shoulder. Had Dorst met her as a child? Had he been one of the masses of counselors, care providers and social workers she'd dealt with before leaving the system?

No. The look in his eyes revealed the fault in her logic. He might have gotten through to her with such an expression, saved her from herself and her teenaged rebellion. Had she truly met him then, she would have fallen sway to the mysterious trust she already felt for him. They hadn't met.

Then how the hell do I know him?

A couple of blocks shy of the hotel, Whiskey caught a whiff of grilling steak. Her stomach cramped in hunger, a sharp ache so strong it made her feet lurch. She licked her lips, eying the small diner from which the most delicious aroma came. She'd told Dorst she'd return to the hotel room to sleep off whatever effects occurred from the chant. It would be a small detour. "He wouldn't want me to starve, right?"

Entering the restaurant, the scent of food made her belly cramp again. She sank into the first chair she came to, fumbling her pack to the floor.

"Are you okay?"

She quelled her rebellious stomach enough to look up at the server. "Yeah, just give me a minute."

He gave her a long look, then glanced back at the counter for support from his co-workers. "You can't stay here."

Whiskey scowled at him. "I came here to eat, not loiter. I've got money."

Holding up his hands in a calming gesture, he took a step back from her. "Okay. I just had to say it."

She nodded, disliking his assumption. Not that he didn't have every reason to be concerned about an obviously homeless person taking up residence at one of his tables. If she'd been in his place, she'd be suspicious, too. "You got a special today?"

"Steak and eggs, side of hash browns and toast or muffin."

Her mouth watered at the mention of steak. "I'll take it. And bring a pot of coffee."

He hesitated.

Whiskey rolled her eyes. She pulled out the last of the money Fiona had given her, and tossed it onto the table. Glaring, she gave him a questioning look.

He swallowed, still nervous, but pulled out a pad and pen from his apron. "How do you want your eggs?"

They hassled through the specifics. Whiskey surprised herself by ordering her steak rare; she preferred her meat well done. When he left to get her coffee, she relaxed. Her stomach no longer flip-flopped as she became inured to the smells around her. She breathed a sigh. *What the hell is this about? Reynhard didn't mention anything about getting sick.*

Staring out the window, she watched cars and pedestrians pass by. The sun began to crawl down the sides of the tall buildings in the downtown area. Sunlight reflected from upper windows, casting slivers of brightness to the ground below. Whiskey dug out her sunglasses, already beginning to feel a headache coming on. *Unless it's from the meditation, too?*

The server arrived with a metal coffee urn. He poured her a cup, leaving the urn on the table. She muttered thanks at his back as he fled. She continued to stare out the window, turning the vision over in her mind. The more she went over it, the less vivid it became. Immediately after, she'd called it a memory, but now she couldn't recall ever experiencing what she'd seen. *Was it a memory or a symbolic, idealized piece of crap from my subconscious?* Last week had been the anniversary of her parents' deaths— yet another reason for her tearfulness lately. It made sense for something like this to come out during a meditation now. Wistful, she wondered if the faces she now held of her parents were truly theirs.

More people entered the diner, locals and regulars that came here often. They called to the server and the cook in the back with familiarity, taking their places along the counter and at the tables. They gave her a wide berth, leaving her to her melancholy thoughts. The waiter delivered her food and ticket.

She smelled bitter ambrosia from her plate. The contents of her stomach pitched to one side, but her mouth watered. She cut into her steak with trepidation, not sure she could keep anything down. Her heart raced at the pink blood running along her plate. She took her first bite and, for a brief moment froze as the steak juices hit her tongue. A sensation of exquisite pleasure coupled with a sharp stab of pain hit her. Her stomach turned over once, and she automatically swallowed against the surge of bile. The blood hit her stomach, calming it. A sudden warmth rippled through her body.

"Don't get steak much?"

Whiskey blinked, glancing at the old codger seated at another table. "Not like *this*!" She fell to her breakfast with-single minded purpose.

The old man chuckled, and returned to his paper.

CHAPTER THIRTEEN

Whiskey had every intention of returning to the hotel room after breakfast. Once outside, the sounds and sights of the wakening city distracted her, and she wandered along the street, watching and listening.

Her emotional and physical response to the steak overwhelmed her. It fed a craving she hadn't known she'd had. A surge of vitality came with each bite, a physical rush better than anything she'd experienced before. She'd been up all night. By rights, she should be ready for sleep, but felt restless and jittery. In contrast to the steak, the eggs and toast didn't sit well, her stomach twisting with vague nausea at their inclusion. Why did she still feel hungry? Her stomach full beyond measure, her brain still insisted it needed nourishment.

As she walked down the street, the smells assaulting her

nostrils strengthened—dust, vehicle exhaust, overpowering cologne or sweat from passing pedestrians, acrid tar from roadwork, concrete and treated wood from nearby construction sites. Sound, too, bothered her. Everyone around her yelled rather than spoke, the cars and buses all rode without mufflers, and the canned music from a store across the way blared full blast. Her ears rang. The sun, always an irritant, burrowed into her skull despite her sunglasses. *Maybe this wasn't such a great idea.*

The synaesthesia continued assaulting her senses. She crossed the street, awed to see wisps of orange haze coming from the engine block of a stopped car. Half the time she didn't know if what she smelled was an actual odor or a sudden sound. Her head pounded, fit to burst open. Her stomach pulsed with heaviness. She needed to get off the street, away from the constant barrage of sensation. Against her better judgment but needing the escape, she entered a coffee shop. She found no refuge in the relative quiet. The walls pressed in, and people drank and talked and rustled newspapers in volumes loud enough to split her skull. Fighting the sensation, she ordered a latte. The change hitting the cash drawer stabbed through her eardrums. When the drink arrived, she grabbed it and fled the confining atmosphere for outside.

The establishment had a small courtyard, off the street and somewhat private. She gratefully sank into one of the seats, setting her pack on the ground. Scrubbing at her aching temples, she wondered what to do. The idea of leaving this semi-secluded area to stagger the two blocks necessary to reach her hotel room daunted her. She didn't know if she could make it on her own. *Maybe staying here for a bit will allow things to settle enough so I can move on.*

She sat there, latte untouched before her, for the better part of an hour. Every time she considered getting up to leave, a wave of dread washed over her, the sounds from outside rising in volume. She didn't know if she should take aspirin for the pounding in her head, considering the solid lump of eggs and acid in her stomach. If she imbibed anything, she'd probably throw up.

Slouched in her chair, she found herself staring at her pack at her feet. Thoughts sluggish, she once again evaluated the contents of her belongings. Nothing there to help her. *Unless that flask of whiskey will do the job.* The thought of the fiery alcohol going down her throat made her stomach clench. The flask. The Book. The dagger and water bottle. All gifts from Fiona. The envelope with only the note inside, most of the money spent.

The cell phone.

Whiskey groaned at her stupidity. She had a cell phone! She could call someone.

She rummaged in a side pocket, finding the phone. She considered calling Gin, but wasn't sure enough of her location for Gin to find her. Ghost wouldn't be pleased at sending Gin on a scavenger hunt, either. Squinting against the light of the tiny screen, she tried to focus her blurring vision on the list of contacts. Dorst's name sat at the top. Swallowing against another wave of queasiness, she activated the phone.

"Hello?"

A wave of relief made her feel faint. "Reynhard?" Her voice cracked. *Damn it.*

"Sweet Whiskey. Where are you?"

"I don't know." She fought a lump in her throat, her eyes stinging with developing tears. "A coffee shop near the hotel." She gave him the company name on her cup. "But there are at least three or four of these places around here."

"I'll be there momentarily. Remain there."

She snorted, a watery sound of amusement. "I'm not going anywhere."

"Good." He hung up.

Whiskey struggled with tears and sickness. When she got herself under control, she put away the phone.

Only a few minutes passed before Dorst entered the outdoor seating area from the street. He knelt beside her, taking her hands in his.

"Jesus, that was fast." Whiskey clutched at his hand, ignoring a handful of patrons staring at them.

"I awaited your return at the hotel." His hand brushed her hair aside, his cool palm resting lightly against her fevered forehead. "You ate?"

"Yeah. How did—?"

Dorst smiled. "I smell breakfast on your breath."

Whiskey scoffed. "You're lucky you're not smelling something else."

His hand moved to cup her cheek. "That I am. Can you make it outside? My car is on the corner."

She took stock of herself, and nodded. "I think so."

"Come then. I'll get your things." He stood and picked up her backpack, settling it on his shoulders after an adjustment to the straps. Reaching for her, he helped her stand. They exited the tiny courtyard into the raucous noise of the street.

The sounds beat down upon Whiskey. Her knees buckled, and Dorst quickly scooped her into his arms. Before she had time to protest at being carried like a baby, they were beside his vehicle. He didn't set her down until he had the door open, and deposited her directly on the passenger seat. He carefully closed the door.

For the first time in over an hour, Whiskey relaxed as the barrage of sounds and smells dissipated. Dorst opened the driver's door, causing a sharp moment of distress. She bent forward with a groan, holding her head. She felt strong fingers massaging the base of her neck. After a moment, the headache backed off a little, the sickness following suit with the interior silence of the car. She still heard smothered street noises through closed windows, but they lacked the power to hurt her. Sitting up, she squinted at Dorst. "Thanks."

His dark eyes studied her. "You're welcome. We'll remain here for a few minutes to allow you to collect yourself."

Despite the fact that he'd spoken in a barely breathed whisper, she clearly heard him. It reminded her of Cora's words being heard by Fiona's pack at Malice. "Is it—" She winced against the sound of her own voice, rubbing one temple. Trying again, she spoke in a similar manner. "Is it supposed to happen like this?"

"Yes. The chant has opened neural pathways in your brain that awaited opening. Your brain is attempting to make sense of the data overload, causing you pain, sickness and a certain level of...crossover between senses."

She remembered the odor of the truck engine earlier. "So you don't smell sound?"

Dorst smiled. "Some do, I suppose, but as a whole Sanguire do not."

Whiskey didn't know whether or not to be disappointed. It'd been cool to see the orange mist of an overheated engine block. "How long will I be like this?"

"Once you've slept, your brain should settle into its new pathways. You'll have moments of illness and overload, but as time goes by, you'll adapt." He peered closely at her. "Are you ready to proceed?"

She took stock of herself. The lump of food still sat in her stomach, and her whole body ached along with her head, but it was manageable. Nodding, she carefully reached for her seat belt.

"Close your eyes, dear Whiskey. They need the rest, and you may suffer motion sickness as a result of the mixed signals you're receiving."

Again she nodded, and did as he said.

At the hotel, Whiskey made it to her room by leaning on Dorst's arm. As soon as she sank onto the bed, he left to retrieve her pack from his car. The linens had been replaced, the fresh smell doing much to dispel her nausea. A thick candle burned on the desk, surrounded by a bowl of water, a sprig of pine, and a spray of jasmine. The aromatic collection canceled out the mildew odor emanating from the bathroom, relaxing her further.

She closed her eyes. The aroma of jasmine reminded her of the memory/vision she'd had during the meditation. She heard the music that played as her parents had danced, though she couldn't see more than the fine haze that had surrounded them. *Why did he pick that flower? Why not something else?*

The door opened, as did her eyes. Dorst entered with her pack, closing the door behind him. He set the pack on the floor by the nightstand, and turned to her. "Are you feeling better?"

She recalled the memory of him with long brown hair. "Yeah, thank you."

Dorst bowed. "Do you wish me to stay?"

"I want to know what happened to me."

He cocked his head in thought, and straightened. "I believe we've already covered the pertinent data." Taking the desk chair, he proceeded to sit with his patented flourish. "You have more questions?"

"What was I supposed to see during the meditation?"

He crossed his legs at the knee, gesturing with one hand. "What you were meant to see."

She pursed her lips, not having the energy to pick a fight with him. "What do others see?"

A sly grin crossed his face. "What they were meant to see."

"Damn it, you know what I mean." Dull anger caused her headache to spike. She grunted, and massaged her temples. "What did *you* see?"

Dorst's expression became contrite. "I apologize for exacerbating your condition, dear Whiskey. I did not realize the levels of determination you exercise." He bared his throat.

The pain in her head disrupted her focus, exhaustion seeping into her bones. "Okay. So?"

"It varies from person to person. Some see the past, others claim to see their future. Many see nothing, but experience auditory visions. Yet others can't explain what they do or do not see. The experience is both subjective and personal, relevant to the individual involved." He shrugged. "I can't say much more than that."

Whiskey nodded. She'd suspected something along those lines. While the vision she experienced had faded, the emotions remained strong. "So, was what I saw a memory or a figment of my imagination?"

"Do you remember it occurring?"

"I think so." She rubbed her forehead with one hand. "I don't know."

"It's possible it was a memory then. I assume it was from early childhood?"

"Yeah."

Dorst, his face unusually somber, considered. "Then I would postulate that it was indeed a memory you experienced. Early childhood recollections fade by adulthood. The vagaries of the brain are what cause the occasional unearthing of such things. The process of the *Ñíri Kurám* interrupts the existing neural pathways in the brain, thereby causing a higher likelihood of old memories to rise to the fore."

The fatigue in her body deepened. Unable to help herself, Whiskey lay on the bed, boots and all. The smell of jasmine and clean sheets lulled her, bringing back a ghost of the vision she'd experienced in her trance.

"You need rest. When you wake, you'll feel much better."

Her eyelids sagged, but she turned her head to look at him. "I saw you."

Dorst sat frozen, his already pallid complexion lightening more. His Adam's apple bobbed once. "Excuse me?"

"On the way to the restaurant, I thought of you and I remembered seeing you." She rolled over onto her side to ease the ache in her neck. "We have met before. You looked about ten years younger, and had long brown hair. Did you use to work for social services in Oregon?"

He stared at her with intensity. After a moment his color returned. He cleared his throat, and blinked excessively.

"No." He spoke in a quiet whisper, barely audible to her. "I did not."

Whiskey frowned. "I'll figure it out, yet."

"I don't doubt that you will." Dorst stood and approached the bed. He untied her boots, and helped her out of them. "Sleep, Whiskey. Call me when you waken."

She nodded, her eyes closing against her wishes. "I will." She felt a hand stroke her hair.

The world again became dark, but this time it felt warm and comfortable.

CHAPTER FOURTEEN

Eyes closed, Whiskey drifted in that half-aware space between sleeping and waking, sluggish thoughts keeping her company. Memories of the early morning washed over her, jarring her with their rough texture—the strange sensations, heightened senses, Dorst's arrival and subsequent assistance.

She cracked open one eye, vaguely pleased it didn't hurt to see anymore. She lay on her side, one hand pillowing her cheek, a crimson dragon writhing silently on her arm. The curtains were drawn, so she didn't know the time of day. Dorst must have closed them before he'd left. She rumbled incoherently and closed her eye. More awake than asleep, her mind kicked into gear. She scanned her body for any ill effects, relieved to note her headache and sickness were gone. Still, if she concentrated, she heard pedestrians walking outside, and hotel tenants enjoying the hourly rate. She also heard a muted thumping that didn't have anything to do with the sexual escapades of her neighbors. *What is that?*

When it appeared she wouldn't be going back to sleep, she gave in to a bone-cracking stretch and yawned. Rolling onto her back, she sat up. She delicately walked around the subject of getting out of bed. No sickness met her appraisal. In fact, she felt hungry again.

Whiskey stood, and stumbled to the toilet. The pillar candle on the desk had burned halfway down. She caught her pale reflection in the bathroom mirror. Remembering vampire movies and the actors and actresses she'd seen, she wondered if she'd be just as colorless in the end. *Of course not, idiot. Look at Fiona's crew. They've all been out in daylight.* Annoyed at her stupidity, she turned away from her visage.

She ran water in the sink. Washing her face, she noted odd sensations along her skin. She slowed her movements, and picked up a bar of soap to lather her hands. The strangest sensations occurred as she washed—nerve endings screamed with a combination of joyful pain and exquisite pleasure, an eroticism that increased as her soapy hands slid across each other. She frowned, realizing that the strangeness wasn't gone; it had merely become normal. Dorst had said she'd adapt. Would she always feel like this, or would it eventually fade? A close study of her reflection gave no solution. Whatever the answer, at least she didn't hurt any more. In fact, it occurred to her that having sex with these new sensations would be quite the experience. She had an urge to search the cell phone for Cora's number.

She snorted at the thought. She did *not* want to invite Fiona back into her life.

On a lark, she closed her eyes and concentrated. Someone sang in the next room over, tuneless lyrics partially drowned out by the running water of a shower. Below her feet she heard the expected grunts of fucking. She wrinkled her nose as she smelled the results of the liaison. As soon as she registered the distaste, the aroma faded. On the street, two bums argued over who could panhandle on which corner. Past the sounds of a bus, a telephone rang and someone answered. The caller received a canned answering machine response stating the open hours of the car wash.

That was across the street! Whiskey's eyelids snapped open. She stared at herself.

Leaving the hotel past midnight, Whiskey noted she'd been asleep for over fifteen hours. After several experiments, she came to the conclusion that the bizarre sensitivity continued, her hearing and sense of smell both sharpened beyond normal. Somehow, her mind had stumbled upon a method of control. Her ability to mute the sounds and aromas to manageable levels had become second nature while she slept.

Relieved as well as confused, she wandered along the sidewalk in thought, ignoring other pedestrians. Even at this hour, there were plenty of people on the streets. Testing her newfound abilities, she looked up at an office building, zeroing in on a third-floor window with a light on. She tilted her head to one side, listening intently.

A pleased smile crossed her face as she heard a man on the phone with his wife, explaining why he hadn't come home yet. She heard the wife on the other end of the line, bitching about another dinner ruined because of his job. A louder, closer sound overlapped his voice, one of rustling cloth and a zipper. Raising her eyebrows at an almost indistinct moan, she chuckled. The man hastily hung up the phone, complaining to his companion that his wife might have overheard. A gasp cut off his arguments. Whiskey shook her head, wondering how long it would be before the unknown person had both their clothes off. The muted thumping that permeated everything increased in tempo. She grinned, pulling her attention back from their adultery, and resumed walking.

She'd solved the question of the thumping noises, realizing they were heartbeats. It made an odd sort of sense; if her hearing had increased to such levels, surely she'd be able to hear the heartbeat of people nearby. By extension, the pace of the beat gave a fair indication of how much exertion a person experienced without having to see them.

The cell phone sat silent in her pocket. She'd told Dorst she'd call when she woke up, but she didn't want to be around anyone. Despite her hotel bill being paid for several more hours, she'd chosen to leave the premises for the night. Her newfound abilities beckoned her. Besides, next time she wanted to be where she could immediately crash, thus avoiding the unpleasantness of the aftereffects. She shivered at the memory of her migraine.

What would happen next time? Would other senses become sharper or would the meditation affect the ones already attuned? She weighed the temptation against her last session. It had taken nearly a full day to recover. Would that be repeated? She didn't have the money to remain at a hotel for another night. Dorst had already paid for an extra evening and, while she couldn't shake the impulsive trust she'd placed in him, she didn't like being beholden to anyone. If she made another attempt, it would have to be on her terms and somewhere safe. She'd need a place to sleep.

A niggling worry gnawed at the desire. What would she see this time, more of the same? If anything, the thought of having another dream as intense as the last filled her with dread. She didn't want more memories of what she'd lost. Gaining further abilities didn't warrant the suffering. It wasn't worth it. Maybe she should stop now, let nature take its course. Both Daniel and Dorst had said that the *Ñíri Kurám* occurred on its own over several years when a Sanguire was left to his or her own devices.

What do I want?

Flashing across her mind's eye, she saw the woman from her nightmares smiling across a table at her, verdant eyes bright. Whiskey hadn't seen this scene before. She swallowed, mouth dry as she stopped dead in her tracks, smelling a seductive spicy odor beneath delicate perfume. *I'm smelling a dream?* Her body responded to the scent of its own accord, a gentle pulse of arousal flickering in her belly.

"Whassa matter, honey? You lose yer little friends?"

She shook her head, regaining her mental balance as she glanced at an old-timer leering at her from the corner. Her nose filled with the ripe scent of old urine and dust and sweat. She gave him a thorough once-over before sneering as he rubbed his crotch in lewd suggestion. "Fuck off," she said, walking away.

"Yeah? Fuck off yourself, bitch!" he called after her, not following.

Whiskey decided to head to the U District. The verbal sparring with the old-timer had reminded her that after midnight wasn't the best time for a street kid to be downtown. She had a few dollars left in her pocket, but didn't want to waste it on bus fare. Food was more important. *Should have accepted those bus tickets and food vouchers from the padre.* She could call Dorst, but she still wasn't ready to see him. Besides, he'd acted pretty weird when she'd admitted to remembering him. She needed the time to process his response.

Though she'd come this way a few nights before, she paid more attention to her surroundings, playing with her new senses. She wondered if Paul and his friends had recuperated enough from Fiona's attack to consider retaliation. Whiskey hadn't had anything to do with them getting their asses kicked, but she'd be the one to pay the price if they found her. Some other homeless kid might run into him first, and receive the beating reserved for her. School *was* still in session. Maybe they'd had a three-day weekend from school. Tonight was Sunday. They couldn't be out cruising for trouble at this hour. *Yeah, you thought that on Thursday when they grabbed you. Better hope it isn't a four-day weekend.*

She made certain to use her newfound senses as she walked.

Finding a fast-food restaurant, she ordered and paid for something to eat. Rather than sit in a brightly lit dining room where anyone passing by could see her, she left and ate on foot. As she walked, she drifted through the business district and into an industrial region. Quieter here, her sharpened ears picked up the sound of vagrants and occasional cars on the nearby streets. Crushing the wrapper of her burrito, she tossed it in the general direction of a Dumpster. She heard the paper bounce off the rim, and scuttle down the side. A rat scrabbled away from the sound, dashing down the gutter. She smelled water, Lake Union only a half mile away. Boat launches and fishing businesses loomed ahead, with a smattering of nice waterfront homes interspersed between them. Once she crossed the bridge, she'd be in the U District and home. Her shoulders relaxed at the thought.

Whiskey heard the motorcycles before she saw them. Several smooth engines drifted in her direction. They'd started ahead, and to her right where the residential area began. She dismissed the sound, knowing that Paul and his friends had borrowed a parent's car. If they'd had their own wheels before, they wouldn't have been in a sedan when they attacked her. When the cycles were a couple of blocks away and nearing her position, she focused more attention upon them. Headlights rounded a corner ahead, five of them. Two bikes had double occupants, each with a scantily clad man and woman. The rest held a single rider each. Most had face-covering helmets, except for two riders with spiky mohawks. She barely registered long red hair beneath the helmet of one as that motorcycle pulled to the side of the street beside her. *Shit.*

All of the vehicles came to a stop. Whiskey recognized Manuel and Bronwyn by their tattoos, and Zebediah and Alphonse from their hairstyles. Seconds later, they took off again, leaving Fiona, Cora and Daniel behind.

Fiona swept off the helmet. "My little *lamma*. What a surprise to see you here." She put down the kickstand on her vehicle.

"Whiskey!" Cora jumped from the back of Daniel's Triumph. She removed her helmet, setting it on the motorcycle seat before rushing toward her. "Where have you been? I've missed you so." She slipped into Whiskey's arms, and gave her a long welcoming kiss.

When Whiskey could breathe again, she said, "I've been a little busy."

"Yes, you have." Fiona had left the motorcycle. She circled Whiskey. "Your *Baruñal* has begun guiding you along the path of the *Ñíri Kurám*." She completed her circuit, smile wide as she regarded her. "And how is *Sañur Gasum* Dorst?"

Did something reveal she'd begun the meditations? *No way. She brought Reynhard to me for this purpose. She can smell him on me.* "He's good." She quelled Cora's wandering hands with her own, not wanting the distraction. "I was just heading to the U District to meet him. We're going to work on the next chant."

Fiona had a knowing smile. "I doubt that. Not enough time has passed. You cannot hurry the *Ñíri Kurám* any more than our *ensi'ummai* have already succeeded in doing. Your body needs to recuperate from the taxing sensations you've generated." She slid one hand up Whiskey's tattooed arm, her smile widening as the skin pebbled beneath her touch. "They are wonderful sensations, are they not?"

Calling attention to the changes in Whiskey's senses magnified them. Before she could answer, Cora leaned in for another long, protracted kiss that left nothing to the imagination. Cora's body squirmed against hers, and a rush of lust made Whiskey moan. She easily caught a whiff of her arousal, delighted to realize she also detected Cora's.

"Oh, yes," Fiona whispered. "Sumptious."

Whiskey broke off the kiss, blood flushing her face. Despite her embarrassment, she met Fiona's eyes, tucking her chin.

Fiona's eyes glittered. "Have you ever driven a motorcycle, my little *lamma*?"

Whiskey almost expected the change of topic; it appeared to be a standard technique of Fiona's, used to derail her opponent's train of thought. Forcing down her libido, no easy task, she cleared her throat. "I've ridden them a couple of times, but never driven one myself."

"Then it's time you learned." Fiona turned to Daniel, who still straddled his bike, his helmet in his lap as he watched the proceedings. "Whiskey will take my Ducati. If you'd be so kind—" She gestured to her bike.

Daniel nodded, and pulled his bike onto its stand, shutting down the engine.

Cora freed herself from Whiskey's hold, and helped her out of her shoulder straps. Whiskey debated the wisdom of letting Fiona run roughshod over her again. The lure of learning this new skill seduced her away from her common sense. *Take more than you can give.*

Soon Whiskey eased down the empty street with Daniel riding behind her. She easily picked up the mechanics of gears and balance, gas and brakes. Most of her difficulty came in keeping the heavy bike upright when she stopped. Daniel assured her that her upper body strength would improve with experience. Exhilarated, she sped along with the wind in her hair, almost forgetting the sensation of Daniel's hands at her waist. She was half tempted to dump him, take off and not come back. *Would Fiona call the cops to report a stolen bike?* Whiskey doubted it; at least it wouldn't be reported to conventional authorities. *Are there Sanguire cops?*

After a spin around the industrial area, she returned to their starting point. Fiona lounged against Daniel's bike with arms crossed beneath her breasts. Cora stood guard over Whiskey's belongings on the sidewalk. As Whiskey pulled to a halt, they both approached. Daniel clambered off the back, and Whiskey fumbled with the kickstand.

"No, dear Whiskey." Fiona held up her hand to forestall her. "You'll ride this one tonight."

Whiskey shook her head, preparing to get off the motorcycle. "I really should—"

"Be still, little *lamma*." Fiona placed a hand on Whiskey's shoulder, halting her attempt to fully stand. She leaned close, her tone softening to a whisper. "You have nothing to fear from me, child. We do not kill our young."

Whiskey didn't know which shocked her more, the erotic touch of Fiona's breath along her ear and neck, or the revelation of her underlying fear that Fiona would rip out her throat. She stuttered a moment, unable to think of what to say.

Fiona stepped back, and located the second helmet strapped to her bike. "Here you go, dear Whiskey. As much as we prefer to ride without, it's best not to taunt local law enforcement any more than is prudent. Besides, I sincerely doubt you have a license to operate a motor vehicle."

Unable to do more than nod in response, Whiskey took the proffered gear. The motorcycle shifted beneath her, and she glanced back to see Cora attaching her pack to the backrest. She then retrieved her helmet from Daniel and put it on, eagerly climbing onto the back of the bike with Whiskey.

Fiona had already donned her helmet, and regally joined Daniel on his bike. "Shall we go then? The night is young."

Daniel started his engine, and gunned it once.

Whiskey felt Cora's hands slide seductively about her waist. Take more than you can give, she reminded herself. *But how long before Fiona demands too much?* She swallowed and hit the ignition button.

CHAPTER FIFTEEN

Whiskey waved at the intermittent buzzing noise for the third time. She sensed it had been going on for a while. Her mind sluggish, she tried to figure out how long, unable to come up with an answer. It buzzed again, loud and obnoxious, too loud to be an insect. Maybe. With her sharper hearing, it could be a simple mosquito, not the jumbo 747 that rocked her aching skull.

The bed shifted, sheets sliding along her sensitive skin. Naked flesh brushed hers, and she sighed and groaned with both pleasure and annoyance. The unknown person climbed across her, reaching for whatever made that sound. Whiskey's breathing became labored at the extra weight across her chest.

"Hello?" a sleep-furred voice said. "Yes, *Sañur Gasum*, she's right here. Please hold."

Whiskey opened her eyes as Cora slid back to her side of the bed. Her head pounded, and her mouth tasted of shit. She squinted at the cell phone Cora brandished at her.

"It's for you."

Groaning, Whiskey took the phone, and cradled it to her chest. She closed her eyes. They seemed full of glass slivers, and her head pounded with her heartbeat. "Reynhard?" she asked, her voice barely above a whisper.

Cora caressed Whiskey's abdomen and hip, waking other more pleasant sensations. "Yes, *Ninsumgal.*"

Whiskey nodded. She remained prone on the wrought iron bed, not willing to try sitting up at the moment. Cora slipped from the linens. Whiskey opened her aching eyes to watch Cora swagger to the bathroom, the faint remains of a bite mark marring her otherwise delicious ass. Licking dry lips with an equally arid tongue, Whiskey brought the phone to her ear. "Hello?"

Dorst's musical tones greeted her ears. "My dearest Whiskey, how do you fare this afternoon?"

"Afternoon?" She tried to remember when they'd gotten back to Fiona's house. The sun had already been up when she'd driven the Ducati into the garage. *Driving without a license and while intoxicated? Jesus. Talk about living dangerously.*

"Yes, afternoon. I trust you had an enjoyable interlude with that seductive blonde on your arm?"

Whiskey swallowed, casting around in her mind. They'd been at Malice again, staying long after the place had closed, drinking and dancing until dawn. "You were there?"

Dorst laughed. "No, dear Whiskey. But Fiona's tactics have remained unchanged for forty years or more. Your interest in Cora has been noted, and steps have been taken to ensure every opportunity for you to be entertained by her charms."

Light footsteps approached, and Whiskey looked up to see a smiling Cora. She held out a tall glass of water and two pills. "Your moisture-deprived tissues need nourishment," she whispered.

Whiskey forced herself to sit up, biting back another groan of pain. At least her stomach wasn't upset; just her head beating against her nerve endings. "Hold on, Reynhard." She dropped the phone on the bed. Taking the pills, she downed them. Ambrosia against her parched tongue, she drained the entire glass. "Thank you."

Cora took the empty glass, and bowed before turning away.

Whiskey watched her go, puzzled. It reminded her of her memory of the long-haired Dorst, bowing and backing away. She picked up the phone. "I'm back."

"When you failed to call from the hotel, I took the liberty of searching for you. I'm glad you found your way to the safety of Fiona's care."

The water had helped to wake her a bit more. In the bathroom, she heard the shower running. "Safety?"

Dorst made a noise. It sounded suspiciously like a snort of amusement. "I'm calling to arrange a meeting with you this evening. It's time to translate the next chant."

A sliver of dread and excitement shivered through Whiskey's chest. "Where and when?"

"Since I've awakened you, I'll give you time to collect yourself. Two hours from now at a coffee shop in the University District? There's one located in an alley near University and Lincoln Way."

She looked at the nightstand clock. Nearly five now. That would leave her time to clean up and get away from here. If she caught a bus within the next hour, she'd be there before seven. "All right, I know the place. I'll be there."

"Excellent. I look forward to seeing you again, my *Gasan*. Until then."

Whiskey stared at the cell phone. "Great. Another fucking word to learn."

Cora did her level best to distract Whiskey from her purpose. Whiskey resorted to making her request a command, tucking her chin and glaring at Cora before the minx would leave her alone. She worried Cora would take umbrage at the treatment, not certain why it mattered. Relief and dismay surged through her when Cora winked coquettishly, leaving the suite with a decided slink in her step. Forty-five minutes later, Whiskey entered the kitchen showered and clothed.

Bronwyn stood at the stove, flipping pancakes on a griddle. Whiskey guessed that cooking duties were rotated among Fiona's followers. She set her pack in a corner of the dining room, intent on a cup of coffee. Bronwyn ignored her, but the corner of her lip lifted in a slight sneer. Whatever problems Manuel had with Whiskey were mirrored in his girlfriend. He sat at the table next to Fiona, focused on his breakfast. More than happy to return the favor to both of them, Whiskey sat at the opposite side of the table from Fiona with a vague sense of *déjà vu*.

"Did you sleep well, dear *lamma*?"

"Yes, thank you." Whiskey glanced at the wineglass, wondering if it were a juvenile affectation, a way for Fiona to appear more adult than the rest of her pack. She sampled the air, smelling the alcohol content of the red liquid, coupled with something more metallic and intriguing. The faint copper smell of blood caused her mouth to water, and she quickly dampened the smell.

Fiona smiled at her, lifting the glass in toast before taking a drink.

Cora sauntered in from the living room. She paused to give Whiskey a thorough kiss. The ever-present arousal, coupled with the strange effect the aroma of blood had given her, fired Whiskey's lust. She broke off the kiss with some effort, pushing Cora away. Her lover blithely smiled, and went into the kitchen. Whiskey glanced at her table companions, face reddening. Manuel's dark eyes glittered with malicious humor before he returned to his meal.

"I can imagine you did." Fiona smirked at Manuel. "I'm so glad I installed that soundproofing, aren't you?"

He grunted a reply. In the kitchen, Bronwyn snickered. Whiskey licked her lips. It wouldn't do her any favors to get into a pissing contest with Fiona, but she'd be damned if she'd act contrite over the jibes. She made a determined effort to appear nonchalant, leaning back to slouch in her chair.

Fiona smiled in amusement, conceding the point. She gestured with her glass to the corner where Whiskey's pack lay. "Going somewhere?"

Cora returned to the table. Placing a plate of pancakes in front of Whiskey, she ran a proprietary hand through Whiskey's hair, then sat down with her own breakfast. "The *Sañur Gasum* called. He wishes to meet with our *Gasan* to begin her next lesson."

Whiskey muffled her surprise. Of course, Cora had overheard every word of the phone conversation with her superior senses. "We meet at seven in the U District." She availed herself of the butter and syrup on the table.

"That's hardly a reason to take your worldly belongings, is it?" Fiona raised an eyebrow. "You'll be safer going through the *Ñíri Kurám* here. We can protect you."

Like I feel safe here. Whiskey didn't respond, digging into her food instead.

When she failed to answer, Fiona pouted. "At least take the Ducati. I'd feel better knowing you had transportation."

Whiskey stared at her. "What?"

"You'd prefer the Lexus or the Porsche?"

"No!" Whiskey shook her head, peeved that Fiona's change of conversation had disrupted her intentions again.

"Then take the bike. The keys are in the ignition."

Whiskey's mind turned, wondering how she could get out of accepting the offer without appearing rude and ungrateful. "That's really not necessary. I can catch the—"

"Take the Ducati," Fiona intoned, glaring at her.

Manuel watched the proceedings, eagerness apparent in the strength of his gaze. Whiskey wondered what he thought would happen if she refused Fiona's order. Oddly, she felt the attention of both Bronwyn and Cora without looking at them. No doubt, Bronwyn's expression mirrored Manuel's, half feral as she waited to witness a fight.

Whiskey's mantra whispered in her mind. *Take more than you can give.* Having the bike would make it easier to get around, at least for a day or two. *I don't have to come right back with it.* She decided to play it coy. It wouldn't do to give in at Fiona's initial command. Whiskey's future compliance would come to be expected. "I don't have a license. What do I do if I get pulled over?"

Fiona's countenance softened as she sensed capitulation. "You have my phone number. Give me a call, and we'll take care of things."

"You'll pay bail?"

"Certainly." Fiona glanced fondly at Manuel. "It's not like I haven't done so in the past."

His lips twisted into a frown.

After a long moment's consideration, Whiskey raised her chin. "Okay, I will. Thank you."

The tension eased. Manuel snorted, and returned to his breakfast. Bronwyn cursed; the pancakes had burned during the minor power struggle. Cora reached under the table, and stroked Whiskey's leg.

Fiona's voice was silken. "You are most welcome, sweet Whiskey."

CHAPTER SIXTEEN

Whiskey roared down the street on the motorcycle. Having been dependent on her feet or public transportation for most her life, she enjoyed this ability to go anywhere she wanted at any time. Though Fiona's home skirted the U District, Whiskey had left early to enjoy the bike, ranging far and wide along the major thoroughfares before finally heading to her appointment with Dorst. She'd leave the bike in a parking lot near there, and the keys with Dorst. He could return the vehicle to Fiona, saving Whiskey the trip.

She located the corner Dorst had spoken of, and pulled to the side of the street. As he'd said, the establishment centered in the alley, sharing the spot with a funky little dress shop. Two scooters already occupied a spot across from a tiny outdoor seating area, so she parked beside them. It took a moment of fumbling before she managed the helmet storage lock by the rear wheel. Eventually she got the bike locked up, pocketing the keys and retrieving her pack.

A literal hole in the wall, the place held seating for half a dozen people at most. Dorst sat at the only occupied table. Whiskey walked past the coffee bar that took up half the business's space, and sat across from him.

"Interesting choice of vehicles, *Gasan*." A smile perched upon his gaunt face. "Did you enjoy the ride?"

Whiskey grinned. "Yeah! It's fantastic. I've never driven one before last night."

"How fortunate for you." He gave her a regal nod, then slid a porcelain cup across the table to her. "I took the liberty of ordering for you. I hope you don't find my actions too presumptuous."

"No, that's cool, thanks." Whiskey picked up the drink, and took a sip, rich chocolate filling her mouth. "It's very good."

"Only the best, *Gasan*."

Whiskey set the cup down. "What does that mean?"

"*Gasan*?" He considered a moment. "Many of our words can mean many things, depending on the inflections involved. With you, I use it as a term that translates to 'lady,' similar to a lady of ancient times as opposed to the generally accepted term of the modern era."

"And *Ninsumgal*?"

Dorst grinned. "Dragon lady."

Whiskey blinked, wondering why Cora would refer to her in such a way. Her hand rubbed the arm with the dragon tattoo, hidden beneath her jacket. Cora had used that word *before* she'd gotten the tattoo. *But it was Cora's suggestion that it be a dragon.*

"Additionally, it could mean 'lady of all' or 'lady sovereign.'" He shrugged. "Unless it was utilized as 'monster of composite power.' Somehow I doubt that was the usage you overheard. It's been several hundred years since anyone has had reason to speak that particular phrase."

"One word means all that?"

Dorst made a noise of agreement as he took a drink from a porcelain cup of tea.

"It's going to take forever for me to learn the language."

"You have time, sweet Whiskey." He chuckled. "You have the Book?"

"Yeah." Whiskey located the leather-bound volume in her pack. Her eyes narrowed. *Why the hell is it warm?* She handed it to Dorst, wiping her fingers on her pants after she released it to his care.

They spent the next hour going over the second chant. Again, Whiskey learned more of his native language, and the strange angular writing known as cuneiform. When she could ably recite the words with their proper intonation, Dorst pronounced her ready.

"Do you have someplace safe to conduct this meditation?" He closed the Book.

Whiskey hesitated. "Not yet. I'm still looking."

"And Fiona's residence is out of the question?"

Dread filled her heart at the thought of being surrounded by Fiona's people. "Am I supposed to be looking for someplace that *is* safe, or a place where I *feel* safe?"

Dorst cocked his head at her. "Most definitely the latter, sweet Whiskey."

"Then Fiona's place is out of the question."

His lips quirked in a faint smile. "Understood."

Whiskey chewed her lower lip. "Are all—" She broke off, considering her words. "Do all our people live like Fiona and her friends do?"

He lifted a hairless eyebrow, tilting his head to one side in thought. "You mean as opposed to the nuclear family arrangement you are familiar with here in North America?"

"Yeah, I guess." That wasn't quite what she meant, but it would do as a start.

"Some do, some don't. Humans live together, raise children, and send their children into the world. Their limited life span makes this a convenient arrangement. Sanguire, however, live significantly longer. Our death toll would no doubt skyrocket if our children remained with us until they reached, say, two or three hundred years of age."

Whiskey imagined that would be true. "You said that Fiona has been using the same tactics for forty years. How old is she?"

Dorst smiled. "Perhaps you should ask her. Sanguire women are just as sensitive about their age as Human ones."

She scowled at his nonanswer, taking the Book from him to put away. The leather was still warm, and her fingertips tingled.

After studying her a moment, he said, "You wonder if the living situation of Fiona and her friends is the norm?"

"Yeah." Whiskey closed her backpack. "To be honest, I don't get why Cora or Daniel hang with her. If they have their own families and contacts, why put up with her shit?" Privately, she thought Bronwyn and Manuel were right where they wanted to be; they had more in common with Fiona than anyone else in the pack.

"Ah," he said in sudden comprehension. "When you're farther along the *Ñíri Kurám*, you will understand the way of things. As you walk the Strange Path, you'll develop an ability to feel the strength of other Sanguire about you. Fiona leads because she's the eldest and the strongest among them, nothing more than that."

"Strong?" Whiskey considered the various pack members. "Manuel or Alphonse can snap her like a twig. Hell, I saw Cora take out a guy with a single punch to the kidneys. How can she be weaker than Fiona?"

Dorst leaned forward, tapping his temple with two long fingers. "Mentally strong. You'll understand better when you've finished the meditations. While Fiona is a slight woman, she can easily lay waste to everyone there."

Whiskey shivered at the implications. "When I'm finished with this...*Ñíri Kurám*, will she have power over me?"

"It's highly probable."

"Can I combat it? Stop it?"

His serious expression faded to sympathy. "Fiona does not usually compel her people. They are there of their own accord. Unless she's changed her strategy, if you do not wish her to have power over you, you may simply leave."

Whiskey felt both relief and concern. "So there's a way to 'compel' other Sanguire?"

"It has been known to happen. It's not an easy task to

undertake, and she would have to use her full concentration to keep you yoked." He tilted his head. "It is not something that can be done lightly or for any length of time. This sort of ability is used primarily for immediate gratification rather than long-term situations."

She sighed, eyes restlessly scanning the interior of the coffee shop, the cozy little place a trifle claustrophobic.

Dorst covered her hand with his, bringing her attention back to him. "Do not let it concern you so, sweet Whiskey. Your primary goal is to get through the *Ñíri Kurám*, nothing more. There will be plenty of time to plan for your future."

His touch comforted her. Considering the strange turn her life had taken, she felt herself becoming more and more dependent on him. A part of her found such a situation perfectly acceptable; he would never lead her wrong. The street kid, however, the homeless wanderer whose desires to belong had disappointed her so many times in the past, knew better. This kindness was false, a prelude to an obligation she couldn't even begin to perceive. Her obligation ran pretty deep with Fiona, what with the toys and money. This emotional connection with Dorst was worse.

She forced herself to pull her hand away from his.

Despite Whiskey's original decision to hand the Ducati over to Dorst, he didn't give her the opportunity. She left to utilize the bathroom, and returned to an empty table. The barristo, as mystified as she, insisted he hadn't seen Dorst leave. She didn't know whether to be annoyed or amused. *How can he get away while looking and dressing the way he does?*

Astraddle the motorcycle, she contemplated her options. She needed a safe place to conduct the next meditation. But where? Starting the bike, she pulled to the mouth of the alley, idling there as she watched traffic and pedestrians wander past. A bus blew by, the advertisement on the side panel suggesting she shop at MegaMart Grocery to save money. Her eyes latched onto the sign, following it intently until the bus turned the corner.

Gin's street family had stayed at an abandoned building near that store. Gin had told her at Tallulah's that they'd found another flop somewhere else, thereby vacating that one. She hadn't said that the police raided the place.

A possible safety net realized, Whiskey drove the motorcycle into the street. If her luck held, the building remained empty. She could hole up in one of the smaller rooms upstairs once she finished the chant.

CHAPTER SEVENTEEN

Whiskey wiped her palms on her pants, staring at the small Book in her lap. She sat in a wooded area of the university campus, darkness surrounding her, a refreshing breeze ruffling her hair, filled with the scents of earth and wood and greenery. Hidden beneath, subtler in texture, the smell of human habitation marred the illusion of privacy. The University Village Shopping Center stood just beyond the wall of trees.

The Book pulsed with hidden energy at her touch. Its warmth bled through the cloth of her pants, heating her thighs. She found it oddly intriguing that, although it beat in time with her heart, she detected no corresponding sound. Tentative, fingers shaking, she brushed the leather cover. A tingle greeted her, coursing up her arm, thrilling her heart. If she didn't know better, blood pumped just beneath the soft leather surface. She swallowed, pulling away.

She hadn't thought to ask Dorst if this was normal or not. *What if it isn't? What if I'm really not Sanguire, and that's why this thing feels like this.* Could something go wrong with the process? Daniel had said a Human couldn't become Sanguire. Could he have been wrong? Can a Human go through the motions and be changed? And if she did, what would happen to her? *There's only one way to find out.*

Whiskey sighed, forcing herself to relax. Using a lighter for illumination, she whispered the words twice more until it burned hot in her hand. Satisfied, she flicked the lighter closed, and gingerly dropped it beside her. She left the Book in her lap, wanting it ready in case she needed to refer to the words, and began the meditation.

As before, her first run-through awakened something within. This time, she kept her eyes open, curious to see if the words did indeed become as visible as they felt. They didn't. Despite her disappointment, a rush of excitement gushed through her veins that didn't correspond with the environment.

The second repetition triggered an ache in her belly, a combination of hunger and lust that left her dizzy. The little light available in the clearing coalesced about her, a bubble of heat that tightened with each passing second, surrounding her, filling her. Unable to keep her eyes open, she closed them, beginning her third round. With no visual distraction, she felt as before that the words tasted and smelled different. This time, they were spicy and wet like a woman in rut. Her body sang with answering desire as she started the fourth and final recitation. Again sparks of fire crossed her closed eyes, coalescing into shining images. Again she heard music, calling from a distance, urging her close. Again, she lost sense of time and place, tumbling into a vision.

Flash.

"Who is she?"

"One of the O'Toole clan."

The music welled up around Whiskey as she watched a young version of the woman from her nightmare dance about a ballroom, emerald dress flowing gracefully behind her. She waltzed with a dapper young man who paid her very close attention as they whirled around. Others also watched them dance, mostly envious young men. Understandable since she was undoubtedly the most gorgeous woman in the room.

Scanning the crowd, Whiskey found herself inexplicably bored though she'd never attended a function such as this. She barely gave the odd clothing, all formal dress, a second glance. As the dancers moved closer to her position, she realized she sat on a stage of sorts, a long table stretching out to either side, detritus from a rich meal scattered on a plate in front of her. Before she could focus on her tablemates, the woman flowed past directly below.

"I want her."

"Yes, my *Ninsumgal*," a familiar yet strange voice said. "I'll see to it."

Flash.

Whiskey stood on a balcony, enjoying a cool spring evening. Peripherally she noted a city beyond the stone wall, her gaze remaining in the garden below. A handful of young women teased, and giggled among themselves as they played in a fountain. Their laughter rang off the walls, inviting her to smile in vicarious longing. She sensed that it had been some time since she'd felt as carefree as these women, despite the fact they were of an age with her. The women were either daughters of nobility or their handmaidens. At this point the determination of rank was impossible, as all manner of haughty decorum had been long abandoned in light of the water play.

Musicians played somewhere, their music less stuffy than in the previous vision. Torches flickered here and there, providing illumination as the sky turned gray and then a deep blue. Stars slowly spread across the darkening sky, jewels across the vast quilt of night. None of them sparkled as much as the jewel in the garden.

Whiskey remained in shadows, watching the intriguing woman from the dance floor as she stood dripping beside the fountain, her dark hair damp, wilted ringlets about her face, generous lips opened in laughter at the antics of someone else. Her dress, a simple affair of burgundy, hung tight against her body, showing off a delectable feminine form. Whiskey tested the air, searching, locating her scent, a spicy odor that promised fire and sweetness. As if aware of her audience, the woman paused in her play, looking up at the balcony. Several moments passed, Whiskey's eyes meeting hers, knowing the woman detected her outline in the shadows.

The woman's glance dropped away, decorous, a delicate blush coloring her skin. Another girl ran by, startling her and she automatically splashed her playmate, receiving a thorough drenching in response. When she looked up at the balcony again, she held an inviting shy smile.

Whiskey felt the full effect of arousal flood through her body.

"I want you," she whispered.

Flash.

Whiskey sat at a small table in her room, fire blazing nearby, a light repast spread out before her. Across the table, brilliant green eyes regarded her in unskilled flirtation. Whiskey's heart trilled as she remembered this scene; she'd seen this moment the night before when leaving the hotel.

The woman's lips curved into a smile as she tasted something or other from the meal before them. "These are very good, *Ninsumgal.*" Her voice held a musical lilt, one Whiskey identified as Irish.

She didn't answer, too intent on this vision licking her rich red lips, something she vowed to do herself before the morning dawned. She leaned back in her armchair, lazily swirling the contents of her glass as she watched with hooded eyes. Both of them knew it was a matter of time before Whiskey took her.

They had plenty of time.

Flash.

Those lips, swollen from many kisses, opened as the woman cried out. She leaned against the corner of a four-poster bed, one hand holding the carved wood, steadying herself. The other buried in Whiskey's hair, the fingers digging into Whiskey's scalp. The woman's naked thighs spread wider, hips hitching as Whiskey expertly tongued her.

Whiskey breathed in the scent of spice, pleased at her catch.

The woman writhed against her touch, the sight and sound setting Whiskey's heart pounding uncontrollably. Unable to hold herself away, she dived back into the heady taste, slaking her thirst with the liquid fire of her lover's arousal.

Flash.

Whiskey burst from the dream state, panting with uncontrollable lust. Her body on fire, she still tasted the woman on her lips, smelled her on her fingers. Gasping, she stumbled to her feet, the Book tumbling to the mulch below. She shook with the effort of calming herself, soothing the rampaging desire until she could think.

What the hell was that? Breathing deep, she banished more of the yearning, sinking weakly to the ground. Her traitorous body still cried out to be touched, and she forced her hands beneath her thighs, effectively pinning them. Catching her breath, she did her level best to not squirm.

It couldn't have been a memory. Whiskey knew she'd never have forgotten bedding the woman, not with these emotions boiling so close to the surface. Another wave of need raced through her as she recalled those throaty cries. Growling, she closed her eyes and shook her head. The vision, the sounds, the smells would not be dispelled. *Who the hell was that? Who are the O'Tooles?*

She pushed her thoughts to the earlier part of her vision, the dinner and dancing. Now she recognized the clothing. She'd seen them in movies and television. *The Middle Ages?* Uncertain of the exact time period, she concentrated, remembering the tunics and trousers of the men, the gowns of the women.

The woman's emerald gown flowing by the dinner table.

What had she said? *'I want her.'* But who had answered? The man's voice seemed familiar to her then, but not now. *'I'll see to it, my* Ninsumgal.'

Scoffing, she released her hands from their prison, and crossed her arms. So now she was past life royalty? Who had she been, Henry the VIII or something? No, she felt as she did now, a woman. If it were a past life memory, would she have felt a difference being a man? Besides, her voice had been her own in the vision.

"Shit!" She couldn't believe she entertained such a preposterous idea. Reincarnation was as hokey as witchcraft, as ethereal as the existence of God, one of a hundred other theories that had been created to make humankind feel above the piles of crap to be slogged through during a lifetime. That didn't make any of them true. Dorst hadn't said anything about this being a possibility. He'd said people saw their futures or past. Whiskey had never seen any of this. *Some sort of hallucination? Is that an option?*

Her emotions and body once more under her control, she grabbed up her belongings. She stuffed the Book back into her satchel, refusing the dwell on the sensual feel of the warm leather. Her lighter remained out long enough to shakily light a cigarette before she stuffed it into her pocket. She needed music and dance, and something to drive the images away.

CHAPTER EIGHTEEN

Whiskey slid through the crowd, flashing lights illuminating her path. With Tallulah's closed, she'd come to Malice on a hunch. The bouncer with the golden/brown eyes had immediately allowed her entry. She knew he'd probably call Fiona, but at this point she didn't care. The vision had left her with unspent arousal; Cora's arrival would be a welcome relief. At the bar, she handed over her backpack and ordered a drink. The bartender recognized her, equably securing her belongings and sliding a glass of Chivas Regal toward her.

No one touched her, the dancers in her path stepping aside automatically with seemingly no thought about why her presence caused them to shift out of her way. She grinned, wondering at this newfound power. Reaching a corner of the dance floor, she set her drink on a nearby table, and began to dance. The music pounded in her blood, crashed against her skin, and raised her to a more familiar trance-like state. Nothing but bass and drum and guitar, techno and rock and pop. So much better than those bizarre chants; clean, pure, true. She relaxed into the known, sighing in relief that this had not been sullied. Eyes closed, she felt alone and separate. Her senses crooned to her, whispered the truth of her surroundings; the nearness of other dancers, the smells of food and sweat and sex. Time had no meaning. A rejuvenation coursed through her, her separation of self fading the longer she danced. Reveling in the moment, she feasted on the excited, youthful atmosphere around her, somehow gaining sustenance in the process.

She drew attention. She couldn't tell how she knew with her eyes closed. Perhaps it was an extension of what had happened at Tallulah's with Dorst, or maybe seeing the woman of her dreams in the garden had triggered this knowing. The thought of the woman derailed Whiskey's sense of self for a split second, a vision of the woman crying out in passion overloading her. Whiskey shook her head, pushed it away. The subtle aura of the dancers reaffirmed itself and shifted, a bubble of intensity focusing in on her, drawing closer. She ignored it for the moment, too drunk on the music and lust, almost wishing for the change to go away. She had enough to deal with tonight. Surrounding her, insistent, the bubble condensed.

Opening her eyes, Whiskey saw an older woman circling her, dancing separately but mimicking her moves. Whiskey looked her over. She couldn't be more than twenty-six or so, no taller than her, maybe an inch shorter if the boots were any indication. The woman's Levi's and tight Henley shirt fit her well. Dark brown hair curled around the collar, while brown eyes regarded Whiskey with a speculative smile.

Whiskey breathed in again, almost swooning at the smell of the woman—a mixture of cologne, soap and musky excitement. Her body's arousal flowed through her with liquid heat. She quirked her lips in a welcome smile as she acknowledged her dance partner, adjusting her steps to include the woman. On a different level, she felt the bubble coalesce around them, closing out other noises and voices. Emboldened, the woman eased closer, dark eyes flickering over the lithe body before her, an answering grin on her face.

Previous experience dictated a very short dance. Most adults looking for an evening's entertainment rarely stayed long after a choice had been made. Not wanting to prolong the seduction, Whiskey stepped forward, pressing against the woman, arms lightly draped over her shoulders. Hands found her waist, riding her hips as their bodies melded into each other.

Feeling the woman against her heightened sense of touch, Whiskey gasped at the physical rush. The hands at her waist slid easily beneath her camisole, fingers gently massaging the skin of her lower back, easing down over her cargo pants to squeeze her rear. She pressed against the thigh between her legs, grinding in time with the music. Burying her hands in dark brown curls and tasting the woman's lips, Whiskey delved deeply with her tongue. Around them, dancers continued their gyrations, making the couple sole occupants in a circle of sound.

The woman tugged her through the dark doorway. "This way."

Whiskey followed her into a small living area. She saw comfortable mismatched furniture, a fireplace with a hearth that spanned the width of the room, and a small entertainment center *sans* television. The woman, unable to see, moved tentatively, one hand questing before her toward a lamp. Whiskey smiled, releasing her hand.

Turning, the woman reached out, but Whiskey stepped aside. "Okay," she said with a laugh. "Stay there, and I'll light some candles."

Whiskey found the woman's giggle irritating. She ignored the flash of displeasure. "Don't bother." She moved behind her, slipping her hands forward to caress the woman's belly and chest. "I see all I need." Her vision had sharpened as much as her hearing and smell. She couldn't quite explain the difference to herself other than the available light from a distant streetlamp provided plenty of illumination. She found it curious that the woman couldn't see much at all.

Her need pulsed stronger with each heartbeat as she slid her hands under the Henley. Any thought of prolonging this liaison fled from the rush of heat in her groin as the woman accepted her control, relaxing against her, gasping as Whiskey pinched and massaged her breasts. Whiskey nuzzled the lithe neck, unable to resist the temptation to nibble. She roughly cupped the woman's sex through the jeans, finding the material slightly moist as she squeezed.

The woman's hips hitched, and she groaned aloud, panting. She brought her arm up to caress the long hair behind her, baring her neck for further attention in the process. Her free hand slid down Whiskey's arm, pressing the hand at her crotch as close as possible.

Lost to the smells and sounds and sensations, Whiskey soon had her partner naked. The woman was splayed across the couch, playing with her breasts as Whiskey concentrated on other areas. On sensory overload, her mind and body were one, a wall of fiery need that blotted out everything else. Beneath her lips and tongue, she felt as well as heard the rapid pulse of her conquest. Heated skin against her cheek, liquid desire beneath her mouth, the essence she desired pumping just under the surface.

A scream and a curse forced her out of her fugue. The woman scrambled backward along the couch away from her. Whiskey, disconcerted, tried to engage her partner again as she moved forward, the copper taste in her mouth inciting her passion. The resounding slap drove her back, clearing her head.

"You *bitch*! What the fuck are you doing?"

Whiskey rocked back on her heels, shaking her head. The woman fumbled with a lamp, switching it on. Whiskey winced, and covered her eyes at the sudden blinding. She heard another angry curse, and peered through her fingers.

"Christ! I'm bleeding! You fucking *bit* me!"

A smattering of blood flowed from a puncture on the woman's inner thigh, sluggish and glittering in the lamplight. Whiskey licked her lips, tasting the copper mixed with musky lubrication. She felt another rush of need wash over her, the woman's blood calling her soul. Sudden disgust rolled through her, and she stumbled back.

"What are you waiting for? Get the fuck out of here before I call the police, bitch!"

Whiskey barely had the sense to collect her shirt and pack before stumbling from the apartment, leaving the door standing open. Behind her, she heard the woman swearing, threatening police and legal action. By the time Whiskey reached the fire exit down the hall, the apartment door slammed shut and two locks clicked into place. She burst through the stairway door, and staggered down, struggling into her shirt as she went. The coolness of the evening washed over her as she stepped outside. Letting the door close on well-oiled hinges, she leaned against the wall beside it, panting.

What just happened?

Licking her lips again, she tasted the last of the woman's blood. It exploded across her taste buds, awakening a hunger she hadn't known existed. She used her fingers to search for more around her mouth that she may have missed. Dizziness swept over her. She crouched against the brick, putting her head between her knees to keep from fainting. Several moments passed before she felt strong enough to move. A distant siren brought her head up, wondering if the woman had made good on her threat. Whiskey didn't need an assault charge on her record. At eighteen, there'd be no juvenile detention for her; she'd spend her time in county jail. Even Fiona couldn't save her from this.

She pushed away from the wall, and walked briskly away, strapping her backpack around her waist. Her thoughts and emotions swirled into a muddy cloud, making it impossible to think. She sped up, instinctively trying to outrun the miasma of confusion only to have it keep pace with her. Soon she trotted, then ran, lungs and legs and shoulders burning with the exertion. She ran until she could run no more. Legs heavy, knees and hips automatically pumping despite hot iron pokers probing the joints with every movement, she lurched into an intersection. A loud horn and a curse barely alerted her in time as a car screeched to a halt. Her forward motion pushed her to fall across the hood.

"God damn it! What's the matter with you!" the driver yelled out his window. "Get the fuck off my car and pay attention, idiot! The light's green!"

Rage washed over her. She opened her mouth, and hissed at the driver, baring her teeth. His face blanched in response, and she heard his heart sputter in fear. She smelled the terror coming from him. Her mouth watered, the bizarre response causing her to shake her head in befuddlement.

He laid on his horn. "Fucking psycho! Go on! Get outta here! Jesus!"

She tottered around the vehicle, stumbling onto the curb as the driver pulled away with a screech. Leaning against a signpost, she noted her location. She'd run toward light and human occupation, coming to a halt on University Way. She gasped, trying to catch her breath. It wasn't as late as she'd thought. Several bars were still open, and the traffic fairly heavy. Pedestrians wandered the sidewalk; couples leaving late dinners, barhoppers roaming to the next establishment, a rare handful of street walkers showing off their wares to passing vehicles.

Finally able to breathe, she wiped an arm across her forehead, feeling the heat from the exertion. She refused to think about what happened, focusing her mind on getting back to the flop she'd chosen for herself. The motorcycle was still at Malice. It would be easier for her to catch a bus, and pick up the bike tomorrow. As if in answer to her thought, a bus blew by, stopping a block away before continuing on. She forced herself forward, her legs rubber, cursing her luck. It'd be at least a half hour before another came by.

Maybe I should call Reynhard.

Abrupt relief weakened her knees again, and for that reason she rejected the idea. Dorst might have the answers, but she'd go to him on her own terms, not because she'd freaked out. Besides, she was two for two—he'd told her to retire immediately after each meditation, which she hadn't yet done. She couldn't expect him to clean up her messes, especially when she willfully defied his instructions.

Whiskey made it to the bus stop, and sank onto a bench. Traffic whizzed past, all lights and noise. Her oversensitive eyes ached, and she closed them, grimacing at the oncoming headache. Her stomach gurgled, but she ignored it. She wasn't about to repeat her error from last time by getting something to eat. While she waited, she wondered why it had taken so long for the illness to catch up to her. After the first chant, she'd come down with the migraine within the hour. It'd been three hours or more tonight.

Still puzzling over the question when the bus arrived, Whiskey boarded the transport and paid her fare. Normally she'd head for the rear seats, but the lights were too bright back there. Instead, she dropped onto the bench behind the driver. She curled up there, sunglasses on, staring at the passing city.

"What's done is done," a man said.

"Stay with me, *'m'cara*! We will get you to a healer and soon you will be fine."

Whiskey shook her head, her laugh a wasted echo of what it should be. "Nay, Margaurethe. It is beyond that; we both know it." She coughed, the spasms causing her blood to flow a little faster from the deep wound in her thigh.

"No! You cannot die, Elisibet."

"Apparently so, *minn 'ast*. Will you forgive me?"

"There is nothing to forgive."

She shivered. "It is so cold, Margaurethe. Hold me."

The world went dark.

Whiskey sat upright, breathing rapidly. Late afternoon sunlight slid through the warped plywood nailed across the window, illuminating the lazy dance of dust motes. Beyond the flimsy divider, she heard rush hour traffic passing the flophouse. After a futile search for the mortal wound on her thigh, she slumped with a sigh, cradling her face in her hands. That stupid nightmare would not go away. *Weird how I suddenly know what they're saying.* Last night's meditation must have had something to do with that. Somehow, the dream and the vision had crossed wires in her mind. That didn't mean either of them were real, just that her subconscious picked up pieces of both and mixed them together. The woman—*Margaurethe O'Toole*—had an Irish accent in the dream this time.

Whiskey frowned. *We weren't speaking English. How would I know an Irish accent from a Chinese one in a language I've never heard?* Trying to reason that shit out made her head throb, and she put it aside. Neither the nightmare nor those visions were real. Dorst had said the chants were created to restructure the Sanguire mind to adulthood; these fancies were just her brain's attempt at making sense of the crap going on inside her head.

Pleased with her deduction, she took stock of her body. Starving, but that wasn't anything new. No headache, no sickness. She didn't have any obvious new abilities. Her hearing and sight were just as acute as they were the day before, maybe more so. She heard conversations spoken a block away inside an office building, regardless of the rumble of vehicles on the street outside. Her eyesight allowed her to zero in on a tiny fly in the uppermost corners of the room. Concentrating, she heard the soft burr of it rubbing its legs together.

"Wow." She pulled back her attention, a smile on her face. "Wicked."

Her stomach reminded her how long it had been since she'd eaten. A quick check of her pockets netted a grand total of three dollars and forty-six cents. Enough for a burger at a fast-food joint. Not enough for the rest of the night, though. She could always head downtown to Malice, pick up the Ducati, and head over to Fiona's. Frowning, she nixed the idea. She couldn't treat Fiona as an easy resource, something that would always be there. Her experience argued otherwise. There might always be social services in some form or other to access for assistance, but depending on private individuals was too dangerous.

Besides, she still didn't know about Fiona's motives.

She decided to go to the Youth Consortium a few blocks away. Not only could she pick up some food vouchers, and maybe a leftover boxed lunch, she could see how far the padre had gotten on her birth certificate. She folded and rolled her sleeping bag.

CHAPTER NINETEEN

The sidewalk outside the consortium building looked vacant. Whiskey, who didn't own a watch, swore to herself as she neared. Her suspicions proved correct when she saw the Closed sign on the glass door. "Damn it!" Grabbing the handle, she gave the door a rattle, knowing it wouldn't do any good. "Fuck."

She used her hand to block the glare of sunlight, and peered inside. Beyond the entry alcove with its free newspaper stands and cluttered community bulletin board, she saw the darkened waiting room. She squinted, focusing on the wall clock at the far wall. Her new visual acuity kicked in, zooming her vision until the numbers blurred from the extreme magnification. She wavered on her feet, grabbing at the handle to remain standing against the vertigo. "Whoa!"

Whiskey removed her sunglasses and rubbed her eyes before trying again. This time she managed it with less abruptness.

The clock confirmed the consortium had been closed for over a half hour. Disgusted, she pushed away, and continued down the street. She admitted to herself that she'd wanted to see the priest again more than anything. Her life had taken such a weird turn, the idea of chatting with someone safe and separate from the madness had been alluring. Getting food vouchers had been secondary to seeing a familiar face.

At the corner, she looked down the east side of the consortium building, seeing the high office windows. A smile quirked her lips. *I wonder if he's still in there?* She rounded the corner, and peered at the windows, pleased to see ceiling lights on in some offices. *If I can just narrow down which one is his...* Centering her attention on the windows, she allowed her hearing to sharpen.

Several of the offices still held people. She heard papers rustle, file cabinets opening and closing, phone conversations, and the muted clicking of keyboards. Everyone still in the building was intent on getting their work completed to go home, rather than chat with each other. There was no way she could tell who was who of the silent ones. Maybe if she focused more. Dropping her pack on the sidewalk, she leaned against a light pole and closed her eyes.

Questing like this seemed different somehow, almost as if she wasn't only using her ears in the process, but a part of her mind. She couldn't exactly "see," but she began to create a mental picture in her head. Here someone sat at a desk in a small room—she knew the size because the paper sounded different here than that in the waiting area, more muted. A file cabinet closed, and steps led away, an office chair gently whooshed when sat upon, a steady heartbeat. A bigger office, with more space. A copy machine hummed and clicked as it worked, another heartbeat and flipping papers indicating the operator remained there to go over the print job.

Hearing a small refrigerator open, Whiskey pulled back her attention to focus on the sound. She heard the slight hiss of carbonated air escaping a bottle. Grinning, her nose delivered the fresh smell of root beer. *There he is!* Amused with the game, she continued to scan his office with her senses, comparing her newfound abilities with what she knew from firsthand account.

She remained riveted upon Castillo, feeling something ethereal grow between them. *What the hell?* The more she concentrated, the more it grew. Somehow she sensed him, not just the sounds or smells he created. He felt like warm dark chocolate, not overly sweet, the edge of aged cocoa bitterness counteracting the saccharin. She explored this sensation with avid curiosity. *Maybe this is what changed this time. I wonder if everyone feels like that.*

She pulled away from the priest to find someone else with whom to experiment. Before she located anyone, the sensation she equated with Castillo intensified, seeming to surround her. It held a questioning essence, though she couldn't register how she knew. Confused, uncertain what to do, she stood there agape. *Is he doing this?* How did he know she spied upon him? After a moment, Whiskey zeroed in on his office with her hearing again. He'd left it, though the chocolate perception remained strong. A door opened, and Whiskey's eyelids flew up.

Castillo stood at the fire exit door, staring at her. "Whiskey?" Incredulity colored his voice.

Nervous, Whiskey picked up her pack, preparing to run. "Padre."

He held up his hands in a calming gesture. "Can we talk?"

She glanced at the building, suddenly feeling more trapped than safe. "I guess."

"Not here." He looked up, and down the busy street. "I'll buy you dinner at the Mitchell Café, okay?"

Nodding, Whiskey nibbled her lower lip. *It's the padre, for Christ's sake, idiot! He's safe enough.* "Okay."

He took a step toward the still open fire exit, and paused. "You'll wait for me here?"

A faint smile crossed her lips. *At least he's not the only one freaked out here.* "I'll wait."

"Promise me."

She rolled her eyes in exasperation. "You know me too damned well." When he didn't respond, she threw up her hands. "I promise! I'll wait here for you."

Satisfied, he gave her a nod, and slipped back inside.

Whiskey sighed, adjusting her pack strap. The padre hadn't acted weirded out about the sensation, but about her presence.

Are there Sanguire hunters? The sudden thought disconcerted her. Castillo was a priest, and the Church always fought vampires in the movies and books. Would he want to kill her? She knew better than to rely on popular media for the answers. This had to be just as ridiculous. *Daniel would say so. I could call Reynhard and ask.* Before she got the cell phone from her pocket, Castillo came around the corner from the front of the building. Still uneasy, she joined him.

The café enjoyed a lull as neighborhood workers fled the area for their homes, and students headed for their dorms to drop books and assignments. Castillo chose an outdoor table, causing Whiskey to smile. *He does know me well.* They didn't conduct much small talk, preferring to study the menus and order dinner.

Once the waitress left them to their table with their drinks, Whiskey braced herself. She knew what she'd felt, but still didn't know how he knew what had happened. He would have to start the ball rolling before she'd volunteer anything. She leaned casually back in her chair. "Thanks for this. I didn't realize the time. I was hoping to pick up some vouchers or a leftover boxed lunch."

His elbows on the table, he rested his chin on clasped hands, and studied her.

Whiskey swallowed at the intent gaze, but didn't react until the dark chocolate essence of Castillo washed over her. Heart pumping, she felt a flush crawl up her face, unable to stop its progress. She almost lifted her chin in defiance, but remembered Fiona's capitulation. Instead, she lowered her head, and stared back at him.

Castillo blinked.

The warm sensation faded a little, stuttered. She raised an eyebrow at him. "Padre?"

"Do you know what's happening to you?"

Whiskey stared in surprise. He spoke the question as if he knew, and she didn't. She looked away from him, watching the cars pulling up to the streetlight. "You're buying me dinner. You wanted to talk."

"Who gave you the Book?"

Her gaze shot back to him. No longer nonchalant, she sputtered. She almost heard the leather-bound volume in her backpack thump with her mirrored heartbeat, fast and thready in shock. "What...what're you talking about?"

He relaxed his shoulders, and sat back, dropping his hands to his lap. "I'm talking about the *Ñíri Kurám*. Your feet have been placed upon the Strange Path by someone, you're becoming an adult."

"How do you *know* these things?"

Castillo rubbed his forehead with one hand. "I've been *Baruñal* to one or two younglings in the past. I know the symptoms."

"*You've* been—you're Sanguire?" Was that the difference in her? She could now sense other Sanguire around her?

"Yes. I'm James Castillo. I was born in the year 1629."

Whiskey's mind buzzed from the information, drowning out other considerations. *He's almost four hundred years old?* Shaking her head, she tried to concentrate on his voice, for he'd continued speaking.

"Who is your *Baruñal*? I can't believe he or she would just let you roam around the city in this state. Whoever it is needs to be reported to the *Agrun Nam*, at the very least the *Maskim Sañar*."

The Sanguire words sparked a surge of irrational hatred. They were alien to her ears, yet she knew to the core of her being that the *Agrun Nam* couldn't be trusted, that Dorst had approached her outside of their influence, and that Castillo must work with whoever they were. Acting on instinct rather than knowledge, she slapped the table to regain his attention. "Why are you here? Have you told the *Agrun Nam* about me?"

Castillo's ranting ceased, and he stared at her. After a long pause, he said, "Yes and no."

Whiskey's eyes narrowed. "You'd better clarify that, Padre."

He sighed, his fingers restless as they traced the woodgrain of the table. "When I first met you, I had my suspicions that you were Sanguire. You weren't very forthcoming with your personal information, so I couldn't conduct a genealogical search to find your family. I notified the *Agrun Nam* at that time."

"What did they tell you to do?"

"To watch and listen, to see if I could get more information to locate your family."

Biting betrayal turned her blood and anger to ice. She couldn't ignore the unreasonable depth of emotion. "You bastard." She'd spent years skirting the Human social services system, and now the European Sanguire had her name and birth date.

"Whiskey—"

"You fucking bastard. You knew what I was, and you never told me. Instead you went running to the *Agrun Nam*, spilling your guts all the way." She thumped the table with her fist, their drinks wobbling. "I gave you my name!"

A passing pedestrian gave them a startled glance. Three patrons at a nearby table looked warily in their direction, then returned to their conversation with muted voices.

Castillo kept his head bowed, looking properly chastised. When she didn't continue to harangue him, he met her gaze. "The *Agrun Nam* doesn't have your name, Whiskey. I never gave it to them, and I don't plan to without your consent."

Her cold fury faltered. "Why not? Don't you work for them?"

"Work for them?" He chuckled. "No. I'm one of thousands of expatriates scattered across the globe, living our lives as we see fit."

She frowned at him. "Then why did you bring me to their attention in the first place?"

He appeared apologetic as his fingers returned to tracing woodgrain patterns. "You have to understand that finding a Sanguire child alone is unthinkable to us. Our people do not have children often, so each is precious and cherished. For one to be living on the streets of a city with no support, no family?" He shook his head, raising his eyes to hers. "First, we had no record of a family losing a child in the last two decades, nor were there any deaths of which we were aware. You presented a mystery."

Whiskey considered his words, conceding the logic of them. "So you contacted them to see if they had records of these things? To try and find my parents?"

"Yes."

She tucked her chin, glaring at him. "But why did you think I was Sanguire to begin with? How are Sanguire kids different enough from Human ones to tip you off?"

Castillo sighed. "They aren't. You happen to bear a striking resemblance to...someone of historical significance."

Dorst's last language lesson came to mind. *"It's been several hundred years since anyone has had reason to speak that particular phrase."* She murmured his translation. "A monster of composite power."

The waitress interrupted Castillo's response. Several long minutes went by as she completed her task. When she left the table, he whispered, *"Ninsumgal* Elisibet Vasilla."

She felt her world slide away for a brief moment. *Elisibet? The name she knew from the nightmare. Which means...what? Margaurethe O'Toole existed?* A sudden rush of longing coupled with the shock of Castillo's news made her feel faint. *Can she still be alive? She was no older than I am now.*

"Whiskey." He gripped her forearm. She felt his warm, chocolate essence envelope her. If she didn't know he'd already sold her out to the *Agrun Nam,* however inadvertently, she would have welcomed the comfort. Instead, she fought it, her anger returning as she pushed him away, both physically and mentally.

He pulled his hand away as if burned.

"Don't touch me," she growled.

"I won't." He held both hands up in surrender, raising his chin. "May I continue?"

Whiskey considered demanding a to-go container for the food. Ravenous and needing to refuel, she elected to stay. She wanted to hear what he had to say. Sanguire or not, Castillo had never struck her as a violent man. The information she received here might give her the edge she needed against Fiona's manipulations. "Yeah, go ahead." She began working on the french fries.

"I have a copy of your birth certificate in my office. Your parents were Gareth and Nahimana Davis. You were born in Dixon, North Carolina, near Jacksonville."

The fries clogged her dry mouth. She took a long drink of

water to get them down. She tasted their names with her mind, committing them to memory, greedy in her mental caresses. "Nahimana?"

"I think she may have been American Indian, which would make you of dual nationality." Castillo smiled. "I have no connections to the *We Wacipi Wakan*, their elder council, so I don't know if I'll find her family. I have a friend in Europe who's looking for your father now. I'll have something more concrete in another day or two."

North Carolina. It fit with her rudimentary knowledge and the first vision she'd had—a warm spring night, jasmine on the air, her father's drawl when he spoke, her mother's eyes and hair black as night. *Which means if the first vision was true, the second might be, too.* She had so many questions. It made her angrier with Castillo's connection to the *Agrun Nam.* He would have been a more trustworthy source of information than Fiona if it hadn't been for that.

"These people you've been hanging with," Castillo ventured. "They're Sanguire?"

Whiskey applied herself to her dinner. "Yeah. They saved my ass from a beating a few nights ago, and sort of adopted me."

"Don't trust them."

She snorted. "I'm supposed to trust you instead?"

He took his heavy crucifix in his hand. "As God is my witness, Whiskey, I will always tell you the truth."

The earnest expression on his face unnerved her more than thoughts of the *Agrun Nam.* Take more than you can give, she reminded herself. *Doesn't mean he'll keep information from the Agrun Nam, whoever they are.* "You say you've been a *Baruñal* to others? Tell me what happens during a meditation."

Castillo frowned. "You mean yours hasn't said? Of all the irresponsible—" He trailed off his rant, visibly collecting himself. "Over the course of thirty or forty years, a Sanguire youngling's brain chemistry alters. This forges different pathways, and activates other areas of the brain that Humans do not use with any regularity. The chemical 'imbalance' changes the body's physical makeup." He leaned his elbows on the table, in full lecture mode. "There are organs in the body that Humans consider vestigial, throwbacks from their time as proto-humans. The appendix is one, as are a number of the glands. To Humans they are a mystery. To us they are essential for survival. As the brain chemistry evolves, signals are sent to those organs, increasing their capacity and...waking them."

Whiskey stared at him. She'd meant the strange visions of an unknown past, not this science lesson. "All that?" she blurted.

"Yes, all that." He gave her a rueful grin. "The meditations simply accelerate that process to a short, and more intense, format. It causes wild hallucinations of various senses, illness, vertigo, and the like, but it's over in a week or two rather than several decades."

She sighed. "What about the visions themselves? What are they?"

His expression shifted into regret, dark eyes portraying concern and sympathy. "No one knows. Each person has a different experience. Some have no comprehensive visions, while others claim to see their future or their past."

Damn it. That's the same thing Reynhard said. "What did you see?"

Castillo looked apologetic. "My parents were killed in a fire when I was very young. I was raised Human. I didn't go through the *Ñíri Kurám*. I didn't know I was Sanguire until I was thirty-seven years old."

Whiskey slouched back in her seat.

"Perhaps you can tell me what you've experienced?" he asked, tentative. "I can compare it to what I know of others' meditations."

She felt a strong temptation to share. The raw and unfamiliar emotions resulting from the chants confused her. She could really use the guidance of someone she'd known longer than a few days. But he had contact with the *Agrun Nam*. She suspected that if the European Sanguire knew she had visions of their "monster of composite power" her life would become much more complicated. If Castillo would tell them of her existence because of her resemblance, which way would he jump if he knew she may have Elisibet's memories?

She couldn't even ask the padre about the woman in her

dreams, or more information of this Elisibet Vasilla without tipping her hand. If she looked enough like the woman to cause Castillo to take notice, what would happen if anybody heard about her visions? "No."

He raised his chin in deference. "I didn't think you'd concede, but I had to ask."

Whiskey's lips twitched in a grin. "You don't know everything about me."

"Whiskey, I know who you are, what you've dealt with. I understand why you don't trust me, though I swear to you that I'm not a threat." He leaned forward, putting his hand on the table, not quite touching hers. "These other Sanguire you've found, don't trust them any more than me. I don't know how they found you, or what their plans are, but it can't be good."

"Because of who I look like?"

He nodded. "Exactly."

She bit her lower lip, wavering. "How much do I look like her?"

"She died before I was born, but I've seen official portraits. The only difference I see is the color of your eyes. Hers were such a light blue, they were almost white, and yours are pitch black."

She felt excitement as the needed piece of the puzzle fit into place. Fiona had seduced Whiskey with the sex and toys for this reason. Once Whiskey became an adult Sanguire, Fiona could compel her to remain in the pack, using her to gain power. Trotting out their dragon-lady monster on cue could be a hell of an advantage. "Thank you, Padre." She closed the distance between them, patting his hand before pulling away. She pushed her chair away from the table.

He stood along with her, reaching into his pocket. "Here's my card. I know you already have it, but this one has my home number on the back. If you have any problems whatsoever, call me. Day or night."

She took the business card, glancing at the information before sliding it into her pocket. "Okay."

"I mean it, Whiskey. Call me. At the very least I can give you a safe haven to conduct the *Ñíri Kurám*."

"I said okay." She didn't know if she should be steamed with his adamant tone, or amused. Right now she had too much to process.

Castillo stuffed some bills in her hand. "There. That should get you through the next day or two."

A lump developed in her throat as she pocketed the money. "Thanks, Padre." She hefted her pack, using the action to regain some control over her emotions. When she knew she wouldn't start crying, she looked at him. The waitress approached with their ticket. "I've got to go. I'll see you around."

"Take care. Jenna."

Warm chocolate surrounded her rather than the hug she knew he wanted to give. She sniffed and nodded, pushing away from the table, and into the flow of pedestrian traffic.

CHAPTER TWENTY

Whiskey walked several blocks, mind whirling, before she found a piece of sidewalk upon which to loiter. She chose the back door of a recycled clothing store to drop her pack, knowing they probably wouldn't be coming through the security gate until closing. She needed a little time to figure out her next step.

The easiest thing to do would be to get downtown to Malice. With any luck, the Ducati still sat in their lot. She could take off for Oregon or California, maybe go to the east coast, and start fresh. In reality, her chances of getting away clean weren't good. Fiona would have to put out a stolen vehicle report on the motorcycle. *If there are ruling councils for the European and the Indian Sanguire, won't there be some sort of justice system in place, too?* Running with the bike would get her out of immediate danger with Fiona, but what new can of whup ass would it open?

Whiskey had some ability at avoiding Human legal authority; she'd be flying blind in Sanguire society.

She needed answers.

Sliding her back down the wall of the building, she dug out her cigarettes and lighter. She needed money to get out of town. Dorst was her *Baruñal*, supposedly there to protect her from others and herself while she went through the *Ñíri Kurám*. If she called anybody, it would be him. The padre had sworn on his God that he wouldn't lie to her, but he didn't say he wouldn't turn her in to the proper authorities. She swore, angry again at his perfidy. It didn't help that she didn't know why she felt so negatively about the *Agrun Nam*.

She needed answers.

Why had she dreamed of Elisibet Vasilla, of dying as Elisibet for weeks? How had she died? Was it a cut to the artery of her thigh? Was Margaurethe really there? What did that have to do with the meditation visions? She'd had this discussion with Dorst already, getting nowhere. Maybe the visions a youngling had were confidential, unable to be revealed. That could be why Castillo wouldn't give her examples, but asked for hers to compare.

Answers.

Whiskey dug the cell phone out of her pocket. She'd turned it off before leaving Fiona's house the day before, not wanting to lose the charge. Now she switched it on, listening to the musical tones as it connected to the phone service. There were three voice mails and two text messages. She didn't have the password for the voice mail, so she skipped past them. Both texts were from Cora. The first held a lewd suggestion of what she wanted to do to Whiskey, sent not long after Whiskey had left the house; the second expressed concern, asking about her health. Whiskey deleted them. Running through the electronic menu, she found the call list. There were multiple calls from Fiona, and one from Dorst.

She took a final drag from her cigarette, tossing the burning embers to the curb. Bracing herself, she activated the phone, and called her *Baruñal*.

"Dearest Whiskey."

She bit her lip against the shiver of relief his voice aroused in her. "Reynhard."

"I'd begun to despair hearing from you today. Are you well?"

Whiskey almost laughed. She swallowed against the returning lump in her throat. "Physically, yes."

"Ah, but not mentally." In the background, she heard street noises that abruptly muffled after the sound of a closing car door. "How may I be of assistance?"

Castillo's disgust with Dorst's methods came to mind. "Why have you let me run around town? Aren't you supposed to be keeping me safe and sound until I'm through this shit?"

"For most, that is the process, yes."

"But not me?"

"You have had a more strenuous childhood than most our children enjoy. I adopted a less...repressive method in your case." He chuckled. "You don't strike me as needing to be coddled. Was I wrong?"

She smiled, and wiped her nose with her free hand. "No. You were right."

"Then I have not insulted your integrity and ability. That is good." He paused. "You have more questions for me?"

"I do."

"Must we do this via the impersonal contraptions of the modern world? Is meeting with you out of the question?"

Whiskey sniffed, blinking back tears. "I'd like to see you."

"Would you deign to visit me in my abode? It's a simple apartment near the University, corner of Northeast 41st and 12th Avenue."

She'd already slept in the devil's den, and found a viper at the Youth Consortium. Why think Dorst was any more of a danger than Fiona or Castillo? She nodded, though he couldn't see her. "Yeah, okay. That's not far from me. I can be there in about fifteen minutes."

"I look forward to seeing you again, sweet Whiskey."

Not knowing what to say in response, she cut the connection. Staring at the phone, she nearly dropped it when it buzzed in her hand. Another text message. She accessed it, seeing Cora's name again.

Where r u? R u ok? I miss u Ninsumgal. F is frantic. Call. Please.

Whiskey's heart trembled in her chest. She didn't need Fiona in her face.

Pocketing the phone, she stood and picked up her backpack. Moments later she crossed the street at the corner, heading for Dorst's apartment.

Whiskey easily located the apartment building. She paused at the security door, finger poised over the button next to Dorst's name. The fresh tape indicated he hadn't lived there long. A college student shoved past her, arms full of books, and used his key to enter the door. She caught it before it closed. After a quick glance at the street, she followed him inside.

She felt him as soon as she stepped off the old elevator onto the fourth floor. She even smelled him thick in the hall toward her right. His essence held the richness of amber cut with fine steel, a dichotomy of hot and cold, mellow and sharp. It seemed familiar in a way that Castillo's hadn't been. She felt Dorst's attention focus on her, wondering what she felt like to him.

When she arrived at his door, it opened. "Welcome to my humble abode, dear Whiskey." Dorst stepped back with a deep bow, waving her inside.

Unsettled, she skirted around him, and entered a small kitchenette. Beyond it, she looked into a studio apartment. The furniture consisted of a neatly made bed, mismatched nightstands and dresser, two empty bookshelves and a small table with chairs. Hearing the door close behind her, she turned. "Nice place. Comes furnished?"

"Yes. Being so near the college, the tenants are rather transient in nature. It suits my purpose."

He looked different. A coatrack near the door held his leather trench. She'd never seen him without his accessories. Now he stood before her without the trench, spiked knee guards, or the training harness he usually wore. It surprised her to see well-defined muscles in his arms and chest beneath the T-shirt. For some reason she'd thought he was as emaciated beneath the garb as his facial structure indicated.

"Please." He gestured for her to enter the main room. "Set down your things, sit. Would you like some tea or hot chocolate?"

Moving further into the room, she shucked off her backpack. "Hot chocolate would be good." She moved across the room to the single window, setting the pack against the wall beside the table.

While he bustled around his kitchen, she circled the room. The missing knee guards were on the dresser, along with a brush, a wad of money and two sheathed knives. One sheath appeared plain and functional. The other held a silver crest and several red gems. Whiskey frowned and looked closely at the more drab of the two blades. She'd seen it before.

"You like weapons?"

Whiskey started, pulling her fingers back from the aged hilt. "Kind of. It's always good to have something on hand to defend yourself."

Dorst set two cups on the table. "Very true. You have a knife?"

She shrugged, and stuck her hands in her pockets. This talk of weapons made her wary. She could almost feel the burn of a blade opening her thigh. "Not often. Fiona gave me one."

"That was sweet of her."

Whiskey couldn't imagine a time or place where Fiona could be considered sweet. "Um, yeah."

Dorst gestured to a chair. "The chocolate's ready."

"Yeah, okay." Whiskey sat down with Dorst across from her.

"Please pardon the presentation." He waved a slender hand at the steaming mug. "I had no real time to prepare for your visit."

"No! It's fine, thanks." She sipped obediently at the chocolate. "It's great."

His smile sarcastic, he bowed his head in acceptance of her

words. "How have you fared since we last spoke? You seemed a bit...uncertain on the phone."

Whiskey stared into her chocolate, reviewing the last twenty-four hours. "It's been— It hasn't been easy." She peered at him.

"No?" He gave her his undivided attention. The concern radiating in his dark eyes offset the sardonic grin on his lips.

"No." Her gaze slid to the window, and she watched traffic go by on the street. "The visions are really tripping me out. I didn't go sleep it off afterward, either."

"Really? Wherever did you go?"

She bit her lip. "I went dancing at Malice." Her words were met with silence, and she glanced quickly at him.

His expression remained one of amused interest. No hint of disappointment marred his face. "And?"

"You're not mad?"

Dorst's smile widened. "No, Whiskey. You're perfectly capable of making your own decisions in life; you've been doing so for years. If you follow my instructions, the transition will go easier on you, but you're responsible enough to deal with the repercussions of your choices."

She felt a little light-headed, surprised at how much she'd been worried over his reaction. "Oh."

"So. Dancing at Malice. What next?"

Whiskey braced herself, and told him of her encounter with the woman who'd picked her up. "I— I bit her! Is that normal?"

"Perfectly. Your body is making essential changes, and its instincts are for the nourishment Human blood can give you. It is rather unfortunate that it happened in the heat of the moment, as it were, but rest assured your control will improve."

"That's good to know." She blushed at his chuckle, a simmering irritation bubbling in her abdomen.

Dorst waved at her, still amused. "My apologies, *Gasan*. I mean no disrespect."

She conceded the point, taking a longer drink of chocolate to mask her annoyance.

"I assume you were able to locate a haven to sleep off the effects of the meditation?"

"Yeah, about a mile from here." She stared out the window,

wondering how to steer the conversation to what she wanted to know.

"You said on the phone you have questions?"

Leave it to Reynhard to cut right to the heart of the matter. "Yeah, I do. I met someone who's not too impressed with your technique as *Baruñal*."

The amused atmosphere evaporated in an instant. Dorst's essence expanded to fill the room and, Whiskey suspected, the building. Her mouth dropped open, and she sat back, seeing the dangerous Sanguire man hidden beneath the foppish behavior he affected.

"Who?" he demanded.

Whiskey swallowed. "The padre at the Youth Consortium." After the automatic response left her mouth, she regretted speaking. *What's going on here? Is this because of Elisibet?*

"The padre." He stared out the window. "I'm afraid I haven't had the pleasure of meeting him. Dark hair, beard, wears a cassock. What's his name? You say he works at the Youth Consortium? How long have you known him?"

"His name's Castillo." She leaned her elbows on the table, and studied him. "He's been my social worker for three or four months. Why?"

"Three or four months. That makes sense." Dorst deflated, his essence fading to a more manageable level.

"What makes sense? Tell me what's going on."

"What did you tell him, Whiskey? It's very important."

She scowled at him, not falling sway to his perilous demeanor. "He wanted to know who gave me that Book, but I didn't say."

"Then there may still be time." Dorst stood and went to the dresser, collecting his things. "Where is he now? Do you know?" He picked up the decorative blade, pulling it out to check the edge against his thumb.

Heart in her throat, Whiskey leaped to her feet. "What do you think you're doing?"

"Your friend is not your friend, *Gasan*. Now that he knows you're on the Strange Path, he must be stopped before he can spread the news." He resheathed, and pocketed the knife.

"To who? The *Agrun Nam*? He's promised he won't inform them, and I know he'll keep his word."

Dorst froze in the act of walking away from her, turning to stare. "You know of the *Agrun Nam*?"

Adrenaline still rushed through her body, and she swallowed. "I know they're dangerous and not to be trusted."

"Yet, you trust this priest who told them of your existence?"

She blinked. "How do you know he did that?"

"I have my sources."

Whiskey narrowed her eyes. The feelings of betrayal and anger she'd experienced with Castillo were fresh, easily resurrected for this new indication of treachery. She swelled with fury, watching Dorst pull back from her. "Have you been in contact with the *Agrun Nam*?"

He studied her a moment, not acting intimidated, though she distinctly felt it from him. "That would depend on your definition of 'contact,' my *Gasan*."

She ground her teeth. "What's yours?"

A small smile graced his lips. "If you mean direct face-to-face meetings with the members of the *Agrun Nam*, telephone conversations to them or any of their multitude of aides and assistants, or written missives discussing the current political state of affairs among the European Sanguire…" He drifted off, pausing for dramatic effect. "Then, no. I have not. At least not in the last four hundred years. A full half of them have been replaced since the time I was a regular visitor in their halls."

Whiskey breathed a little easier, the anger fading once more to mere irritation. *He's always been a drama queen.* How she knew this briefly crossed her mind, a question she quashed. "Then how do you know the padre told them about me?"

"As I said, I have my sources."

She considered this new information from all sides while he stood before her, not moving. Castillo had claimed to be under four hundred years of age, and Dorst hadn't officially been to the *Agrun Nam* "halls" for over that amount of time. Dorst spoke with smooth familiarity of them, and had a capability to disappear at will from both Humans and Sanguire. She recalled Cora calling him by his title, *Sañur Gasum*, and the words suddenly made sense to her.

The second she understood their meaning, she saw a memory of the long-haired Dorst, bowing as he backed away from her. She recognized the same room as her dream, the room where Elisibet died. He wore tunic and trousers in black and burgundy. "You're an assassin," she whispered. "A spy. I remember."

The world went dark.

CHAPTER TWENTY-ONE

The sharp pain in her thigh woke her.

Whiskey sat bolt upright with a hiss, grabbing her leg. Immediately, the pain receded. "Damn it!" She saw she'd been laid on Dorst's bed. He sat alert on a chair beside it, watching her. "How long have I been out?"

"Not long, *Gasan*. No more than twenty minutes."

She rubbed her face, and scooted to the edge to swing her feet over. "I'm surprised you didn't leave me here to find the padre."

"Your last words before losing consciousness were somewhat enigmatic. I decided to remain here for clarification. Have you been learning our language from Fiona or Cora?"

Brow furrowed, she tried to remember what she'd said before passing out. "No."

"You spoke Sanguire in your sleep."

She gaped at him. "Was I repeating a chant?" What kind of damage would it do if she repeated a meditation? Had anyone ever done it before? The thought both intrigued and terrified her.

Dorst slowly shook his head. "No. You were carrying on a conversation with someone." He leaned on his elbows, coming within inches of her. "Who was it?"

Whiskey debated with herself. What if he was the one who had killed Elisibet in the first place? She shivered. Again she heard the voice in her dream, the man saying, *"What is done is done."* That wasn't Reynhard's voice. Why would he be her *Baruñal* if he meant her harm? Why would she instinctively trust him without knowing him if he'd been responsible for her past death? Her mind reeled from that. *When the hell did I accept what I've been dreaming is real?*

"Whiskey, you are safe with me. I will not betray you."

She examined him, letting his image blur slightly in her vision. He told the truth. "It's a nightmare I've been having for months. I'm in a study of some sort, and I've been wounded. I hear a man's voice, then a woman leans over me, crying. We talk to one another, and I get really cold. Then I wake up."

"Where is the wound?"

"My right thigh." She ran her hand along her uninjured leg. "I think the artery is nicked. There's lots of blood, but I don't die quickly."

"You've been having this dream for months you say?"

Whiskey nodded.

"And they speak Sanguire?"

"I guess so." She shrugged. "I didn't understand a word of it until last night. That was the first time I heard it in English."

He raised a hairless eyebrow. "I don't believe you heard it in English, *Gasan*. While you were unconscious, you spoke our words fluently. Somehow, you've subconsciously picked up the language. I'm uncertain how that could happen."

She nibbled at her lip. "There's more."

Dorst leaned back in his chair, a slightly amused air about him as he regained his equilibrium. "Do tell."

"This is going to sound stupid."

"Considering the revelations I've received from you over the past few minutes, I highly doubt that. Please continue."

"I have visions during the meditations. My first one was from my childhood. I saw my parents." *Gareth and Nahimana Davis.* Glancing at Dorst, she saw his attention appeared politely interested. His eyes intent on hers, however, revealed the lie of his demeanor. She sensed his fascination. His interest bolstered her flagging confidence, and she continued. "The second one—I saw…" She trailed off with a groan. Thinking she'd had visions from a past life was crazy enough. Announcing them aloud sounded even more insane. *He's going to lock you up in a Sanguire nuthouse.*

"Whiskey, I will not judge your visions. As I said, each is personal to the individual. No one will ever hear of them from my lips."

She nodded. "In the second one, I—I'm Elisibet Vasilla."

Dorst looked as if someone had gut punched him. His careful control faltered, and his face slackened in shock. It was hard to imagine he could become any more wan, but what little blood remained in his face drained completely. "What did you say?"

"I'm Elisibet Vasilla," she repeated. His response alarmed her, and she began to babble. "I'm at a dance or something, and I see a woman there, the same woman that leans over me in my nightmare. Her name's Margaurethe O'Toole. I tell someone that I want her, but I don't see who answers me. Then I'm overlooking a garden where she's playing with other women her age. After that, she's in my suite, and we're having something to eat." She blushed hotly at the memory of what happened next, shutting her mouth with a snap.

He stood with such abruptness that she flinched back from him. He stalked away from her. Leaning over, his hands gripped the small table with such force, she heard the wood fibers creak. One of the cups overturned, spilling the dregs of chocolate to pool and drip to the carpet below. He stared out the window, his heart beating rapidly in his chest.

Whiskey relaxed. Her instincts had proved true; he hadn't hurt her, and she still believed he wouldn't. Whatever he felt wasn't directed at her. Comparing his scent to that of others she'd smelled over the last few days, she recognized a faint odor of fear. She didn't have enough experience with her senses to understand what other emotions he felt.

Several minutes passed before the rhythm of his heart slowed to normal. The table stopped shaking. When he spoke, his voice was gruff. "*Zaz ne za tud?*"

Her eyes narrowed as she considered the gibberish. She almost asked him to repeat it again when something connected in her brain. "Do I know who I am?" He didn't move or answer, forcing her to seriously consider his question. "A few hours ago, I would have said yes. But now, I don't know. It can't be possible, Reynhard."

He straightened, inhaling deeply. "What can't be possible?"

Whiskey scoffed. "The shit going on in my head!" She tapped her forehead with a finger to accentuate her words. "I was a Sanguire queen several hundred years ago in a past life? And now, I just happen to remember it while going through meditations designed to physically change me into a being that drinks Human blood to survive? It sounds like a movie, or maybe an elaborate hoax. Where the hell's the camera crew?" She dropped her head into her hands. "I'm going crazy. That's all there is to it. I'm already in the psych ward at Swedish or something, and this is just a drug dream."

"Your sanity is not in question, yet." Dorst left the table to kneel before her. "What is your true name?"

She peered at him. The name she'd so carefully guarded throughout her adolescence rolled off her lips without a qualm. "Jenna Davis."

"It is a pleasure to meet you, Ms. Davis."

Whiskey couldn't resist smiling at the absurd introduction.

He bowed his head. "I, Reynhard Dorst, Master of Spies and Chief Assassin, recognize *Ninsumgal* Jenna Davis as my liege and ruler. My dagger, my blood, my heart is yours, my *Gasan*, to do with as you will."

Her mouth dropped open. She stared at the three strips of black hair atop his pate.

When she failed to respond, he lifted his head and grinned at her. "Well? Do you accept me?"

Whiskey closed her mouth, eyes wide. "Um. Yeah, I guess." She forced herself to the task at hand. This required something formal, though she hadn't a clue how to go about it. "Your dagger, your blood, your heart are mine to do with as I will. In return," and here she momentarily faltered. "In return, I swear to treat you as you treat me, respect with respect, trust with trust, loyalty with loyalty."

"Not bad." He appeared impressed. "This will have to be repeated with the proper witnesses. Until then, may I rise?"

"Oh! Yeah." Dorst did so, and resumed his chair. "What just happened?"

"I swore fealty to you, my *Gasan*. I'm honored to be the first of what will hopefully be many."

Slightly suspicious, she wondered if it meant what she thought it did. "What's 'fealty?'"

"Ach, American education is sorely lacking these days." His voice took on a lecturing tone. "Swearing fealty is an act of swearing my loyalty to you. The word was used extensively in the Middle Ages, usually sworn by vassals to their feudal lord. I have, in effect, sworn my life to you so that you may use it as you deem necessary."

"Your life?" Her head swam at the impact of his statement. "Then it's real? These visions and dreams are real?"

"I believe they are."

She shook her head to clear it, her distrustful traits rising to the fore. "You know, skipping past the impossibility of the whole thing, how do you know I'm not just a plant? From what the padre told me about my resemblance to Elisibet, I've already figured out what Fiona's plans are for me. It could just be coincidence that I look like her, and am Sanguire."

Dorst nodded slowly. "Excellent point, my *Gasan*. However, you're not taking one thing into consideration."

"What's that?"

He smiled. "I knew *Ninsumgal* Elisibet. I have personal experience with the nature of her being."

Whiskey pursed her lips, not getting the distinction.

"Tell me, how did you discover the priest was Sanguire?" He crossed his legs, and perched his hands upon them.

She remembered the dark chocolate warmth. "I felt him. Like I felt you when I got to this floor." Reaching out with her mind, she easily engaged with the steel and amber she'd sensed before. "Like I'm feeling you now. Does every Sanguire feel different?"

"Yes, they do. It's subjective, as well. How I feel to you is different than how I feel to Cora. Sometimes it's just a matter of degree, but the nature of an adult Sanguire is similar to a person's appearance—each is varied from individual to individual. No two will ever feel, smell, sense or sound the same."

"So." She considered a moment, the thought dawning as he spoke again.

"*Ninsumgal* Elisibet's essence was a heady mixture of roses, as is yours." He frowned in thought a moment. "I've always wondered if the fairly non-threatening essence of her being had something to do with her rather violent nature." He shook his head, and waved it away with an elegant gesture. "No matter."

Violent? "You're saying I feel like Elisibet?" The bond between them grew stronger as Dorst focused once more upon her. It wasn't uncomfortable, but she imagined it had the ability to be so with the wrong person.

"To a good degree," he pronounced. "There are some slight differences, a hint of water and blood that I don't remember experiencing. All in all, however, your nature is strikingly similar to hers."

"Would that mean anyone else who'd known her would find something similar?"

He smiled. "To my knowledge, no Sanguire has ever 'returned,' so to speak. Perhaps so."

Whiskey digested this information. The offhand manner in which Dorst had mentioned Elisibet's violent personality disturbed her. She was a "monster of composite power" to these people. Castillo had immediately notified the *Agrun Nam* when he'd seen her. Fiona, subtle threats aside, wanted Whiskey under her thumb. *But Reynhard says I feel different than her.*

Dorst waited for a response from her, calmly watching her.

Why wouldn't I feel different? I'm me, not her. Why would

Castillo, a self-proclaimed "expatriate," notify the leading European council upon seeing her? Why would Fiona think she could use Whiskey just because of her appearance? *Why would Reynhard swear...himself to me? I'm just a screwed-up street kid!*

She said, "There's something missing here, something you haven't told me. I get that I look like this badass bitch from your past, but what does that have to do with anything? I'm guessing you think I'm the person you've been searching for all this time. You said at Malice that you'd thought you'd found her a couple of times, but hadn't. You just said this has never happened before, so Sanguire don't reincarnate. Are you here to test me like the Dalai Lama or something?"

He chuckled. "No, my *Gasan*, I will not trot out a favored bowl or pen that *Ninsumgal* Elisibet enjoyed to test you." He glanced over at the bland knife still on the dresser. "Though, had I done so, you'd already have passed the test."

"That was hers?" Whiskey stood and stared at it, her body suddenly edgy with the desire to take it from its resting place.

"It belonged to her father, one that he wore all his days. She did, as well."

Whiskey forced herself to resume her seat, tearing her gaze from the knife with an effort. "You haven't answered my question."

"After my *Ninsumgal* was assassinated several bad years passed. They are now known as the Purge. Anyone who was truly loyal to or a patron of Elisibet was hunted down, put on trial, tortured, or outright killed."

A vision of Margaurethe O'Toole being tortured or killed made Whiskey dizzy. "You survived. Did others?" she demanded, her voice strained.

Dorst cocked his head at her. "If you mean *Ki'an Gasan* Margaurethe, have no fear. She lives."

Whiskey's heart pounded. *She does exist. She's alive.*

"Shall I continue?"

"Yeah."

"The *Agrun Nam*, in all their wisdom, decided to forego a monarchy, and rule in the *Ninsumgal's* stead. Thirty-two years later, a trio of *ensi'ummai* attended a public session. Their leader,

Mahar, proclaimed that Elisibet may be dead, but her spirit lived. She would return to bring order to chaos, compassion to corruption, and peace to warring peoples."

"Oracles?" She concentrated on the name. "I don't recall Mahar."

"Mahar was ancient, one of the oldest Sanguire alive even then. Some said she lost her mind to senility in the shrouded history of our past. Others thought she was someone to venerate for her visions and wisdom." Dorst gave a light shrug. "She rarely made public appearances, so you can imagine how her words went over with the council."

Whiskey smirked. "Not well."

He mirrored her expression. "Exactly. In any case, because the session was a public one, word of Mahar's prophecy spread far and wide in no time. Hence, my search for you."

"And also why Fiona thinks she can get something out of me, and the padre let the *Agrun Nam* know when he saw me."

"Yes, my *Gasan*."

It made sense, even if everyone had it wrong. She wasn't Elisibet reborn. She wasn't a full-blooded European if Castillo had the right information about her mother. It meant her life was going to be that much tougher in the long run as she dealt with this Elisibet's long-term mess. "So what now?"

Dorst raised a hairless eyebrow. "Now we begin your lesson for the third meditation."

Of course.

CHAPTER TWENTY-TWO

They spent the next two hours going over the chant. The farther Whiskey went through the process, the more the slim volume loomed sinister in her mind. What used to be a simple book now became the Book. Had she been raised Sanguire, she supposed she'd have assumed the veneration that Dorst and Castillo gave the item. Her lack of cultural experience didn't change her growing physical aversion. She sensed it inside her backpack, beating in sync with her heart, a sensation of blood coursing beneath the surface of the leather cover. The more she handled it, the more alive it felt, somehow attuned to her body rhythms.

Do all Sanguire feel this way, or is it just me? Can Reynhard feel the Book as easily as he feels me? She shivered, and pulled her focus away from the thing. *More than enough other things to worry about.*

She'd left Dorst's apartment with strict instructions not to conduct the third meditation until the next day. He'd also given her a key to his door, advising her to return whenever she wished. She walked down the street in a light daze, hardly seeing the people and vehicles around her.

Dorst had answered her immediate questions, but she still had a hundred more. It unnerved her that he took the strange developments with such aplomb. He seemed pleased with the situation. After searching for four hundred years, having the end in sight had to be a relief. His endorsement of her strange visions and newfound memories didn't ease her discomfort. *He's got to be wrong. What happens when he figures that out? Hell, when I figure that out?*

She yearned to talk over this mess with someone she knew, to vent or get a second opinion. As much as she trusted Dorst, he had an utter devotion to his *Ninsumgal*, a requirement to have kept looking for so long. Not even Margaurethe O'Toole had searched with such diligence. Whiskey experienced that same worn yearning she'd held her entire life, finally connecting it to its origins. The idea that she had spent the majority of her adolescence pining over a woman she hadn't known existed frightened her. She shoved those thoughts away. It would have been so cool to talk to the padre about this. Regret and annoyance washed over her. *Damn him.* The sky began to darken. She looked up to see cloud cover. Maybe tomorrow would be overcast. She certainly hoped so. The days of sunshine hadn't helped her mood, or the transition.

With nightfall coming and no place in particular to be, her feet automatically took her to Tallulah's. Cora's text message had been somewhat agitated; going to Malice was out of the question. Probably for a very long time. Too bad. Whiskey had liked the music there. The illicitness of being underaged in an adult bar hadn't hurt, either. She chuckled to herself as Tallulah's came into view.

Being a Tuesday night, local high school students didn't spend much time here. Slipping past the pool tables to the back, Whiskey nodded to some kids she recognized. She saw a couple of adult men trolling for jailbait at the bar, the aging chickenhawks ludicrous in their hip-hop clothes as they flashed money and made eyes at the homeless boys on the dance floor.

Whiskey grinned when she saw Gin at a table, a heavy load rising from her shoulders at the mere sight of her. There were six others from her street family there, but no Ghost in residence. She could talk to Gin about this. *Maybe she can help.* Her step quickened as she approached.

"Hey, *chica*!" Gin stood up, a welcome smile on her face. "Where you been? I missed you."

"Around." Whiskey sank into the hug in a way she never did with anyone else, feeling a sense of comfort and affection similar to what she'd felt in her parents' arms in the first vision. Her mind automatically reached out to connect with her best friend, as it had with Castillo and Dorst, recoiling when no essence met her quest. She stiffened at the blankness between them, feeling disoriented at the lack, bringing other senses into play. It took a moment before she realized what she heard. *Two heartbeats. Reynhard was right.* Pulling back, gripping Gin by the upper arms, she stared. "You are pregnant."

Gin's mouth dropped open, one hand reaching for her belly. "How did you know that? I haven't told Ghost, yet."

The confirmation told Whiskey everything she didn't want to know. Releasing Gin, she stepped back, her world slowly crumbling to her feet. "I just do." *I can't drag her into this, not with a baby on the way.* She doubted Fiona would hold off using Gin as a bargaining chip in the future. If Whiskey continued her defiance, Fiona would utilize every opportunity to keep her in line.

Gin studied her with a puzzled expression. "Are you okay? You seem...different."

"I'm fine." Whiskey took off her backpack, and set it on the floor beside her, feeling more weary than anything else. She remembered Dorst saying that Humans naturally steered clear of Sanguire, and wondered if that's what Gin now noticed.

"You sure?" Gin looked around the area. "You still hanging with those punks that gave you the money and tattoo?"

Whiskey looked away. "No. They're bad news."

Gin reached out, and gently cupped Whiskey's cheek.

"I thought they were. Nobody gives out *mucha dinero* for nothing."

Staring into Gin's caring eyes, Whiskey fought back tears. Had Fiona and Dorst found her six months ago, all would be well. She'd at least have had a friend by her side through this, someone she could trust. That avenue had closed forever with the advent of Ghost, and a baby on the way. *I can't endanger my closest friend in the world, and her unborn child. I'm on my own with this shit.* A different emotion built in Whiskey's chest. Not wanting to analyze her feelings and thereby deny herself, she leaned into Gin and kissed her. For just a second, Gin responded as she'd often done in the past. Emboldened, Whiskey pressed her case, tongue teasing full lips.

Gin pulled away.

"What the fuck's going on here?"

Gin quickly snatched her hand away as Ghost stormed up to them. "Nothing, *mi corazón*. Whiskey just got here."

"Looks like she was getting there, yeah." Ghost pushed Gin back away from Whiskey, inserting himself between them. Gin stumbled against a chair, almost falling.

"Hey! Watch it, asshole." Whiskey tried to move past Ghost to support her friend, but he blocked her, shoving her back.

"*You* watch it, dyke. I'm sick of you hitting on my girlfriend. I heard you slept together while I was gone."

Whiskey scanned the crowd, noting several of Ghost's street family had arrived with him. A loose circle of street kids surrounded them. Dominick, the young kid nicknamed Spot, grinned at her, leaving her no doubt as to who had passed on that bit of information.

Gin slipped her arm through Ghost's. "That's all we did, *muchacho*. Whiskey crashed at the flop with us, nothing more. Don't you trust me?"

He wouldn't be put off. "I trust you just fine. It's this bitch I don't trust for shit. She still acts like you're cut buddies when you're not."

The scent of anger and betrayal rolled off Ghost, enveloping the two of them. It triggered an echoing fury in Whiskey, startling her with its intensity. Ghost could kick her ass with little trouble. Fear would be the usual cause for the adrenaline pumping into her system, not wrath. The difference confused her.

"We're not cut buddies anymore, *mi corazón*." Gin tugged lightly on his arm. "Just friends."

Ghost violently shook her off, almost causing her to fall again. "Bullshit!"

Whiskey's rage increased. She didn't know what she could do. Street fighting wasn't her strength. If she attacked, she'd be beaten to a pulp. *Better that than Gin losing the baby.* "You'd better tell him, and tell him now," she said to Gin. "Or I'm going to do something I'll regret."

He swelled larger, suspicion in his eyes. "Tell me what?" he demanded, looking at his girlfriend.

Gin hesitated.

"Tell him!"

"I'm pregnant!"

Gin's words filled the tableau, sharp and surprising. Ghost's skin flushed light pink before immediately fading to its normal albino white. Around them, his street family stared in various states of shock.

"What?" He choked, voice rough.

Gin slumped into a chair. "I'm pregnant. I just found out yesterday. I went to the free clinic while you were in Portland." She held her face in her hands, and began to cry. One of the girls knelt beside her to comfort her.

It took everything Whiskey had not to rush forward to support her friend. A lump developed in her throat in sympathy, complicated by the knowledge that this moment ended their friendship. She scowled at Ghost, who looked more like a fish out of water than a soon-to-be father. "You'd better take care of her, you bastard. If I find out you didn't, I'll kill you." It didn't faze her that she meant every word.

Taking up the gauntlet, he turned back to Whiskey. "You stay the fuck away from us."

Whiskey swept up her backpack, and turned away. The spectators, both his street family and other bystanders, parted to allow her out of the immediate area.

Goodbye, Gin. Take care of yourself.

She fought a losing battle with the tears, feeling them spill over as she left the bar area and weaved through the pool tables. Gin's sobs remained strong in her ears, a perverse part of her not wanting to let go of even this small connection between them.

She clearly heard Ghost speak to his family. "Anybody sees Whiskey anywhere around, take her out."

"I can take her." That was Dominick's eager voice. "Let me do it now."

"Whatever."

Whiskey picked up her pace as she headed for the door. It had finally happened; Ghost had put a hit out on her. That didn't necessarily mean he wanted her dead. A simple beating would do just as well on the streets. *Like I don't have enough troubles.* Behind her, she heard footsteps in pursuit. *Shit.*

Bursting out of the club, she ran, scattering a handful of kids loitering outside. She got a half block away before Dominick and two others exited, looking for her. Glancing back, she saw one of them point, and call to the others. The trio pelted after her. Laden with a backpack, she knew they'd overtake her. Rather than search for a useless hiding place, she scanned the street for anyplace that would give her some tactical advantage. She ducked into a tight little alley, pleased to see no illumination except the streetlight on the other side. With her newfound abilities, she had no problem locating a clear path. They might not be able to find her in the dark. If they did, there wasn't enough room for all three to attack at the same time.

"In here!"

Whiskey ducked into the heavy shadows of a Dumpster, pulling the hood over her head to hide her blonde hair. She forced herself to stillness as she listened to the stealthy approach of her pursuers. While she concentrated on being invisible, she frowned. She smelled ashes. It grew stronger by the minute. Ashes and saccharin sweet flowers of some sort. She jumped at a loud crash, biting her lip to keep from yelping in surprise.

"I know you're in here, bitch. You didn't have enough time to get out the other side before we came around the corner."

She ground her teeth at Dominick's snide voice. Her anger

hadn't dissipated with the immediate threat of a thrashing. There were three of them to one of her. She wasn't stupid. The smell of ashes and flowers grew stronger, and she wrinkled her nose. There were other odors and sensations developing, too. Puzzled, Whiskey tried to locate where they came from, not finding anything in her immediate vicinity to explain the increasing potency. With her nose, she easily picked up rotting food, cigarette residue and dust. Her eyes widened. *That's not a smell. That's Sanguire.*

CHAPTER TWENTY-THREE

As soon as her mind made the shift, the variety of essences grew stronger. She sensed relief, pleasure, and not a little anger mixed within the tumult. Whoever they were, they were near, and glad to have found her. She didn't feel Castillo's dark chocolate or Dorst's amber and steel among them. It had to be Fiona and her pack. Remembering what they'd done to Paul's group of friends a few nights ago, Whiskey stood. *These guys are toast!*

"There she is!"

Whiskey left her hiding place, approaching the three street kids. "You got to get out of here." She held up her hands in a peaceful gesture. "Someone's coming—"

"Damn right someone's coming." Dominick marched up to her, and took an immediate swing.

She ducked, struggling with her pack.

"You guys watch for cops," Dominick ordered. "I'm going to make this bitch hurt." He swung again.

Whiskey dropped her pack on the ground, keeping clear of his fists. "I'm serious, man! You need to get out of here now." She assumed a defensive posture.

One kid went back the way they'd come, and the other skirted around them in the close confines of the alley. He didn't make it far. Whiskey heard a scuffle behind her, and Dominick glared beyond her shoulder, confusion on his face.

"Who the fuck are you?"

"Look, Manuel, my little *lamma* has found entertainment for us. Wasn't that sweet of her?"

Whiskey dropped her head upon hearing Fiona's silky voice. Manuel grunted a response. She stepped back from Dominick, turning to see Manuel dragging the unconscious street kid toward them by the collar of his shirt. "Leave," she growled at Dominick. "You still have time."

"Not before I kick your ass." His voice cracked at the end of his sentence, and he flushed.

Her eyes flickered to movement behind Dominick. Daniel neatly took out the second kid with a roundhouse kick. He paused long enough to pull the body into the darkness before approaching. "Too late."

Cora rounded the corner behind Daniel, and rushed forward. "*Ninsumgal!*"

Manuel dropped his baggage behind Whiskey with a meaty thump. Cora brushed past Dominick to throw herself into Whiskey's arms. Bronwyn appeared out of the darkness next to Daniel. She winked at Whiskey, fangs on display. Considering how little Bronwyn cared for her, the smile didn't ease Whiskey's nerves.

"Such big threats from such a little man." Fiona studied Dominick. "And threatening a woman, no less. Your parents must be proud."

He glared at her. "Fuck you. This is between me and her. Nobody else."

Fiona appeared taken aback. "Is this so, sweet Whiskey? I certainly wouldn't want to interrupt your playtime."

Whiskey scowled at her, mind whirling. "Yeah, it's between me and him. It's personal." She eyed Daniel and Bronwyn behind Dominick. "Let him out of here."

"We're not finished," Dominick said.

Fucking macho idiot!

"I think not," Fiona said simultaneously.

Whiskey smelled the fear rolling off Dominick. They both knew he was in over his head here, but his disagreeable personality wouldn't allow him to back down. Try as she might, she couldn't think of a way to get him out of the alley, and still save face with himself and his street family. If he walked out unscathed, the other two having been knocked unconscious by unknown assailants, it'd look like he'd run from a fight.

Undaunted by his abrasiveness, Fiona grabbed him by the shoulder and shoved, demonstrating quite a bit of strength as he stumbled away from Whiskey. He cursed at the rough handling, rubbing his arm.

Cora relinquished her hold on Whiskey, and joined her friends as they circled him, taunting and jeering at him. He turned with them, trying to keep them in sight. They reached in and pinched or poked him when his attention fled elsewhere, laughing as he yelped out in pain, and whirled to catch the perpetrator. Whiskey scowled at their antics. They played with him, like a pride of cats with a tiny, defenseless mouse, each trying to outdo the other, escalating their attacks as they went. She looked back at the street, wondering if anyone heard his calls.

"Will you not join us, my little *lamma*?" Fiona called. "This is for your benefit."

Dominick looked at Whiskey, his face a mixture of shame and withering hope she could get him out of this, his strawberry birthmark stark against his pale face. Hell-bent for a little action, Fiona's pack bristled with fervor. Maybe if she assisted, she could control the outcome. *It's not like the snitch doesn't deserve a beating anyway.* Disgusted, collecting her annoyance and irritation with their victim, she focused on getting the two of them through the next few minutes. It didn't take much to arouse the simmering anger that had been with her since she'd discovered Castillo's betrayal.

Forcing a grin, she became part of their circle. Stepping forward, she slapped Dominick hard. "You fucking idiot." He spun away from her, right into Bronwyn's arms.

Her attack sealed his fate as the pack's onslaught became rougher. Each successive assault caused more damage, the women more vicious than the men in their midst. They took their time about it, prolonging his suffering for their amusement. Whiskey knew better than to pull her punches, and gave as good as the rest of them. At the very least, if Dominick became unconscious, they'd leave him alone. To that end, she sent a good number of attacks to his head and face in an effort to knock him out. As the assault continued, Whiskey's fury turned to exhilaration. A cloud of blood and fear settled around him. It pulled at her spirit, releasing her from her initial inhibitions regarding the situation. Excitement flowed through her, overpowering the ache of sore knuckles, and the distant part of her that abhorred the torture she inflicted.

A cell phone rang, and Fiona stepped out of the circle to answer it. Several minutes later, she rejoined them. "Let's wrap this up, children. Alphonse and Zebediah are waiting at the car."

Dominick reeled in their midst. Blood ran down his chin from a broken nose. His eyes were nothing but black hollows in his face. His thin T-shirt had ripped, stained red with his blood. He staggered in their little arena, hardly conscious.

Whiskey caught a flash of metal in Cora's hand, realizing she had a knife. Did Fiona mean to bring this to a more final end? Sudden fear shot through Whiskey, dissipating the bloodlust. She didn't want to be involved in a murder. She stepped in front of Cora, and punched Dominick with everything she had. "Drop, fucker!" Sharp pain shot through her hand as her knuckles split.

He didn't fall.

"Do it, *Ninsumgal*." Cora shoved the knife into her hand.

Rage pulsed through Whiskey. *Why the fuck doesn't he go down?* Rather than use the blade, she punched him again, her fist ramming his broken nose. With her sensitive ears, she heard the bones and cartilage break more, a gruesome crackling sound that would stay with her forever. Dominick stared at her with eerie, dead eyes. Whiskey shivered. If she didn't know better, he was already unconscious, his body failing to take his physical state into consideration. He slowly crumpled to the ground, his head hitting the concrete with a significant thump. The smell of blood grew stronger, but relief flowed through her. *Maybe they'll leave him be now.* "Shit, that hurts."

Manuel paused to spit on their victim before giving Whiskey a once-over. "Not bad for a—you know."

Whiskey frowned in puzzlement.

"That was a compliment, sweetness." Fiona stepped over Dominick's prone form as if he were merely a puddle to bypass. "Shall we leave? I expect someone will have heard enough to call the authorities."

Feeling drained, Whiskey followed them. She heard a groan in the shadows from the kid Daniel had felled. Bronwyn stomped his head hard enough for Whiskey to wince. She glanced behind her, pleased to hear his heart still beating. Casting farther back, she tried to locate Dominick's pulse. She saw blood oozing from her knuckles. *Why can't I hear his heartbeat?*

Cora gently removed her blade from Whiskey's hand, spiriting it away to God knew where. Her touch familiar and intimate, it distracted Whiskey, arousal pumping through her already singing veins.

"This way, my *lamma*." Fiona waved them down the street.

Whiskey felt a measure of relief that they walked away from Tallulah's. A handful of street kids loitered outside. A couple had kept their eye on the alley, and now ducked inside when they saw her. In a few minutes, other members of Ghost's family would come out to see what had happened. Getting away from here was a fine idea, but not if it meant heading back into the serpent's lair. "I've got somewhere else to be."

Fiona turned to look at her, eyes hard as diamonds over a serene smile. "You'll not be joining us?" she asked. "A hot bath after your strenuous evening, a soft bed to rest in, and a warm body to keep you company?"

"No," Whiskey stated.

The cloying sweet stench of flowers expanded around her,

leaving her no doubt as to whom the essence belonged. She recalled Dorst speculating on the connection between Elisibet's violence and the innocuous nature she held, and wondered the same. Perhaps Fiona and Elisibet were more alike than different. The idea repulsed her. She pushed the smell away from her, like she'd done with Castillo at the café earlier that evening. Fiona's eyes narrowed and, for a brief moment, a cold abrasiveness slid against Whiskey's senses. Anger flared in her chest. She physically stepped forward, shoving hard with her mind. Fiona faltered, retreating, face pallid. The smell of flowers dissipated to nothing, and Whiskey took a deep breath in a vain attempt to dispel the last of it.

After a long examination, Fiona raised her chin. "Then allow us to at least escort you to someplace less...hazardous."

Whiskey nodded, hearing a commotion at the youth club doors. "Good idea."

They walked the rest of the way in silence. She wondered if they'd force her into the car. When they arrived at the Lexus, she saw Alphonse and Zebediah lounging upon the hood.

Cora slid enticingly into Whiskey's arms. "Are you certain, *Ninsumgal?*"

The wave of lust nearly overwhelmed her. "Yeah." Unable to help herself, she gave Cora a blistering kiss. "I'll see you around."

Cora smiled. She pressed closer and gave Whiskey another long, moist kiss. "I certainly hope so."

Whiskey forcibly reminded herself that this seductive woman had wanted her to knife someone. "Thanks."

"Just remember us, *Ninsumgal.*" She reached up to trace Whiskey's lips. "I know I'll remember you."

Whiskey shouldered her pack, surprised they'd let her go so easily. Cora sidled to the passenger door. Most the others were already inside the vehicle, but Fiona leaned against the driver's door.

When she had Whiskey's undivided attention, she strolled closer. "Keep the Ducati for now. It's not safe for you out here."

Whiskey almost snorted at the humor of the situation. *Like I'd be safer with you?* She knew honest appreciation would appease the woman's dominant streak. "Thanks for everything, Fiona. You guys saved my ass again tonight. I'll never forget this."

A satisfied smile crossed Fiona's lips. "That's all we can ask, my dear little *lamma*." She leaned up, and gave Whiskey a peck on the cheek.

Whiskey watched until the taillights disappeared around a corner several blocks away. Blowing out a breath, she took in her surroundings. She couldn't go to back to Tallulah's any more than she could Malice now. She had enough money left over from Castillo's donation for a meal or two, and the keys to a motorcycle currently parked three or four miles away. She had no friends, only enemies and opportunists waiting in the darkness for her blood. She had a whole host of complete strangers who would take one look at her, and assume she was the reincarnation of some dead bitch come back to wreck havoc once again.

"Christ. What the fuck am I going to do now?"

CHAPTER TWENTY-FOUR

Not wanting to waste time, Whiskey continued to put distance between herself and Tallulah's. While she walked, she considered her dwindling options.

Ghost's family had been at the flophouse a few nights earlier, Whiskey with them. Once they found Dominick in the alley, the hunt would be on. It wouldn't take much to have someone check the abandoned building for her. The youth shelters were closed for the night. It wouldn't do to get spotted in one of them anyway. She'd do herself no favors seeking asylum in a shelter— no street kid would come in to get you, but you couldn't stay forever. They'd be waiting outside. Besides shelters didn't call the police even if asked by their patronage to do so, something about making sure their clientele felt "safe" to come to them for assistance without being ratted out to the authorities.

Fiona had told her to use the motorcycle for her own purposes. Parked downtown, it might as well be a world away. Cruising that area at this time of night begged for further complications. The old-timers would make mincemeat of Whiskey. Besides, once she had the bike, where would she go? If she abandoned the *Ñíri Kurám*, what would happen to her?

While woefully ignorant of Sanguire society, she knew that the *Agrun Nam's* knowledge of Elisibet's doppelgänger made things more difficult. Once she disappeared from their radar, she wouldn't be surprised if a general all-call went out to every European Sanguire living in North America. Where the hell could she go to get away from them without a birth certificate or state identification? How far did Elisibet's influence and memory go? Would Whiskey be safe if she, by some bizarre chance, relocated to China or something?

An abrupt vision crossed her mind, a laughing Asian woman dressed in a traditional Japanese kimono. It stopped Whiskey in her tracks. She carefully examined the image, catching a nostalgic whiff of ginger root, and realized the woman was Sanguire. *Fuck! How far did Elisibet get back then?*

Sirens in the distance brought her back to the present. She glanced guiltily over her shoulder, and started walking again.

Digging her hands into her pockets, she felt a strange set of keys. They were to Dorst's apartment, the ones he'd given her before she left this evening. God, had it only been a couple of hours? She pulled them out to examine them. Maybe he'd let her crash there tonight. He might know what she should do now, too.

Relieved at the alternative, Whiskey stuck the keys back in her pocket, and looked around her surroundings. She could be at Dorst's place within the hour, putting her farther from Tallulah's. *Icing on the cake.*

Whiskey fidgeted at the outer door for a moment, then pushed the buzzer. It had to be almost one in the morning. Better give him some warning. She waited a full minute, receiving no response from the speaker, or the subtle click of the lock opening. Maybe he wasn't home.

She turned away and studied the street, considering. He'd said to come by at any time. Granted, he probably hadn't meant a few hours after leaving, but the circumstances didn't allow for much else. She chewed her lip, digging in her pocket for the keys.

"You are a difficult woman to keep up with."

Whiskey jumped, looking into the shadows cast by decorative bushes and trees. Amber and steel washed over her, and she dropped her guard. "Reynhard, you scared the crap out of me."

Dorst eased out of the darkness, his face dimpled in delight. He made one of his elegant bows. "Sincerest apologies, my *Gasan*. It still remains a pleasure to see you so soon."

She sensed an expectant air from him. "Did you know I was going to be here?"

"I had hopes." He shrugged lightly, reaching for the keys in her hand.

Whiskey released them, and he opened the outer door, holding it for her. She entered the foyer. She asked, "Has Fiona talked to you?"

"No, not for a few days. Why? Has something happened?" He led them to the elevator.

She wondered how to explain the disaster the night had become. "I almost got into a fight tonight, and she showed up with her pack." The elevator pinged and opened for them.

Dorst gestured for her to precede him. "Almost?" He pushed the button for his floor. "I assume her fortuitous arrival was beneficial?"

"For me, but not for him." She recalled the crackle of bones and cartilage as she hit Dominick that final time, the barren look in his eyes. She shivered as the elevator opened, distracting her from the memory.

He led her down the hall, using her keys to unlock the door. "Do tell."

Whiskey stepped into the apartment, shrugging out of her backpack. "That albino guy you saw the other night, my friend's boyfriend?" He nodded, and she continued. "He put out a hit on me tonight, and someone tried to collect."

The amber and steel swelled in the small apartment, and Dorst bristled. "Clarify."

"It just means I'm a walking target for a beating on the streets," Whiskey said, making calming motions. "Not like a 'hit' in the movies. After a couple of days, maybe a week, it'll die down."

His demeanor mellowed, but a dangerous edge clung to him as he whipped off his trench coat. "And Fiona's pack arrived in the nick of time?"

"Yeah."

"Had she any reason to believe you'd be in the area of Tallulah's?"

Whiskey sat without invitation at the small dining table. "Not that I know of. If she asked around the street, she'd know about it. I'm not sure she'd think to, though, or that anyone would tell her."

"I doubt it, as well." He joined her. "You still have the cell phone she gave you."

His words were a statement, not a question. "Yeah. Why?"

"Because it has a GPS tracking unit built inside. Plainly, Fiona has discovered its unique code, and has been using it to locate you." He looked impressed. "One of her younglings is quite handy with today's electronic surveillance equipment. I may just have to recruit him."

Whiskey's blood chilled. "You mean she knows I'm here?" She turned to stare out the window at the street, half expecting to see golden Sanguire eyes in the darkness.

"She knows the phone is here, therefore you must be, as well. That can be easily remedied." He held out his hand. "The phone, my *Gasan*."

She fumbled the cell phone out of her pocket, and gave it to him. "What are we going to do?"

"I'm going for a long walk, my *Gasan*, and perhaps a short drive until I find a proper resting place for this little boondoggle. You are going to remain here and sleep."

Whiskey scoffed. "Are you kidding? I can't sleep, I'm too freaked out!"

Dorst smiled, his expression slightly apologetic. "You'd be surprised." He stood, gesturing for her to do the same.

"Reynhard, I know you just want me to be safe. No worries, dude. No way am I going back out there tonight."

"I concur." He swept into one of his special bows. Then with a swiftness beyond Human abilities, he straightened, reaching out to touch her temple. "Sleep."

Whiskey's eyes slammed shut. She noted a distant sensation of falling. Amber and steel enveloped her before she hit the floor.

Light and sound woke Whiskey. She squinted her eyes, trying to figure out where the sound of birdsong came from. Instead, memories flowed into her mind, her heartbeat increasing with each new scene—Castillo's confession, Gin's pregnancy, Fiona's crowd beating Dominick to the ground, fleeing the scene of the debacle with a proverbial sword hanging above her head, Dorst's sudden appearance and his attack.

She sat upright, looking around for her *Baruñal*, unable to locate him. Unless he hid in the closet, she doubted he was here. Blinking, she remembered her newfound ability to touch other Sanguire. Her questing thoughts met emptiness, and she relaxed.

Whiskey yawned and stretched. She found the obligatory alarm clock on the nightstand. It read a little after nine o'clock; the brightness outside made it morning. In the middle of the apartment, she looked around. She saw nothing ominous. Her pack sat under the table by the window, undisturbed. On the table sat a cell phone and a piece of paper. Whiskey picked up the note.

Dearest Whiskey,
I hope the morning finds you well. My sincerest apologies for forcing the issue, but it was required for both your safety and my peace of mind for you to nap a bit. Please, feel free to enjoy my humble yet temporary abode for as long as you wish. As they say in other parts of the world, "Mi casa es su casa."

It would be best for you to remain off the streets as much as possible, though I realize that may be too much to ask of such an active youngling as yourself. If you should choose to leave, keep safe, keep the keys, and call me no matter the reason.

Remember, this afternoon you must attend to your third meditation. Regarding the recent situation among your peers, both Human and Sanguire, you might consider conducting the meditation in my apartment. I will gladly vacate the premises for your comfort.

I've left this cell phone for your express use. Do not concern yourself with its security. I've taken the liberty of cloning all relevant data from the old one to this new unit. You have no need to worry about Fiona finding you with the GPS link.

Faithfully yours,
Reynhard

Whiskey shook her head. *Like I can sit still that long.* As early as it was, she'd be safe for the time being. Ghost's street family probably left Tallulah's upon its closing three hours ago. They'd been at their flop a couple of hours at most. She had a good five or six hours to kill before it would start getting too dangerous to be out there.

Her stomach rumbled.

With no idea of when Dorst would return, she decided to get something to eat. Once she tamed the beast her stomach had become, she could think more clearly. Maybe Dorst would be back by the time she returned. They could discuss what her next step should be. Curious, she went to the closet and peered inside, eyeing a handful of clothes. One hanger held a crimson silk shirt, and she pulled it out to get a better look.

Take more than you can give.

CHAPTER TWENTY-FIVE

Whiskey squinted as she stepped out of the Mexican restaurant with her purchases. She set her breakfast on an outdoor table, and brought her sunglasses down to cover her eyes before divesting herself of her pack. Though the morning was overcast, she had difficulty dealing with the light. Still, better to be here than boxed up inside Dorst's apartment or the restaurant. She sat down to enjoy her first meal of the day, confident she had a few hours of safety ahead.

The tacos tasted like cardboard and the burritos too gummy for words. She forced herself to finish, and drank the syrupy soda with a grimace. Around her, traffic swept past on the busy street. Hardly giving the vehicles a second glance, she concentrated on the pedestrians as she kept an eye open for anyone from Ghost's street family. By all rights, they should be asleep, but she didn't want to take any chances. Dominick had been totally worked over last night, but he or his companions could easily point the finger at her. The damage had been serious enough that they might have decided to spend the morning hunting her down rather than sleeping.

Ever vigilant, she nevertheless dismissed the people climbing out of an expensive car across the street until she felt a faint touch along her mind. The dry, grainy sensation of ashes spun around in her head. *Aw, crap. Don't they ever sleep either?*

"*Ninsumgal!*" Cora said with a laugh as she threw herself into Whiskey's lap, forcing Whiskey to hold tight to prevent the blonde from falling. Cora's hands, ever restless, stroked the silk shirt Whiskey had appropriated from Dorst's closet. "Mmm, I love this."

"It certainly does become you." Fiona approached with a bit more elegance. She'd traded riding leathers for a flowing emerald green dress, tight and sheer in all the right places. Behind her, Daniel drifted along, wearing tight leather pants and a collar, his tattoos readily visible. "You've obviously fared well since last night."

Not about to reveal where she'd ended up, Whiskey grinned. "It's been pretty good."

"I missed you last night." Cora contrived a pout, playing with the buttons of Whiskey's shirt. "You should have come home with us."

"I missed you, too," Whiskey half-lied. Having a willing woman in her lap played hell with her overactive libido. Instead of pushing Cora away, Whiskey nudged her closer.

"She's been positively broody since your departure." Fiona came around the table to run her hand along Whiskey's shoulders. "How are your dragons faring?"

The stench of sweet flowers overpowered her. She sensed a questing connection along the physical touch. Half-panicked, Whiskey did the same thing she'd done the night before, somehow pushing with her mind. She must have done it harder than necessary, because Fiona pulled away with a hiss of pain. The flowers gave way to ash. Whiskey's mouth dropped open. *Did I cause that?*

Hesitant, Cora caressed Whiskey's cheek, distracting her. Daniel watched them carefully, his body thrumming with sudden tension.

Whiskey saw a flash of fury in Fiona as she looked away from her. *The ashes are Cora.* Only when Fiona's expression returned to its cool superiority, did Whiskey relax. She cleared her throat. "Uh, the dragons are fine."

"My apologies for being forward." Fiona's voice wasn't as faded as her complexion, nor was it as confident as it had been in the past. "I only wished to impress upon you how much we worried about your well being."

Whiskey's eyes narrowed, knowing the words for a lie. "I'm fine, Fiona, but thanks."

Fiona lifted her chin.

"May I see the dragons, *Ninsumgal*?" Cora asked.

Nettled by the title, Whiskey said, "Don't call me that." Her tone sharper than she intended, she felt a stab of guilt as Cora ducked her head. By way of apology, Whiskey tilted Cora's head up, and kissed her brow. She began to roll up the sleeve of the silk shirt.

Soon the women admired the tattoo running up Whiskey's forearm. Daniel decided things were safe once more, and returned to lookout status, watching passing people and vehicles.

Having regained a measure of her haughtiness, Fiona smiled. "Would you like to finish it this morning? It's healed well enough to continue."

Whiskey wondered how she could get away this time.

Cora leaned forward, whispering, "I'd certainly enjoy checking your piercings later, sweet *aga ninna*. Perhaps they've healed, as well?"

A rush of arousal swept through Whiskey at the offer, and her nipples tightened in response. Common sense kicked in before her libido took over her mouth. She had to go through the third meditation today, and there wasn't a chance in hell that she'd feel safe enough in Fiona's clutches to do so. Yet the lure of a finished tattoo warred with the violent memories of Dominick's beating. It didn't help that she'd enjoyed her participation in the conflict once she'd gotten involved.

"Fresh meat."

Daniel's words were whispered, but Whiskey heard them over the noises of traffic and conversation. She turned her attention to where he stared, her heart sinking as she saw Gin and Ghost walking up the street with his pack.

"Shit."

"Do you know them, sweet Whiskey? Are they a danger to you?" Fiona asked, drifting around to stand between the table, and the approaching street kids.

Whiskey didn't want to tip Fiona off to endanger her friend. "No."

Daniel kept his attention on the approaching group. "Are you certain? They smell very much like the toy we played with last night."

"Fuck." Whiskey wondered if she could sink under the table without being noticed. Ghost probably wanted her blood for Dominick's injuries, and the Sanguire surrounding her were eager to have another go at the street kids. Not only could Gin get hurt, endangering her baby, but Ghost could be killed. That would leave Gin without even that much support for her unborn child.

Gin held Ghost's hand as they walked, speaking to him in a low, serious voice. Whiskey easily located the sound, followed by his as he added something to the conversation. Behind them, three others tagged along. Gin glanced ahead, and saw Whiskey. Her expressions rushed through a gamut—from initial pleasure, concern and relief, to a look of revulsion. Her dark skin whitened, and she came to a dead stop. Whiskey heard her say, "*Mi Dios.*"

Whiskey grunted as Gin's expression closed, and her friend looked away.

Cora turned toward her. "Whiskey?"

Whiskey had to separate them before something happened. "I think getting this tattoo finished is a great idea." She stood, hoping to draw Fiona's and Daniel's attention.

Concerned, Ghost looked from Gin to the restaurant. Despite his dark glasses, Whiskey knew when he registered her presence by the stiffening of his body. His heart rate increased, and anger caused his white skin to pink. Behind him, his three friends also bristled. Ghost radiated a fury so thick, Whiskey smelled it over the vehicle exhaust fumes and rancid grease from a nearby garbage can. He traded places with Gin, keeping himself between his girlfriend and Fiona's people. He released her hand in the process, balling both up into fists, and began walking again.

The two groups eyed one another as they neared, though the Sanguire hardly changed their stance. Daniel sat on a table, his manner that of a lounging panther. The swelling excitement from Fiona was palpable, flowers overpowering Whiskey's senses. Whiskey remembered the swift and devastating attack of Fiona's pack against the rich boys threatening her when they'd first met. Knowing there would be bloodshed if the two groups met, Whiskey snapped, "Fiona! Daniel!"

The two turned as one to stare at her, eyes glittering.

"Let's go. I want to finish this tattoo." When they made no movement, she dropped her chin and pushed with her mind. "Now."

Fiona blinked in surprise at the order. Uncertainty crossed Daniel's face and he stood, taking a step toward Whiskey.

The tableau broken, she glared at them. "Is the tattoo parlor open already?" she asked, more to keep their attention than anything else. She watched the street kids from the corner of her eye as they continued past. *Thank God for that!*

"Of course, dear Whiskey." A smile tugged on Fiona's lips as she glided closer, the Humans forgotten. "Most artists have their doors open by noon, but I know one or two who will gladly be available at this hour for the right amount of money."

Behind Fiona, Gin and Ghost passed. Whiskey breathed a sigh of relief when they chose to keep walking rather than force a confrontation. Her heart sank at the look of loathing on Gin's face.

"Whiskey?" Cora asked again, linking her arm through hers.

With a sigh, Whiskey forced a smile. "Can you think of anything else that needs piercing?"

Cora smiled, brushing her breasts generously along Whiskey's arm. "I'm sure I can think of something."

"Daniel." Fiona, back in control, directed the man to get Whiskey's gear. "Shall we, my little *lamma*?"

Whiskey allowed herself to be escorted to the waiting Lexus, wishing she'd stayed put at Dorst's place. She preferred starvation to this. At least she had the cell phone he'd given her; she doubted Fiona would begrudge her calling her *Baruñal*. She felt the eyes of the street kids glaring at her back. As she climbed into the backseat, she risked a glance in their direction. Ghost stared at her, hands still fisted. His mouth moved, and though he spoke quietly, she easily heard the word.

"Murderer."

CHAPTER TWENTY-SIX

Whiskey sat in a daze as Cora chattered on about something, unable to let go of her last sight of Ghost. Whiskey wouldn't put it past him to yank her chain this way, alluding to her responsibility for a murder. If it had just been him or one of his buddies, she'd consider it a trick. Gin's expression of loathing burned away that illusion. A wave of queasiness swept through Whiskey. *We killed him? I killed him?*

She replayed the last minute of the fight. *Fight? That was a slaughter.* The smell of blood had been strong, mingling with the essences of the Sanguire around her, making it difficult to pick out individual sources. Dominick had stopped fighting back, only responding to the violence being inflicted on his body with grunts or soft *woofs* of expelled air. The look in his eyes when she'd hit him that final time gave her the shivers. She'd thought he'd already been unconscious, but had he been *dead*? Again she heard the crackle of bone and cartilage. Bile burned the back of her throat.

Fiona pulled the car into a parking lot next to a ratty building. "We're here, children."

Whiskey pulled out of her fog and got out of the vehicle. She regarded their surroundings. "This isn't where we got the first part done."

Cora stroked her arm. "You've healed far too fast for that, *aga ninna*."

"I'm sure that adorable little artist might have some questions for you if we were to return so soon." Fiona breezed past them, and into the tattoo parlor she'd selected.

Whiskey allowed herself to be drawn into the establishment. The place had a deserted feel. In the reception area, the overhead lights were off, the only illumination coming from the soda cooler in the corner. It gave the tattoo parlor an abandoned look. On the floor by the door lay the daily newspaper. Whiskey seized it, and went to the counter to search for information. A grizzled older man came from the back, wiping his hands on a towel. While he and Fiona dickered over the job, Whiskey dragged out the local section and scanned headlines.

"Are you all right, Whiskey?" Cora caressed her back and shoulder, radiating ashes and concern. "You're pale, and you seem upset."

"Do you know what happened to that kid last night? The one we beat up?" Whiskey looked up from her search. "Did anybody go back to see?"

Cora tilted her head in puzzlement. "There was nothing to see, *aga ninna*, and we'd already fed. There was no need to go back."

"But what happened?" Certain she'd get no answers, Whiskey continued to flip through the pages, checking the smaller articles toward the back.

"I expect those Human children who saw us leave called the authorities." Cora paused, a thoughtful look on her face. "Perhaps not. They seem to be less reliant upon governmental agencies than most."

"Did we kill him?" Whiskey demanded.

"No."

Whiskey's knees trembled, and she leaned against the counter for support.

"You did with that last strike." Cora's eyes lit up. "At first I was surprised you didn't use the knife I gave you, but now I know it was because you wanted the visceral experience of killing him with your bare hands."

The relief disappeared with a puff. Whiskey struggled to remain standing. Her stomach gave her little warning. She looked wildly around, seeing a nearby trash can. Dashing to it, she vomited up her breakfast, sagging to her knees on the floor. She continued until nothing remained in her stomach, dry heaving for several minutes afterward.

Cora knelt beside her, holding her hair back, whispering calming words. Whiskey finally sank back, pushing the can away. Daniel squatted close by, handing her a wet hand towel. She accepted it gratefully, covering her face with the warm cloth.

Behind Whiskey, Fiona explained the situation to the Human tattooist. "A little too much last night, you know. I'm surprised she's lasted this long, really."

"If she's drunk, I can't legally work on her, even if it is just color."

Fiona chuckled. "Oh, she's not drunk. The hangover finally got the better of her, that's all."

Whiskey scrubbed her face with the hand towel. *Oh, Jesus. I killed him!*

"*Ninsumgal.*"

She pulled the cloth away to see Daniel holding out a paper cup of water. She rinsed the nasty taste out of her mouth, spitting it into the mess in the trash can. *He's never called me that before.* She didn't know if she should laugh or be furious at this additional portent of her future. "Thank you."

He bowed his head in deference, and stood. Cora still lightly held her, her hands gently stroking Whiskey's shoulders.

Whiskey didn't have time to deal with this. She couldn't count on Fiona not having overheard her conversation with Cora. Her equilibrium shot to shit, Whiskey didn't think she'd be strong enough to hold Fiona off if she tried to leave now. Fiona would gladly use it against her. Forcing the knowledge of Dominick's demise away, Whiskey finished wiping her face. She dropped the cup into the trash, and stood. Cora attempted to assist, but Whiskey shook her head and gave her a gentle nudge away. Once she'd regained control, she turned to Fiona and the tattooist with a smile. "Sorry about that. Sometimes I don't know my limits."

Fiona flashed a feral smile. "Isn't that the truth?"

The tattooist gave her a commiserating grin. "I've been there. I can give you a couple of minutes to get your shit together before we get started."

That might take a damned long time, pal. "No, I'm good. Let's get going." *The sooner we're done, the sooner I can get away from these people.*

"I'll get you something to drink, *aga ninna.*" Cora opened the door on the soda cooler.

As the Human led Whiskey to the back of his shop, Fiona's soft laughter followed them.

I killed him. Still shaky, Whiskey fumbled at the buttons on the silk shirt.

Before she could protest, Fiona slid into her personal space, brushing her hands away. "Allow me, sweet Whiskey."

Unsettled, Whiskey didn't put up a fight. As soon as the buttons were undone, she stepped back and stripped out of the shirt, ignoring Fiona's amused smile.

When he got a look at the dragon the tattooist whistled in appreciation. "I recognize the artist. She sure does excellent work." He half circled Whiskey, studying the tattoo. "Must have taken quite a few hours."

"Yeah, it did." Whiskey draped her shirt over a nearby chair.

A *hiss* of escaping carbonation heralded Cora's arrival. She held out a soda to Whiskey. "For you, *aga ninna.*"

"Thank you." Whiskey drank deeply. The sugars and effervescence did wonders for the nasty taste in her mouth. It served to settle her stomach to a degree. *I killed a Human being, a kid.* Nothing would help the sickness in her soul.

"Have a seat." The Human gestured to a chair. "The dragon is red, right?" He peered at his equipment and inks, shuffling things around on the tray. Pulling a pair of latex gloves from a box, he put them on.

"Yes." Fiona settled in an armchair, her expression indulgent. "Perhaps when these are healed, we'll add another to the other arm. Black or gold?"

Whiskey sank onto the tattoo chair, grateful to get off her trembling knees.

Cora clapped in happiness. "That would be wonderful!" She pulled up another chair to sit beside Whiskey. Smiling, she caressed Whiskey's thigh. "Don't you think so, *aga ninna*?"

Distracted with removing one strap of her camisole for the tattooist and her churning thoughts and stomach, Whiskey took a moment to answer. The Sanguire words Cora now called her suddenly became clear in her mind. *Aga ninna* literally meant a crowned and fearsome lady. Fiery anger burned through the anguish. *I've got to get it through to these people that I'm not Elisibet!*

She didn't snap at Cora again, uncertain what the protocol would be if she humiliated a Sanguire adult in front of a Human witness. A boy had already died due to her involvement with these people; she didn't want to endanger another innocent bystander. Forcing herself back to the conversation, she cleared her throat. "We'll see. No promises."

Cora accepted that with a grin.

The tattooist started work on Whiskey's arm, beginning a running commentary on tattoos he'd done in the past. He concentrated on bringing the red dragon to life, adding a touch of fire from its mouth onto Whiskey's shoulder. The eye gleamed a deep gold that sparkled with life.

Cora remained at her side, making small talk with him, alternating between holding Whiskey's free hand, and caressing her thigh. Daniel had disappeared as soon as they'd moved to the back, but he hadn't gone far. Whiskey felt him, an odd combination of flowering plums and smooth vanilla, just outside. Fiona remained in her armchair, her fond expression grating on Whiskey's nerves almost as much as the cloying sweetness she exuded.

Whiskey watched the proceedings with grim thoughts, forcing herself away from the raw emotions regarding Dominick. Getting away from Fiona was paramount. She'd bail as soon as the tattooist finished, letting Fiona know she had to do the next meditation. She'd have to call Dorst. Even if no one spoke to the cops last night, word would get around that Dominick had been after her when he'd died. Sooner or later the authorities would start searching for her. Maybe Reynhard could get her out of town. Her emotions lightened. Maybe he could get her out of the country!

She sank back into despair at the thought. That move might keep her safe from the immediate repercussions of a homicide investigation. She'd still be hip deep in shit among the Euro Sanguire. Like it or not, she had to deal with this situation. She'd be damned if she knew what to do. Any Sanguire she met would either want to kill her on sight, or use her as a power base.

Since that bizarre repelling incident this morning at the restaurant, Fiona had kept her mental distance. Whiskey picked up her flowery essence because she sought it out. She still didn't know how Fiona and Dorst were connected, let alone what she'd done to push Fiona away. *Come to think of it, didn't I do the same thing to the padre?*

A wave of yearning washed over her at the thought of Castillo. Maybe she could confess to the padre, and turn herself in to the *Agrun Nam*, explain—what? That they'd made a mistake four hundred years ago? That she wasn't who they thought she was? Whiskey almost laughed aloud at the idea. *Somehow, I don't think they'll believe me once they hear about these visions I've been having.*

CHAPTER TWENTY-SEVEN

Cora and the tattooist carried on their conversation over Whiskey as the minutes turned to hours. Her churning thoughts analyzed every avenue of escape, unable to come up with a definitive answer. She rarely felt the pain of the needle, returning to the present only when it grazed near wrist, elbow or shoulder bone.

"There you go. Finished."

Surprised, Whiskey came out of her rumination with a start. She stared at her arm, surprised to see the depth of life portrayed. Adding color and definition made the dragon much more realistic. It twined along her skin, shielding her arm with its scales and wings. "Wow. That's fucking killer." She blanched as soon as the word left her mouth. *You're the killer now.*

"Thanks." He scooted back to clean his work area. "There's a mirror over there if you want a closer look."

Cora helped Whiskey to her feet, and escorted her to the mirror. "Very nice. We can start the design on your other arm today."

Whiskey lightly touched the tender skin with a grimace. "We can do it next time."

Pleased, Cora kissed her with a full body contact that left Whiskey breathless.

"Enough of that, children."

A sudden flash of annoyance crossed Whiskey's emotions. She'd had enough of Fiona telling her what to do. *It's because of her I couldn't get everybody out of the alley last night. Spot might be alive now if I had.* "I'll decide when it's enough." For good measure she pulled her willing partner into another deep kiss. When she finished she raised an eyebrow at Fiona.

Fiona's eyes had narrowed, but she gave a slight lift of her chin in concession. "As you wish, dear Whiskey."

Cora smiled angelically at Fiona, an expression that set off alarms in Whiskey's head. *What the hell am I doing? I don't belong here. The last thing I need is to get involved in the pack's internal politics.* If Whiskey succeeded, she wouldn't be around to defend Cora in a power play against Fiona. She released Cora. "Are we done?"

"Yes," Fiona agreed. "I've already paid the artist. We're free to leave."

"What about the piercing?" Cora asked, trailing after Whiskey as she made her way to the front of the shop. The lights had been turned on, and the establishment had opened for business during the hours Whiskey had been under the needle. Three Humans stood at the counter, and pored over a book of photos with another artist. Nearby, a heavily tattooed receptionist spoke on the phone.

"Some other time." Whiskey felt a pressing need to get out of there, and pushed through the door. The sun had passed its zenith outside. It was well into the afternoon, past time for her to begin her next meditation. She heard a car door open, and looked to see Daniel stepping out of the Lexus where he'd lazed the hours away.

"Shall we head home, sweet Whiskey?"

She glanced at Fiona, seeing the tips of her fangs in the savage smile. "I have to go."

Fiona's smile quickly turned into a scowl. "Your obstinacy wearies me, little *lamma*. I'm beginning to think you're incapable of making appropriate decisions for yourself." She stepped forward, a glare in her eyes. "While I may be temporarily hobbled in my ability to compel you to a course of common sense, it is only because I do not wish to do you harm before you've completed the *Ñiri Kurám*."

Whiskey backed away. Fiona had never directly threatened her before. It disconcerted her. "I've been making my own decisions for years. I've lasted this long."

"And not much longer, at this rate. On the off chance your *Baruñal* hasn't informed you, the stakes are considerably higher the longer we wait."

Stumbling on an uneven section of sidewalk, Whiskey looked around. Fiona herded her into the parking area beside the tattoo parlor, a lot surrounded by three buildings. She didn't think Fiona would try anything violent in broad daylight with busy traffic on the street. Cora and Daniel circled around to flank Whiskey. They slowly steered her toward the car.

"Come home with us, *aga ninna*." Cora reached out to take Whiskey's hand.

She pulled away. "No. I have to start the third meditation now. I have to go."

"You'll come with us, whether you wish it or not," Fiona said. "Daniel?"

He stared at Whiskey for a long moment. "It is unsafe for you, *Ninsumgal*. I will guard you. Where do you wish to go?"

The sweet, sickly sensation of flowers swelled, matched by Daniel's essence. Whiskey saw Fiona almost physically expand. "She's a child. It is not her place to make that decision, Daniel. You will get her into the car, and we'll discuss this at home."

Sweat popped up on Daniel's brow. He dropped his chin, and stepped between Whiskey and Fiona. "I'll gladly discuss this with you later, but right now she'll do as she wishes. She *must* complete the *Ñiri Kurám* in the proper frame of mind. You know the consequences if she does not."

Whiskey's heart double-timed at the ominous implications. "What consequences?"

"He's right, Fiona." Cora took her place beside Daniel, providing a united front. "We must support our *Ninsumgal*."

Fiona scoffed, placing her hands on her hips. "Oh, please. You don't believe that prophetic drivel any more than I do." When neither answered, she mocked them with a feigned expression of surprise. "Why, wonder of wonders, I think you do! Had I realized how gullible the pair of you were, I'd have left you to your pauper families in Europe."

Realizing that the prophecy of Elisibet Vasilla worked in her favor, Whiskey kept her mouth shut. Better to have her questions about consequences answered by Dorst in any case. At least she'd get a more truthful response from him.

The four of them remained still for several minutes. Whiskey's newfound abilities were unable to pick up the subtle nuances of their confrontation. She caught a few movements between the three of them, tasting the battle as Daniel's and Cora's essences converged to strengthen one another. Not wanting them to fight her battles, she made a clumsy attempt to offer help, questing forward into the fray with her mind. They blocked her intrusion. Stung by the mental perception of plum and ash, Whiskey frowned at her defenders.

"Fine." Fiona crossed her arms over her chest, lifting her chin. "Take her where she wishes to go. We'll discuss this when you return home."

The battlefield immediately cleared. No longer focused on the Sanguire sensations, Whiskey marveled at the volume of sound and richness of smell that hit her from the street. *Concentrating on that kind of fight would leave you open for a physical threat pretty easily.* She filed it away for future consideration.

Daniel bowed deeply to Fiona, and Cora curtseyed.

Fiona glared at Whiskey. "Give me the Ducati keys."

Whiskey dug into her pocket and retrieved them, handing them to her.

"This isn't over, little *lamma*. Your world has been small and inconsequential for a long time. That is going to change. You'd do well to allow me to protect you."

Feeling somewhat secure, Whiskey shook her head. "I know why you want me. I won't be used. By anyone."

Fiona suddenly smiled. "You'd be surprised."

Whiskey frowned, once again confused by Fiona's change of demeanor.

"Take the car, Daniel. I'll take the bike home." Fiona turned to Cora, with a raised eyebrow.

Cora slid her arm through Whiskey's. "I'll be home with Daniel."

"So be it." Fiona turned, and strolled away.

Daniel watched her go until Fiona disappeared from sight. Turning to Whiskey, he raised his chin. "Where do you wish to go?"

Whiskey stood a moment, at a loss. Dorst said she could use his apartment for the meditation, but she didn't want any of Fiona's people knowing where it was. She doubted she'd be able to get rid of Daniel so easily if she asked him to drop her in a public place. "Can you get me a hotel room somewhere? Maybe in Queen Anne?"

"Of course." He bowed, and gestured to the car.

Soon they were on their way. Whiskey stared out the passenger window, ignoring Cora who cuddled against her side. They pulled to a stoplight, and her gaze wandered over the pedestrians moving through the crosswalk.

Something tickled her senses. She focused on a man standing on the opposite corner. Dusty brown from head to toe, his clothes and boots and trench coat matched various hues of the color. Dreadlocked hair fell to his shoulders, ragged and wild, and black sunglasses perched on his nose. Without seeing his eyes, she knew they held an aura of devil-may-care. He stood there, statue-still, a vague grin on his face as he stared at her.

Whiskey had the oddest sensation that she knew him.

Fear and distaste fluttered in her belly. She knew him to be dangerous, but couldn't place him. She watched him warily as the stoplight changed color.

As soon as the car pulled beside him he moved, a startling blur of motion. She gasped at the speed, grasping at the armrest of the door. One moment he stood, arms loosely at his side, grinning. The next he had turned toward her, one hand at his sunglasses, holding them down as he peered at her over the rims, his amusement still evident. At this distance, she saw his eyes were hazel, as dusty brown as everything else about him. They were full of sardonic humor, grim sadness and something else.

Betrayal.

An answer echoed in Whiskey's heart. She felt a combination of pleasure and rage fill her, the anger by far the stronger of the two. She opened her mouth, and hissed at him through the glass.

"Whiskey?" Cora tugged on her arm, peering out the window. "What is it?"

They were already past. There was nothing for Cora to see. Whiskey, blood pumping, looked out the back window. The man stood in the same spot, now facing the back of the moving car. His glasses returned to cover his eyes, a lone sentinel among a mass of humanity shuffling past him.

"Whiskey?"

"*Ninsumgal*? Shall I turn around?" Daniel asked.

She watched until the man vanished. "No." Adrenaline made her shaky as she settled back into her seat. "No. Keep going. Let's get to that hotel."

"Yes, my *Gasan*."

Did Elisibet know him? If so, then her "coming out" party among the Sanguire approached too quickly. Whiskey blew out a breath. *This day's just getting better and better.*

There were no further complications on their trip to a hotel. Cora was the more presentable of the two Sanguire adults, having the benefit of at least being fully dressed. She escorted Whiskey inside to pay for the room while Daniel remained in the car. Once the transaction was complete, Cora handed over the key, and took Whiskey back outside.

While Daniel retrieved Whiskey's pack, Cora wrapped her arms about Whiskey's waist. "Are you sure I can't entice you, *aga ninna*?"

Whiskey's desires were split between wanting to lose herself in the soft curves of the agile woman, and running to the hills to become a hermit. "I'm sure, *lúkal*." She wasn't sure where the

Sanguire endearment came from, but Cora's amorous intentions were bypassed as she blushed at the word. "I have to get through this alone."

Cora gave her a squeeze. "I know. We all do."

"Do you wish us to remain nearby?" Daniel set her backpack beside her feet.

Whiskey shook her head. "No. You've done way too much already. Fiona's going to skin you alive when you get back."

"She can try." Daniel studied the hotel. "You should be safe here. That's paramount when conducting a Ñíri Kurám meditation. You have my phone number in your list of contacts." He turned to Whiskey, an earnest expression on his normally stoic face. "Call me if there are any problems. I swear to you that I will not willingly give Fiona your location."

Whiskey wondered about his motivations. "I will."

Satisfied, Daniel bowed, and returned to the car.

Cora gave her another hug. "Don't forget me."

Whiskey saw Cora hand her a knife in a dark alley, heard her sweet laughter at a vicious punch, and her voice urging her to stab a boy. She barely controlled the urge to shiver as her empty stomach flip-flopped. "I could never forget you, Cora." She received a pleased embrace.

Eventually, she extricated herself from Cora's hold, and got her into the car. She gathered her belongings, and headed for the main door of the hotel, waving at them as she entered. Remaining several feet back from the glass, she waited and watched.

As the Lexus pulled out of the lot and into traffic, Whiskey felt an overwhelming urge to leave. If she weren't in a world of shit after last night's— She trembled, a wave of revulsion forcing her to swallow against the bile in her throat. It didn't matter that two of Fiona's pack mates knew where she was. She had nowhere else to go, no flop house would be safe with Ghost's family searching for her. By now, the word would have been broadcast on the streets. Any other street families out there with political ties to Ghost's would be looking for her, too.

Whiskey marched to the elevator, ignoring the expression of distaste from the front desk clerk.

CHAPTER TWENTY-EIGHT

Whiskey finished her meal, a ham sandwich and french fries from room service. Wadding up her napkin, she tossed it onto the plate. She washed down her last swallow with a swig of bottled water. Her stomach felt better with something in it. As long as she didn't think about last night, it remained settled. Rising from the desk, she went to the armchair in the corner and sat down. Late afternoon sunlight trickled through the window. Despite being a few blocks from the major thoroughfares, she heard a steady stream of traffic from rush hour.

Unable to put off any longer what she needed to do, Whiskey picked up the Book sitting on the end table. An electrical surge from the leather surface jolted her fingers. If she were one to personify inanimate objects, she'd have to say that it was enthusiastic. *That's ridiculous.* Pushing the thought away, she opened it at Dorst's bookmark, flipping the black ribbon aside to look at the next chant.

Curious at what she'd soon see, and intrigued with how she might change, she felt a combination of eagerness and trepidation. The last two meditations had been done with little thought, little focus. Tonight she planned on concentrating on a single person while she chanted—the brown man on the street. She needed to know if he had some connection to Elisibet, if that explained why she felt she knew him. She didn't know if it would work; nothing Castillo or Dorst had said gave her the impression she controlled the visions she experienced. They'd never suggested she'd be picking up past life memories, either. She had a fifty-fifty shot at this experiment working.

After going over the words for the meditation, Whiskey breathed deeply a number of times in an attempt to relax. Her heart thumped heavily in her chest. Licking her lips, she closed her eyes, and spoke the words aloud.

Before the second word left her mouth, the well-known sensations rushed through her, a wave of intensity accompanying them that she both desired and loathed. Her mouth dry, she nearly faltered at the onslaught, barely keeping up with the chant until she gained some equilibrium. As with her previous experiences, she became lost in the words, a hallucinogenic fog covering her, pulling her, leading her somewhere else in time.

Flash.

She looked away from Margaurethe seated beside her, heart full of indulgent pride for her young lover as she returned her attention to the two men on the floor beneath her throne. Both knelt in her presence, one far older than herself, and the other a mere stripling. The younger man's skin reflected dusty brown, as did his hair and clothing.

"*Ninsumgal,* I'd like to present to you Valmont, my protégé," the older man said.

"So, this is the youngling you've had sequestered away, Nahib." Her voice sounded both familiar and not. A distant part of her recognized and hated the indulgent tone she'd heard Fiona use much of the time. "I've wondered whether you'd present him at court, or keep him locked away in your library until he died of old age." Others laughed politely at her jibe though she knew it wasn't humorous. She felt annoyance at their artificiality, and satisfaction that her people wished to keep her appeased.

Nahib, however, did not respond as the others. Whiskey cocked her head at him, wondering whether she should take offense at his refusal, or respect his level of integrity. Deciding on the latter, she listened to his response.

"Nay, my *Gasan*. Valmont is of a mind to serve his *Ninsumgal* to the best of his ability."

"And you, Valmont. What abilities do you have?"

Again a round of decadent chuckles from her court, all assuming she made a vulgar jest. She felt Margaurethe's hand on her arm, and relaxed. Let them chatter and gossip as they would. It meant nothing to her.

Valmont raised golden cinnamon eyes to look at his liege. "I have a strong sword, *Ninsumgal*, and a willingness to follow you to the ends of this earth and beyond."

Whiskey raised an eyebrow at his sincerity, flicking a glance at Nahib who smiled in return. Around them, the courtesans laughed over his words, expecting their ruler to make lewd jest of his "strong sword." Eyes narrowing, she glanced about the room. "Be silent!"

In the abrupt hush, she returned her gaze on this youngling kneeling before her. "Beyond the ends of this earth?" she asked. "That would be a long way indeed, would it not?"

"Perhaps so, my *Gasan*. But it would be a trip well worth taking."

He spoke true; her senses picked up no ulterior motives, no falsehood, no deceptions. She found this young Sanguire rather refreshing in the scheme of things, still unsullied by the intrigues of her court. "Rise and be welcome, Valmont. Tonight you shall dine with myself and *Ki'an Gasan* Margaurethe."

Valmont flushed, and bowed his head. "Thank you, *Ninsumgal* Elisibet! I am most honored."

"As am I, Valmont. As am I."

Flash.

A clatter of metal on metal where there should be none drew

Whiskey around the corner. The three guards with her had their weapons drawn. She waved them to remain behind her.

Valmont traded blows with another dark-skinned man in the wide corridor leading to her private quarters. His skill was evident though his opponent couldn't claim the same. Bleeding from many injuries, the man he fought had slowed, weakening. Whiskey wondered if he'd ever been on the attack, or could only defend himself from Valmont's dancing sword.

"Hold!"

Her young friend stepped backward, but did not let down his guard. "My *Gasan*."

The other swordsman's eyes widened at her voice. He panted heavily as he put his back to the wall, holding his blade out to dissuade an attack from any of them.

"Valmont, perhaps you can explain why you're playing with one of my people?" Whiskey said, idly stepping forward.

"Is he one of yours?" Valmont asked, pointing the tip of his weapon at the man. At her faint grin, he bowed low. "My apologies, *Ninsumgal*. From the words pouring out of his mouth, I thought he was a lying sack of shite rather than Sanguire."

"Really?" Her gaze pinned the other fighter. "Ghedi, isn't it?"

The other man barely nodded, swallowing hard as he kept his sword before him.

"Ghedi, why would Valmont accuse you of such a thing? I, for one, have never heard you speak a word of dishonesty. What did you say?" The man remained silent, and Whiskey looked at Valmont. "It seems Ghedi doesn't wish to defile my ears with any lies. Perhaps you'd be kind enough to repeat his words?"

"I'd be most happy to, *Ninsumgal*." Valmont grinned. "He said—"

Ghedi, dripping with both sweat and blood, yelled and attacked Whiskey. His movements fast, he could not hope to match her. Far older than he, she had many decades of experience upon which to draw. Compelling him would be too easy, making the task droll and unpleasant. Instead, she slipped sideways, grabbing at his arm as he passed. He screamed as his forearm broke with a loud snap before he stumbled against the far wall. Physical confrontations were always so much more satisfying.

Again Whiskey waved the guards back. She dusted her hands. "I can assume by Ghedi's response that it was less than flattering, these words he's reputed to have said?"

"He is of the opinion that you are an evil blight upon the Sanguire, *Ninsumgal*. When he refused to recant his statement, I offered to remove his tongue for him." Valmont smiled ferally. "As a gift for you, of course."

Whiskey could feel her teeth elongate as she regarded the wounded man cradling his arm. Her voice low and dangerous, she growled, "Then by all means continue, Valmont. Far be it for me to interfere in the offering of gifts to your liege."

Her young friend eagerly stepped forward, hefting his sword.

Flash.

Whiskey watched her best friend and her lover chase each other across the garden. She sat beneath a towering oak on a marble bench, laughing as Margaurethe drew Valmont along. The game ended when her lover came too close, and Whiskey reached out to grab her, pulling her into her lap.

Valmont dropped to the ground at their feet, panting and happy. "Let that be a lesson to you, *Ki'an Gasan*." He waggled a finger at Margaurethe.

Giggling, she stuck her tongue out. "There's been no lesson, sir. You've yet to catch me."

"Ah, but I've caught you." Whiskey tickled the woman in her arms until she begged for mercy.

The laughter soon died, and they sat in contented silence. Overhead, the full moon well illuminated the garden, causing white lilies to glow.

Whiskey basked in the simple contentment surrounding her, an alien but intoxicating sensation. This was as it should be— trusted friends, loved ones, and peace among her people. That the peace came from her iron grip mattered not at all. Some things had to be sacrificed to keep her people safe.

"Valmont, what are your plans for the day after tomorrow?"

He looked up from the twig he shredded, a grin on his

handsome face. "That's the night of Ostara, yes? I'll be at the ball, dancing with many eligible and not-so-eligible women."

Margaurethe snickered. "It's the not-so-eligible you should be worried about, Valmont. Soon or late, someone's husband will get the upper hand with your philandering ways."

"Ah, they'll have to catch me first," Valmont said, grinning. "And then they'll catch my blade."

Whiskey smiled. "I'll send my tailors on the morrow. I want you to wear the finest of outfits."

"Thank you, Elisibet. But why? I've clothes enough, and if I had my druthers, I'll be out of them and in some vixen's bed while the night is young."

"Because I plan on elevating you, Valmont. How does *Sublugal Sañar* sound? I've an eye on some land that will be bestowed upon you as well as the title." Whiskey paused, feigning deep thought as she tapped her chin. "Defender of the Crown."

"I like that." Margaurethe hugged her. "It's quite fitting."

"What say you, Valmont?" She forced herself not to laugh aloud at the expression on his face as he tried to find his tongue.

Sputtering, Valmont finally said, "I'd be honored, my *Ninsumgal*."

"Good. Consider it done."

Flash.

"Oh, come now, Valmont! The man spoke out against me. I had no choice but to silence him." A combination of confusion, and regret washed through Whiskey as she tried to fathom the nature of the problem.

He fumed as he stood before her, eyes cold. Valmont appeared older now by a few years, past the blush of youth, and into early manhood. "He was your *Nam Lugal*, and my friend." His voice shook with emotion.

Whiskey rolled her eyes at him. "His position as senior on the *Agrun Nam* was the primary reason for his public execution. Certainly you must know that." She turned her back to him, wondering if he'd control his anger, or attempt an attack. Pouring a goblet of wine, she continued. "If Nahib hadn't been fool enough to flap his gums, it wouldn't have happened."

"Fool enough...?" Valmont took a step forward. "He only spoke sense, Elisibet! You no longer care for your people. Your only desire is blood and chaos."

Whirling around, Whiskey pointed at him. "Watch yourself, Valmont. You may be a friend this moment, but I'll not listen to rabble rousing from you, the *Agrun Nam*, or anyone else." She drank half her wine in one swallow, and thumped the goblet onto a table. "Don't think our friendship will save you any more than Nahib's position saved him."

"He was a good man. He did nothing to deserve the gory end you sentenced him to."

Whiskey's eyes narrowed at his hypocrisy. "Really?" she asked, her voice sweet with anger. "I seem to recall many gory ends to which you've sentenced people. Remember just a month or so ago? That beautiful young man in the dungeons? We had an enjoyable time with him, didn't we? And he said much the same things as Nahib, if I recall. Do you remember what you did to him?" She circled Valmont, appreciating the tense shoulders, the smell of his fury. "I believe Nahib got off rather lucky in comparison."

"It's not the same—"

"Why?" Whiskey asked sharply, coming back around to face him. "Because he led the *Agrun Nam*? Or because he was your mentor?"

Valmont snarled, face red. "Yes!"

"No one is allowed to speak against the Crown," she said. "You helped me enact that particular law decades ago. And in case you've forgotten, that means all Sanguire, to include you."

He lowered his chin, refusing to concede as he glared at her. "You threaten me? Your Defender?"

Whiskey sighed, and relaxed her aggressive stance. Her hand went to his upper arm, grasping the trembling muscle firmly. "You're my best friend and greatest ally, Valmont. I do not wish to lose you over something so inane. We make laws to perpetuate peace among our people. Some are sacrificed because of these laws, but overall they work to instill common sense."

"No, Elisibet. They instill fear, not common sense." He

pulled away from her, stepping back and out of reach. "You sicken me."

A wave of fury rolled over her, smothering her. She felt her teeth unsheathing in her mouth, heard his heart pumping in his chest. "Guards!" Six burly soldiers immediately stepped into the room. "You'd do well to look in a mirror, *Sublugal Sañar* Valmont. What sickens you is that you're just like me."

"Never!"

"Guards, see this man out before I lose my temper."

Flash.

Searing pain along her thigh, the familiar taste of blood, sweaty, weak, stumbling as a sword blocked her attack, knocking her weapon away to clatter against the marble floor. Looking up, Whiskey saw Valmont stumbling toward her. Unable to move, she watched as he stood over her prone figure, a sword reversed in his hands as he prepared to skewer her.

"Get away from her!"

Valmont, distracted by the voice, turned and spoke. Not waiting to listen to his words, Whiskey grunted as she rolled over, attempting to crawl away. She heard a flurry of movement, a crash of bodies hitting the floor, the sound of Valmont's sword skittering away. Swallowing against the nausea and pain, she felt her life's blood seeping away as she concentrated on her escape.

Familiar hands stopped her progress, gently turning her over. Above her, Margaurethe's green eyes scanned her injuries, filling with tears. Valmont's voice drifted over them.

"What's done is done."

Margaurethe hissed at him, protecting her. "Stay with me, *'m 'cara*! We will get you to a healer and soon you will be fine."

Whiskey knew her lover lied. She'd always been able to tell when someone spoke dishonesty. She found herself chuckling at the irony of her death occurring in her lover's arms. "Nay, Margaurethe. It's beyond that, and we both know it." The words were hard to speak, her breath coming in gasps as her body shut down. She coughed, gripping at the woman's arm as she tried to hang on for just a little while longer.

"No! You cannot die, Elisibet."

"Apparently so, *minn 'ast*. Will you forgive me?"

"There is nothing to forgive."

Whiskey's one regret was leaving Margaurethe. Nothing else mattered but this beautiful woman's love. Odd she should come to the realization now when she'd lost everything. She shivered. "It's cold, Margaurethe. Hold me."

The world went dark.

Flash.

Whiskey came to herself slowly. The darkness of an ancient death dissipated as sunlight from outside the window brightened. Her vision blurry, several minutes crawled past before she realized tears coursed down her cheeks. Her awareness of them spurred them on, and she held herself, rocking where she sat, salty drops hitting the cover of the leather Book in her lap. *It hurts.* God, it hurt though she knew it was just a dream, and nothing had really happened. It must have killed Margaurethe to hold her as she lay dying. How long did she suffer? Did she ever heal, or find another lover?

As she gained control of the sadness, Whiskey's anger began to burn. The more visions she had, the more real they became, as if she had experienced them herself. Whoever Elisibet had been, Whiskey felt closer to her now than ever before.

And Elisibet yearned for Valmont's blood.

CHAPTER TWENTY-NINE

Hours later, Whiskey groaned and rolled over in the darkness. Similar to the first chant, she had become ill not long after the visions had ended. This time it wasn't brought on by a result of incongruent sensory simulation, however. A fever rushed through her body. Her skin burned, and her head pounded. She'd long ago lost her impromptu lunch, barely having the strength to drag herself into the bathroom. Her stomach cramped in avid displeasure as it rumbled with deep hunger. Immense pain in her belly rolled over her, wave after wave crashing down, threatening her consciousness. Sweat beaded on her forehead, and she took those few minutes between cramps to decide what to do. *Call Reynhard.* Her *Baruñal* would understand what was happening. Maybe he'd be able to stop the pain.

Though comforted by the thought, Whiskey didn't think

Dorst had any control over the issue. She'd yet to go through the aftermath of a meditation without dealing with the physical repercussions; why would this time be any different? Dorst would come and collect her, and she'd suffer just as much in his apartment as she did here. At least here she had some sense of privacy and dignity. She already knew that the one thing that would stop the pain would be to go through the final chant. That wasn't possible for at least another twenty-four hours. Whiskey gritted her teeth, feeling another swelling need to vomit wash over her.

Her hearing had zeroed in on the heartbeats in neighboring rooms. Try as she might, she couldn't stifle her awareness of them. Between bouts of cramps, she daydreamed of soft skin and pulsing blood. Her mouth watered. She remembered the taste of blood and sex from her abortive pick-up on Tuesday night, and her stomach rumbled dangerously, sending a wave of pain through her. Clutching at her belly, she folded over with a groan.

Maybe food would help. Didn't people eat crackers or something when they had the flu? This wasn't the flu, but it might work. She looked at the only illumination in the room, the bright red numerals of the bedside clock making her squint. Nearly five in the morning. The sun would rise soon. With room service closed, perhaps she could do a little begging with the front desk.

A half hour later, Whiskey nibbled crackers in bed. The night clerk was a lot nicer than the asshole who'd checked her in yesterday afternoon. He'd also brought up a bottle of soda and some Pepto-Bismol from the gift shop. Had she felt well enough she might have tipped him, but she couldn't take her eyes from his throat, almost tasting the blood flowing beneath the skin. Her stomach had cramped hard, ending the whispered hallway conversation.

The caffeine-free soda felt cool and pleasurable against her tongue, yet simultaneously unwelcome as it reached her throat. Her body craved something thick and warm. She nearly choked on the liquid, her stomach making an abortive attempt at rejection before accepting her offer. The next expected wave of cramps arrived. She fought the pain, pleased to note it had lightened in intensity. Maybe the carbonation was settling her stomach. Whiskey didn't know if the aches lessened, or she had become inured to them. She sincerely hoped the former.

As the pain subsided, she had an overwhelming urge to see Margaurethe O'Toole. The thought of her gentle touch and soothing voice made Whiskey feel better. *That is so fucked up.* She'd never even met the woman. Any feelings or history she thought she had were Elisibet's. *Quit thinking of her as your cut buddy.* That reminded her of Gin, and the look of disgust she'd given Whiskey. Tears of frustration, fear and loneliness spilled over. She clutched a pillow over her face, allowing herself to mourn the deaths of Dominick, her innocence and her friendship.

The sun had risen when Whiskey staggered to the bathroom. She'd dozed between stomach spasms, getting at least a little rest through the morning. The pain had tapered off. It stabbed at her when she focused on blood or hunger, so she kept her thoughts away from such things, enjoying what little peace and quiet she could get. The mirror showed her haggard visage, wild hair and deep shadows beneath her eyes. Red and green splashed across her light skin, her dragon the only bright thing in the reflection. Rubbing the tattoo, she realized it had healed twelve hours after completion. The initial line work had taken three days to mend. There were definite benefits to being Sanguire. *But will they outweigh the crap you'll have to deal with?* She frowned at herself, wishing she had a picture of Elisibet Vasilla for comparison. *Is plastic surgery an option? How fast will I heal when the Níri Kurám is finished?*

Another cramp assailed her, its intensity much more manageable. She leaned against the bathroom counter until it left her, forcing herself to think of something else.

Valmont.

Flash.

She stood in what could only be termed a dungeon. Flickering torches illuminated stone walls, and several ominous instruments on a wood table. Dirty straw littered the stone floor, soaking up body fluids. Chains hung from the ceilings and walls. A large brazier burned merrily in the center of the room, several blades and brands glowing cherry red in the coals. A naked Human hung before her, his golden skin slick with sweat and blood. She circled his dangling form, pleased to note he remained conscious as he panted from the exertion of his torture. His body showed signs of his interrogation, patches of missing flesh and hair, welts along his thighs and belly, her brand angrily blistering on his left buttock.

"Again."

"As you wish, Elisibet." A young Valmont stepped forward, grinning. In his hands he held a knife, liberally stained crimson. He used it to peel away a thin strip of skin from the prisoner's back, dropping the flesh to a small pile nearby. The smell of fresh blood sharpened in the smoky room, and she licked her lips in anticipation, watching her quarry as he struggled to keep from screaming.

Flash.

Whiskey swallowed thickly, half-disgusted and half-swooning from the rich aroma of blood. She suffered another cramp before pushing away from the counter, and left the bathroom. At the very least, the soda and crackers had remained in her stomach. That gave her some sense of relief. Perhaps this would pass as quickly as the last time. If that were the case, she'd be clear of it by evening.

CHAPTER THIRTY

Her stomach had stopped cramping. She didn't know if it was because of the Pepto-Bismol and food, or the passage of time. It helped that she forcibly kept her mind on other things besides blood when awake. Every time she thought of blood it triggered another round of pain. She felt bruised and delicate around her abdomen, but none the worse for wear. She'd slept most the day before finally rousing enough for a shower. Clean, warm and feeling much better than earlier, she perused the room service menu for dinner. Despite the gastrointestinal upsets, she still felt normal hunger. Crackers just didn't cut it anymore.

Once she had eaten, she planned on calling Dorst. They could go over the next meditation after he picked her up here. She hated the thought of putting him out of his bed again. Maybe she could con him into springing for another hotel room.

The sickly sweet essence of flowers washed over her.

Whiskey slammed the guest directory closed. She swiftly turned off the lamp, and moved to the window. Peering outside, she saw a Lexus across the street, a familiar redhead leaning against its side, watching the hotel with flashing golden eyes.

"Dammit!" She let the curtain fall back in place. Fiona had gotten her whereabouts from Cora or Daniel. Neither of them were strong enough to defy her on their own. Fiona merely needed to get one of them alone, and compel that person to give up Whiskey's location.

She looked wildly around. Her belongings were scattered about the room. No time to pack; she'd have to abandon everything she owned to get out of here. Fiona wouldn't tip her hand unless there were others of her pack in place to grab Whiskey. She stopped, questing toward the door with her mind, finding the pungent essences of sulfur and pepper. Manuel, with Bronwyn not far behind. God knew where Alphonse or Zebediah were; she wouldn't even know what their natures felt like, having never felt them before.

Whiskey snatched the knife and cell phone from her pack, and went to the door. Cracking it, she peeked into an empty hallway. Wherever Manuel was, he wasn't on this floor yet. She bet one came up the stairs, and the other on the elevator. Not wanting to get cornered so early in the chase, she took her chances on the stairs. The pepper taste on her tongue grew stronger, leaving her no doubt who thundered up the stairwell. She heard the thud of booted feet and, for a moment, wondered if Alphonse and Zebediah were behind Bronwyn. She hesitated, positive she couldn't get through three Sanguire on her own. Reaching out with her mind, she found no others in the vicinity. *Is it possible to hide your essence from another?*

Ding. The elevator doors opened. Whiskey barely noted shadowy movement down the hall. She rushed into the stairwell.

Bronwyn rounded the corner at the next landing down. She grinned at Whiskey, pointed teeth sparkling in the fluorescent light, and dashed up the last steps.

Whiskey dropped the cell phone, using that hand to stabilize herself on the steel banister. In sheer desperation, she launched herself, feet first, into Bronwyn. Her actions were inhumanly fast, and more controlled than she'd expected. Her opponent hadn't anticipated the attack, either. Bronwyn took the brunt of Whiskey's weight in the chest, and fell backward with a yelp.

Stumbling to her feet, Whiskey hauled herself back to the main landing by one hand. She glanced down at Bronwyn, piled in a heap on the next landing, trying to stand. Before Whiskey could chance going upstairs, the door behind her flew open. Sulfur filled her nostrils, though she knew the smell wasn't really there. Arms wrapped around her from behind, pinning hers to her side.

"Gotcha!"

The anger from her visions, that which she associated with Elisibet Vasilla, roared to the surface. "I don't fucking think so, bitch." She elbowed him hard in the ribs, and stomped on his instep, causing one side of his grip to weaken. Her free hand went to the knife sheath. She turned in his lightened grip, unsheathing the blade, and rammed the knife into his stomach. His essence immediately dissipated, and his hold on her disappeared. Now their hands interlocked about the hilt of the blade, he trying to pull it out, she forcing it in as deep as it could go.

Whiskey twisted the knife, causing Manuel to grunt. Hot blood spilled over their joined hands. Whiskey inhaled deeply to catch the heavenly aroma. Her fury abruptly failed as a devastating cramp clenched her stomach. Rather than release the knife to Manuel's tender mercies, she pulled it free. He let go, and fell backward to the floor, grunting.

There came a wordless cry of anger behind her. Whiskey spun around. Bronwyn careened up the steps toward her. Whiskey sidestepped, and grabbed one outstretched arm. She tugged hard, her bloody grip slipping a little, pulling Bronwyn past her to crash into the wall beside the door. Bronwyn dropped to the floor beside her lover.

Panting, Whiskey stood over them, bloody knife in one hand. Bronwyn's eyes were glassy; she'd put a fairly decent dent in the wall with her head. Manuel kept his hands on his wound, holding it closed while it healed. Whiskey considered how fast her tattoo had healed. She didn't think it'd be long before they'd be able to come after her again. By now security had been called by other guests. Their struggle hadn't been a quiet one.

Whiskey half ran, half stumbled down the stairs, leaving bloody prints on the banister and walls as she went. Four floors down, the steps ended. She looked left and right. Two doors led out of the stairwell. The one with a window in it showed the darkness of night. Bolted at eye level, a bright red sign stated an alarm would go off if opened. The other probably led into the lobby. She looked down at her bloodstained hands, the blade glistening with crimson wetness. Somehow, she'd lost the sheath. Running into a public place like this would do her less good than just blowing through the outer door, and setting off the alarms.

She heard noises upstairs and looked up; footsteps, a door, unfamiliar voices, static from a radio. Security had found Bronwyn and Manuel. She saw a smear of blood she'd left on the wall at the next landing up, and cursed. *Nothing like leaving a fucking trail. Cops will be here soon.* She barged out the exterior door, a loud hooting alarm resounding in the concrete and metal stairwell behind her.

The fire exit let out onto a side street. The front of the hotel and Fiona were to Whiskey's left. She turned right, and ran across the street, hoping to lose herself in an alley or courtyard along the way. Her eyes scanned for Alphonse or Zebediah, not seeing anything out of the ordinary. She skirted a large sidewalk fountain, aiming for the shadows of a small parking lot. Using her mind, she sought any others of her kind, especially Bronwyn or Fiona. None were close.

Whiskey almost made it to the darkness when a sense of being smothered swept over her. *What the fuck?* She stumbled, tripping over the curb, and crashed to the ground. The knife skittered under one of the decorative bushes encircling the lot. It took her several moments to realize she breathed freely despite the sensation of a pillow over her face. She heard footsteps behind her, and groped for the lost weapon.

Alphonse came to a stop before her, his blue mohawk stiffly upright. He held his hands out in a calming gesture. "We're only here to take you back home. We're not here to hurt you."

As Whiskey stood, she realized that what she felt was

Alphonse's Sanguire nature. She fought against it, pleased to see him wince. "I'm not going anywhere with you. Tell Fiona to back off."

Another set of footsteps neared, and she whirled to see Zebediah arrive. "Cops and paramedics are on their way. Fiona took the car for a spin until it clears up." He nodded his head at Whiskey. "She really messed up Manuel."

Whiskey waved the knife. "Same's going to happen to you if you don't leave me alone."

"We can't." Alphonse took a step closer, prudently keeping out of reach. "Fiona wants you home, and that's where we're taking you. You can stab us if you want, but it's not going to kill us. We'll just keep coming for you."

"What? Are you fucking zombies?" The anger in her heart exploded, and she reached for Alphonse's mind. "I know how to kill a Sanguire." She forged a connection with him, overcoming the smothering sensation with little discomfort. It felt good to let the fury have its head, and she smiled as she watched him bend over with his head in his hands.

Zebediah swore, and reached out with both his fists and his mind. Whiskey felt herself immersed in cool water, a questing liquid that searched for and linked with the smothering sensation. On automatic, she intercepted Zebediah's physical attack, grabbing and twisting his forearm until she heard the snap of the bones. The water receded, but grew stronger as it joined forces with the suffocation.

For a moment, it seemed the two would overcome her with their abilities. Whiskey felt her consciousness fading, and had a fuzzy vision of crashing to her knees. A frenzied rage washed over her. "Fuck this!" Working on instinct, she fought her way through their combined attack, piercing through the cloud around her mind. Using the breach as her focal point, she shoved with all her might, exhilarated as the pinprick hole ripped and expanded. The men dropped to their knees. Whiskey might have released them to escape, but euphoria took over her common sense. She continued to work on them, gathering every little bit of the fugue she came in contact with into a little ball. Once she had it all, she squeezed with her mind.

Her heart soared with joy at their screams of agony. She could listen to this music forever. To prove it, she jabbed again at the remaining wad of their natures, laughing as they voiced their pain. She wanted to do it again, but something stopped her, an emotion she wasn't used to feeling in circumstances like this. Pausing in her mental torture, she cocked her head, trying to chase it down. *There it is. What is that?* She focused on the feeling, finding it both alien and familiar.

Compassion.

Whiskey staggered, the storm of madness disappearing. Repulsed, she released her victims, taking a step back. Alphonse and Zebediah collapsed to the sidewalk, panting and moaning. One of them had vomited during the attack, and they both writhed slowly as they lay there.

She stood frozen in place, staring at the result of her handiwork. She didn't know what to do, who to call for help. Digging in her pocket, she couldn't find her cell phone, belatedly remembering that she'd dropped it on the stairs when Bronwyn came at her. *Besides, if I call emergency services, can they do anything for Sanguire? Can Reynhard?* A car drove slowly past. She glanced at the driver, nervous. The vehicle wasn't one she knew, but the wide-eyed driver suddenly hit the accelerator. The police would be here soon regardless of her indecision.

Zebediah pushed to his hand and knees with a groan. Whiskey went on the defensive, holding the knife in front of her. He cradled his broken arm, and looked up at her. "Damn."

"I am so fucking sorry," Whiskey babbled. "I didn't mean for that to happen." Alphonse showed some measure of returning consciousness, and she stepped out of his reach, as well.

Gingerly holding his arm, Zebediah rolled his head on his neck. "How old are you?"

Whiskey felt a giggle rise in her throat at the inane conversation. "I just turned eighteen a couple of weeks ago."

Alphonse grunted and rolled over, swearing under his breath.

Zebediah glanced at his companion, then peered at her. "How far have you gotten on the Strange Path?"

She debated telling him, knowing he could use the information against her. "Third chant."

He blinked. "You're fucking with me."

"No. I did it yesterday afternoon after Daniel and Cora left me here."

"Jesus." Alphonse groaned, reaching up to rub his head. "No wonder it hurt so much. Never did that before?"

Whiskey swallowed. *This is stupid! You're letting them get their shit together so they can go at you again.* "No."

"We need to get out of here." Zebediah staggered to his feet, raising his uninjured hand to show surrender to Whiskey. "I think I heard a car go past—?"

"Yeah, a couple of minutes ago."

Zebediah helped Alphonse stand up. "You okay?"

The blue mohawk dipped once. "I will be." Alphonse looked over his friend's broken arm. "You?"

"It'll heal."

Whiskey backed away, gathering the energy to defend herself once more, disgusted with the eagerness swelling in her chest. She now knew why Elisibet Vasilla had been so violent; it had been invigorating to toy with their minds. They both turned their attention to her, and she braced herself for round two.

"We brought our bikes. They're parked about three blocks from here. Where do you want to go?"

She blinked at them. "What?"

"Where do you want to go?"

Whiskey felt her jaw drop open. She'd just kicked these guys' collective ass, her one to their two, and they acted as if it happened every day. She heard a siren in the distance, and realized there wasn't much time to make a decision. "I want you two to go away, and leave me the hell alone."

"Can't do that."

Alphonse nodded. "It's not safe for you."

"Story of my life."

Zebediah chuckled. "Maybe so, but it's twice as bad now. If any of our people find you, you'll be mincemeat."

Whiskey scowled. "Why now, and not before?"

"Because you hadn't started the Ñíri Kurám. No one knew for sure you were Sanguire." Alphonse shrugged, then twisted his head with his hands until his spine crackled. "Now they'll know."

She couldn't argue with their logic. Still, if they wouldn't let her leave alone, she couldn't go to Dorst's apartment. With a lot of mileage between here and the U District, she could try to lose them. *Where can I be safe with a street hit out on me, a future murder rap in the works, and Sanguire hunting me?* After Fiona, her next immediate threat was Ghost. There was one part of town close enough that she could hide for the night from street kid vigilantes. That'd give her time to think of a way to ditch these two without compromising Dorst's location.

"No bikes. We're going on foot."

Neither of them disagreed with her order. Zebediah carefully twisted his arm until the bones grated back into place. "Where to?"

"Downtown."

CHAPTER THIRTY-ONE

Whiskey sat on the sidewalk, legs stretched out and crossed at the ankle. She leaned against a brick wall, watching people pass. Her foot rocked in restless agitation. At one o'clock in the morning, the cool breeze felt wonderful against her still overheated skin. Foot traffic had faded to a trickle. There might be another rush of pedestrians when the bars closed, but by then the city transit would be stopped. A bus stop to her left saw people arriving and departing regularly, more going than coming at this hour. The transit area held a handful of Humans waiting for their next transport.

Beside her were the empty wrappings of her most recent meal—a microwaveable container of chicken and noodles, a plastic spoon and a half finished box of crackers. Not quite what her stomach ordered, but it would have to do. At least the food had remained in her stomach to strengthen her. She could almost pretend everything was normal, that she just had a touch of the flu.

Except for the company.

A dozen or so hardened punks, resplendent in leather and chains and violent hairstyles, hung out nearby. They left her to her own devices as they discussed who recently pounded whom and which band had the best music. Most of them were homeless, and had probably heard of the hit out on her. None of them cared much for the skater kids whom Ghost and Gin hung with, so she felt a measure of safety in their midst. When Alphonse and Zebediah greeted these people like friends, Whiskey thought it would be a fine place to park it for the time being. While surrounded by anarchist punks, even the old-timer street people wouldn't mess with her. Besides, she'd been on the fringes of their cliques for years, and several recognized her. Regardless, she kept a close eye on her self-appointed guardians.

It had taken an hour to get here from the Queen Anne suburb. She'd confiscated their cell phones when they'd begun ringing. Both men easily turned them over without a fight. She'd thrown them as far as she could into someone's backyard. Neither of her companions put up a fight at the loss, either. Considering their lack of response, she knew she was missing some vital piece of information, but was too tired and messed up to try and make sense of things. On the way here, they'd stopped at a convenience store to stock up on beer and food. Most of the beer had been consumed by the punks, doing much to appease their volatile nature.

Shrouded in silence, Whiskey listened to the conversations of those around her, a distant voyeur. Occasionally, the group would become sullen as police drove through the area. Discussion would then turn to the latest round of busts and stories of juvenile detention or county jail. Eyes would slide in her direction, but no one brought up rumors of slain street kids.

Bored with the posturing and boasts, she directed her hearing elsewhere. She concentrated on a couple she saw walking a block away—he whined about his job and she bitched at him for getting fired again. Sighing, she tried another conversation, her mind drifting with her senses. The longer the night became, the more she wanted to be up and moving. But she couldn't go anywhere until she ditched her unwanted companions. She felt a yearning, but didn't understand what she needed.

Hooting and teasing interrupted her rumination, the punks rudely talking about a man wearing a dress. Blinking in surprise, she looked up, seeing Castillo smiling and jesting in response. He glanced at her, and his grin widened. The urge to run into his arms disconcerted her, conflicting with an equally strong desire to flee. She almost stood, but didn't know which way she'd jump if she did. With nowhere to go and no time to work through the confusion, she swallowed and forced herself to remain in place.

Castillo approached with obvious pleasure. "Whiskey!"

Before he got close, Alphonse and Zebediah blocked his way. The Human punks looked on with interest, some beginning to eye the priest with fresh suspicion. "Maybe she doesn't want to see you," Alphonse suggested. Beside him, Zebediah's red mohawk dipped in an agreeable nod.

No one moved. Whiskey sensed a struggle between them. Similar to the one she'd witnessed between Fiona, Cora and Daniel, this one seemed more refined than her initial foray into such a battle. The tableau broke when Alphonse sagged, reaching out to stabilize himself against Zebediah's shoulder.

"Are we finished?"

Zebediah stared at Castillo, his eyes dark hollows within a milky complexion. When he made no move to intercede, Castillo bypassed them and approached Whiskey, sitting beside her. "I've been looking for you."

"Really?" She attempted to sound casual. The rest of the punks resumed their conversations, their curiosity evident as they kept an eye on their visitor. Zebediah and Alphonse conferred and then took up positions to watch both the Humans and the priest.

"Yes." Castillo leaned forward, and dropped his voice. "I heard about what happened at Tallulah's. Are you all right?"

Whiskey chuckled. "As well as can be, considering. What's the word?"

He stroked his beard, watching her. "You know how it is on the streets. There are rumors all over the place. The most predominant is that 'someone' lured a poor street kid into the alley, and beat him to death."

"Bullshit!" Her anger flared, and she felt her lip curl. "Ghost got jealous, and put out a hit on me. Dominick and two others pinned me in that alley to beat me."

"But that's not what happened."

A wave of regret flowed through her, dampening her hostility. "No. Those Sanguire found me, the ones I've been hanging with. They took out the other two kids. Dominick wouldn't back down. So they beat him instead."

Castillo glanced over his shoulder at their silent audience. "Were these two involved?"

She looked at Alphonse and Zebediah. "Would it matter if they were?"

He returned his gaze to her. "It would to me."

Whiskey flushed under his kind scrutiny. *I don't deserve that kind of look. I'm the most guilty.* "They weren't. Their friends were, though."

"The police are still gathering evidence and testimony. It's just a matter of time before your name comes up." A sudden frown transformed his features, and he looked at the punk Sanguire again. "Don't tell me one of these is your *Baruñal.*"

She rolled her eyes. "No, neither of them. I don't know why they're here. An hour ago I took them out in some sort of mental fight, and they've been sticking to me like glue ever since."

"A mental fight?" Castillo's brow furrowed further, and he stared at her. "What do you mean?"

Great. Don't tell me I'm the only one who can do that. She immediately negated the thought. *That's stupid. I've seen others do it. Hell, Alphonse and Zeb just attacked the padre that way.* "You know what I mean." She pitched her voice low, so that only he could hear her. "That mental thing they just pulled on you? They tried it on me, too."

"And you bested them?"

She blinked at his intensity. "Well, yeah. It took some work, but I kicked their asses." His behavior spooked her, so she didn't bring up knifing Manuel in the hotel, or putting Bronwyn into a concrete wall.

Castillo sat back, mouth open, eyebrows raised. "That's impossible."

"Why? Why is it impossible?" Everyone knew things, had basic information that she lacked. These things were happening to her. She leaned forward, the frustration of not knowing feeding her annoyance. "Why are they protecting me from the person who leads them? I don't understand."

"You haven't completed the *Ñíri Kurám*. You don't have the power to defend yourself from a joint attack."

She scoffed. "Yes, I do. Ask them." She waved an arm in the direction of her guardians.

"It was like a battering ram," Zebediah informed Castillo, rubbing his temple with one hand.

Alphonse nodded. "What she lacks in finesse she makes up for in brute strength."

Whiskey scowled at the pair of them. "Why are you following me?"

Zebediah shrugged. "You lead."

"That's the shit I get when I ask," Whiskey said to Castillo. "I don't get it. Up until an hour ago, they were trying to kidnap me and bring me to their home base and pack leader. Now they act like I'm the fucking president, and they're the Secret Service."

Castillo visibly floundered a moment before gaining control. "With age comes strength among Sanguire. A youngling, one having not finished the *Ñíri Kurám*, is the weakest of all. Anyone a year or so older can overpower their minds."

Whiskey gnawed fiercely on his words, digesting them, drawing as much information as she could from them. "What are you saying?"

"If you can overcome two joined adult Sanguire before coming to adulthood yourself..." He trailed off. "It's almost unprecedented."

She picked up one word. "Almost?"

Castillo shifted, uncomfortable. "It's happened once before. It was thought to be a fluke due to the nature of the *Ñíri Kurám* involved. The individual was given the Book much too young, before attaining adolescence. She completed the Strange Path as one of the strongest Sanguire in history."

Whiskey braced herself, knowing what he'd say next. She spoke the name with him. "Elisibet Vasilla."

He stared at her with a concerned expression. "What's happening, Whiskey? You look like her. You're exhibiting power like her. Is there anything else?"

She wanted to tell him the truth, felt the words at the back of her throat as they yearned to be spoken. *He told the* Agrun Nam *about you.* Her eyes narrowed, remembering the brown man on the side of the street by the tattoo shop. "Valmont."

Castillo shook his head as if he didn't hear her correctly. "What?"

"Valmont is here in Seattle. I've seen him."

The priest's face drained of color, and her barely formed suspicions were confirmed.

"You've seen him, too, haven't you?"

"You know *Sañar* Valmont?" He rocked back, eyes widening. "He hasn't mentioned...officially meeting you."

"We haven't been formally introduced."

Castillo's composure returned. He cocked his head. "Then how do you know he's here? You say you saw him; do one of these people know him, too?"

Whiskey looked away, watching the punks posture and boast in blissful ignorance. Her next words would tip her hand. Either Castillo would run once more to the *Agrun Nam,* or he'd keep her secret. How else would Valmont know to come here unless the padre went back to the council, and told them more about her. She needed so badly to trust in him, watching as everything that connected her to her old life crumbled into ash. He'd said he'd keep her confidence as best he could. What if the decision had been taken out of his hands? Valmont was at least three or four hundred years older than him.

When she didn't answer, he reached forward to touch her forearm. "Jenna?"

She decided to take the plunge, her tender stomach swooping as if she'd leapt from a tall building to the street below. "No. No one needed to point him out. I remember him from when he was presented to Elisibet at court."

Silence.

Whiskey risked a glance at him. She thought he'd turned pale earlier, but his swarthy skin had whitened enough to rival Ghost's. Mouth open, he gaped at her. His friendly demeanor had whisked away, leaving behind a man stumbling through the dark, unable to find his God for solace. She regretted causing his distress, though a small, vicious part of her wanted to drive the knife deeper just to watch him squirm.

"You—" He choked and cleared his throat. "You saw him? At Elisibet's court?"

Gathering her wits about her, she shrugged in an attempt to appear nonchalant. "Yeah. I saw Margaurethe O'Toole, too."

"Dear God." He swallowed convulsively, pulling away from her. "I've got to do something."

Anger surged through Whiskey. Deep inside, a tiny voice of reason tried to dissuade her, to take a logical approach to what Castillo probably felt. But rationality had gone out the window— these visions, these people, these sensations. She was done being played with, and damned if she'd let him rat her out to Valmont. What had Castillo said? *"He hasn't mentioned...officially meeting you."* Which meant Valmont and Castillo had been in contact, spoken recently.

Instinctively, she forged a link with him, just as Alphonse had done with her, fighting through the warm, dark chocolate. On the periphery of their struggle, she felt Alphonse and Zebediah offer their assistance. She refused them, curious to see just how much power she had. She and Castillo scuffled for control between them, a more difficult struggle than her previous encounter. Castillo had the benefit of experience, and nearly gained equal footing a number of times. Whiskey's rage and natural talent gave her enough of an edge to retain control.

"What do you think you're going to do?" She kept a tight rein on his mind.

Castillo sweated, drops springing up on his lip and forehead, but his eyes remained calm. His essence felt skittish, but held firm. "I don't honestly know."

"Don't even think about telling the *Agrun Nam* or Valmont about me."

"That was never my intention."

"You've spoken to Valmont. What did you say?"

Flash.

Whiskey suddenly *was* Castillo. She saw through his eyes as he walked down a sunlit street near the Youth Consortium. A feather touch of request crossed her mind, letting her know of the presence of another Sanguire, one who wanted something. She looked over her shoulder, scanning the sidewalks and street for the new arrival. A man lounged against the corner across the street, arms crossed as he stared at her. *Valmont.*

"Father James Castillo?" His voice had an odd accent, one she both recognized, and couldn't place.

"Yes," Castillo's voice said. Whiskey shivered at the strangeness.

"My name is Valmont. The *Agrun Nam* sent me."

Her heart dropped to the pit of her stomach, just as quickly rising to clog her throat.

Flash.

"When did you first see this woman?"

They were sitting in a bar, and she stared at Valmont across the table. "Nearly six months ago. She's like those children to whom I was speaking, living on the streets." The oddness of hearing the padre's voice while she spoke almost upset her control. *Is this normal?*

"Originally, your only evidence was a likeness to Elisibet, correct?"

"At the time, yes. The images I have of her are copies of her official portraits. By all accounts, the only difference is the color of Whiskey's eyes which are almost black."

"Whiskey." Valmont shook his head, face sour. "Have you discovered if she's Sanguire or not?"

"Yes. She's begun the *Ñíri Kurám.*" When Valmont cursed, she felt a stab of pleasure, knowing somehow that it was hers, and not Castillo's.

Flash.

Back at the bus stop, she stared at Castillo. His white face inches away from hers, he trembled with the effort it took to close off her investigation of his memories. "Why is Valmont here, Padre? You must have said something to someone. The *Agrun Nam's* known about me for months, you said. Why send him now?"

Despite his physical distress, he appeared chagrined. "My utmost apologies, Whiskey. I think my friend in Europe had something to do with that. Either he was compromised, or my phones are tapped." He bared his neck for her. "It's my fault."

Unable to help herself, she listened to the rush of blood coursing through the large vein in his throat. The memory of that woman's blood and sex on her tongue caused a sudden vicious cramp, and her control over the link faltered. Whiskey fought the sickness away for several precious seconds, returning to the present to find Castillo holding their bond open. Soft confusion grew in place of her uprooted anger. She stared at him. "Why are we still connected? You could have cut me off, defeated me."

Castillo smiled kindly. "Would it have done any good? You're stronger than I already. Besides, this way you can see the truth of my words as I answer your questions." He chuckled. "Though I would advise against forcing bonds in the future; it's considered the ultimate in bad manners."

"Bad manners?" She snorted laughter, a tinge of hysteria in her voice. "You're saying it's impolite to force this...bond on others? Do you know how many times I've had someone attack me in just this way the last couple of days, Padre?"

His smile faded to a worried frown. "Whiskey, you must come with me. I can keep you safe." Castillo leaned forward to take her upper arm.

Whiskey's amusement disappeared, and she pulled violently away. She was getting really tired of hearing that from people. Scrambling to her feet, she sent a wave of anger along their link, pleased to see him wince, and grab his head. "Don't ever touch me again, Padre."

As he struggled against the pain, she walked backward toward the bus stop. The punks cleared out of her way, silent as they watched the drama. Alphonse and Zebediah drifted along with her, ready to assist.

"You don't understand, Whiskey! I can protect you!"

The bus pulled up just as she reached the curb. "You two keep him from following me."

Alphonse raised an eyebrow. "You need someone with you."

"I'm going to my goddamned *Baruñal*, okay? I'll be safe with him." She prodded both of them with her mind, wondering what the limits were to her power. *Surely I should be reaching the end point, right?*

Zebediah raised his chin, and stepped away from the bus.

"C'mon! Either get on or get away from the door," the bus driver ordered.

Alphonse gave her a curt nod. He followed his companion.

Keeping tight control on the bond between them, keeping Castillo off-kilter, Whiskey boarded. Only when the doors closed, and it pulled away from the stop, did she release him. She felt the combined essences of Alphonse and Zebediah take over, knowing they'd never be able to hold him long. But long enough.

Slumping onto a seat, she stared at passing scenery, unable to formulate a plan of action.

CHAPTER THIRTY-TWO

Nowhere near her intended destination, Whiskey watched the bus pull away from the transit station without her. The bus she'd boarded in Seattle had brought her to the outskirts of Tacoma instead. A major neighboring town *cum* suburb, the area had long ago been stuck with the moniker "The Aroma of Tacoma" by the old paper factory. These days it held a decent sports stadium, and much work had been done to renovate it, but the seedier aspect of the area still remained.

Hers had been the last bus for the night. She had five hours or more before the morning routes began. At least no one searching for her would think to look here, not even someone who'd seen the bus she'd ridden. She needed to find something to eat and a place to hole up for a nap. Numb to her bones, she stepped off the platform, deciding to put as much distance between her and the station as possible. She didn't think Castillo would attempt to follow this bus route to its end, but she didn't want to take any chances.

She wasn't sure where to go. What if Valmont decided to look up Castillo again? Very much a predator, her old friend could easily locate her the same way she'd seen his meeting with the priest. She froze, midstep. *"My old friend?" Christ, I'm going crazy.* Berating herself, she continued walking, aimless in her travels.

Her path took her toward habitation and activity. The lights of a twenty-four hour convenience store beckoned from a half block down the street, and she headed in its direction. Her stomach remained tender. So long as she didn't think of—her mind automatically veered away from the term blood—that, she was fine. She wondered how long she'd be able to play these head games with herself before it would overwhelm her again. "Next time put the cell phone in your pocket when you're attacked by vampires." She snorted.

Some time later, she sat on the curb outside the store, eating a sandwich. Beside her were a large plastic cup of soda, and a bag of chips. The food tasted like plastic, leaving a vague burning sensation at the back of her throat. Beggars couldn't be choosers. She washed the thing down with her drink. The chips were relatively better and she sighed, her stomach rumbling slightly in discontent.

What would Castillo do? Did he own a car to search for her? She'd taken his outward appearance, the simple priest slash social worker he portrayed, for granted. At four hundred years old, he probably lived as well as Fiona did, regardless of his standing in his church. Did the Church know he was Sanguire? She shook her head, not pursuing the thought. It'd be too easy to lose the focus of her predicament going that direction.

By now Alphonse had probably called Fiona. Or would he? He and Zebediah had said she led them now. Would that change if she wasn't there to oversee them? Was that why they lived with Fiona? It'd be a lot easier keeping tabs on everybody if they were under the same roof. While that made some sense, she had to wonder. They couldn't all avoid older Sanguire, could they? How would anything get done if every time you met an elder, you'd be directed from your purpose? *Damn, I wish I knew Reynhard's number.*

A car pulled into the parking lot, and a laughing couple clambered out. Whiskey ignored them as they entered the store, refusing to acknowledge their curious glances. Her meal finished, she crumpled the wrappers and stood to deposit them in the trash can by the glass doors. Looking inside, she saw the couple split up. The man headed for the beer cooler while the woman perused the snack foods. The woman's dark hair caught the overhead fluorescent lights, illuminating a touch of reddish highlights.

Flash.

She crushed a younger Margaurethe against a wall, pinning the woman's wrists above her head with one hand as she leisurely explored bared flesh with the other. The torch light caught the red tones of her dark hair, and Whiskey nuzzled it, smelling herbs, the spicy trace of her lover's scent, and the musky odor of arousal from both of them. Margaurethe's heart thumped fast and heavy. Whiskey saw the blood moving through the vein at her neck. She breathed into Margaurethe's ear, pausing to suck a tender earlobe into her mouth to nibble, enjoying the lithe body squirming against hers.

"Please, Elisibet," Margaurethe murmured, twisting her head to one side. "Please."

Whiskey smiled, and licked her way to the pulse point. She felt an odd sensation in her mouth, like she had too many teeth. Gently kissing along the thick vein, she whispered, "I love you," before biting down.

The intoxicating flow of Margaurethe's blood in her mouth magnified her lust.

Flash.

Whiskey's stomach rebelled at its most recent meal, and she vomited into the garbage can. She staggered away in defeat when she finished. The taste of blood in her memory ignited the need for more, and the cramps stormed through her with a vengeance. She stumbled, falling.

"Jesus! Is she okay?"

"I don't know. Maybe she's strung out."

"Hey! You'd better call an ambulance. This girl just collapsed out here!"

Whiskey heard the voices, but the roar of their heartbeats filling her ears muted them. Unable to respond, her eyes rolled up, and blissful darkness claimed her.

Whiskey blinked sleepily, wincing away from the dawn pouring through the window. She muttered, crisp sheets scraping across her sensitive skin as she turned over. *Sheets?* Freezing in place, eyes closed, she extended her senses. Someone's heart beat close by, and she heard a muted paging system, muffled and echoing. The antiseptic smells held an undertone of sickness, an after-odor rich and repellent with disease. She grimaced, squinting one eye open. A thin ivory curtain met her gaze.

Fully awake, she struggled to sit up, ignoring the complaint of her sore abdomen. Chrome bars boxed her into the bed, and she found a cable with the controls near her pillow. A nightstand and phone sat beside her, and several electronic devices hung from the wall above her head. She found a medical shunt taped to the back of her right hand, embedded in the thick vein below her thumb.

A hospital?

Whiskey tried to remember what had happened. She recalled being in Tacoma, and eating something. Then came the memory, and severe cramps. Her mind veered away from the vision, glad to note her stomach merely rolled over. Someone must have called the paramedics. How'd she come to be here and not in the emergency room? She didn't have any money. Certainly the admitting staff figured that out early on during the intake process.

The growing sunlight pierced her eyes. She raised a hand to shade them. She fumbled for her sunglasses before she realized she wasn't in street clothes. She wore a shapeless hospital gown of light blue. Whiskey pursed her lips. She had to find her clothes, and get out of here. Who knew what would be found by a thorough exam from a Human doctor? That had to be why

Daniel had studied to be one. The world had Sanguire politicians and police, why not medical personnel to help keep the Great Secret?

It took a few moments before she figured out the railing mechanism. Her knees gave a perilous wobble when she slid out from beneath the covers. She swallowed a thrill of fear. *God, I'm so weak. Can I make it out of here without fainting?* Her bladder asserted its dominance. She shuffled across the room, wondering if she'd fall before making it to the can. Peering past the curtain, she saw an open door leading to a bathroom, and hobbled inside.

She left the bathroom with a bit less haste, pausing at the door to glance around. Another bed occupied the room, its occupant snoring softly. A green exit sign glowed above the other door. Moving gingerly back to her side of the room, Whiskey located a small closet, relieved to find her clothing inside. She tossed her things onto the bed, and prepared to dress.

"Here now, you can't leave quite yet."

Guiltily, Whiskey glanced over her shoulder to find a nurse bearing down upon her.

"Watch me." She began to untie the flimsy hospital gown.

The nurse, obviously used to dealing with stubborn patients, scooped up Whiskey's clothes. "Not yet." She easily kept them out of reach. "You need more rest, and to eat some breakfast. The doctor will be by later in the morning."

"Give me that!" Whiskey stumbled as she flailed for her belongings, disliking the helpless feeling. "I'm fucking leaving, you got it?"

"No, Jenna. You've got to let Dr. Mulligan do his job. He'll no doubt release you this afternoon."

She stopped, glaring at the woman. "How did you know my name?"

Taken aback, the nurse said, "Your brother called looking for you. He's no doubt on his way here."

Brother? Whiskey's sluggish mind prodded at a sudden new relation. *Reynhard?* A rush of weakness washed over her at the thought of seeing him. The nurse barely caught her in time.

"There now. You see? You need to stay in bed for now, and

regain your strength." She helped an unresisting Whiskey back under the sheets. "I'll have breakfast brought to you. The doctor makes his rounds at about seven. In the meanwhile, you sleep." The nurse tucked Whiskey under the blanket, making sure the bed controls were within reach. "If you need anything, just push this button, and one of us will come to you. Okay?"

Whiskey fought the dizziness, barely nodding in response. Her eyelids felt so heavy. She found herself fighting to keep them open with no success. She watched the nurse gather up her belongings, and return them to the closet. She'd try to leave later. Until then, a nap wouldn't be remiss.

CHAPTER THIRTY-THREE

Whiskey didn't know how long she slept. She woke again to the sound of voices, her body feeling somewhat stronger. The sun had risen above the horizon. Fortunately, it now hid behind low-lying clouds, saving her from a potential headache. Not much time had passed. She wondered if Dorst had arrived.

The curtain drew aside, and a middle-aged man in white came into view. "Good morning, Ms. Davis. I'm Dr. Mulligan. How are you feeling?"

"Ready to get the hell out of here." She scooted up in bed. She did feel stronger. Her stomach grumbled with real hunger.

Mulligan smiled, and glanced over her chart. "Well, let's just see if that's a possibility, shall we?"

Whiskey suffered through a round of poking, prodding and a cold stethoscope placed against her skin. Her blood pressure a little low, her skin still a bit sensitive, she still appeared to be in good health. The medical shunt was removed from her hand, leaving a bruise in its wake.

"Do you have any idea what happened last night?" The doctor made notations on her chart.

"Not really. I thought I had the flu. Vomiting, stomach cramps."

He nodded and scribbled something down. "Jenna, did you have any drugs in your system last night?"

She pursed her lips. "No."

"I have to ask. Your blood tests haven't come back from the lab, yet. What about alcohol?"

"No."

Mulligan finished writing. "All right then. Breakfast will be served in a matter of minutes. I want you to eat all of it, if you can. Your lab results should come through in the next couple of hours. Once I've assessed them, I'll let you know what's going on."

"I want to get out of here."

He peered over his glasses at her. "If you'd like, you can get dressed after breakfast. From what I've seen so far, I'll probably release you today."

Relieved at the concession, she nodded. "Okay. Thank you."

"But after breakfast." Mulligan's expression brooked no argument.

He left her, pulling the curtain back in place. As he began his examination of her roommate, the nurse bustled through with a tray.

"Here's the meal I promised you." She placed it on a bedside table, and rolled it into place. She helped Whiskey with the controls until the bed supported her seated form. "Now eat every bit of it."

Whiskey nodded, finding herself hungry for the first time since the meditation. The tray held scrambled eggs, a patty of what could laughably be called sausage, two tiny pieces of toast and a fruit cocktail cup. "Has...my brother come to see me? Do you know if he's on his way?"

The nurse frowned. "Unfortunately, I don't know. You were transferred to this ward after he called the emergency room, and identified you. It hasn't been that long, though. I'm sure he's on his way." She fussed with the blankets, and gave her the television remote. "Visiting hours are at nine, and it's just past seven thirty. I'll let you know when he arrives."

"Thank you."

Ravenous, Whiskey barely tasted her breakfast as she ate. It was probably just as well since the eggs appeared undercooked and the sausage patty was suspect. She knew she should try to go slow to allow herself time to get used to the food, but couldn't help herself. In response, her stomach cramped once or twice, but the pain wasn't of the same nature as before. Lying back, now overfull, she groaned with contentment. Maybe this sickness passed with time, just like the first one. It certainly had taken long enough, much longer than the other two. She didn't want to repeat the incident that got her in here, and refused to dwell on the visions and cravings that would trigger another round of vomiting. Maybe later when she'd had time to digest breakfast, and gain some strength.

An hour and a half before visiting hours. Whiskey wondered if Dorst had already arrived. On a lark, she closed her eyes, and let her mind drift, searching. A tenuous flicker of dark chocolate tickled the edges of Whiskey's mind. *Shit! The padre.* She sat up straighter in bed, scanning farther. Her mind brushed across three other Sanguire presences, none of whom she knew.

To protect herself, she yanked herself back from making full connections with any of them. Other Sanguire? Were they working with Castillo or Valmont? She didn't think the padre would betray her after his many denials, but that wouldn't stop the *Agrun Nam* from watching his every move. Would Valmont have thought to check hospitals, too? Did he send people to all of them in the area to locate her? Or maybe Alphonse and Zebediah had called Fiona last night, filling her in. Maybe these people worked for her.

Her initial complacence gone, Whiskey climbed out of bed. Noticeably stronger this time, she took a deep breath to relax. She had to get dressed. Then she'd debate staying, or going in search of Dorst. He had much more experience and knowledge than she; if anyone could protect her, it would be him.

The flimsy hospital gown soon lay on the bed. Whiskey stood by the window, fully clothed. From her position, she saw past the curtain to the door beyond, and the foot of her roommate's bed. The television droned on, the volume low, portraying a morning news station. A picture of Dominick appeared behind one of the newscasters. Whiskey stared.

"Still no leads on the slaying of a young homeless boy, Dominick Filardo. Filardo, who was fifteen years old, was beaten to death early Wednesday morning in the University District. He was a reported runaway at the time. Current theories range from a revenge killing or drug bust gone wrong. The police are urging anyone with any information to please call." The newscaster gave a number, and the screen changed to a weather map. "Now to Hank with today's forecast."

Whiskey turned off the television. Before she could react, a nurse entered the room, barely noticing her. The woman went to the other bed, and chatted with the person there.

"And how are you this morning, Mrs. Draiman? Did you sleep well last night?"

"Surprisingly, yes. The doctor said my tests were inconclusive this morning?"

"I'm sorry to say." The nurse fussed with some instruments. "I've come to get another blood sample from you. He's got some more tests to run so we can pin down what's wrong."

Whiskey's mouth watered, her senses focused on what happened on the other side of the curtain. She heard the rustling of cloth, the squeak of rubber, and the faint click of plastic on plastic as the nurse uncapped a syringe.

The odor undid her. Rich and thick and sweet, it called to her. She felt an odd sensation in her mouth. Running her tongue along her teeth, she came in contact with fangs where none had been before. The strangeness in her mouth distracted her from the activity beyond the curtain. She flopped into the chair by her bed, carefully exploring the new fangs with her tongue.

Oh, my God! Is this supposed to happen?

Her heart raced. She swallowed, returning her attention to the other half of the room. The nurse had left with her sample, but the smell of it still drifted in the air. Too faint for Human senses, it beckoned Whiskey. She swallowed again, noting her stomach didn't rebel as it had the day before. Instead of cramping, it merely complained of a hunger she hadn't assuaged.

The teeth wouldn't go away. Adrenaline whisked through her as she considered they might not until she'd...fed. Her memory of being with Margaurethe, literally dining on the woman, brought her to her feet. She didn't come to her senses until she was halfway across the room.

Stopping herself, Whiskey gaped at the old woman in the bed. What the hell was she doing? Her stomach growled louder in demand, and she imagined the feel of the flesh as her teeth pierced through. With a grunt, she turned away, stumbling to the door.

I have to get out of here. Now.

Whiskey slipped down the hall. Despite the hour, people bustled back and forth on important errands. Nurses went about their tasks, checking on patients. A pair of uniformed men delivered trays of food to each room, checking a clipboard as they went. Passing close to her, a doctor with a trail of interns rounded the corner and entered a room, looking very much like a mother duck and her ducklings. An elderly patient hobbled along with his IV stand as a walker. Two technicians loitered at the nurses' station, flirting with a little blonde. The number of people helped hide Whiskey's escape attempt; no one noticed her except one intern with an armload of medical files. "Waiting room's over there. No visitors yet."

She nodded, and kept walking, not trusting she could speak with the mountain of teeth in her mouth. Passing the indicated area, she headed for the elevator beyond.

"Jenna."

Too quiet for Humans to hear, the whisper shouted at her. She spun around, eyes wide. Castillo stood in the doorway of the waiting area. Opening her mouth to speak, the fangs got in the way. She clapped her hands over her mouth, blushing as she realized she'd shown them to the padre, and anybody happening to look in her direction. She looked wildly around the area. Too absorbed in their activities, no one had noticed.

"I understand." He sped forward, faster than Humanly

possible, and took her arm. "Let's get you somewhere safe." He pushed the call button.

Despite having heard that from far too many people, Whiskey gladly allowed him to take the lead. She nodded, hand still clasped across her mouth. The elevator door opened before them, and she stepped inside.

Castillo took her to the hospital parking structure, guiding her to a car. She knew he'd have one. She'd dropped her hand from her mouth, but the fangs were still there. Secure inside the vehicle, she explored them with her tongue, leery of the sharp scrape across her skin.

"Are you all right?"

Unable to help herself, she laughed, teeth flashing. "Sure thing, Padre." Her words slurred with inexperience. "Happens all the time." She waved at her mouth in explanation.

Castillo started the engine, heading toward the exit. "You will be able to control it, I promise."

"Will I?" An edge of panic flickered along her smile.

He glanced at her, sending a gentle brush of warm, dark chocolate against her mind. "Yes, you will. We all do."

She closed her mouth, the mental caress igniting tears, and stared out the passenger window.

Castillo paid the attendant, and pulled out into traffic. "I'm going to take you to my home." He glanced at her. "Not the rectory, nowhere near the U District. I swear on God's grace that you'll be safe while you're there, and free to leave at any time."

Whiskey continued to watch the passing scenery.

"Is that okay with you?"

"Can you get a message to my *Baruñal*? I lost the cell phone that had his number."

Disapproval colored the edges of his sincerity. "Yes, I will. I can't wait to meet him."

She couldn't help the grin crossing her face. "He feels the same way about you." She sniffled, and wiped at her eyes.

Again he looked at her, an answering smile on his face. "Does he?"

Whiskey nodded. "Oh, yeah." She thought a moment, tongue worrying the fangs. "He's older than you."

"I'll take that into consideration." He drove onto the highway, heading north.

"Then it's okay with me." Since she was pretty much stuck with him regardless of her suspicions, she realized she had the perfect opportunity to ask questions. "So you're Sanguire *and* a priest? That seems kind of odd."

"You'd think so, wouldn't you?" He shrugged, watching traffic. "As I told you before, I was raised Human. Like you. I followed in my adoptive family's spiritual footsteps."

Whiskey blinked. "You've been a priest for that long?"

Castillo laughed at her tone. "No, I took the vows about a hundred seventy-five years ago. And don't sound so horrified." He changed lanes to bypass a semi truck. "When you live as long as we do, a hundred years isn't all that much."

She turned that over in her head. Her intentions varied from day to day; wouldn't a Sanguire's, too? Did Valmont come here to assassinate her again, or had he changed his mind? That reminded her of the other Sanguire she felt at the hospital. "What about the others? When I felt you at the hospital, there were others there. I think three of them."

"No one you recognized?"

Whiskey shook her head.

"Chances are they were others who live in that area. Our population doesn't rival Humans, but there are many of us, especially in large urban areas. No doubt a proper census would surprise everyone."

She sighed, and leaned her head against the back of her seat. Her eyes drooped closed for a second.

"You're tired. You need rest. When we get to the house, you can have a nap."

"But, my teeth!"

"Have already sheathed."

Whiskey sat upright, searching her mouth, finding nothing amiss. "How the hell did that happen?"

"The conversation distracted you. Your body's automatic responses took over again. If you concentrate on them, they'll come out again."

She toyed with the idea of doing just that, but sudden fear

tingled down her spine at her lack of control. "I'll take your word for it."

He chuckled. "Right now you have little mastery, but that will pass. Lean back, nap. It'll be another hour before we get there."

CHAPTER THIRTY-FOUR

Whiskey woke in darkness. She lay on a soft bed, snuggled and cozy with sheets and a quilt. For the first time in a while she felt almost Human. Chuckling at the thought, she sat up and stretched. *How fucking bizarre, to feel Human when I'm not.*

"Hello."

Whiskey turned toward the voice with a hiss, automatically crouching on the bed, fangs extended. Her accelerated senses, no longer sluggish from sleep, pinpointed a young woman seated in a chair by the window. Her heart beat strong and steady, not racing as Whiskey's did. "Who the hell are you?"

The woman rose from her chair, and sauntered toward the bed. "My name is Aleya. I'm *kizarus*, a vessel."

"A...a what?" Whiskey recoiled from her confident manner. She scooted away as Aleya neared. The word sounded familiar.

Where had she heard it before? "A *kizarus*. What's that?" Her superior vision focused, noting her visitor's plump frame and heart-shaped face. Castillo wouldn't have allowed her in if she meant Whiskey harm. Would he? Her ever-present suspicion of him soothed her surprise.

Aleya sat on the bed, leaning back on her elbows in a seductive pose. "Some Sanguire don't have the time or inclination to hunt. Instead, they have *kizarusi*, select Humans who find the bloodletting arousing."

Kizarusi. Whiskey heard Fiona's voice in her head. "*They are a group of people who...serve us.*" She swallowed, uncertain whether to move closer, or flee. She tongued her new fangs. "You like getting bitten? Doesn't it hurt?"

Aleya sighed, purring with contentment as she tossed her head back, and revealed her neck. "It hurts. But pain can be a very pleasurable thing." She rolled over onto her side, and studied Whiskey. "It really depends on the Sanguire. Some are very capable of creating an enjoyable atmosphere; a hint of the forbidden, the erotic, goes a long way."

"You're a Goth."

She laughed, delighted. "Yes, I am."

More curious than concerned, Whiskey relaxed her stance, and edged closer. "Aren't you afraid I'll kill you?"

"Kill me?" The question puzzled Aleya before her eyes lit up in understanding. "That's right. Father Castillo said you were very new at this, just now maturing. You can't drain me like they do in the movies and books. Your stomach isn't nearly big enough." Aleya propped her head on her fist, sliding her free hand along the quilt in idle patterns. "Besides, Sanguire don't really need more than a few ounces to survive. Less than a liter every few days, actually."

Whiskey stared at her, anticipation and dread making her swallow. "Why exactly are you here?"

Aleya gave a lazy smile as she continued to caress the bed. "It's time for your first feeding. Father Castillo thought I could entice you."

A wave of heat washed through Whiskey, leaving her slightly sweaty in response. Her mouth watered and her heart thumped, the taste of blood right on the proverbial tip of her tongue. She held herself still, awaiting the expected stomach cramps, but none came. Instead, a strong wave of hunger made her tremble.

This is it, the final step. You'll never be able to go back. It didn't matter that she had no choice. The thought remained. Shaking her head, she backed away until her spine pressed against the headboard. In response, Aleya smiled and rolled over, crawling forward, stalking her. Whiskey didn't want to do this, didn't want to hurt her, didn't want her to leave. Before she could formulate an escape, the *kizarus* straddled her waist.

Aleya tossed her hair to one side, baring her neck. "We need this," she whispered. "You need this to survive. And I need you to do it."

Whiskey swallowed, breathing hard as she focused on the slow, steady pulse beating beneath the skin's surface. Her entire body shook with need. Still she held back. "I don't know—"

"Shhh." Aleya's hand slid behind Whiskey's head, guiding her closer. "You'll figure it out."

Whiskey nuzzled the soft skin. Inhaling, she committed Aleya's scent to memory. Her arms wrapped around the woman's body, holding her close, no longer being guided. She knew what to do. Elisibet remembered.

The first taste of copper was unlike anything Whiskey had ever had before. Ambrosia, an aphrodisiac to her body. Better than her inadvertent biting of that woman a few days ago, better than what she remembered of the meditation visions. Growling, she pressed into Aleya, suckling hard against the tear her teeth had rendered. In her arms, the woman sighed, undulating her hips against Whiskey. Her scent altered, smelling of musky arousal as well as blood, her pleasure ignited by the feeding. Whiskey felt no echoing sexual desire. Parched to the bone, she suffered a deep thirst. Aleya's blood relieved the ache, a soothing balm against the fading undernourished tremors that shook her. As Whiskey drank her fill, her nerves tingled in response, waking from a sleep that had lasted her entire life.

She found herself slowing, stopping. Completely relaxed for the first time in days, she gently licked the wounds she'd left on Aleya's neck. Aleya, smelling heavily of her arousal, hummed in satisfaction in her arms. Whiskey rolled over, setting her gently on the quilt. "Are you all right?"

"Very." Aleya sighed. Her eyes opened, heavy-lidded. She waved vaguely at the chair where she'd been seated. "Could you bring me my bag? I have first-aid supplies there."

Whiskey obeyed. "Do you need help?"

"No. I'm fine." Aleya sat up, seemingly none the worse for wear. She found a gauze pad and some tape. With deft hands, she covered the bite mark, and taped the padding down.

Uncertain, Whiskey stood awkwardly beside the bed, watching. What did you say to a woman whom you just bit? 'Gee, thanks, you were tasty?' She muffled a giggle.

As Aleya stood, Whiskey stepped back from the bed. Aleya tossed the strap of her bag across her uninjured shoulder. Stepping closer, she leaned in, and gave Whiskey a quick peck on the lips. "Thank you. You were very gentle."

Was that good or bad? "Um, thanks."

Aleya smiled, and patted her cheek. "See you around." She sauntered toward the door, hips swaying. She turned back to give Whiskey a wink.

Alone once more, Whiskey sank onto the bed. *That was... indescribable. How often do I need to feed? Will it feel like that every the time, or do I get used to it?* Aleya had said some Sanguire didn't prefer "hunting." What of those who did like to hunt? How did they go about it? Whiskey couldn't imagine Valmont having a *kizarus* or six wandering around behind him.

Whiskey threw herself backward on the bed, staring at the ceiling. Her hands roamed her skin, absently noting differences in sensation. Her teeth had retracted once she'd released Aleya. She used her tongue to explore the normal-feeling flesh. Concentrating, she closed her eyes, and thought of the taste of blood, slicing through skin with her teeth. Her eyes popped open as fangs slowly slid out from their sheaths. For a panicked moment she worried she'd be stuck with them as she'd been when she'd left the hospital. Her heart thumped, and she pushed away the thought of blood. She felt the fangs retract, and her heart slowed. Rubbing her face with her hands, she sat up.

Time to see if Castillo had found Dorst.

CHAPTER THIRTY-FIVE

Whiskey explored ahead with her mind, pleased to feel both the men she sought. At least they hadn't killed each other. Castillo seemed slightly distracted. She heard him tell Aleya goodbye. *That must be why.* With them together, she compared their strength. The difference in vigor between them intrigued her. She knew Dorst was at least three hundred years older than Castillo, probably more. She felt the inequality of their power, but couldn't say how. Maybe Fiona and her pack weren't different enough in age for her to catch it. Or maybe she wasn't far enough along to see it when she was there. There certainly hadn't been time to distinguish the finer points of strength last night at the hotel.

She stepped into the living room, relief easing through her at the sight of Dorst seated prim and proper on the couch. Knee guard and wristband spikes stuck out at all angles. "Better watch it, Reynhard. The padre will have a cow if you rip the upholstery with what you're wearing."

He stood, a tower of creaking black leather. Bending into a low bow, he showed her his partially bald pate. "My *Gasan*! It is truly a joy to be reunited with you."

Castillo, his Human guest gone, paused in the entryway to stare. His swarthy skin a little green around the edges, he looked a little the worse for wear.

Whiskey chuckled at Castillo's expression. "He's just being a smart-ass, Padre. Get up, Reynhard."

Dorst did so. "A wise woman once told me 'better a smart-ass than no ass at all.'"

"Good point." She snorted. Castillo had remained rooted in place. Concern colored her amusement. "Padre? You okay?"

He swallowed, eyes flickering to Dorst for a fraction of a moment. "You failed to tell me who your *Baruñal* was, Whiskey."

She frowned at him. "Did I need to?" She glanced at Dorst for an answer.

The specter gave her an apologetic smile. "It would have helped Father Castillo to understand the significance of the situation. He made the unfortunate error of bursting into my apartment, intent on taking me to task for my incompetence as your guide along the *Ñíri Kurám*."

"Damn." She turned to Castillo. "I told you he was older than you."

"That you did." Castillo finally stepped into the room. "I thought I'd have the opportunity to...explain my dissatisfaction with his leadership before he got the upper hand. Had I known he was *Sañur Gasum* Dorst, I would have gone about it in a more circumspect fashion."

"What happened?"

Dorst gave an elegant wave. "That's neither here nor there. Suffice it to say, the father learned from his error in judgment, and it won't happen again." He raised a hairless brow at Castillo. "Will it?"

They stared at one another for a full minute before Castillo barely raised his chin. "Not without provocation."

A slow grin crossed Whiskey's face; she admired Castillo's obstinacy. Beside her, Dorst put on a show of being miffed, but didn't pursue the topic. She ignored him. "I'm sorry I didn't think to tell you, Padre. It didn't occur to me that it'd be an issue."

"It's all right, Whiskey. I understand. Chances are good I would have believed it was someone attempting to scam you." Nearing them, he held out his hands.

Whiskey took them in hers, squeezing. "It's kind of hard for me to take in. It probably isn't any easier for you, huh?"

"It's had its moments."

Dorst cleared his throat. "Now that the pleasantries are completed, perhaps you can bring me up to date, my *Gasan*? The last time I attempted to call your cell phone, Fiona responded. Considering your lack of faith in her motives, I found that rather surprising. She didn't know your location, and was rather put out at the situation."

They sat upon the comfortable chairs and couch. Whiskey filled them in on what had happened since she'd last seen them. She had to do some backtracking to catch Castillo up with earlier events, but eventually he, too, knew almost everything. Dorst didn't bat an eyelid as Whiskey confessed everything to Castillo. She'd already told him far more than she'd wanted to when he'd searched her out the night before. It seemed right to finish the job now. The only item she glossed over was Dominick's death. She'd admitted to being there with Fiona's crew when it happened, and having a hand in his beating. She hated seeing the disappointment on Castillo's face. How would he feel if she told him she'd personally landed the killing blow on a defenseless Human street kid?

"Where are Alphonse and Zebediah?" Dorst asked.

Whiskey shrugged. "Your guess is as good as mine, Reynhard. For all I know they went back to Fiona's place after the padre got away from them." She looked at Castillo. "You didn't hurt them, did you?"

Castillo pursed his lips. "You didn't leave me much choice. They were determined to keep me from following you. It took several minutes, and I had to put them both down." He looked down at his lap. "It's been a long time since I've had to do that."

She wondered how that would square with Castillo's spiritual vows. "I'm sorry. I didn't want to put you in that kind of situation."

He smiled reassurance. "Don't worry about it. It's just been awhile. I'm more of a historian than a warrior, that's all."

Dorst sipped at his tea. "I doubt they'd return to their former leader. They'd know that Fiona would be furious with them for changing allegiance. While their choice of hairstyle is suspect, they've never struck me as being particularly ignorant."

Whiskey indicated his three mohawks. "You should talk."

He gave her a toothy grin. "And frequently do."

She laughed. Castillo watched them both, keen interest in his eyes. "What are you thinking, Padre?"

"I'm thinking I'm an extremely fortunate man."

Not understanding his burgeoning enthusiasm, she shook her head. "I don't get it."

"Many of our people don't believe in the prophecy. If they do, they don't admit it. Yet, here I sit, watching it unfold before me. Few will be able to claim that in the months and years to come."

Dorst looked on with amusement. "What will you do with this knowledge, Father? Write a book? The memoirs of our dear friend, Jenna Davis, the poor homeless Sanguire—raised among Humans, yet destined to become the greatest *Ninsumgal* our people have ever known?"

"If she'd allow it."

What were they talking about? Whiskey balked at the eager expression on Castillo's face. "No. That's stupid, Padre. Nobody'd read it."

"You're wrong. If you are the incarnation of *Ninsumgal* Elisibet Vasilla, then any book written on the subject will be read by every Sanguire in the world, even non-Europeans."

"Then you people need to find better books." She held up her hand to forego Castillo's further argument. "No. No more talk of a book. I've got more important shit to deal with right now."

Castillo sank back into his chair, an apologetic expression on his face.

"The foremost of which is getting you through the final meditation." Dorst reached into his jacket, pulling out a copy of the Book. "Father Castillo said you had none of your belongings, so I took the liberty of bringing this with me."

Whiskey ignored the tome. "The foremost of which is locating Alphonse and Zebediah, and finding out what happened to Daniel and Cora. Fiona doesn't take rejection well; she's going to keep coming after me until this is over."

"I will gladly search for them in your stead, my *Gasan*." Dorst held the Book out to her. "In the meantime, you must finish the last meditation. You've enjoyed your first feeding; it's time for the *Ñiri Kurám* to end."

She looked at the Book with a combination of enthusiasm and distaste. It was smaller than the one she'd used, the binding a deeper brown, the ribbon bookmark a crimson slash against the pages. Listening carefully, she heard a light heartbeat coming from the item. She almost didn't want to touch it. *What the hell? Is it psychological? Addictive or something?* "There's no time for that."

"Whiskey, *Sañur Gasum* Dorst is correct. You can't go much longer without causing irreparable damage to yourself."

She scowled at Castillo. "What are you talking about? What damage?"

"Forgive me, my *Gasan*, but if you do not step off the Strange Path, you'll become lost upon it. Your mind will continue to make changes, distort your abilities, and alter your perceptions. This final meditation is designed to halt the acceleration process." Dorst looked appropriately sober. "Without it, you'll go criminally insane."

Whiskey couldn't help but quip, "Meaning I'm not already?" Neither answered her as she considered her options. *Not just crazy, but "criminally insane." That would be, what? Elisibet on steroids?* "What are the symptoms?" *Is that what happened to her?*

Castillo audibly ground his teeth together. "Now isn't the time for your stubborn streak to rear its head, Whiskey. This is serious. Your sanity depends upon this."

She physically angled her body to Dorst, giving Castillo the literal cold shoulder. "Answer the question."

"It will be similar to what happened after your first meditation—synaesthesia, extreme sensitivity to everything around you, migraines, nausea. Rather than dissipate, these effects will increase in magnitude until you lose your mind. There will come a point where you'll no longer be able to concentrate well enough to do the final meditation at all." No rebuke glowed in his eyes.

His complete acceptance of her lead bolstered her confidence. "How long before I can expect it to start?"

"At any time. It's rare that anyone refuses to step off the Strange Path, so reports are varied. It could be an hour, or a week. Depending on how fast symptoms develop, you may have days or hours before you'll reach the point of no return."

Castillo sprang to his feet. "What do you think you're doing?"

Dorst gave him a mild look. "I'm answering my *Ninsumgal's* questions, Father. She cannot make an informed choice without the proper information."

"You're her *Baruñal*, for God's sake! You're supposed to protect her when she can't protect herself."

Dorst's tone deepened with warning. "She's my liege, priest. My *Ninsumgal*."

Castillo stared down at him, then turned to Whiskey. "He swore allegiance to you?"

She shifted beneath the power of his gaze. "He called it fealty."

"Dear God in Heaven." Castillo fell back into his chair with a groan.

Whiskey wasn't sure what his problem was, so she ignored him. "Show me the meditation now. I'll keep the Book with me. If things get too bad, I'll do what has to be done."

Dorst accepted her decision, opening the Book to its mark. Castillo remained in his chair, a nonverbal grumble emanating from him every so often. His annoyance palpable, he seemed unable to sit still. It made concentration difficult. Whiskey finally asked him leave the room. He did so, registering a final argument over her decision before going into the kitchen. He continued to bang around there, but it didn't bother her as much. The lesson went quickly, her understanding of written Sanguire coming along as fast as her ability to speak the language.

She closed the Book, and put it into a cargo pocket of her pants. "Will I get sick again?"

"No sickness this time, though you may feel exhaustion."

Whiskey chewed her lower lip. Now what? She rose, and went to stare out the living room window. A typical suburban street filled her unseeing vision, complete with a white picket fence around one house. Kids played in their yards or rode bicycles along the sidewalks, a few cars occupied driveways, and somewhere she heard a rock band rehearsing in someone's garage. Behind her, Dorst remained silent. Castillo had quieted in the kitchen. Only the faint dark chocolate essence let her know of his presence.

Finding Alphonse and Zebediah, while one of her higher priorities, wouldn't do Daniel or Cora much good. Whiskey didn't know how far Fiona would go to get information out of them. If she was anything like Elisibet, they might already be dead. Dismissing the thought, Whiskey chastised herself. Elisibet had the might of an entire European nation behind her. Fiona was a young Sanguire with an addiction to power. There were laws and regulations in place to keep her from going too far. Weren't there? She turned back to the room. "Is there a penalty for murder?"

Dorst's expression flickered in surprise. "There is. A Sanguire accused of murder is turned in to the local Sanguire authorities. Depending on the victim's status, the case may be brought before the Low Court or the High. If a ruling of guilt occurs in the Low Court, appeal to the High Court is an option. The High Court's judgment is final."

"What do you mean, depending on the victim's status?"

"He means whether or not the victim holds office in the government, or comes from a ruling family." Castillo came into the room bearing a tray with sandwiches, and a pitcher of iced tea. He set it on the coffee table, and sat down. "We have no caste system, per se, but some family lines are more highly thought of than others."

"That doesn't sound fair."

"It's not all bad. As *Sañur Gasum* Dorst has stated, the High Court's ruling is final. At least with the Low, you have an opportunity to appeal the first ruling." He poured them each a glass of tea.

Whiskey accepted one. "Do you think Fiona would kill any of them?"

Dorst leaned back, his face a parody of deep thought. "She's a smart woman, despite her apparent anger management issues. I doubt she'd do any permanent damage. To my knowledge, she's never been in serious trouble."

She remembered golden eyes coming out of the night to rescue her, the swift and decisive attack on the Human boys in the clearing. Immediately, Dominick stood before her, staring with his blank eyes, the crunching sound of his nose as she hit him echoing in her ears. A sudden thought occurred to her. "Won't I face charges for Dominick's death?"

"Not in a Sanguire court. You still may have to answer to Human law for your involvement. For the most part, however, we avoid such legal repercussions."

"Of course not." Dorst waved Castillo's words away. "He was Human. Prey."

Whiskey felt the floor drop out from under her. "You're joking."

Dorst raised an eyebrow. "Human law does not apply to Sanguire, my *Gasan*. It cannot. They don't know of our existence; how can we be held accountable within their legal system? What would happen to a Sanguire who received a life sentence for a crime? And, considering our ability to heal, it would take a lot more than the average capital punishments currently in effect to kill us."

Castillo appeared more somber. "It's true. As a race, we've always had separate laws from Humans. Few of our people spend much time with them. Those that do follow the general regulations to blend in. Humans are not seen as equal in any way."

She remembered that Castillo had been raised among Humans, as had she. He showed his displeasure with the accepted point of view. "So, Fiona's not accountable if she kills a Human?"

Dorst at least attempted to look contrite. "No. Accidents happen."

Whiskey growled under her breath. *There's a whole new take on racism.* "So you don't think she's killed Daniel or Cora. What about torture? What if she's hurt them? Would that get her in trouble?"

Castillo fielded this question. "It would depend on the circumstances, but probably not. Sanguire society is different from Human. A *ninna* or *lugal* rules her or his people however she or he sees fit. The individuals in question can always walk away."

"Like Alphonse and Zebediah did."

"Correct."

"I want them found, and brought here. Is that okay, Padre?"

"I'd rather they weren't." The spike of bitterness in Castillo's warm chocolate essence highlighted his ambivalence. "This is a safe house that no one knows exists. Some day you may need to avoid them or the people they become involved with, and this haven will have been compromised."

Dorst tsked. "Providing she stays in the area. Your thinking is so provincial, Father."

Whiskey blinked. The idea of permanently leaving the Pacific Northwest wasn't something she'd considered other than the occasional panicked thought of escape. "I think we're getting ahead of ourselves."

"Indeed we are, my *Gasan*. Should I find the unruly younglings, where do you want them?"

"I need you with me. I want the padre to look for them." Whiskey saw Castillo's shoulders drop, but didn't let it affect her decision. She needed someone completely behind her, and Castillo would argue with her every step of the way. Alphonse and Zebediah were young enough to take her leadership in stride; Castillo had more experience in the world, making him less inclined to follow her regardless of the fact that she could mentally overpower him. "You're better suited to find them; you know the streets, and where people who look like them hang out. Take them wherever you think they'll be safe from Fiona."

"You're going after her."

She wanted to look away from his frustrated accusation. It took everything she had to keep eye contact, and not back down.

"I can't leave Cora and Daniel with her, Padre. And she won't stop. If she doesn't get me under her thumb, she'll inform the *Agrun Nam*. Either way, I'm screwed."

He ran a hand through his unruly hair. "It's a bit late for that, else Valmont wouldn't be here now."

Dorst set his glass of tea down, and stood. "Fiona Bodwrda has a vindictive streak that defies measurement. My *Gasan* is correct in her speculation. Fiona continues to be a danger. She'll have no compunctions about filling the *Agrun Nam's* collective ears with lies until they feel they have no other recourse but to kill Whiskey."

"I should go with you. Maybe I can help—"

"No, Padre." Whiskey put her hand on his shoulder. "I need you to find Alphonse and Zebediah before Fiona does. I need you to set up a safe place for them and the others." She squeezed his shoulder. "I'm hoping I can talk some sense into her, not get into a pissing match."

He looked unconvinced. But after several moments of silence, he raised his chin.

She breathed a sigh of relief, standing. "I don't have my cell phone anymore."

Dorst shrugged. "No worries. I have the good Father Castillo's number, and he has mine."

Castillo stood as Dorst spun, and stalked toward the door. "Whiskey."

She turned to him.

"Be safe. Don't take any chances."

Whiskey smiled. "C'mon, Padre. I've lasted this long on the streets. I'm tougher than I look." She stepped into his arms, startling them both with her newfound easy manner. Something inside had loosened its hold on her during this transformation. For the first time in a long while, she accepted the gesture, returning the comfort it gave her. "I'll be careful. I promise."

"You always keep your promises."

She laughed, and followed Dorst.

CHAPTER THIRTY-SIX

"Are you certain that confrontation is the proper course of action, my *Gasan*?"

Whiskey looked away from the passing scenery to study Dorst's profile. "What else is there? If I am who you think I am, I can't tuck tail and run every time there's trouble, especially in the beginning." *God, I am crazy. I have to be tranked out of my mind, and in a straitjacket somewhere. That's all there is to it. Bring on the happy drugs!*

He gave a slight nod of acknowledgment. "Yet we are going into a potentially volatile situation. I'm assuming you'll wish me to stand aside. Fiona is well over a hundred years old; she may overpower you, could possibly kill you."

Over a hundred years old? Crap! "The padre's almost four hundred. I held him off pretty well." She returned her gaze to the passenger window, analyzing her encounter with Castillo the night before. *I did, didn't I? At least until I got sick.*

"Father Castillo is a self-proclaimed scholar, not used to such tactics. He lives alone among Humans rather than with his own kind. He has little experience in holding his own with an adult Sanguire, let alone a fledgling such as yourself."

"I can't leave it like this, Reynhard!" Whiskey scowled at him. She didn't need him chipping away at her already questionable self-confidence. "Two-thirds of her pack have put themselves in danger for my benefit. I can't repay that by leaving them to their fate. Fiona won't let them be; she's got a vindictive streak that rivals Elisibet's. She'll hunt them down and, if she doesn't kill them, she'll make them wish they were dead."

"They did so because of your unexpected power, not because they owed you anything or felt the need to act on Human principles and ideals."

"Daniel and Cora did it before my power became the issue."

He continued to drive calmly down the highway, her words having no effect. Her mood worsened as the miles passed. She had no plan except to barge into the house, and demand to see Cora and Daniel. Once she verified they were okay, she'd give them the choice to leave with her or remain. Considering some of the memories she'd acquired from Elisibet, she doubted either of them would be in good enough shape to walk out with her.

"You've shown some aptitude for knives." Dorst reached into his coat pocket, extracting a plain blade, the one that had belonged to his previous mistress. "Take this one. It will keep you well."

She reached out, the hilt fitting neatly in her hand. She knew if she pulled it from the sheath, she would see ancient Damascus steel.

Flash.

A younger Dorst knelt before her, long brown hair surrounding his face, the same image she'd had of him before though much clearer. He wore black clothing, and a burgundy sash, with her sigil stitched in silver thread across his chest.

Looking down, she saw the old dagger in her hand, plain and brown, but recognizable—her father's knife, the one he had always worn. She carefully unsheathed it, staring at the random squiggled designs of a Damascus blade.

"I believe he would have wanted you to have it, my *Gasan*. It was his favorite."

Flash.

"You gave this to Elisibet. That's where I've seen you before."

A slow smile grew on his face. "I did. It wasn't long after her *Ñíri Kurám*. Her father hadn't been buried for more than a month. In the rush of preparing her to lead, and keeping up with matters of state, everyone forgot she was a child mourning the loss of her father."

Whiskey swallowed against a lump in her throat. "How old was she when he died?"

"Twelve. Her mother passed the veil when Elisibet was four. She'd been traveling the province, and been discovered by a pack of Humans." He paused a moment. "They tortured, and killed her."

She couldn't help but see the correlation between Elisibet's childhood and her own. Both parents dead, suddenly thrust into the middle of a situation over which she had no control. At least she was eighteen. She couldn't imagine the mess she'd have made of things if this had happened when she was twelve. "I guess that could be why she hated Humans so much."

"After the attack on his wife, *Ki'an Gasan* Solveig, *Usumgal* Maximal would allow no non-allied Humans on our lands. *Ninsumgal* Elisibet carried on what her father had begun. She widened our territory, and set up treaties with other Sanguire in the world. I think she hoped to create a permanent homeland for us."

"Did it work?"

"Not really. Humans outstrip us when it comes to reproduction. For every one of us, there are hundreds of them. We may not be easy to kill, but it can be done." He took the upcoming off-ramp. The car slowed down as he continued. "That was part of the reason the *Agrun Nam* began agitating against her policies. In response to our expansion, the Humans became more organized in their resistance. Many of us died in what could be termed as guerrilla attacks."

They drove through a familiar suburb. As much as Whiskey wanted to continue her history lesson, now wasn't the time. They'd arrive soon. Having both Dorst and Castillo at her disposal would be intriguing, providing she survived this. One man firmly believed the party line, and the other held a more liberal inclination. She'd get a chance to see issues from two sides, be able to sort through the propaganda, to understand the bigger picture and how it related to her.

"How do you wish to do this, my *Gasan*?" They were a few blocks away.

As quickly and safely as possible. "We'll go in together, but you hang back. I don't want Fiona thinking you're running the show here. She needs to deal with me."

"As you wish, *Ninsumgal*. I will not promise to remain completely aloof, however. If she attacks, I will defend you."

The house loomed in the windshield. "I'm hoping it won't come to that." She reached out with her mind, locating the sickly sweet flowers. Beneath it, a vague sense of ashes fluttered. *At least Cora's still breathing.* Of Daniel she found nothing, but the sensation of sulfur and pepper told her Manuel and Bronwyn were both in attendance.

Dorst pulled into the driveway. "Let's do this," she stated. She slid the knife into her pocket. They climbed out of the car, and walked to the front door. Considering the reason for their visit, Whiskey thought it ridiculous to ring the bell. Instead, she opened the unlocked door and entered, Dorst at her heels.

She'd never stood in the entryway before. The living room looked odd from this angle, but still recognizable. Manuel sprawled on the couch, playing one of the video games on the large screen television. He gave Whiskey a look of utter hatred. Shirtless, a white bandage covered his abdomen. She saw no one else. A quick scan with her mind showed Bronwyn somewhere on the second floor.

Stepping forward, she heard Dorst quietly close the door behind them. "Where's Fiona?"

Manuel ignored her.

"Fine, I'll find her myself." Whiskey opened her mind, detecting Fiona's presence beneath her feet. *Great. Didn't realize this place had a basement.* She had a stab of memory from her last meditation; Elisibet and Valmont in a dungeon working over some poor Human. Faint surprise washed over her as the expected stomach cramps didn't recur. Of course they wouldn't. She'd fed today. She was starving yesterday. That's what the sickness was. "You know where the basement entry is?"

"Possibly through the kitchen?" Dorst suggested. "That is the American architectural standard."

She nodded, and led the way. The dishwasher hummed along, the counters freshly wiped down. If she didn't know better, this was any normal suburban household. She wondered if the pack did the cleaning, or if Fiona hired a maid service. *Duh. She's rich.* Shaking off the mundane distraction, she glanced around to see a door in the corner. Cracking it open, her superior vision saw stairs going down. "Here."

Dorst pulled the door open further, and slipped past her. "May I, my *Gasan?*"

While she didn't think Fiona would set up a literal ambush down there, better to placate Dorst. He hadn't yet become difficult, but that didn't mean he couldn't. He'd be far less likely to roll over than Castillo. "Go ahead."

He slid into the darkness, his leather jacket sucking in the little available light.

Whiskey kept her attention split between the rooms below, and the rest of the house. Manuel and Bronwyn would be part of a trap, coming up from behind to block their escape. Manuel hadn't moved from the couch, continuing to play the video game. Bronwyn also remained in place. Whiskey felt no reassurance. Seething anger rolled off Bronwyn, dark and pungent with her peppery essence. Whiskey felt a mental urge to sneeze at the nonexistent aroma.

Dorst opened a door at the bottom of the stairs. A sound of rubber on rubber, and the strong smell of blood wafting up indicated a good insulation seal had been installed around the frame. Now bathed in a warm, yellow glow, he asked, "Would you care to join us, Whiskey?"

She followed him down into the darkness.

CHAPTER THIRTY-SEVEN

Dorst waited for her to reach him before stepping into the basement. His form partially blocked her view until she moved to one side.

The right half of the basement resembled a family room. Thick granite tiles covered the floor, decorated by a sectional throw rug of burgundy and gold. In the far corner a fireplace crackled, warm and inviting behind a glass screen. An over-stuffed black leather couch and loveseat pinned the rug down, both angled toward an oak entertainment center with a large screen television. The accent tables were of the same granite as the floor, polished and gleaming in the golden light of two lamps.

The smell came from the other side of the room. Burgundy velvet curtains had been hung to section off the two halves, but the heavy material had been gathered aside, and tied back to the walls. The granite tile abruptly cut off, revealing coarse concrete beneath. The cement floor sloped ever so slightly toward a drain, rusty and stained with what was clearly both old and fresh blood.

Daniel hung here, unconscious, his naked torso streaked with crimson gore. It looked so much like Whiskey's vision of Valmont and Elisibet in the dungeon, she automatically glanced at the floor for a grisly pile of skin. She swallowed in relief upon seeing none. Could Fiona go that far without getting into trouble with Sanguire law?

Beyond him stood four steel-barred detention cells. Each no more than five feet square, they held no available facilities beyond a plastic bucket in a corner. Two stood empty, silent sentinels to the macabre activities taking place here. One door stood open, presumably the cell within which Daniel had been imprisoned. The other held an occupant. Cora knelt with her forehead on the floor. A false ceiling of metal bars had been lowered from above. Locked in place, it forced her to remain crouched with three feet of headroom. Strong rope bound her forearms to her body, and metal shackles encircled her bloody wrists. Her clothes were the same she wore two days ago.

Disgusted, Whiskey slipped past Dorst, intent on freeing them both. Swift movement from the seating area caught her attention, and she paused.

"*Sañur Gasum* Dorst, what a pleasure to see you again." Fiona glided from where she'd been seated on the couch to stand between the new arrivals, and her prisoners. "And you brought my wayward child home, too."

Whiskey stepped closer with a growl. "I'm not your child." Her blood pulsed with anger, throbbing in time with a dull pressure at her temples.

Fiona made a show of looking around the room. "Do you see anyone else with a better claim?" When Whiskey didn't answer, she continued. "You are still a child, my little *lamma*. A headstrong, recalcitrant one, but a child all the same. You need strong adult guidance, and an education before you can...take your proper place among our people. I'm the best choice for that."

"Bullshit."

"My point exactly." Fiona dismissed her, turning her attention to Dorst. "Unless you take prior claim? You did call me when you arrived here in search of her."

The last bit of the puzzle fell into place. Fiona and her pack had been actively hunting for Whiskey on Dorst's request. They hadn't accidentally stumbled upon her when they did. They may have been following her for some time before they decided to intercede on her behalf against the boys who'd kidnapped her. Whiskey felt a lightening in her soul, her supposed obligation to Fiona not weighing quite as much as it had.

Dorst lifted his chin. "I have no claim here."

Fiona smiled, and made a welcoming gesture toward the seating area. "Please, sit and relax. I'll have Bronwyn bring down a snack. Unless you'd prefer—" She glanced innocently behind her at Daniel's hanging form.

"That is entirely up to my *Gasan*; I'm here at her disposal."

A flash of confusion crossed Fiona's face.

Whiskey enjoyed the expression, a grim smile on her lips. "Get Daniel down from there."

Dorst paused no more than a second, before moving to comply with Whiskey's order.

"No!"

Fiona raced forward, and cut him off. The smell of sweet flowers filled Whiskey's mind, counteracted by amber and steel. Whiskey almost saw the vapors of power emanating from each of them. Fiona glared at Dorst for half a minute before going white. The flowery essence faded, and Dorst stood there with a gentle golden glow about him.

That's a first. What the hell is that?

"Do not mistake my position as weakness, child." He moved around Fiona, reaching Daniel's side with no more opposition.

The kindness in his voice caused Fiona to flush to the roots of her red hair. She snarled and strode forward, stopping just out of Whiskey's reach. "Who are you to give him orders?"

"Who do you think I am?"

Fiona stared at Whiskey. "You can't be serious!" She glanced over at Dorst who now had Daniel in a fireman's carry, bringing his unconscious form to the couch. "This is ridiculous! She's a child, a cheap imitation. The prophecy is nothing but the codswallop of an ancient witch who should have done us the favor of dying a thousand years ago."

Dorst laid Daniel down. Ignoring Fiona, he awaited another order from Whiskey.

"Get Cora out of that cage." He bowed his head, and proceeded to cross the room. "Do you need the key?"

He chuckled. "Even if I did, I doubt you'd get it from her without a fight."

Fiona tucked her chin, glaring at Whiskey.

"I think you're right." Had she known it'd be this easy, she'd have been here hours ago. She silently swore, wondering how much grief she could have spared Cora and Daniel if she'd arrived earlier. Fiona's arrogant voice brought Whiskey out of her self-castigation.

"You are not Elisibet Vasilla reborn."

Whiskey shrugged, noting for the first time how bright the lamps were in the room. Her skin burned from the exposure, almost as bad as being outside in sunlight. "Maybe not. We'll see what happens. We both know I look like her, though. That's why you wanted me as part of your sick little family." A squeal of metal caused her to wince. Dorst had the cell door open. The pressure behind her eyes grew, not quite becoming an ache.

"I see. You wish to play the game on your own." Fiona smiled, baring her teeth. "Tell me, little *lamma*, how do you plan to do that? With him?" She indicated Dorst with a sharp nod of her head. "He is the master of manipulation, sweet Whiskey. How do you know he's not going to use you in a similar manner?"

Dorst ignored her jibes, though he clearly heard them. He had Cora out of the tiny cell, and untied. She lay on her side, whimpering as she unfurled from her forced fetal shape. He produced a lock pick for the manacles at her wrist.

Whiskey couldn't deny Fiona's suspicions. She'd had them herself, needed them to survive in a world that didn't give a shit about a throwaway orphan kid. She'd given up trying to explain the depth of her confidence. She shrugged. "I don't. I trust him not to, that's all."

Fiona burst into laughter. "My goodness! How naive for such

a street-hardened youngling." She turned to Dorst, attempting to bring him into the conversation. "You'll have an excellent time with this one, *Sañur Gasum*. Perhaps, when you're finished with her, you will allow me the privilege of killing her for you."

The manacles popped off Cora's wrists, clattering to the concrete floor. Dorst helped her stand, offering a solicitous arm, ignoring Fiona's words.

"Get them out of here, Reynhard," Whiskey said. "Take them upstairs."

"That will not be possible, my *Gasan*. I cannot leave you here alone." He escorted Cora to the loveseat.

Whiskey's stomach soured. *Honeymoon's over.* "That was an order," she said with a growl. "Get them to the car so we can leave."

Dorst gave her a deep bow. "Perhaps you could escort our new friends to the vehicle. I'll remain here with dear Fiona. We have so much catching up to do."

Fiona's already pale complexion blanched at his veiled threat. The wicked smile on her face disappeared, and her eyes flitted around the room. She backed away from Whiskey, teeth bared.

Pinching the bridge of her nose, Whiskey tried not to let her anger take hold of her. "Did you or did you not swear fealty to me?" She ignored the strangled sound from Fiona.

"I did." Dorst's voice held both a defeated, and regretful tone.

Whiskey raised her head to glare at him. "Then you will take Cora and Daniel out of here, put them in the car, and make certain Bronwyn and Manuel don't get any wild ideas. Understood?"

He studied her for a long moment, before lifting his chin. "As you wish, my liege."

"No." Cora's whispered word was clearly audible as Dorst helped her to stand. Able to keep her feet without faltering, she'd need blood and time to heal.

"Do as you're told," Fiona snapped. The panicked expression had left her face.

Whiskey smiled at Cora, taking in the fearful look. "I'll be fine. Go with Reynhard; help him with Daniel."

"If she can't have you, she wants you dead!"

Moving away from the door would give Fiona an escape route. Whiskey remained where she stood. "That's not going to happen, Cora. Trust me." She reached for Cora's mind, soothing her emotions. "You asked me to remember who assisted me. I do remember. Take Daniel and get out."

Unshed tears made Cora's eyes glassy, but she complied. Dorst picked up Daniel again, who moaned at the jostling, and Cora led their way to the door. When she passed behind Whiskey, she reached out, and caressed her arm.

Whiskey loosened up when the upper door closed softly behind them. *Another obligation bites the dust.* Turning her attention to Fiona, she saw she wasn't the only one relaxing her guard.

"Isn't this cozy?" Fiona strolled to an end table, retrieving the glass of blood wine she'd been drinking when Whiskey arrived. Looking up at the ceiling, she traced the path of footsteps to the door. "It's just as well. They were both far too weak to be here. Not like the others." She sat on the loveseat with graceful ease. "So, tell me. Was *Sañur Gasum* at the hotel? Is that what happened to Alphonse and Zebediah?"

Startled pleasure rolled through Whiskey. *She doesn't know!* A slow grin crossed her face. "No, he wasn't."

"Certainly you must have had some kind of help then. A youngling such as yourself could not have taken on four adult Sanguire."

"I don't know. I did well enough with Bronwyn and Manuel." Whiskey came around the couch to perch easily on its arm.

Fiona made a face. "Yes. They didn't take into account your increased physical strength and flexibility. Neither is too happy with the outcome."

That set off warning bells. Whiskey didn't care for either of them, but it didn't mean she enjoyed the idea of them being tortured for fun and profit by Fiona. "What did you do?"

She arched an eyebrow in response. "What any good matriarch should do. Manuel is still healing, but I made certain his paramour understood the result of her failure."

Whiskey shivered. Alphonse and Zebediah had done the

smart thing by not coming back. Cora and Daniel had remained by Fiona's side despite their differing opinions, and look what it had gotten them. If Fiona punished the people who were loyal to her, what would she do to those who were complete traitors? She forced herself to return to the conversation. "Alphonse and Zebediah won't be back, I think."

Fiona's eyes narrowed. "And how do you know this?"

"Because they helped me get away from you. Last time I saw them, they were pinning down another Sanguire so I could escape."

Whiskey savored the long moment of stunned silence. It almost counteracted the growing headache pulsing in her temples. The grin returned to her face as Fiona stared at her.

"What...?"

Whiskey laughed aloud. It didn't help when Fiona's pique showed, a thin line creasing the smooth skin between her eyes. Whiskey laughed harder, pointing at her. Her head throbbed vigorously, but seeing Fiona's perplexed reaction made it worth the pain. "Oh, my God! This is hilarious! This is just totally fucking with your head." She slid from the arm, and onto the couch, holding her abdomen as she let her mirth carry her away.

Fiona held her chin to her chest, glaring at the amused response. "Alphonse and Zebediah would never follow your lead, child."

Still chuckling, Whiskey made a show of wiping her eyes. "They would if they'd been overpowered."

"By who? You said *Sañur Gasum* Dorst wasn't there."

Whiskey stretched out, thumping first one boot, then the other onto the coffee table. She crossed her ankles. "By me." She suppressed another round of chortles as Fiona stared at her.

"By—"

"Me."

The annoyance faded from Fiona's face as she considered this information. She sipped lightly at her wine, staring at nothing.

Whiskey wondered how long she needed to keep up the arrogant facade. Dorst had gotten Cora and Daniel out of the house. They waited for her to join them. Questing with her mind, she felt her *Baruñal's* strong presence as he dissuaded Manuel from getting involved. Of Bronwyn, there was only the light sensation, still in another part of the house. Whiskey understood why she had a headache and saw strange things; they were the symptoms of the *Ñíri Kurám* going too long. She had to get the final meditation out of the way before long. She needed to get out of here. She had what she came for; no reason to make things worse.

Something stopped her. Seattle was Fiona's stomping grounds. She'd been here with her pack of sycophants when Dorst first arrived on an indirect tip from Castillo's report to the *Agrun Nam*. Maybe Cora and the others would be free of Fiona, but she'd be here to collect more twisted Sanguire rebels. *What if Valmont finds her?* That wasn't a pleasant idea. Someone several hundred years old working with Fiona to take care of old grudges? *She can tell him I started on the streets here. He might be able to locate the people I hung out with.* Considering what Whiskey "remembered" about Valmont, he'd ruthlessly use Gin as leverage if he ever found her. He'd been trained by the worst monster, Elisibet Vasilla. *I have to put a stop to this before it starts.* A chill washed through her. She had to deal with Fiona before she left this house. When Fiona spoke, it brought Whiskey back to the conversation with a jolt.

"I don't believe you." Fiona waved vaguely with her glass. "Granted, you're stronger than I expected considering your stage of development, but that means nothing. I exhibited abnormal strength when I went through the *Ñíri Kurám*. It's no stretch of the imagination that others do, as well."

The words spilled out of Whiskey's mouth before she realized what she said. "How about a little one-on-one, just for comparison's sake?"

Fiona froze, glass halfway to her lips, staring over the rim. "What do you mean?"

What the hell am I doing? "You and me, no weapons, no holds barred."

"I do not grapple in the dirt like a common peasant, *puru um*." Fiona's words dripped with acid.

It took a moment for the translation to work its way through

Whiskey's brain. Had she just called her a...hillbilly? She was going to have to ask Reynhard or the padre about that one. She put her feet on the floor, and scooted to the end of the couch. "No, idiot. This isn't the WWF. I'm talking no holds barred here." She tapped her temple for emphasis.

"No."

Whiskey looked to see that Dorst had returned. Delaying the inevitable, she asked, "Are Cora and Daniel safe?"

"Yes, my *Gasan*. Manuel has decided to remain in the living area, and Bronwyn is unable to leave her room. It's time for us to vacate the premises."

Wondering why Bronwyn couldn't leave her room, Whiskey shook her head. "Fiona and I aren't finished. Go back to the car, and wait for me."

"I will not leave you here alone. You're making a mistake."

Whiskey ignored him, and looked back at Fiona. *Wouldn't be the first time, pal.* "If Reynhard swears to butt out, what do you say? Do you think you're stronger than me?"

Fiona studied her, her expression speculative. "I know I am. But would he stand by his word? He has a reputation for deviousness."

"I trust his vow. He has never gone back on his word, not in all the centuries he's been alive."

"*Ninsumgal—*"

"Shut up, Reynhard." She stifled surprise when he did. A thrill of pleasure vied against a strange sadness. He'd sworn fealty to her, he'd do as she said, no matter what it entailed. As much as she wished he could be her friend and confidante, that would never, ever be. Dorst would forever remain a servant. *What the fuck! I don't have to go that route. I'm not the Sanguire Second Coming!*

After a long pause, Fiona spoke. "I'll take you up on that." She pointed at Dorst. "But he swears more than to stay out of it. He'd better swear to allow me to leave when I win."

Whiskey stood, and turned her back on Fiona. "Reynhard, swear to me that you'll stay out of our little contest here and, should Fiona win, you'll give her twenty-four hours head start."

"And if I say no?"

The smile on her face contrasted with her lowered chin. He was putting on a show for Fiona. *Reynhard's always about the drama.* She glared at him through her bangs. "I'm not asking."

Dorst showed little emotional response to her demand. His dark eyes reflected unhappiness, but no rancor. He raised his chin in supplication. "I swear to stay out of your little contest. On the off chance she's lucky enough to survive the encounter, I'll give her twelve hours head start before I hunt her down, and eviscerate her."

Whiskey smiled, and glanced over her shoulder. "Good enough?"

"You trust him?"

Her eyes met Dorst's, and her next words were spoken very softly. "With my life."

Fiona gauged their sincerity. "All right. It's a deal."

"I want a vow from you, too. If you win, Cora and the others go free and you leave them alone."

Standing, Fiona smirked at her. "I swear to let my people go free when this is over. They won't want to, but I'll give them the option." She set her glass on the nearest table.

"All right, then." At a loss, Whiskey put her hands on her hips, looking around the room. "So what are the protocols here? Are there rules for this sort of thing?"

"There are." Dorst held out his hand. "All combatants must be physically disarmed."

Whiskey felt a pang of regret as she handed over the plain-hilted knife. "Keep it safe. I want it back."

He grinned, bowing low. "As you wish, my *Gasan*." Pocketing the blade, he glided toward Fiona. "Weapons?"

Fiona smiled coyly at him. "Going to pat me down? At least I know you won't get enjoyment from this. Eunuchs seldom do."

Dorst wasn't dissuaded. "You listen to far too many rumors, *Gasan*. Perhaps you should become more scholarly in your approach to knowledge." He gave her a once-over, his palms barely touching her body. "The pistol in your bodice, please."

Whiskey stared in surprise. "You're kidding me."

"A girl can't be too careful these days." Fiona fished a small gun from her cleavage, handing it over to Dorst.

"And the blade strapped to your thigh."

Annoyance marred Fiona's expression. "Of course, *Sañur Gasum*. You have only to ask." She retrieved the weapon from beneath her graceful skirt. "That's all I carry."

Dorst stepped aside, pocketing the weapons. "Do you wish a second to attend you, *Gasan* Fiona? I can call Manuel down here to be your witness."

Fiona appeared to give it some consideration. "No, it's not necessary. I'll tell him about it when we're finished here." She moved away from the seating section, circling wide to reach the open area where Daniel had been tortured. "Ready whenever you are, little *lamma*."

Whiskey followed, her mind reaching out to meet with Fiona's sickly flower essence. She attempted to access Elisibet's memories as she poked and prodded along the mental wall between them. She'd been panic-stricken when Alphonse and Zebediah had come upon her the night before, and furious at Castillo. Willfully attempting an attack wasn't as easy. She felt Fiona's mind surge against hers, and met her push for push. It took very little effort to keep her at bay. *Am I really that strong? How is this possible? She's at least a hundred years old.*

Fiona attacked, piercing Whiskey's mind. Pain lanced Whiskey's temples, she barely heard her own grunt of pain. Despite the agony, her mind held Fiona's away, keeping true damage to a minimum. The pain fueled her fear and anger. She physically made no move, but felt the definite vicious shove as she pushed Fiona's essence away from her. Instantly, the stabbing in her temples lessened only to be replaced by another at the base of her neck with Fiona's immediate return thrust. Almost as an afterthought she felt her knees wobble, her body weakening from the onslaught.

No! This can't happen! She can't beat me. Whiskey had taken down both Alphonse and Zebediah, and held a four-hundred-year-old Castillo at bay. Her desperation triggered that which was Elisibet, the strength rising to the surface; memories of situations, feelings and furies mingled with training techniques and strategies with which Whiskey had no experience.

Snarling, she set up blocks, contravening the worst of Fiona's attack, keeping her opponent's mind at bay. As Fiona struggled to find another access, Whiskey felt along her guards, stabbing and prodding where she thought there might be cracks or crevices. One area felt particularly vulnerable, and she concentrated upon it, putting as much as she could spare into opening Fiona's skull like a melon. The horrific visualization helped her focus. Fiona's attack lessened as she attempted to shore up the point Whiskey drove toward. Whiskey found it odd, seeing things from three different angles. She saw the melon in her mind, the rind distorting as she pressed against it, penetrating the skin, the juice dribbling. She saw Fiona standing before her in the small room through a reddish haze, her eyes bulging, her smug face drawn into a grimace as she fought. And she saw a memory, Margaurethe looming above her as she died, cold and dark and so very anguished at the thought of leaving her lover.

The memory gave Whiskey added strength. Her anger blossomed into fury, her mouth watering as she stepped forward, closing the short distance between them. In her mind's eye, the melon burst open as Fiona's defenses failed. Whiskey plunged her essence into Fiona's, shredding everything within her grasp, Fiona convulsed, her body straightening and spasming before beginning to fall. She never made it to the ground. Whiskey stepped forward and caught her compulsively, burying her fangs into the jugular vein. No gentle feeding this; her hunting instincts took over, and she ripped Fiona's throat open, gleefully bathing in the hot splash of blood that spilled over her face, chest and hands.

When she had had her fill of the liquid still pumping sluggishly from Fiona's neck, she dropped the body. Her mind still holding Fiona's fading thoughts, she looked at the pulp with vague curiosity. Something dark grew at the center, spreading as she watched. She pushed her essence closer. A hand on her shoulder pulled her away. Whiskey turned, crouching in preparation for another attack, her mind instantly grabbing the other.

Dorst, gasping, doubled over. "My *Ninsumgal*! You must let her go."

"Reynhard?" She swallowed, tasting the blood still in her mouth. Licking her lips, she felt a rush of power flow through her. Looking around the small room, she saw Fiona on the floor, blood splattered liberally about her corpse.

Still bent over, Dorst quickly recovered from her reflexive attack. "It's all right, my *Gasan*. It's over now."

Not wanting to think, to acknowledge her first Sanguire kill, Whiskey stumbled toward the couch. Her full stomach rumbled with displeasure when she focused on its contents. She swallowed past a lump in her throat, and collapsed into the plush leather.

"Come. We need to get out of here. You must step off the Strange Path."

Whiskey allowed herself to forget for now. She didn't complain when Dorst scooped her up, and carried her out of the basement. Relaxing in his arms, she started to cry.

CHAPTER THIRTY-EIGHT

Whiskey stared out the window, unseeing, at the small courtyard below. The moon had set some time before she'd woken from her exhausted slumber. Castillo had come through for her again, relocating her and her fledgling entourage to a penthouse apartment in downtown Seattle. If she reached out with her mind, she'd feel Cora, Zebediah and Alphonse, as well as Dorst and Castillo. Only Daniel remained silent to her search; he'd regained consciousness at some point during the drive here, but had lost it again not long after she had.

Her headache almost blinded her. Any intelligent person would have begun the final meditation to stop the pain, but she couldn't quite bring herself to do so. It seemed fitting she suffer at least *something* for the things she'd done over the last few days. She could deny responsibility, but the fact remained that two people were dead—one Human and one Sanguire—and four Sanguire were injured because of her.

Dominick had been a jerk, but he hadn't deserved to die. If he'd had one bit of sense, run when she'd told him to, he might still be alive. Regardless, the final blow had been hers. She rated a lot more agony than she currently suffered for that particular punch.

Cora and Daniel had sacrificed themselves for her. She owed them so much more than she ever thought she'd owe to Fiona, it boggled her mind. What little relief she'd felt releasing her obligation toward Fiona was negated when it came to the torture these two had gone through for their choice to defend her. She didn't know how to repay either of them, but she'd do her damnedest. From what Fiona had said in Whiskey's presence, she assumed that both Cora and Daniel came from lower-ranking families among the European Sanguire. Maybe she could find a way to get them home to their families. Everybody needed a family.

Bronwyn and Manuel had stuck with Fiona to the end. Dorst had gone back inside after depositing Whiskey in the car. After several minutes that felt like hours, he'd returned, simply stating that neither wanted anything to do with her, or their former companions. If anyone would cause her future trouble besides Valmont, it would be these two. She knew Manuel would hold a grudge. He'd never leave things as they were. According to Dorst, they were the eldest of Fiona's pack, and had been with her for decades. That was a long time to ignore, even considering Fiona's ideas of friendship. Perhaps they'd decide to lick their wounds somewhere else; she could hope.

Whiskey sighed. She wasn't holding her breath. Her life hadn't been easy so far. Why change now?

She heard the bedroom door close behind her, knowing that Castillo had entered. Every footfall on the carpet pounded into her overly sensitive ears. She took the pain as her due, forcing herself not to grimace. "How are you doing?"

Castillo stopped beside her. His answer came in a faint whisper. "Shouldn't I be asking you that question? You're the one who's had your life turned upside down in a week."

"Yeah. But it hasn't been easy for you either."

He looked out the window. "Perhaps not. But I've grown accustomed."

Whiskey smiled, turning to him. "I don't blame you, you know. You did what you thought was right when you notified the *Agrun Nam*."

Closing his eyes, he bowed his head. "At the time, I thought so. Now I'm pretty sure I screwed things up."

She laid a hand on his shoulder, feeling the pulse of blood beneath the fabric of his black shirt. "Reynhard wouldn't have found me if you hadn't, Padre. I count that as a benefit."

"Nor Fiona, nor *Sublugal Sañar* Valmont, I suspect."

Her head hurt too much to argue with him. She promised herself she'd do so when she got over this.

Castillo must have read her mind. He opened his eyes, and gestured toward the bed. "It's time for you to complete the *Ñíri Kurám*, Whiskey. *Sañar Gasum* Dorst said you were experiencing pain. I can see it in your eyes. You have to complete this before any more damage is done."

She allowed herself to be guided to the bed. After sinking onto it, she realized how shaky her knees had become while she'd stood at the window.

The Book pulsed in her hands, having been thrust there by Castillo, the Book she'd originally begun with. Reynhard must have picked up her things from Fiona's.

The inner vision of Fiona's mind as it split asunder made her shiver.

"Do you wish to be alone?"

Whiskey shook her head. "I've been alone too long, Padre." *Margaurethe. Gin. Mama and Daddy.* Her thoughts were becoming more and more disjointed. It would be easier to just let it happen. Then it would be over. She watched Castillo close the curtains, cloaking the room in darkness. Out in the living area, she heard Alphonse and Zebediah bickering over a video game console they'd installed. Dorst's amber and steel essence mixed easily with his voice as he spoke with Cora over inconsequential matters.

I can't. Not until I set things right.

She opened the Book, and found the next meditation. The

ink hovered above the page, flickering with red-gold light. She needed no light to scan them. When she finished, she set the Book aside. "You'll stay?"

Castillo came forward, and cupped Whiskey's cheek. "I'd be honored, though I cannot participate."

"I understand."

They held the pose for a moment before Castillo dropped his hand. He settled in a nearby armchair, a silent sentinel to her rebirth.

Whiskey steeled herself. Her insides shook, her hands trembling as she plucked at the quilt on the bed. She'd never had a witness to the meditation, and fought a case of nerves along with the physical agony. What would the padre see? She looked into his eyes, and her fears melted away. What he saw made no difference. Castillo would be there to support her regardless of the circumstances, despite the visions of blood and mayhem that always accompanied Elisibet's memories. It occurred to her that she'd done Castillo a disservice. He cared for her over and above any connections to Elisibet Vasilla. After their first meeting, he may have gone to the *Agrun Nam*, but that had been a knee-jerk reaction. She believed him when he said he wouldn't contact them again.

Whiskey made a vow to herself. She would remain true to Castillo, true to herself, and never allow Elisibet's anger and cruelty to control her.

Sensing the seriousness in Whiskey's demeanor, Castillo tilted his head, a gentle question on his face.

With a smile, Whiskey shook her head. "I'm ready now."

"I'm with you."

She closed her eyes, and began the chant.

Flash.

"I want him." Her voice held a higher pitch, the tone petulant and childish. She stared greedily at a litter of puppies suckling at a bitch. The squirming mass of canine life held one solid black pup upon which she focused.

"Certainly, Your Highness," a man said. "But he's newly born. He'll die if you take him now. You must wait a few weeks before he'll survive without his mother."

"I don't care!" She stamped her foot. "I want him *now*." Glaring at the man in the servant's livery, she narrowed her eyes as she'd seen her father do upon occasion. "Do not vex me, Andri. I'll have him now, or you'll answer to the *Usumgal*."

Andri cast a resigned glance at the dog handler, and nodded stiffly. "Yes, my *Gasan*. The black one you said?"

As he pulled the hungry pup from the litter, Whiskey felt a split, a schism within her soul. She felt Elisibet's immature glee at getting her way, uncaring about the consequences of her actions, and how they affected others around her. But for the first time *she* responded to what she witnessed, a sense of loathing filling her heart. Somehow she knew that the pup would last mere hours away from its mother, that Elisibet would become bored with its constant whining, and leave it in a drawer of her room to die a lonely death, starved and suffocated among cast off bedclothes.

Whiskey's gorge rose.

Flash.

She stared at the Book in distaste, its cover worn and dirty. At the very least, she should have been afforded a more presentable copy, one that befitted her status as the new *Ninsumgal*. Primly, she opened it with thumb and forefinger, easily reading the Sanguire writing inside. She'd have to throw this gown away when she finished. Her handmaiden would never be able to get the dirt stains out of the fine linen. At least she would be *Ninsumgal* now. And the first Sanguire to ever follow the Strange Path at twelve. With a haughty toss of her hair, she prepared to begin the first meditation.

Whiskey knew *Usumgal* Maximal had only been laid to rest in the catacombs three days earlier. She searched Elisibet's thoughts and heart for any indication of mourning for the loss of her father, and found nothing. She recoiled from the lack, its absence conflicting sharply with feelings of grief for her own parents, dead a dozen years. How could Elisibet not feel such a thing? What kind of monster was she?

Flash.

Nahib the Traitor's body had been strewn about the *Agrun Nam* public chambers in bloody strips. Witnesses, courtesans and the remainder of the *Agrun Nam* stood in the gallery, all of whom required a reminder of who held power here. Their eyes wide and fearful, she reveled in their terror. This was as it should be.

Searching the room, she found one person who didn't share the feeling. Bertrada Nijmege's hawk face flushed with fury and anguish, her lip curled into a sneer, murder in her heart. With a smile, Elisibet kept the gaze of Nahib's lover, pausing long enough to lick his blood from her fingers. Her only dismay was Valmont's absence. She'd asked him to be here. Where was he?

Whiskey tasted the Sanguire blood, her stomach turning. *Nam Lugal* Nahib had done what he thought right, speaking against the atrocities for which Elisibet was responsible. Considering the time and circumstances, he had been a hero to the Sanguire. Yet, Elisibet's nature blinded her. Mulling over this apparent stupidity, Whiskey realized a very important thing about Elisibet. The *Ninsumgal* was terrified of losing control, and used any means to keep it.

Flash.

She happily got into the backseat of the car, her stuffed bear tight in her grip. Carefully working on her seat belt, she managed to buckle it all by herself. Sometimes it didn't work, and Mama had to do it for her.

The change of time disoriented Whiskey, and it took a moment to understand the switch. No longer Elisibet, she witnessed her own past, a memory she hadn't seen before. The separation, the dichotomy wasn't there anymore. Taking off her hat and sunglasses, she watched her parents climb into the car, and sit in front.

"That waterfall was really big, wasn't it?" Mama asked, looking back to check on Whiskey's seat belt.

"Uh-huh! Upsy Downsy was scared."

Daddy laughed, and started the car. "No reason for him to be scared. He had you to protect him, Jenna."

Whiskey nodded vigorously. "And I had you to protect me!"

Her parents laughed in agreement as they drove through the parking area. Mama talked about the market in Seattle, and the shops she wanted to see there as Daddy prepared to pull onto the busy interstate.

Whiskey felt herself tighten inside, knowing what was coming, and not able to stop it. Her attention distracted by her teddy bear, her father's sudden frightened curse brought her head up. Her mother screamed, automatically reaching back toward her. Confused, Whiskey looked out the window to the left, and saw the grill of an eighteen-wheeler bearing down on the little car. Terrified, she hugged Upsy Downsy to her chest, and screwed her eyes closed, gritting her teeth as she waited for the truck to hit them. Her ears filled with an airhorn blowing long and loud, a deafening crash and the screaming of her parents. Oddly, she felt no impact; only a jarring thump as she landed on the ground.

When the noise died away, she cautiously opened her eyes. She sat on the highway with her bear, cars screeching to a halt just feet away. Bewildered, she winced from the pain of sunlight, wondering how she got out of the car with her seat belt on. Where were Mama and Daddy?

She stood, and looked up the road, finding two thick black lines on either side of her. Horrified, she saw the back of a semi truck, the cab turned at an angle, smoke rising from the front. The driver, a grizzled man in a plaid shirt, stumbled out of the vehicle, and raced around to the other side.

"Mama?"

Flash.

Whiskey gasped, falling forward onto the bed. Arms wrapped around her, strong and familiar. Tears streaked down her face, making vision difficult as she tried to see who it was. She stared into dark eyes.

"Mama?" she whispered.

"Whiskey?"

The male voice brought her out of her confusion. Those weren't the midnight color of her mother's eyes, but those of Castillo. "Padre?"

CHAPTER THIRTY-NINE

Castillo stayed with Whiskey until she cried herself out. She drowsed for a while, hugging a pillow to herself. Eventually she slept, though not much. Awake, her body complained from remaining in one place too long. She forced herself to sit up. The headache had disappeared, as had all other irritants. She had to actively focus on her hearing or smell to locate what had earlier assaulted her. Her body still felt precarious, probably a result of the hell she'd inflicted upon herself. For the first time in hours she felt hungry.

She pushed to her feet, holding out one hand to grab the nightstand as she swayed. Her balance restored itself, and she headed for the door. Somewhere out there, someone fried up eggs and bacon. Her stomach rumbled in anticipation. By the time she arrived in the living room, she almost felt Human again. She snorted to herself, getting her first real look at the place.

The colorful mohawks had brought in a large flat-screen television and surround sound system to go with their multiple gaming consoles. Alphonse sprawled on the couch with one controller, and Zebediah sat on the coffee table with the other. The screen showed them beating the snot out of a horrific creature with red eyes and tusks. Whiskey scanned the men with her mind. She easily saw that they were the youngest Sanguire in the apartment. They couldn't be much older than they physically appeared, not much older than her. She wondered why she hadn't realized it before.

The demonic figure on the screen met a messy end, and Alphonse looked back at her. "Morning."

"Hey. How's it going?"

"Kicking ass. You?"

Whiskey considered the question. "Better, thanks."

Zebediah cut into the conversation. "C'mon, man. Through here is the armory. We can stock up."

She raised her chin at the game, indicating he should continue. Alphonse grinned, and did so. Leaving them to their digital mayhem, she followed the delicious scent of food into the kitchen.

A multitude of paper bags littered the breakfast nook table, evidence of a hasty shopping trip. Several items cluttered the counter. Castillo shoved eggs around the pan with a spatula. Cora stood at another counter, slathering butter on toast, and piling it on a plate.

"You picked up jam?"

Castillo nodded, concentrated on his task. "Yes. Three kinds, just as you requested."

Cora appeared pleased. "Good. Whiskey likes peach, but Daniel prefers strawberry over everything."

At the mention of Daniel, Whiskey glanced back at the living room. Where was he? Was he okay? "How is Daniel?"

Cora whirled about, dropping the butter knife. *"Aga ninna!"* She rushed forward into Whiskey's arms. She buried her face in the curve of Whiskey's shoulder, muffling her words. "I missed you."

Whiskey clutched at Cora more to keep from falling off her unsteady feet. She blushed at Castillo's raised eyebrow. Cora left nothing to the imagination, clinging to Whiskey in barely restrained lust. Having a priest as witness didn't bother her in the least. "I missed you, too." Whiskey carefully extricated herself from the hug. "I'm glad to see you're all right."

Castillo turned away from the intimacy, digging in a cabinet for a stack of plates. "Daniel is well. He's sleeping." Castillo piled eggs and bacon on a plate, holding it out to Cora. "Can you take this to his room, child? It's past time he's eaten."

Cora appeared reluctant to leave Whiskey after so long an absence. A gentle swell of warm dark chocolate changed her mind. "I'd be happy to, Father." Slow to extricate herself from Whiskey's arms, she took the proffered plate, pausing long enough to grab toast and the jar of strawberry jam. "See you soon, my *ninna*."

Having turned back to the stove, Castillo waited until Cora left. "*Aga ninna?*"

Whiskey sighed. "Yeah. I ordered her to stop calling me *Ninsumgal*. That's the result."

He grunted in response. "Better than *ñalga súp*, I suppose."

Her mind easily translated, and she chuckled. "Yeah, I don't think I'm a nitwit."

"Most definitely not." He served up another plate, handing it to her. "You need to eat, and you need more blood to finish healing."

Whiskey leaned against the counter, ravenous. She didn't bother to sit at the small table as she shoveled food in her mouth. Several minutes passed before she could speak. "Aleya again?"

"No, it's too soon for her. I'll have someone else come over."

She ate a piece of bacon in two bites. "That gives a whole new meaning to 'ordering in,' Padre."

He smiled. "Doesn't it?" He broke more eggs into a bowl, added salt and pepper, and whisked them together. "How are you holding up?"

She shrugged, slowing down her pace of eating. "Still kind of numb, I guess. I don't really want to think about it."

"That's understandable. The first kill is never easy." He poured the egg mixture into the fry pan, causing a loud hiss as it hit hot metal.

Whiskey wasn't sure if she recoiled because of the angry sound, or his words. No longer hungry, she dropped her fork onto her plate, and went to the sink. She ran hot water over the remains of her breakfast, washing them down the drain, and into the disposal. Behind her, Castillo continued cooking, not interrupting her thoughts.

The padre didn't know that Fiona wasn't her first kill. She hadn't wanted to incriminate herself in his eyes with Dominick. His opinion of her had still mattered when she'd entrusted him the day before. It mattered more now. *What will he say when he finds out I've killed a Human, too?* A part of her wanted to keep that forever hidden. So much easier to avoid the messy result of confession for as long as possible. Cora and Daniel were both here, though. They'd witnessed the killing blow; Cora had reveled in it. Sooner or later one of them would say the wrong thing at the wrong time. Which was worse? Telling Castillo, or having him realize she'd lied to him by omission? She shivered, holding the edge of the sink for support. *The sooner the better. Get it over with now.* "That wasn't my first kill." The busy sound of the spatula froze with her heartbeat.

"Really?" The spatula resumed its motion.

Castillo's voice seemed too casual. She refused to turn, to face him. "Yeah." Her voice disappeared. She cleared her throat, ignoring the lump developing there.

"Dominick Filardo?"

Whiskey couldn't speak. She nodded, hot tears spilling from her eyes. The pan slid to another burner, the click of the stove turning off loud in the silence. She imagined his face, knowing how disgusted he must be with her. Any minute now, he'd leave the room, leave the apartment, and never come back. He was her last friend from her old life; odd that she would realize it now when the friendship ended. *What a waste. I'm such a fuckup.*

A hand took her shoulder, turning her. She gave half-hearted resistance, knowing Castillo's stubborn nature. He wanted to face her, to tell her exactly how repulsed he was with her actions.

Giving the devil his due, she allowed him to pull her around, let him guide her face up with his fingers at her chin. Flinching away from his fingers, she met his gaze.

Warm chocolate enveloped her. Sympathy and kindness emanated from his eyes.

"Padre." She choked, unable to speak. He wrapped her in his arms and his essence, cradling her, protecting her from her fanciful terrors, accepting her and her past actions. "I'm so sorry."

"Shhh. I know you are. Let it go, Jenna."

It took time before she cried herself out again. Eventually the tears stopped, and she realized they both sat on the kitchen floor, leaning against the lower cupboards. "This is getting to be a bad habit," she muttered, her voice cracking.

"You've had a lot to deal with. This kind of stress has to go somewhere." Castillo produced a handkerchief. "Can you talk about it now?"

She wiped her eyes, and blew her nose. "I didn't know it was me until the day after. I thought I knocked him out." She gave a watery snort. "I was trying to *keep* him from being killed."

"An admirable attempt considering the circumstances. Do you know what went wrong?"

Whiskey nodded, seeing and hearing it happen anew. Cora handing her a knife, her realization that Fiona's people would kill Dominick outright if the slaughter went much longer, and the crunch of his nose as she crushed the cartilage. "I think he was unconscious on his feet. When I hit him that last time, it was enough to knock him down. The smell of blood got a lot stronger afterward. I must have driven the bones around his nose up into his brain."

Silence. She rested in his arms, fear of his rejection causing her to tense. His hold remained warm and close. It didn't retract, didn't react to her words. She swallowed, wondering what he thought.

When he spoke, his voice remained compassionate and calm. "I doubt that's what happened. Killing a person in that manner happens only in movies. It's a myth."

Whiskey sniffled, and pulled back to peer at him. "Then what else was it?"

"You said the smell of blood got stronger afterward. Perhaps when he fell he cracked his skull open on the ground."

She stared at him, unable to process the information. Eventually she found her voice. "Is there any way you can find out?"

A flicker of uncertainty crossed his features. "I can try. I don't have many connections in the local political structure, but I might have an acquaintance close to the *Saggina* who might be able to get some information."

"I really need to know, Padre." She clutched at his shirt. "If you can tell me anything, it'd be great."

"Consider it done."

"Thank you." Hope filled Whiskey's heart. Even if Dominick had died from hitting the ground, she'd be responsible for his death. At least she'd know she hadn't done it herself, that it had been an accident. "I thought you'd be really pissed at me."

"I can't say I'm not disappointed. But it's not my place to judge, Whiskey."

She felt a fresh wave of tears sting her eyes. "Still, what you think means a lot to me."

"What I think is that you've had a rough row to hoe. You did the best you could considering the circumstances and resources you had. I wouldn't have done any better in your place." He tightened the embrace, hugging her. "I think that we all go alone before God, and His is the only judgment that matters. What you do between now and the day you pass the veil will decide whether Dominick's death is atoned."

"Is the furniture not to your liking?"

Whiskey looked up to see Dorst standing in the kitchen door. She wiped at her heating face, scrambling to her feet.

"My *Gasan*." He bowed. "Dear Cora tells me you and the padre were having...an intimate moment, and did not wish to be disturbed. Shall I leave?"

Castillo got up and returned to the stove, sliding the pan of half-cooked eggs back onto the burner.

Whiskey reached for the paper towels. "No, that's okay, Reynhard. We're done." She turned back to the sink, splashing her face with water and drying it with the towels. "Where have you been?"

Dorst gave her a mocking grin. "Out and about, dear Whiskey, doing what I do best."

She sniffed. "And what's that?"

"I am your chief spy and assassin, my *Ninsumgal*," he reminded her.

"Meaning he's been crawling around doing whatever he does to support you." Castillo slid the eggs onto a plate. "Hungry, *Sañur Gasum*?"

Dorst raised an eyebrow, and tilted his head, his grin concurring with Castillo's statement. "Thank you, but, no, Father."

Picking up the centuries old recollection Elisibet had of Dorst, Whiskey scowled. Given an opportunity, Dorst would play political word games for hours, never revealing what his conversational partner wanted to know. She crossed her arms, and glared at him. "That's not an answer."

He gave a slight shrug of apology. "*Sublugal Sañar* Valmont remains in the area."

Whiskey's fangs made an abrupt appearance, a mixture of fear and anger surging through her. She clamped down on her lips, willing them to retract.

"He's currently residing in the luxury suite of the Sorrento Hotel. He's registered there for a month, with the stipulation that he may extend his stay. I've access to his hotel phone records, but he's obviously using a cellular for most of his calls. It may take time for me to get the number." Dorst frowned in thought, tapping his chin with a long index finger. "He's spending a good portion of his night prowling the University District and, when not scaring the bejesus out of the youthful unfortunates living on the streets there, he frequents Crucible for company."

"He's not hurting anyone in the U District, is he?"

Dorst shook his head. "No, no. He's shaking your peers down for information about you. It's only a matter of time before he happens upon the right people who can describe Fiona and her pack. Until then, he's grasping at straws."

Whiskey thought of Gin. "What happens if he finds someone willing to talk to him?"

"Then he can approach the local *Saginna* for more

information. Find out where Fiona has been residing, and what she's been up to."

Castillo, finished with his stint as chef, shut down the stove, and joined the conversation. "It's required by Sanguire law to announce your presence to the local authorities when you're in the area. Considering the nature of our people, it's best in case something happens."

Her heart dropped into her stomach. "Then it's just a matter of time before he tracks me here." She glanced wildly about the kitchen, searching for an exit that didn't exist. "When Manuel and Bronwyn tell the locals about Fiona, I'll be up on murder charges. This...*Saginna* will have to tell the *Agrun Nam* about me, and Valmont will be informed."

"Actually, no." Dorst drew off his jacket, tossing it over the back of a chair at the breakfast nook. He casually leaned his elbows on the counter, studying the plate of bacon. "What happened between you and Fiona was a duel, and accepted by law. No charges will be filed in this matter. Should anyone think otherwise, I'll file my statement as your Second." Picking up a piece of bacon, he gave it close examination as he continued speaking. "Manuel and Bronwyn have had a change of heart regarding the Seattle area. It's so dreary, don't you know. They're already gone, moved away. Rumor has it they're in the company of a certain youngling who's just completed the Strange Path. Poor woman. She bears an uncanny resemblance to our long dead *Ninsumgal* Elisibet Vasilla." Dorst took a bite of bacon. "Pity. They both had such potential as assassins."

"They're gone?"

"Far away." Dorst waved the remaining chunk of bacon at his audience. "Did I mention a horrible fire that occurred not long after they left the premises? Terrible, that. The authorities say someone left the gas on in the house when they left. Decimated the place." He popped the rest of his snack into his mouth.

Whiskey stared at him, unsure whether she should feel appalled or pleased or suspicious. She inhaled, focusing her senses on Dorst, wondering why she hadn't caught the faint scent of burnt wood when he'd entered. *I was crying; my nose was congested.*

"Amazing how that worked out," Castillo drawled.

Dorst nodded. "Isn't it, though?"

She shook her head, trying to look at the situation with a little objectivity. "So, if Valmont does get far enough to find Fiona, he'll think I've gone with Bronwyn and Manuel?"

"One could hope." Dorst pushed away from the counter. "And since I've never registered my presence with the authorities, it's doubtful he'll realize I'm here. There'll be nothing keeping him in the area."

Whiskey inhaled deeply, releasing a slow breath as she considered. "So, what next?"

Castillo answered this one. "Your education. You might have picked up the language well enough, but you need some serious schooling in our ways, our history, our law. If you are to take over as the *Ninsumgal* of the European Sanguire, you need to know as much about our politics as possible."

Take over? The idea repulsed her. She'd seen what having that kind of power had done to Elisibet. Granted, the woman had been a spoiled brat without an ounce of compassion, but running the whole show certainly hadn't done her any favors. *Last thing I want is to become like her.* She knew that her life experiences wouldn't allow it to happen, but she also remembered the feral joy she'd felt as Fiona's mind broke beneath her attack.

"Whiskey?"

She glanced up at Dorst, realizing he'd asked a question she missed. "What was that again?"

"While our dear Father Castillo schools you in our etiquette and protocol, what would you have me do?"

Whiskey almost laughed. *I'm only eighteen years old. What the hell do I order a seven hundred-year-old spy and assassin to do?* Her heart stilled in her chest as a thought occurred to her. "I want you to find Margaurethe O'Toole and bring her— No. Ask her to come here."

CHAPTER FORTY

She didn't see the warning signs until it was too late. How could she not see them? The tension in the palace had been all but impenetrable after *Nam Lugal* Nahib's grisly execution. Valmont had refused a direct order to attend the proceedings, and had gotten into a shouting match with Elisibet afterward. It had been three weeks since he'd left the palace and the capital city for *Aga Maskim Sañar* Bertrada Nijmege's estate, taking half of Elisibet's disaffected royal guard with him.

Someone had seen him in the palace. Today.

When had the halls become so endless, so wide and empty? They went on forever, seeming to expand before her as she went. She dashed through them, holding her skirts up without decorum, a stitch needling her left side. Nothing appeared out of place, nothing odd, except the sound of her tortured breathing, and the fear choking her throat. She held out hope that the brainless, nameless ninny who'd reported seeing Valmont in the kitchens had been wrong. The chance of a misunderstanding were small; he was a distinctive man, well known in the palace environs.

As she rounded the corner, her heart leapt into her throat before sinking to the depths of her belly. The corridor to the royal wing wasn't simply unguarded. Had it been so, she would have assumed Elisibet was elsewhere in the palace, conducting business. The smell and sight of blood put lie to that supposition. One hand in her skirts, one clutching the suddenly constricting collar of her gown, she slipped past the pooled blood. Streaks marked the floor, leading into a nearby room. She didn't bother to check for survivors, instead pushing on, attempting to run faster. *No time!*

A thump. A crash. The blood smell faded with distance, and then grew stronger. She sprinted for the ornate door that marked Elisibet's personal audience chamber, cursing that it was closed. The sounds of a fight echoed and reverberated from behind the heavy wood, causing sharp pain in her ears and head. It seemed hours before she finally reached the door, and burst into the room to confront her worst nightmare.

Valmont weaved on his feet, the black devil still holding his weapon. His back to the door, he didn't see her arrival. He towered over Elisibet's prone, crawling form, sword raised in two hands.

"Get away from her!" Her headlong motion, so slow for so long, abruptly sped up. She crashed into him as he turned. They fell to the ground with a crash, his sword skittering away on the marble.

With the immediate threat stopped, she wasted no time on the enemy. She scrambled to her lover, pained to see the amount of blood smearing the floor as Elisibet crept away from her attacker. *It's too much! It's everywhere!* She reached Elisibet, turned her over, calmed her, cradled her. Tears stung her eyes. *I can't stop this. What can I do?*

Behind her, Valmont spoke. "What's done is done."

She leaned protectively over her lover, turning to hiss and

bare her teeth at him. He wiped the blood from his blade, and sheathed it. For a long moment, he stared at Elisibet, both revulsion and longing on his face. He spun around.

As he strode away, she turned back to Elisibet. "Stay with me *m'cara*! We will get you to a healer and soon you will be fine."

It was a lie. They both knew it, though she still tried to convince herself of its truth.

Ice blue eyes regarded her, and Elisibet had enough energy to laugh. "Nay, Margaurethe. It's beyond that, and we both know it." It was hard for her to speak, her breath coming in gasps. She coughed, tried to hang on for just a little while longer.

"No! You cannot die, Elisibet." *I cannot live without you!* How could she fix this? Where was the healer? Why didn't anyone follow her as she ran past them? Certainly someone had to have witnessed her indecorous gallop through the palace corridors.

"Apparently so, *minn'ast*. Will you forgive me?"

She focused on Elisibet. "There is nothing to forgive." *Not to me.*

"It's cold, Margaurethe. Hold me."

She gathered Elisibet into her arms, hugging her close. It wasn't much longer before the panting slowed, paused, tortured and rattling as Elisibet struggled to breathe. A lethal quietness followed. The hand holding Margaurethe's arm relaxed, and fell away. The body lightly twitched in her grasp until it came to its mortal rest. The silence didn't last long, soon broken by a keening escorting her Elisibet, her heart, her life past the veil separating this life from the next.

The world went dark as she realized the lamenting wail came from her.

Margaurethe O'Toole sat upright, gasping for air. Her frantic hands searched for her lover among the bed linens. No blood, no cold marble floor, no cooling body. She looked wildly around in the darkness, searching for Elisibet. Instead, she saw the murky depths of her bedroom. No elegant sitting room, no exquisite artwork, no cool black marble. A slight gap in the bed curtains illuminated a fire gone cold in the hearth, and polished wood furniture. She saw her robe draped haphazardly over the foot of the bed. No overpowering smell of blood met her indrawn breath. The scent of roses filled her nostrils.

That damned nightmare again. She slumped, shoulders and head down, eyes closed. After almost four hundred years, it still had the power to plague her. Over the centuries it came and went with irregular frequency, but the last decade had shown an alarming increase of nightmare nights. A week rarely went by that she didn't wake in the throes of grief and fury, suffering the loss anew.

She drew in a shaky breath, calming herself. Fully awake, she rubbed sleep from her eyes, and climbed from bed. She slid her fingers through her hair, settling the worst of the snarls before donning her robe.

Moments later, she entered her private office. A silver tray on her desk held a porcelain cup and teapot. Steam drifted from the cup, the aroma of ginseng driving away the memories of blood. She pursed her lips, glancing back at the door. *I must have cried out loud again.* She hated when she did that. It had begun happening too often. She hadn't called out during her nightmares since the late sixteen hundreds. This would make it the third time this week.

Disgruntled, she drifted to the window. Moist fog clung to the ground this morning but she easily saw the brick wall in the distance that marked her property line. The grass would soon need cutting, and new green looked to be budding on the trees. Spring awakening was just around the corner. Her eyes caressed the rose bushes. There'd once been a full garden on this side of the estate, but she'd had it removed. Too many memories. None she wished to lose, but all far too painful to endure even three hundred eighty years later. She'd never part with the roses, however. Those memories she wished to retain for the duration of her life.

She sighed again, the smell of the tea calling her, and sat at her desk. At a touch, her computer screen lit up. She accessed her email and Internet programs, and began to catch up with the morning's news. While she waited for her messages to download, she sipped her tea and marveled at how far technology had advanced in the last seven hundred years. In the days of her youth, a courier took weeks to get messages from her family's homestead to the palace. Now it was a matter of typing out a missive and hitting the send button. Instantaneous.

Sometimes, especially after the vivid reminder of her nightmares, she wondered how Elisibet would have fared in this day and age. It had taken centuries of struggle for her to hold onto four hundred thousand kilometers of territory. At the time, she'd been one of the most successful and ruthless leaders of their people, rivaled only by Tairo-no-Mitsuko in Japan. In her foolish moments, Margaurethe daydreamed that a contemporary Elisibet would be a more merciful ruler, less subject to violence as a tool of control. Those thoughts withered in the blistering light of Elisibet's true nature. Her admittedly low level of compassion was reserved for an elite few—Margaurethe and Valmont, for the most part. Margaurethe's nose wrinkled at the thought of him. She pushed him from her mind, and began to peruse her messages.

In the last century, she'd invested money in several technological advancements that had flourished. Many of her peers and elders floundered in the modern age, preferring to sequester themselves away from the rapid advancements. Elisibet had been a strong proponent of new things, and Margaurethe had honored her memory, taking the modest stipend from her parents, and turning it into a financial empire. An active board member in one software and two computer hardware companies, her stock portfolio showed a keen understanding of the market, and she held majority interests in two satellite communications companies. If she were to liquidate her earnings and holdings, she'd have three times more money than Elisibet had ever held in the royal treasury, even accounting for current day inflation.

She used the next hour and a half to go over the messages, answering those that required an immediate response, filing the informational ones, and deleting those of no consequence. This afternoon she'd attend to those from her family, and those missives requiring a more focused response. She spent another hour going over the daily newsfeeds, and stock exchange data.

By the time she completed her morning routine she'd emptied the teapot, and the sun had burned off most of the fog.

A knock at the door took her unaware. She raised an eyebrow at the door, staring. Her staff never bothered her at this hour unless it was an emergency. Other than her personal assistant delivering tea, no one would ever approach until she left her private suite for the public rooms. She reached out with her mind, simultaneously picking up the phone. Amber and steel met her mental touch, an essence both familiar and alien, one she hadn't felt in several hundred years.

"Yes, *Ki'an Gasan*?" a voice on the phone asked.

Margaurethe's hand shook. "Nothing. Never mind." She hung up on the speaker before he formulated a reply. "Reynhard, come in."

The door eased open, and in walked a garish ghost. Reynhard Dorst's formerly long brown hair had disappeared, leaving three strips of black that bristled four inches above his scalp. She watched him carefully close the door behind him, his dark eyes glittering with humor. He wore leather and silver, head to toe, and he threw the tail of his trench coat backward as he gave her a patented Dorst bow.

"*Ki'an Gasan* O'Toole, how wonderful it is to see you once again. You've been well, I trust?"

Suffering through the recurring nightmare had her on enough edge. She had no patience for his excessive cheer, and verbal dueling. "I haven't seen you since—" Her face heated. Even now she couldn't say it. "—since before the Purge. I thought you were dead."

His expression became apologetic. Rising, he moved closer to her desk. "I do hear that quite often. I had hoped you, of all people, had more faith in my abilities."

The last time Margaurethe had seen him, he'd spirited her away from the palace after Elisibet's funeral. Had she stayed behind, she would have been killed by the mob that raged through the city hours later.

She made a production of shutting down the programs on her computer. "If you're looking for a thank you for saving my life, you have it. Will there be anything else?"

He tsked. "Lies? I thought we were dear friends."

"We've never been friends, Reynhard." She glared at him. "Don't ever mistake tolerance as friendship."

"May I?" He gestured to a chair, then sat without invitation. "We both know you'd have preferred to remain in the palace that night. You wanted to die."

The words, so close on the heels of the dream, stabbed her heart. She bared her teeth at him, reaching for the phone. "Get out. I'm calling my security."

"Alas, I cannot leave until I've done my duty." He attempted a mournful look, but the light of laughter in his gaze ruined the affect.

"And what duty is that?"

"You've been summoned to the Colonies, *Ki'an Gasan*. Someone there wishes to meet you."

Summoned. Despite Elisibet's assassination and the Purge that followed, the *Agrun Nam* had upheld Margaurethe's title of *Ki'an Gasan*, "beloved queen," at least in name. The only ones allowed to summon her were the *Sañar* themselves. *Unless*—

Margaurethe felt the blood drain from her face, suddenly cold in her robe and nightclothes. The sun sparkled brightly behind her, but her soul felt the icy mist of the early morning. She opened her mouth to speak, to ask, but her throat made no sound.

The joyful mockery fled Dorst's expression. His smile was genuine, his eyes sympathetic. "Yes. I've finally found her."

Whiskey started awake, her Sanguire eyes seeing every nuance of the dark bedroom. Cora muttered, still asleep, and shifted to pull her close again. Whiskey allowed it though the warmth of another person beside her did nothing to calm her rapidly beating heart. Whispering through her memory, she heard Margaurethe's voice. *"There's nothing to forgive."*

Alone despite the woman in her arms, Whiskey murmured, "I miss you, *minn'ast*."

Glossary

Aga Maskim Sañar - Judiciary of the High Court of the *Agrun Nam*; currently held by Bertrada Nijmege.

aga ninna - fearsome crown, ["the crown" and "fearsome lady"].

Agrun Nam - council ["inner sanctuary" and "fate, lot, responsibility"]; the ruling body of the European Sanguire.

amiga - Spanish, friend [feminine].

Baruñal - midwife to the *Ñíri Kurám* process.

caja - Spanish, literally box; slang for a woman's vagina.

chica - Spanish, girl.

ensi'umma, ensi'ummai - oracle, oracles.

gasan - lady, mistress, queen.

gracias - Spanish, thank you.

hola - Spanish, hello.

Ki'an Gasan – beloved lady mistress, ["beloved" and "lady, mistress, queen"]; title of Margaurethe O'Toole.

kizarus, kizarusi - vessel ["large vessel" and "to tap" and "blood"], vessels; the Human chattal that feed the Sanguire.

lamma - female spirit of good fortune; Fiona's nickname for Whiskey.

lugal - male leader of small household unit.

lúkal - dear one.

m'cara - beloved (Gaelic derivative); an affectation of Marguarthe O'Toole for Elisibet Vasilla.

Maskim Sañar - Judiciary of the Low Court of the *Agrun Nam*.

mi corazón - Spanish, literally my heart; term of endearment.

minn'ast - beloved (Indo-European derivative); an affectation of Elisibet Vasilla for Margaurethe O'Toole.

mucha dinero - Spanish, literally a lot of money.

Nam Lugal - chief counselor of the *Agrun Nam*.

ninna - fierce lady, female leader of small household unit.

Ninsumgal - lady of all, sovereign, dragon, monster of composite power; official title of Elisibet Vasilla.

Ñíri Kurám - the change, the turning, ("path" and "strange"'and "to take/to traverse"); the final step a youngling Sanguire takes to adulthood. It occurs naturally over decades, or can be hastened via chants and trances.

puru um - idiot, hillbilly.

Saggina - local magistrate of the European Sanguire; a political office that answers to the nearest embassy.

sañar/sanari - councilor of the *Agrun Nam*.

Sañur Gasum - eunuch assassin ["eunuch" and "i will" and "to slaughter"]; Reynhard Dorst's title.

Sublugal Sañar - military equivalent of the *Nam Lugal*, military leader; Valmont's title.

Usumgal - lord of all, sovereign, dragon, monster of composite power; official title of Maximal Vasilla, Elisibet's father.

We Wacipi Wakan - Lakota, ["blood" and "dancing" and "sacred"]; the leading council of the American Indian Sanguire.

zaz ne za tud - literally, do you know who you are?